COLD AS ICE

Lee Weeks was born in Devon. She left school at seventeen and, armed with a notebook and very little cash, spent seven years working her way around Europe and South East Asia. She returned to settle in London, marry and raise two children. She has worked as an English teacher and personal fitness trainer. Her books have been *Sunday Times* bestsellers. She now lives in Devon.

COLD AS ICE

LEE WEEKS

**SIMON &
SCHUSTER**

London · New York · Sydney · Toronto · New Delhi

A CBS COMPANY

First published in Great Britain by Simon & Schuster UK Ltd, 2013
A CBS COMPANY

1 3 5 7 9 10 8 6 4 2

Simon & Schuster UK Ltd
1st Floor
222 Gray's Inn Road
London WC1X 8HB

www.simonandschuster.co.uk

Simon & Schuster Australia, Sydney
Simon & Schuster India, New Delhi

A CIP catalogue record for this book is available from the British Library

B Format ISBN 978-1-84983-860-3
Trade Paperback ISBN 978-1-84983-859-7
Ebook ISBN 978-1-84983-861-0

Typeset by M Rules
Printed and bound by CPI Group (UK) Ltd, Croydon, CR0 4YY

To the staff and volunteers of the
Devon Rape Crisis Service.

Chapter 1

It was the first week in December and for three weeks the temperatures in the UK had plummeted so low that now the Regent's Canal had completely frozen over. The gloomy silence was fractured by the boom and bellow of a massive building works programme going on in King's Cross. Most days the sky played battlefield to giant industrial cranes but today visibility was limited to just twenty feet; it was just far enough to see across the canal, where it narrowed towards the gates then dropped eight feet and widened into a basin. The water hadn't been flowing for two weeks and the canal boats were stuck, moored in ice.

A group of six lads walked down towards the frozen canal. Mouse, nicknamed a year ago when he was the smallest member of the gang, before he grew into a lanky skulker, dragged his feet, kicking the loose stones as he sloped along the towpath, hands deep in the pockets of his black hoody. He was nervous today. A lot was expected of him.

Leon, the leader of the boys, moved back along the ranks until he came level with Mouse. Mouse lifted his chin in the direction of the new boy. 'I don't see you asking him to do it?'

'That's cos he needs to wait his turn.'

The others sniggered and Mouse gathered phlegm and rolled it round his tongue before he spat the globule onto the path.

'Anyways—' Leon moved closer and walked alongside Mouse – 'he don't know how it works with the old man on the till. He don't know how to distract him.'

Mouse's eyes were furtive beneath the rim of his hoody. He shook his head. 'No, man, he knows me; he won't let me in the shop.'

'He will.' Leon put his arm around Mouse's shoulder. The other boys turned and grinned at one another.

He shrugged Leon off. 'I'm telling you he won't. I tried to buy something for my mum last week. He wouldn't even let me do that.'

'You scared of the old man?'

Mouse tried a laugh but it came out shrill and false in the frozen air.

'You need to stay calm. Stay cool.' Leon sucked in the air through the gap between his big front teeth. 'Be happy; don't worry.' As he talked he leant his weight on Mouse and they stepped closer to the canal's edge. One of the boys picked up a stone from the towpath and threw it across the frozen water.

'Oi! Stop that!' The man stood at the other side of the canal and stared at them. Another stone skimmed over the top of the ice, leaving a frosted trail. 'What the bloody hell do you think you're doing?' he shouted again.

'What's it to you, old man?' Laughter rang out amongst the obscenities as one of the lads prised up a loose slab from the side of the towpath and launched it across the ice.

'I work here, that's what. It's dangerous. Now bugger off home.'

Mouse joined in the whistling and the jeering across the canal. When he turned his attention back to his mates he found them standing in his way, corralling him in; his back to the canal. A play-fight ensued between him and Leon. Mouse struggled to slip his wiry frame from Leon's firm grip and finished being tipped backwards towards the ice, dangling. He tried to laugh as he clung tight to Leon, who seemed about to haul him in but instead dropped him. Mouse bounced on his back and then slid across the surface. His friends whooped with delight as they watched him struggle to get to his knees, fall and slip sideways. He tried again, still managing to see the funny side of his predicament, inwardly so grateful that the ice had held his weight, but now all he wanted was to get off it fast. He steadied himself, turned over onto his knees and placed two hands down on the frozen surface and then stopped laughing. He scrambled to move away from that spot. His hands began to stick to the ice. His face was just an inch from the surface and his eyes slowly focused on the scene beneath his hands. He was winded, he couldn't scream; he couldn't talk. He heard the sound of his friends laughing. He tried to make out the shape he was looking at: the first thing he saw was the grinning mouth, the next her eyes, swollen lids opening just wide enough to stare back at him. There between his hands, inches from his face a woman stared up at him through the frozen surface of the canal.

Mouse's scream was lost in the wail and boom coming from the building site nearby.

Chapter 2

By midday, the day was as light as it was going to get. Freezing fog shrouded the canal above St Pancras Lock. It wrapped around Detective Inspector Dan Carter's thick-set frame like a wet blanket. He tucked his stripy cashmere scarf into his overcoat and pulled the collar up around his neck.

From where Carter was standing he could see the naked legs of a young woman's body. Her swollen white limbs had a blackish hue.

He looked up as Detective Constable Ebony Willis came striding back along the towpath towards him, tucking her notebook back inside her jacket as she did so. He thought how she didn't seem to notice the cold, didn't feel it like he did. Today the cold and damp in the air sank into his bones; he just couldn't get warm. Ebony didn't even have gloves on. She was wearing her self-imposed uniform of black trousers and a fitted black quilted jacket. Her afro hair was scraped into a ballooning ponytail at the back of her neck.

He waited until she reached him. 'What's the score?' he asked, keeping his voice low and banging his leather-gloved hands together to counteract the cold.

'Basically – he says she wouldn't have gone far in this canal.'

Carter looked past her to the man in the dark overcoat walking away.

'Is he the lock keeper?'

'No, he's the man who was here when the boys were messing about and fell onto the ice. But he knows all about the Regent's Canal – he works in the Canal Museum just down the road. He said that different types of locks allow for different water levels and movement between sections of canal.'

Carter swivelled on his heels to look around him and get his bearings. 'Plenty of ways to get down here, especially with all the development that's going on. There's two acres of Camley Park on the other side of the canal for a start. Did he mention if there was any CCTV?'

'The nearest is two hundred metres away, Guv.'

Carter stepped closer to the side of the canal and knelt to pick up a piece of the broken ice.

'Got to be two inches thick.' He turned it over in his hand. 'We'll need to wait for the ice to thaw before we can get the divers in to search.'

'Yes, Guv – forecast isn't good. No more snow for a few days but then it's coming back.'

Carter's thoughts were interrupted by the arrival of journalists on the bridge that spanned the canal up to their right. He could just about make them out: dark shadows moving through the fog. He heard them clanking their equipment as they hurried down as far as they were allowed onto the towpath. They stopped fifty metres away from where Carter and Ebony stood; just near where their car was parked. Next they heard an officer on the edge of the crime scene talking to them, directing them to where they could stand. Carter scowled.

'They didn't take long to find out.'

'No, Guv. The canal man said the lad who fell on the ice took pictures on his phone; his friends wouldn't help him out till he put it on Instagram.'

'Little bastards. Where is he now?'

'In a cell; he's given his statement already. Now he's waiting for someone to be free to tell him he can leave.'

'Good. Make him sweat for a few hours.' He shook his head, trying to shake off a headache. He'd spent the evening reminiscing with an old friend and a bottle of JD and now he was beginning to feel the hangover start. He rubbed his face and sighed. 'What's the matter with people? Should have respect for another human being. Now we've got the frigging newspapers before we've even had a chance to assess the situation, let alone inform the family.'

Carter pulled back the entrance to the crime scene tent and stooped as he stepped inside; Willis followed. The smell hit Carter so hard that he was in danger of throwing up. He instinctively drew his scarf up over his nose.

'Doctor Harding?'

A blonde-haired woman in a white forensic suit was kneeling beside the remains of the woman, which were bloated and blackened by the water. The woman's head was inside a polythene bag. She had wounds as big as teacups that had eaten into her body.

Doctor Harding looked up and nodded. She didn't smile. She wasn't one for automatic gestures of politeness. 'Willis ...' She handed Ebony a pair of gloves. 'Help me with the body.' A police photographer moved around and between them in the small tent as he took pictures of the body.

Carter spoke from behind his scarf. 'How old do you put her, Doc?'

'Mid-twenties.'

'Any birthmarks, operation scars? Anything that might help us to identify her?'

'There's a tattoo running up the outside of her left ankle.' Harding turned the victim's left leg over. 'I think it's something written in Norse. I saw something like it once before, on a bald-headed man. That time it turned out to be an ancient proverb meaning: *A cleaved head no longer plots*.'

'Yeah,' said Carter. 'I remember that guy – had it around his crown, didn't he? Drug dealer from Croydon, came up to deal with the Turks on Caledonian Road. It proved to be a perfect guideline for someone to cut the top of his head off like a boiled egg. Let's see if our mermaid shows up anywhere on the system.'

'Yes, Guv,' said the photographer.

'Whoever she was, she's definitely undernourished,' said Harding.

'How long's she been in the water?' asked Carter.

'A few months, at least. She went in when the water was warmer. Decomposition started but then slowed right down.'

Carter hovered nearer and looked directly down

over the body at the plastic bag covering her head. 'Her face looks like something from a waxworks horror museum,' he observed. He moved closer. 'It looks like it's made of cheese.'

The photographer stood where Carter had been to take his shots of the head. Carter pulled back.

Harding nodded. 'It's called adipocere – the absence of oxygen and plenty of moisture inside the bag have caused the fats from her face and her brain matter to fuse, turning her face into soap.'

'Prostitute maybe?' asked Carter. 'A client went too far: got carried away with the bag, and killed her by accident then dumped her here?'

'Pretty risky getting undressed in the middle of King's Cross,' Harding answered as she turned the woman's head towards Ebony and searched for the best place to begin cutting open the bag.

'People enjoy taking risks,' Carter disagreed. 'Might have been a warm summer evening. Maybe this was an experimental sex session gone wrong – he asphyxiates her and then dumps her body straight into the water.'

Harding decided on an entry place for her scalpel and Ebony held the plastic out, away from the woman's face, whilst the doctor slit down the centre of the bag and peeled it back gently. She finished cutting the bag through. Ebony moved the clumped strands of dark auburn hair away from the woman's face and neck for Harding to get a better look. She splayed them out, medusa-like.

'Except ...' She turned the head to one side – 'she wasn't asphyxiated; she was strangled and the bag was an afterthought. Someone used huge force too; they crushed her windpipe, and broke the vertebrae in her neck, snapping her spinal column – usual injuries we see in someone who's hanged themselves, but there are no rope lesions. But there's a necklace, protected by the plastic,' Harding added as she worked a chain loose that was embedded in the flesh of the neck and eased it free. Turning it till she found the clasp, she pulled two rings around with it, threaded onto the chain. The photographer leant over the body whilst Ebony rested the rings on her open palm so that they could be photographed. Harding undid the chain and handed it to Ebony to bag up. Ebony showed Carter the rings as she did so.

'Two very different types, aren't they?' he said.

'Of rings, Guv? Yes, I think one is an antique, maybe worth something. Think the other one is cheap.'

'Anything else on her?' asked Carter.

'Not that I can see,' answered Harding.

'She look British to you?' asked Carter. 'What about the hair? Red hair is very popular with Eastern European women. We have a lot of those living in London.'

'Yeah, but this wasn't dyed,' answered Harding. 'Celtic, maybe.'

Ebony was still kneeling beside the body, studying the woman's face. Carter stood back and watched. He was marvelling how Ebony could get that close to the smell and not seem to notice it.

'What is it, Ebb?'

'She's got make-up on.'

Harding rubbed the woman's cheek with a swab of cotton wool and looked at the resulting red stain on it.

'You're right. Must have been industrial-strength to survive this.'

'There are remnants of blue eye-shadow,' said Ebony. 'She's even got some sort of black eyelashes painted above her eyes. It's as if she were going to a party.'

'Dressed as what? A pantomime dame?'

Harding looked down the length of the woman's body. 'She's had a tough life, whoever she is. The fish have capitalized on the decayed flesh.' She stopped at the largest of the wounds on the woman's thigh. 'But all this tissue destruction wasn't done in the water.'

'Could you walk around with that kind of open wound?' asked Willis.

Harding shook her head in response. 'Can't see how.' She parted the frayed flesh and opened the edges of one of the wounds on the woman's left thigh; the bone was visible.

'What can have caused so many different sites of infection, and so deep?' Carter asked as he took photos of the injuries with his phone. Willis helped Harding to turn the body on its side.

'I think these wounds started as ulcers.' Harding turned the victim's arms at the elbows to take a look. 'No obvious needle marks but these large open wounds might have started with skin-popping – injecting contaminated heroin under the skin.'

'If she's got that kind of drug abuse history we might find her fingerprints on file or she might be known at the needle exchange. We'll check it out.' Carter said as he moved back from the body. Ebony continued her fascinated examination of the woman's face. Harding stood to allow the photographer better access.

'Can you do the post mortem examination today?' Carter had seen enough. He felt the need to get out of the confines of the tent. He wanted to breathe in something other than the putrid flesh of a body that had been at the bottom of the canal for months. Carter knew Willis would be happy to stay another hour or two. She came alive around the dead.

'Yes. This afternoon. I'll give you a call when we're ready to start.'

'Thanks.' They left Harding in the tent.

'The tattoo's got to mean something to someone, Ebb,' said Carter as he and Willis stepped back over the crime scene tape and walked back towards the detectives' pool car: a black BMW. 'We'll get Harding to take a biopsy. The inks used might help us narrow it down to certain tattooists. Did you ask the canal man if he'd seen anything suspicious? He might have seen someone coming to try it for a location. Did you get a statement from him?'

Ebony nodded. 'Yes, but nothing suspicious.'

Carter pushed past a journalist who called out 'Excuse me, mate?' as he passed.

'Christ – no – you can't have a frigging interview.' Carter squared up to him. 'If you vultures don't get out of the way I'll do you for obstructing a police investigation. And I'm not your frigging mate – got it? MOVE.'

The reporter backed off with two hands in the air in a mock show of compliance.

'Just doing our job.'

Ebony looked across at Carter as he shook his head, annoyed. They'd worked together for a year. She knew him well. She knew he'd be cross because the reporter was right and, on most days, Carter would have chatted to the journalists, got them on his side. But today Carter was somewhere dark in his own head. He looked across at her and shook his head, exasperated.

'Sorry.'

'You all right, Guv?'

'Yeah. Sorry – got a lot going on at the moment, Ebb.'

'Guv?'

She raised her eyes towards the car to show where they'd left it and to show Carter that he was going in the opposite direction.

'I know, I know,' he snapped irritably.

Carter got into the driver's seat and waited till Willis shut her passenger door and then reversed at speed, almost hitting the photographer who had just stepped off the kerb to get a photo of them leaving. Willis stayed quiet. She looked across at him. She'd worked with him long enough to know he'd tell her in his own time. She was waiting for him to calm down and get back to what he was good at. Carter was the best 'people person' she knew. Today was an 'off' day.

'You want me to attend the post mortem on my own, Guv? It's no problem.'

'What, and let you have all the fun?' He smiled

gratefully. 'No, I'll be all right, Ebb. Nothing like the smell of a post mortem to get things in perspective.'

After the black BMW had passed him on the bridge, the man turned back to look at the white tent below. The fog was just beginning to thin and he could see it shine bright in the wisps of white. He smiled to himself. He was breathless. Something told him today was the day she would finally rise through the dark water to reveal herself to the world – reborn. And the game would begin again.

Chapter 3

Tracy Collins was still in her dressing gown watching telly while she got ready for work. She was on a late shift today. She worked on a cosmetics counter at Simmons department store on Holloway Road. Because Christmas opening hours had just begun, her shift started at two today and would go on until nine.

Her husband Steve had left for work already so Tracy didn't have to bother about anything other than putting on her face for work. She liked the noise of the television to keep her company while she got ready. She listened to the news as she wandered in and out of the bathroom between applying layers of make-up.

'*Damn.*'

It all seemed to be going so well then she dropped an eyelash just as she was about to glue it into place. Tracy knelt on the lino and tried to pick it up between her finger and thumb but her acrylic nails were too thick at their ends. Instead she licked the pad of her forefinger and pressed it down on the lash. She stood back up and deposited it on the side of the sink, stopping to listen to the reporter on the telly in the other room.

'Today a woman's body was found beneath the ice in the Regent's Canal at King's Cross.' Tracy walked back into the lounge, looking at the TV screen – at the image of the fog and the frozen canal. 'Police are not yet able to identify the woman and are treating her death as suspicious. They are appealing for any witnesses and anyone with any information to come forward and ring the number on the screen.'

Tracy moved closer to the screen to get a better look at the canal and the crime scene tent. She knew the area well. She'd had many walks along the canal. She knew that exact spot. As she swung her head in disbelief and squinted at the images of the crime scene tent she caught a glimpse of an Italian-looking detective with immaculate black shiny hair and a stripy scarf pulled up around his chin. Then, a few seconds later, she saw a blonde-haired woman in a white forensic suit emerging from the tent. Just as she was absorbed with watching the report the phone rang and made Tracy jump. She ran and grabbed it from the bathroom where she'd left it on top of the toilet cistern.

Her heart thumped as she looked at the number on the screen.

'Yes?' she said abruptly.

She hadn't meant to sound so jumpy. The news, the disturbance to her routine had done it. She was jittery.

'Is it a bad time?' It was a woman's voice on the other end of the line.

'No. Sorry. You just caught me, that's all. I'm getting ready for work.' She closed her eyes and took a deep breath.

'Is it still okay for today?' the woman asked.

'Yes. Yes, of course.' Tracy said, her voice metre swinging too high. 'I'm looking forward to it. But – I'm sorry – I don't have long. It will just have to be a quick chat today. You do understand? It's Christmas opening hours and we're going to be really busy in the shop.'

'Yeah. You said before.'

'Oh sorry ... of course ... I'm just nervous. Are you still bringing your son with you – Jackson, isn't it?'

'I don't have a choice. He only goes to school in the mornings.'

'And you know where it is?'

'Yes.'

'That's fine, as I said, there's a Christmas Fayre just around the corner from me. We can meet there by Santa's Grotto.'

'Okay. See you there.'

'But I don't know what you look like.'

'I'll know you,' the woman answered.

'Oh ... all right. Well, I'll see you at four then. I'm looking forward it.' Tracy was just about to ask her how she would know *her* when the phone went dead. 'Hello? Danielle?' Tracy looked at the phone in her hand for a few seconds. Had she handled that well? Had she come across okay? She sighed and set about saving the number: new contact.

Tracy felt butterflies in her stomach. Some of it was guilt. She hadn't told Steve what she was up to. She didn't know why but it didn't seem a good idea; not until she was sure what would come of it. She went back into the bathroom and applied fresh glue to the eyelash on the side of the sink. As she waited for her hand to stop shaking she looked at her reflection. Danielle must have come into Simmons and seen Tracy behind the counter. What had she thought? She always tried to make a good impression and to look her best. Had she looked okay that day? She must have, she supposed, otherwise Danielle wouldn't want to see her, let alone bring her son.

Tracy paused, eyelash on her finger, and looked into her reflection. She felt old suddenly. She looked at herself and frowned. Thirty-six wasn't old. Deep inside she was still the same girl she used to be. She still wore the same make-up she'd worn as a teenager. Her hair was dyed to keep it looking vibrant. Her skirts were longer now. But inside she was the same girl who'd got pregnant at fifteen.

Chapter 4

Carter and Willis returned to Fletcher House, where they were part of the thirty-eight-man Murder Squad. Fletcher House was at the back of Archway Tube station and joined onto Archway Police Station. Just a door separated the normal goings-on of a police station from what they called 'The Dark Side'. It was home to Major Incident Team seventeen, MIT 17, along with three other MIT teams that served Londoners north of the Thames. Each MIT team had its own, identically laid out, floor. MIT17 was on the third floor.

'Sir?' Carter knocked and entered Detective Chief Inspector Bowie's office door. Since the retirement of Superintendent Tanner, Bowie was the most senior detective in MIT 17.

'You got a callout this morning?' Bowie asked from behind his desk. The desk itself was messy, littered with papers and personal effects. In pride of place were photos of his wife and kids.

Carter came to sit down opposite him. Despite his expensive suit and three-hundred-quid shoes, Bowie always had a dishevelled look; his shoes needed cleaning and his suit didn't sit properly on his bony shoulders. He struggled to keep weight on. He was pale, tall and blond with watery blue eyes.

'A woman pulled out of Regent's Canal at King's Cross, Sir.' Carter took off his coat and scarf and hung them over the back of the chair.

'Any idea who she is?'

'Not yet. She's pretty distinctive with long auburn hair, youngish – early twenties. She has a tattoo which we're hopeful about.'

'How did she die?'

'She'd been strangled. Probable sexual motive. She had a plastic bag over her head.'

'Maybe a sex game gone wrong?'

'I was thinking the same.'

'Dismembered?'

'No.'

'Heat of the moment then – he panics and throws her into the canal.'

'Yeah,' agreed Carter. 'Except Doctor Harding says the bag was put on after death.'

'You're SIO on this investigation. Operation Sparrowhawk.' Carter nodded. Murder Investigations were named in alphabetical sequence, they followed groups. The last group had been towns in Australia; this time it was birds of prey.

'Still, I think a prostitute seems likely,' said Carter. 'We'll get officers out on the surrounding streets with a photofit of her and see if any of the regulars recognize her. SOCOs are out searching the surrounding undergrowth and along the towpath for any items of clothing or ID but I'm not expecting great results.

Doctor Harding estimates she'd been in the water a couple of months, maybe three.'

'Was she wearing any clothing?'

'She was naked except for a chain around her neck with two rings on it. One of them is worth money – we're running it through lost and stolen property files now.'

'What's the condition of the body?'

'The drop in water temperature has kept it from decomposing too far. Skin is still there but it's lifted and most of her fingers are gone. But she was in a bad way before she ended up at the bottom of the canal.' Carter took out his phone and handed it to Bowie. 'She has these wounds over her body.'

Bowie took the phone from him and slid his finger across the screen as he viewed the shots.

'Nasty. Aren't they caused by the pond life?'

Carter shook his head.

'What does Doctor Harding say they are?'

'She says they started out as ulcers left untreated – it's possibly down to some contaminated heroin injected under the skin.'

'Better see if there is some on the streets that's capable of that.'

'Yeah – doing it.'

'Anyone interviewed the lad that found her yet?'

'We took a statement from him earlier, much earlier.' A smile crept across Carter's face. 'We're holding him for a bit longer just in case we remember anything else we want to ask him. Then maybe he'll remember his civic duty next time and call us first instead of posting a photo on Instagram.'

'Jesus Christ – little fucker. Let me know what you need after you talk to Robbo. Let's get it all set up. When's the post mortem?'

'Harding said she'd get started in about an hour. I'm heading over there shortly.'

'Okay, keep me in the loop.'

Carter left Bowie's office and walked down the corridor to the largest office in the department – the Enquiry Team Office. Willis was sitting at one of the six long desks. Jeanie Vincent the Family Liaison Officer sat diagonally opposite her. When the office was full there were twenty detective constables and five detective sergeants in it.

Ebony was scanning through Missing Persons records.

Carter stopped at her station and looked over her shoulder at the screen. 'Anything in Mispers?' His eyes drifted up to nod a hello to Jeanie. Jeanie smiled back.

'Not yet, Guv.'

'Okay, you ready? We don't want to be late for Doctor Harding.'

'Ready.' Ebony stood and picked up her jacket. 'Are we walking over, Guv?'

Carter didn't answer so Jeanie did. 'Don't be silly. Of course not.' She rolled her eyes. 'You know he hates what the damp air does to his hair, Ebb.'

Ebony smiled.

'And don't forget you're coming to Sunday lunch soon. Peter's cooking it so you're safe. It'll be edible this time.'

'Nice to know some things never change,' said Carter as he waited for Ebony to shut down her PC.

Jeanie nodded. 'Yep. It's never a good thing to admit you can cook to a man – slippery slope. How are your parents, Dan?'

Carter nodded. He looked ready to say something and then changed his mind.

'Give them my love.' Jeanie's eyes lingered on him. 'Will do.'

They caught the lift down to the car park. Ebony looked across at Carter. She was used to the awkwardness between Jeanie and Carter. They had been a couple long before Ebony began working at the Murder Squad. They still found it difficult to work together. But Ebony had seen the way Carter hesitated at the question about his parents. She knew something wasn't right. She'd met his parents many times when she and Carter had called in after work and been fed or given a coffee. She was very fond of them. She hadn't been around to their home in Finchley for a couple of months.

He turned to see her watching him.

'My dad's really ill. He's got throat cancer.' Carter smiled sadly and shook his head. 'Cigars have done it. That and a few brandies every night.'

'Is he having treatment?'

'Yes. He's having an operation to remove what they can. It's a terrible thing to feel so helpless. I can't do anything to help him. He can't eat. He sits in his chair in the lounge and he pretends to be fine about it but I can see the panic in his eyes. He's scared.' Carter started up the engine. 'Still, where there's life – there's hope, huh? He's a fighter.'

'He'll be all right, Guv.'

'Yeah – let's hope so, Ebb. And at least he didn't end up at the bottom of a freezing canal.'

The fog had cleared and the man walked away from the canal bridge and back through the new building works in King's Cross. He stopped to look through a peep hole at the massive construction site that encompassed the whole of King's Cross Station and the surrounding area. The day stretched pale blue and a giant crane swung in the air. The ache and groan of steel being driven into the earth made him feel exhilarated. He felt the blood pump around his body as he stood watching the huge machinery languidly move its metal limbs and lower and lift.

A group of Chinese students passed, all chattering together. They didn't notice him. A woman passed walking too fast for her skirt. She was in a hurry – going somewhere. She glanced his way; he stared back. He saw beneath the make-up, he peeled her open like an onion, folding back the layers of skin, fat, muscle and severing tendon and ligament, snapping bone.

She came level with him and he smelt her perfume. It made him want to grab her by the neck and pin her to the wall, squeeze her neck, lift her feet from the ground as he cut off the oxygen to her brain. He would watch her eyes widen, panic, stare at him, drift and lose focus and roll back in her head and he would part her thighs and enter her at that moment and the last thing she would feel was him inside her, the pleasure and the pain in death and ecstasy.

The woman stared back at him as if she knew what he wanted to do and was inviting him to try. *Just fucking try.* He smiled at her. She tossed her chin in the air and walked on by.

Didn't she realize who he was? Didn't she realize she was in the presence of greatness? He had complete control over other human beings – over her, if he wanted it. He had power at his fingertips that she would never know because she wasn't worthy. He picked the women he chose to play his game very carefully. He handpicked them and he decided their fate from that moment on. He decided how they lived and how they died.

He turned back to watch the magnificent machines he loved. The massive cranes stretched up to the sky and prepared to do battle with one another, lowering and lifting their mighty heads. His head hurt with the pleasure of it all.

'Got a light, mate?' An art student from nearby Saint Martins interrupted his thoughts. The student had a hand-rolled cigarette in between his fingers. His hands were dotted with paint.

'Got a light, mate?' he mimicked. The young man scowled and turned his head away for a few seconds as if considering his reaction.

'Got a light? Got a light?' he parroted again.

For a second the two men stared at one another.

'Go fuck yourself.' The young man shook his head and started walking away. 'Fucking weirdo.'

Chapter 5

Doctor Jo Harding had a reputation for being as cold as the corpses she cut up. She was brittle inside, steel outside. She worked exclusively for the Murder Squad. She carried out the forensic post mortems in her laboratory in the Whittington Hospital mortuary department which was just a few minutes' walk from Fletcher House and Archway Police Station.

Mark, the mortuary technician, knocked and entered her office as she was looking at the X-rays.

'Inspector Carter and DC Willis are on their way over, Doctor.'

She pushed her chair back and looked up from her desk. 'Okay – you can begin. I'll be out in a minute.'

Mark left her office with a nod and went to get changed before going through to the body store and wheeling out the body from the canal. He waited to unzip the body bag. For him there was a ceremonial aspect to the disrobing of the victim. He showed reverence, in deference to the deceased person. He was a sensitive soul. He already smelt the odour of advanced decomposition. He kept his eyes lowered as he opened the zip all the way and then his eyes took in her injuries one by one and he felt a heavy sadness that was the same today as it had been the first time he'd seen a dead body, the day he started work at the funeral home where he had worked for eight years before joining Doctor Harding. He sadly peeled the edges of the bag back and looked at the auburn-haired woman, her face moulded into a mannequin of horror, her auburn hair snaking out and he thought how beautiful she must once have been. He moved to the top of the table and laid out the necessary tools on the tray above the sink.

Harding picked up the post mortem forms before going through to get changed into new scrubs and an all-in-one suit, white boots. Then she picked up visor and gloves and joined Mark in the post mortem room. The body was waiting on the stainless-steel dissection table.

She signalled to Mark to help and together they slid out and folded up the plastic sheet that the body had been wrapped in, ready to be sent to the crime lab. Harding carefully peeled away the last of the polythene from around the victim's neck. 'We'll get the preliminaries done ready to start the examination when they get here. Start by brushing and washing her hair, eyelashes, eyebrows and pubic.'

Mark nodded that he understood and began gently combing her hair. He eased out the tangles and used a syringe to squirt water onto the scalp, flushing the debris into a bowl.

Harding was watching him from the corner of her eye. They'd been working together for three months now and were still getting used to one another's ways.

He washed the victim's hair as if he were in love. He tilted his head one way and another as if mesmerized by the strands of colour in her hair. Harding coughed. She saw his hands speed up – efficiency replace sentiment – and watched as he finished up before removing the tray full of the washing liquid. He began combing through her eyebrows and eyelashes, and removed the make-up that had been hiding the swollen cheese-like texture of her face. Her bulging eyes were lovingly wiped clean of blue eye-shadow with cotton pads, her cheeks cleaned of red stain. When he finished the face he moved down to comb through her pubic hair.

Harding looked up from behind her plastic eye shield as Carter and Willis approached wearing full forensic suits. Harding handed Willis the camera with a querying look. Ebony nodded and took it. She switched it on and checked it was working before moving silently around the body photographing. After Harding, Ebony knew more about forensic pathology than anyone else in the room. And, although her degree was in criminal justice and law, forensics had been a hobby all her life.

Mark switched on the extractor fan beneath the table as Harding began official proceedings.

'The diener here is Mark Langham; he has washed and prepared the body for autopsy,' Harding dictated as she moved along the side of the dissection table. 'We have collected hair samples and will continue with the exterior examination. DI Dan Carter and DC Ebony Willis are in attendance at the post mortem examination of the victim, a woman found dead this morning, pulled out of the Regent's Canal. DC Ebony

Willis will be recording the visual account of the autopsy. We are looking at a white female, approximately twenty-four years of age. She is five foot six and weighs six stone seven pounds. She has yet to be identified. She's been in the water for approximately twelve weeks. Decomposition and submersion in water for a period of several months has caused a blackening of the skin which is lifting and separating from the muscle, on her body and limbs. Her abdomen is swollen and has a green hue.' Harding halted at the top of the table. 'Her head has been encased in plastic, which has led to it being preserved; adipocere has formed, giving it a tan colour, and causing a retaining of features as the fat melted.'

Harding moved to the side of the table and picked up the woman's hand. 'All but two of the fingers are missing on her right hand; they were probably lost while she was in the canal.' She looked at the two ragged ends to the fingers and nodded to Mark, who had already anticipated her needs and handed her a scalpel and specimen tray. 'We've already taken fingerprints.' She began to cut away each of the nail beds from the two fingers, and deposited them onto the tray. She turned the woman's arms over.

'No obvious signs of the use of needles.' Harding stopped dictating. She looked across at Carter.

'Any luck with the jewellery or the tattoo?'

'Not yet.'

'What about the heroin?'

'No reports of any problems on the streets, Doctor.'

'Maybe she came from abroad and brought it with her,' answered Harding.

'If she did we might never find out about it – or her,' replied Carter.

'Really?' Harding said sarcastically. 'You surprise me, Inspector. So defeatist.'

Carter glanced Ebony's way. They both knew what the sharp end of Harding's tongue felt like. She rarely thought before she spoke. She didn't see that she needed to. She was cocooned in the mortuary world where she was queen and reigned supreme.

She continued her examination: 'Overall, the body is in a very poor state. I count ... three infected ulcerated sites on her torso, a further six on her limbs. The largest of the wounds is on her left thigh.'

Mark followed her silent instruction as he moved into place and laid a paper tape measure down the length of the wound. 'Twenty-four centimetres top to bottom, width sixteen point five. Depth ...' he said as he placed a Q-tip into the wound and gently prodded the base until he found the lowest point then he slid his fingers down level with the surface and took a reading – 'seven centimetres deep in the centre.' He slid the Q-tip around, prodding the sides of the wound. 'Underpinning of the wound at ten o'clock, depth of ...' he measured it the same way as before – 'five centimetres.'

Harding handed him a pair of tweezers. 'Any debris inside there?'

He took the tweezers from her and got down level with the wound to have a look. His fingers disappeared inside the tunnel and re-emerged with the remains of a small eel.

'Must have been having his breakfast when she was pulled out,' Carter said.

Harding proceeded to cut away a section at the side of the wound and place it into a specimen tray. 'She would have been in huge pain from these wounds,' she said. 'Some of them are showing signs of trying to heal. I can't imagine she could have carried on normal life with these. We'll have to wait until we have the blood results back to know what she had in her system but it will take longer to find out about these infected sites. It's not a quick process; it involves growing a culture to identify it. The only time I've seen this amount of ulceration in random sites like this is in cases of MRSA, the flesh-eating bug. But, without doubt, left untreated like this, this many infected wounds would have led quickly to organ failure and death: I'm not quite sure why they didn't.'

Harding moved down to the woman's abdomen. 'Skin slack – a child maybe? Rapid weight loss evident. There is bruising around the pelvis area.' She lifted the woman's right knee up and outwards. She began a detailed examination of the genital area. She opened the entrance to the vagina and examined a short thick scar.

'She's had a child within the last few years. She was given an episiotomy.' Harding waited whilst Ebony photographed. 'We'll turn her over now.'

Carter helped Mark turn the body over.

'We have one ulcerated site on her lower back section which is similar to the wounds on her front,' said Harding. 'But we also have deep grazing on the pressure points: shoulder blades, buttocks and calves.' Mark handed her a scalpel. She cut down the centre of the back and across to free the area of skin over each shoulder blade and then lifted the flaps and cut them free to examine them. 'Some sort of organic material, splinters or fibres of some kind, are growing into the flesh. She must have rubbed against something over a long period of time and it's implanted and taken root in her flesh.' She placed the skin on trays before lifting the victim's right knee upwards and parting the buttocks.

'There is tearing of the tissue around the anus and bruising around the inner thigh and leading up to the vagina, but this has also become the entry point into the body for the feeders in the canal.' Harding inserted the end of a swab into the anus and looked at the end of it – minute particles of decomposing flesh mixed with a grey sludge from the canal were clinging to it.

'Can there be many fish living in the canal?' Willis asked

'Carp, eels, perch, pike even.' Carter answered. 'Someone caught a seventeen-pound carp in the Regent's Canal just near here a while ago. I used to fish there with my dad.'

'Don't they all die if the canal freezes over? asked Willis.

'Survival of the fittest, Ebb,' answered Carter.

Harding discarded the swab into the specimen tray. 'I'm going to take a biopsy of the rectum via the anus. It tears easily and there might be something embedded inside.' She took a scalpel from Mark and cut into the side wall of the anus and took a sample of tissue.

When she had finished, Harding changed her gloves and indicated that Ebony should come across to stand where she was for a moment, level with the woman's head, to photograph as she cut into the flesh of the neck.

'I'm now going to make a detailed examination of the injuries that led to her death.' She pulled the magnifying lens and spotlight down over the victim's neck and carefully cut into the crushed trachea with a scalpel. She opened up the neck and exposed the splintered bones, then turned the woman's head and examined the neck closely. 'All seven cervical verte-brae are broken. The discs and ligaments are crushed, compressed. The large muscles of the neck are torn. To do this much damage it would take continued and immense pressure. There are no signs of a tourniquet, which would show where the initial pressure emanated from, where the screw was turned, so to speak.'

'Maybe the killer used a length of something smooth, rubber tubing perhaps,' said Carter.

'Yes, perhaps,' Harding answered. 'It would have to be wrapped several times around the neck and then squeezed slowly to achieve this kind of result. Almost like a blood pressure monitor when it squeezes your arm – even, strong pressure all round.' She spoke as she worked at opening up the neck and separating the fused bones. 'Even her collarbone is broken, snapped under the weight of whatever it was that crushed her slowly, cutting off oxygen to the brain simultane-ously.'

Ebony looked up at Carter from behind her visor.

'Not done by the canal's edge then, Guv? He couldn't have done this there and taken the time he needed. What about the make-up?'

Mark answered: 'I took a photo of her face and then I removed what was left of the make-up and I've bagged up the swabs to send to pathology to analyze, but I'm sure it's what we used in the funeral home. It's semi-permanent, waterproof. It's really thick and the pigments are much stronger than normal make-up.'

'So the person who killed her wanted it to be seen,' said Carter. 'Why else would he go to the trouble of preserving the head in a watertight bag?'

'And he didn't choose to weight her down, either,' added Ebony. 'She was always going to rise to the surface.'

'But then we are crediting him with a lot of planning,' said Carter.

Harding looked down the body of the woman with the Titian hair.

'None of this happened overnight. Wherever she's been, she's been through immense pain and suffering in the last few months of her life – she's been to hell.'

Chapter 6

The icy wind blew down Blackstock Road in Finsbury Park. It was three-thirty and dusk. Danielle pulled up her fur-trimmed collar against it as she stood waiting for a number four bus to take her to Holloway Road. She bent over the pushchair and checked Jackson's gloves were still on. She pulled them up and tucked them inside the cuffs of his coat. She knew he was watching her. She looked at him when she finished and kissed his cold cheek.

'Who's going to see Father Christmas?' Jackson grinned, his eyes watering from the cold. She tickled him through his padded all-in-one suit. He squirmed and giggled. Danielle looked up to see a woman who had come to stand at the bus stop. She was watching them, pity in her eyes. Danielle scowled at the woman as she bent back down to Jackson and pulled his hat further down over his ears. Danielle had Jackson out of the buggy, and the buggy folded in an instant, as soon as the bus arrived. She held his hand and pulled him up onto the bus.

The driver winked at Jackson. Danielle swiped her oyster card and deftly made her way through the vehicle, leaving the buggy in the luggage rack. She sat Jackson on her lap and pulled out a tissue. He squirmed as she wiped his nose. He watched her. She mouthed the words 'good boy.'

They alighted halfway along Holloway Road and Jackson stood on the pavement waiting as Danielle took one seamless kick and flex of the buggy to make it ready for him. Jackson was slow getting into it; he was straining to look past Danielle and pointing to the window display across the road in the department store where a massive animated Father Christmas was waving at him. Jackson waved back, star-struck. Danielle looked at her watch. She had a half hour to kill. She crossed the road and stopped outside Simmons department store. Danielle pretended to look at the window display as Jackson sat watching Father Christmas wave his arm and mouth the words 'Ho ho ho'. But her eyes went beyond the display and she searched the cosmetics counter. She watched a woman working on one of the counters that she just knew was Tracy; she felt it inside. She'd stopped at the window many times in the last two weeks. Now she felt a flutter in her stomach. She didn't want to be spotted too soon. She wanted things to go as she had imagined, and so she kept her head down and pushed the buggy on, steering it through the street towards the Christmas market.

The cosmetics department of Simmons was hectic in the build-up to Christmas. The atmosphere was good. Tracy loved coming into work to be rushed off her feet. With so much talk of hardship and recession,

takings had been down all year. This was her chance
to try and prove to herself and to her bosses that,
given the opportunity, Tracy Collins could sell ice to
Eskimos.

She looked at her watch. It was ten minutes to
four. She looked across anxiously at her colleague
Jazmina on the other side of the make-up counter.
*They were both so busy; how could she possibly
leave?* Tracy had watched the shoppers pour in
through Simmons' doors – all day it had been a
steady stream. She had kept her eyes open for someone who might be Danielle. Once she could have
sworn that it must be her when she saw a blonde
woman who looked like a younger version of herself,
immaculately turned out, bubbly, pretty, a little over-
weight, pushing the cutest-looking child: all golden
curls, immaculately dressed – and Tracy imagined
that could be her daughter and grandchild. But no,
they had bought their special Christmas purchases of
perfume and make-up and they had disappeared
from her counter.

'You go …' her colleague Jazmina said as she
wrapped a package for a customer, pulling the ribbon
into swirls with the blade of some scissors. 'It's five to
four – you said you had an appointment?'

'You sure?'

Jazmina nodded – she looked as excited about it as
Tracy.

Tracy had not told Jazmina exactly who she was
meeting but she knew it was important and Tracy
wanted to look nice for it. Jazmina had jumped to
her own conclusions and believed that Tracy had

finally decided to ditch boring Steve and find herself a new man and was about to embark on a steamy affair.

Tracy turned the mirror round on the counter and checked herself: her lippy was still intact. She looked at Jazmina one last time to make sure. Jazmina nodded eagerly.

'You look great – just go for it . . .'

'I'll be as quick as I can,' said Tracy with a frown. She wondered if she'd missed something with Jazmina.

'You take an hour; you're entitled,' Jazmina replied, giving Tracy the 'don't think for one moment I won't cope' look. 'Just enjoy yourself – you only live once.'

'I couldn't possibly. I'll be back in half an hour – promise.'

Tracy grabbed her coat and bag and slipped out from behind the counter. She left the shop, turned right then right again and onto the busy crossroads that marked the start of the German Christmas Market. She walked past the sweet counters and the mulled wine and looked around her. The place was heaving with mums pushing prams. She passed a stall selling Christmas-themed jewellery next to Santa's Grotto. The sound of Bavarian carol music pervaded in the air, along with the smell of burnt caramel, mulled wine and Bratwurst sausage. At the exit from Santa's Grotto she found her way suddenly blocked by a young mum pushing a little boy with Down's syndrome. In his hand he had a pink pig. His face was flushed. Tracy looked back up from him to the young woman, who was staring at her, waiting. Tracy smiled, tried to pass. The young woman moved the buggy to block her again.

'Tracy?'

Tracy's heart stopped. Was this the daughter she'd given up when she was fifteen? Was this the little girl whose existence had haunted her for twenty-one years? 'Danielle?' Tracy did her best not to look shocked. 'And this must be Jackson?' She recovered fast, bent down to talk to Jackson, who stared up at her in awe, fascinated by her bright red lips and her inch-long eyelashes. 'Who have we got here?' Tracy tapped her fingernail on the pink pig.

Jackson held it aloft for her to see. 'Peppa Pig,' he said, turning back towards the Grotto and pointing, struggling to sit up and turn around to show Tracy where he'd been and where the pig came from. 'Father Christmas give it to me.' He held the toy up in front of her face.

'We got here early,' Danielle explained. Tracy stood and took a few seconds to take a good look at Danielle. She wasn't as she imagined she'd be. As far as Tracy could make out, she didn't look like Tracy at all. Danielle was skinny and dark and two inches taller than Tracy. She had her hair scraped back in a ponytail and not a scrap of make-up on. Tracy's mind was in a spin – the baby in her arms. The birth, the terrible wrench she felt at giving up her baby. Was this her baby? How could she be sure?

'You lucky boy. You must have been awfully good to get that.' Jackson nodded, large proud nods of his head. Tracy smiled awkwardly. 'We better find some-where that's not so noisy to talk. I only have half an hour – I'm sorry. It's the busiest time of year.' She was apologizing again. 'I've left my colleague to cope alone.' They walked past the Christmas stalls. 'Can I get you a coffee?'

Danielle shrugged. 'Okay.'

She pushed the buggy forward until they found a bar that had a few busy tables and a side stall selling coffee. They stood in the queue. 'Glad you could spare the time,' Danielle said as she pulled Jackson's hat down further on his head. Tracy was momentarily flustered. She'd promised herself she wouldn't get emotional. She would stay calm, stay focused. She had so wanted her daughter to be living the dream – Tracy's dream. She wanted her to have the perfect life. It was what Tracy had made the ultimate sacrifice for, after all. *Did this girl look like she was living the dream*? thought Tracy. No she didn't. She looked lost, tired, pale and cold.

'I mean – I'm glad you decided to meet me and Jackson.'

'Of course,' she said. 'I would have tried to find you as well but I didn't want to ... intrude ... you know what I mean?' Tracy tried to relax her mouth, her frozen smile. She could feel her face was so tense that she must look like she was about to cry. Danielle stared back at Tracy with a confused look of pity and anger on her face. Tracy breathed deeply, tried a new smile. 'I didn't think I had the right to ... You had your life.' Tracy got to the front of the queue and ordered coffee. She turned to Danielle and pointed to Jackson: 'What about him? Does he want anything?'

'No. He's got his drink.'

'What about something sweet for him?' She smiled at him.

'No. He has to watch his weight.'

'We can get him out of the buggy if you like. There's a kids' skating park just at the end of the stalls.'

Danielle didn't answer. They collected their coffees. Tracy carried Danielle's for her while she pushed the buggy and they moved off towards the end of the Fayre. They walked towards the sound of laughter and music coming from an area that had been a car park and was commandeered for use as the kids' ice rink. It had been iced over and kids held on to metre-high plastic penguins that guided them around the frozen playground helping them stay upright. There was a queue but Tracy had already decided it was as good a place as any to talk. She knelt down the talk to Jackson.

'Would you like to skate with the penguins?' He nodded and pointed excitedly at the skating rink. 'Is that okay?' She looked up at Danielle who nodded. 'You'll have to take him on though?' said Tracy. 'I'm not really dressed for it.'

Tracy bought the tickets; she paid for one adult and one child. They sat at the side waiting for their turn. Tracy had the privilege of a box to sit on as she sipped her coffee and watched the children skating around the frozen rink. Tracy took the opportunity to study her daughter's profile.

She was looking for traces of her own. Their colouring might be different: Danielle was darker, but still somehow reminded Tracy of herself, the way she'd been all those years ago when she'd fallen pregnant at fifteen. *A skinny girl, just a slip of a thing,* thought Tracy. *Looks like she could do with a good meal.* People used to say that about Tracy – not now of course! Something else ... Tracy's heart surged a little – yes – Danielle had her father's nose, his chin. Yes – she looked like him.

Danielle turned from squatting beside Jackson, who was playing with his gloves.

'I didn't think you'd want to see me,' she said as she glanced Tracy's way, held her gaze for a second and then turned back to look at Jackson.

Tracy didn't know what to say. She looked down at Jackson; he was pointing at the penguins in delight.

'My goodness.' Tracy shook her head. 'Why on earth not?'

Danielle shrugged. She looked down at her coffee and didn't answer.

'How old is Jackson?' She was struggling to think of safe ground.

'Four.'

'And he's at school?'

'Just started this term. He goes in the mornings. He's working up to "all day".'

'Does he enjoy it?'

'Yeah, he likes it a lot. He's quite shy. He has difficulty communicating sometimes. People don't understand what he's trying to say. School's done a lot for him, brought him out of his shell. He doesn't see many people besides me.'

'What about his grandparents – the couple who adopted you, Marion and Gerald? The Fosters?'

'My mum Marion died last year. My dad, Gerald,

doesn't talk to me. He doesn't want anything to do with me or Jackson – never did.'

'Oh dear; I'm so sorry to hear that.'

'My mum was lovely but she was sick for so much of my life. She got one form of cancer after the other.'

'Oh . . . I'm sorry. It must have been hard.'

'You never had any kids then?' Tracy shook her head, didn't know what she should say. She was searching for a tissue in her bag. 'Will you?' Danielle persisted. 'After all, it's not too late, is it?'

'No, I suppose not; Steve and I – we're just not in a good position to right now, financially. Steve's my husband. We've been married for fifteen years. He works for a storage company. Things are not easy for us, financially – well, it's a difficult time for everyone, isn't it?'

It had crossed Tracy's mind that if Danielle should ask for money Tracy better make sure she understood that there wasn't any to be had.

'Is there ever a good time to have kids?' Danielle asked.

'No, I suppose not. So you never see him then – your dad?'

'No. I haven't seen him since he chucked me out when I got pregnant.'

Tracy felt an overwhelming surge of pity – it hadn't been like that for her when she got pregnant. Other people took over the problem for her. They took it away.

'I'm sorry, Danielle, really sorry.'

'Yeah . . . I went to live with Jackson's dad but he wasn't the best either.'

'Where do you live now?'

'I have a flat, housing association. It's a high-rise and the estate's old, bit rough. But it's ours for as long as we want it. Jackson and I have been in there nine months now.'

'But, Jackson's dad? Surely ...'

'Yeah – well, we're doing fine, aren't we, J?' She squeezed Jackson's leg to make him giggle.

Tracy was struggling to stay calm and to understand what was happening. She had rehearsed this meeting so many times but none of the times resembled the reality of it. Jackson's turn came to go on the ice. Tracy stood and straightened her coat. She took Danielle's empty cup from her and stacked it inside her own.

'I'm really sorry I can't stay longer. I have to go back to work.'

Danielle looked at her with the wounded eyes of a child, quickly obscured by a practised indifference.

'Sure. Thanks for coming. You have my number. It's up to you if you want to see us again.'

'Yes of course; I'd love to.' Tracy said it but she wasn't sure she meant it. 'I'll ring. Sorry. It's all a bit of a shock, isn't it? I'll phone you later if that's okay?' When she looked back she saw Danielle leaning over Jackson, he was straining to get out of the buggy and take his turn on the ice; Danielle was watching Tracy as she walked away. Tracy couldn't wait to get back to Simmons and the Christmas rush. There were dozens of Christmas orders to box up and tie with ribbons. Jazmina would be desperate for her return.

Back at Simmons, Jazmina didn't bother asking Tracy if things had gone well at her appointment – she could see by her face that they hadn't. Tracy would normally have been in her element, bustling behind the busy counter, but she found herself staring out of the window past the back of the animated Father Christmas; her heart wasn't in it; nothing felt right and there was so much to think about. Memories came flooding back: they were painful and they made her eyes well up. They were things she hadn't allowed herself to think about for many years. She watched the mothers push their buggies up to the window and the kids waving at Father Christmas and she couldn't help but feel devastated.

Danielle held tight to Jackson as he gripped the penguin and pushed his way around the ice very slowly. He was getting in others' way as the older children whizzed past and swerved in front of him. He ignored it – he was happy. Danielle moved around the ice rink in a dream, trying to get her head around the meeting with Tracy. She wasn't sure that they had really connected. Danielle had expected some sort of deep affinity, an unspoken bond. Tracy was nice enough but Danielle felt like she was being talked to as if she'd come to buy a mascara – as if she were a customer. Tracy smiled a lot, was polite, but she did what she had to and then she left as fast as she could. Danielle wondered if she'd ever hear from her again.

It was nine o'clock when Simmons finally closed for the evening. It had been slow the last hour and there were only so many ribbons Tracy could curl ready for decorating Christmas boxes on her shift the next day. All the shelves were replenished; everything was laid out in order and in sequence and in its place.

Tracy walked with Jazmina back to their bus stop where they separated and caught different buses on their opposite ways home. Jazmina lived in Camden, Tracy headed north to Hornsey Rise where she and Steve lived in a ground-floor flat that they rented. Tracy sat on the bus listening to the music coming from the iPod of the boy sitting next to her. She turned to look out of the steamed-up windows and thought about Danielle. Tracy was having a hard job understanding what had motivated Danielle to look for her. Danielle was a tough young woman, prickly – sharp-tongued. She felt let down. She had so wanted it to be wonderful. She had so wanted it to be easy. The reality was that it was awkward and difficult.

But Danielle seemed to want something from her. At the same time she was an angry young woman. Angry at Tracy and angry at everyone. It was her and Jackson against the world, so far as Tracy could see. Tracy had a lot of thinking to do. Is this what she wanted – a single parent with a Down's syndrome child, living in a high-rise on benefits? Did Tracy need that in her life? Someone who didn't even seem to like her very much? How was that going to work out? She could just walk away now. Maybe tell Danielle that the most she could give her was the occasional tenner for Jackson.

She could hear the sound of the television coming from the lounge as she opened the door. The flat was only a little warmer than outside – no matter how much they spent on heating it, it was cold and damp and the landlord did nothing about it. But Tracy did everything she could to make it a home. She stood in the hallway, hung up her coat and took off her shoes and examined the gap where Steve's shoes should have been. She pulled on her fluffy slippers then went into the lounge where Steve was watching the television, the remnants of his dinner on a tray on the floor beside him.

She leaned in to give him a peck on the cheek and pick up the tray. 'Steve … I don't know why you can't pick up your tray and take it out to the kitchen.' Steve didn't move. He grunted. 'And Steve, there's mud or some dirt walked all through the flat.' She didn't use the dreaded term 'dogshit'. 'Did you forget to put your slippers on?' She looked accusingly down at his feet and his dirty shoes, then went back to the door and came back with a pair of Homer Simpson slippers that she'd bought him the previous Christmas. They were just meant to be a joke but she'd been really trying to have a little dig at him – it hadn't worked. He took the slippers from her with an irritable sigh and put them on his feet. Tracy also sighed, but she hid it beneath a sweet smile as she took his shoes and put them next to the front door then she went into the kitchen and came back with a bowl of soapy water and began scrubbing the stains off the carpet.

After a few minutes Steve went out to the kitchen and Tracy paused from scrubbing to listen to the familiar sound of the fridge opening and the clink of a bottle touching another.

'Steve, can you pour me a glass of wine please, love, and is there any of last night's dinner left?'

Steve didn't answer. Tracy heard the pop of the wine bottle and Steve came back in and handed her a glass while she was scrubbing at the brown stain on the carpet.

'Can you put it on the table please, love? I'll be finished in a minute.'

He didn't answer as he took his beer back to the chair.

'I didn't hear what you said about dinner? Is there any out there for me?' Tracy came to stand in front of him.

'No. Sorry. I didn't think you'd want any. I finished it off.'

Tracy finished up and took the bowl out to the kitchen. She emerged with a ham sandwich and picked up her glass of wine.

'Steve, love, can we talk?'

Steve looked accusingly at her. 'What about?'

'I just wanted to have a chat, that's all. How was your day? Is it busy at work? You haven't told me about the Christmas "do" yet.' She sat on the arm of his chair.

Steve eyes went back to the telly as he drank his beer. He looked irritated. 'Can we talk later? I'm watching the match.'

'Yes, of course.' Tracy got up from the chair. 'I'll go and do something else if you don't mind – you know how I hate sport of any kind.'

He grunted his agreement and Tracy walked into the bedroom. She sat on the bed and smoothed her hand across the cover, so silky and creamy white – such good quality. She was lucky to get a thirty per cent discount at Simmons. That meant she could afford the luxury brands. Since Steve wasn't keen on holidays any more, or even going out anywhere, Tracy found herself buying for the home. She took another couple of bites out of her sandwich before abandoning it and just drank her wine instead. The cold wine hit her almost empty stomach. She lay back on the plump pillows and thought about the events of the day. All afternoon she had mulled over the meeting with Danielle.

She shouldn't blame herself for feeling disappointed: she had thought everything would be perfect. She couldn't be blamed for feeling shock about Jackson even; Tracy knew nothing about Down's syndrome. The minute that thought came into her head she scrunched her face and frowned. No . . . it wasn't that simple. It wasn't about that – she was just anxious, that was all. She didn't want to let anyone down – not again. But – she needed to take it further. It wouldn't be right to say 'no thanks' until she gave it a chance.

She took out her phone and stared at Danielle's last text message telling her she would be bringing her four-year-old son Jackson. She smiled as she thought of Jackson with his toy from Father Christmas. She took another large gulp of wine and then she rang Danielle's number. She was just about to hang up when it seemed like no one was going to answer, then Danielle came on the phone, breathless.

'Sorry. Jackson is taking ages to go to sleep.'

'I expect he's excited about Christmas after going to the Grotto today and getting his little pink pig.'

'Yes. He loves Peppa Pig.'

'I could see – very sweet. Danielle – it was lovely to meet you today. I just wanted to tell you that. It's not easy for me.'

'I know. I appreciate that.'

Tracy closed her eyes and clutched the cold glass. 'It was never an easy thing, you know, to give you up?'

'No?'

'No. It wasn't easy, in those days.'

'You're not *that* old. You make it sound like it was the Dark Ages, not the Eighties.'

'No. You're right. But I was only fifteen. My parents were conservative. They thought it was for the best ... But I want you to know something ... I loved your dad.' Tracy heard her voice quiver. 'I don't know why I'm telling you this.'

'Telling me what?'

'He was my first love. True love. Do you understand?'

'So you're telling me you weren't a slapper.'

'No, of course not. I mean yes – that's right. I wasn't. I was in love ... for the first time.'

'Why didn't he want to keep me?'

'It wasn't as easy as that, Danielle. He was the same age as me. We had no idea how to bring up a baby. We talked about it. We cried about it, but both sets of parents were adamant that we had to give you away.'

'You could have had an abortion.'

'I left it too late.' The words hung in the air and Tracy regretted them instantly.

'So you would have done if you could?'

'Yes, maybe.' Tracy shook her head as she held the phone tight. She hadn't meant it to come out like that. She opened her eyes, smiled, clenched her fist in her lap and dug her nails into the palm of her hand. 'But who knows? Maybe it was just meant to be. I thought I was doing the best thing for you, Danielle. I thought the Fosters, the couple they found to adopt you, were lovely.'

She heard silence. She heard Danielle breathing.

'Gerald? He wasn't much of a dad – when I was little maybe. But he became a complete psycho when I hit my teenage years. Nothing I did was right. He shouted all the time, kept me locked in my room. I know it made Mum sicker than ever hearing all the constant rowing. It turned me into someone like him: always shouting, always angry – bitter. Until I had Jackson, that is – then things changed. They do, don't they? When you have a child? Yeah ... well ... it doesn't matter anymore. Jackson asked about you.'

'What do you mean?'

'He likes you. He doesn't like many people. He doesn't often take a shine to someone but he likes you.'

Tracy was mid slurp of wine when it caught in her throat. 'He's a lovely little boy.'

'Yeah ... he has his moments.'

Tracy relaxed a little. 'Shall we meet again?' she asked.

'I'd like to.' Danielle's voice was quiet.

'I have a half day tomorrow. I can meet in the morning, about eleven?'

'Okay. Can we meet near my home? Finsbury Park is just across from me. I can meet you at the main entrance?'

'Of course.'

'Sounds lovely. See you tomorrow.'

Tracy closed her phone and put it back in her bag. She sat on the edge of the bed. She could hear Steve shouting at the television as his team went down at home again. Tracy waited until she heard him get up and go into the kitchen for another beer then she picked up her wine and walked into the lounge. Steve came back into the room and sat back in his chair to listen to the half-time commentary.

'Did you find something to eat?' He kept his eyes on the screen but directed the question her way. He was irritable, resentful. 'Bloody ref. Never seen such a biased decision in all my life.'

'Yes, don't worry.' She came to stand beside him. 'I'm hardly wasting away.'

Steve glared at the telly as a replay of the incident that led to his team's striker being sent off was replayed and analysed. He glanced her way. His eyes ran down her figure.

'No, you're right, you could do with losing a stone. We both could.'

Tracy stared at the side of Steve's head. All the years they'd been together Steve had never realized how hard she tried to fulfil his vision of female perfection and how much it hurt that she knew she would never make it.

She went back into the kitchen and washed up the few things and then she stood looking out into the blackness peppered with orange streetlights beyond the kitchen window. She wiped her hands, sighed loudly as she poured herself another glass of wine, closed her eyes and took a deep breath, then walked back into the lounge. Steve was flicking through the channels as he waited for the analysis to stop and the football to resume after half-time.

'Steve. I need to talk to you about something.' Tracy went to sit to his right on the small silk-covered sofa that she had bought at a large discount from Simmons. Steve watched her. She sat on the edge of the seat and held her glass in two hands.

'It's about the child I gave up for adoption.'

Steve sat back in his chair. He picked up his beer. He kept his eyes on Tracy.

'Well you know that I had a child, a baby girl, when I was a teenager and you know that I gave her up for adoption.'

'I didn't know it was a her?'

'Yes . . . yes . . . it was a girl.'

'Okay and?' He shook his head, confused, irritable now that he was missing the start of the second half.

'She got in touch with me. She said she wanted to meet up.' He looked at her dumbfounded. 'Well, I saw her today.'

'What, you met her?'

'Yes.'

'You didn't think to talk to me about it before you met her?'

Tracy shook her head, flustered. 'I tried to. I thought about it. But I didn't know if she would turn up, if it would actually happen.'

Steve shook his head. He looked at Tracy with an expression of betrayal.

'What the hell, Trace?'

'But, Steve, you have to see ... I had no choice. And I didn't want to worry you in case it came to nothing. You seem so worried about everything these days.'

'And now?' He glared at her. She felt her shoulders rise, her gut tighten. She opened her mouth to answer but nothing came out. Tracy longed to rush over to him; to cuddle him; she wanted him to hold her and reassure her. But she knew that was her job in their relationship.

So she stayed where she was and sat upright on the edge of the sofa: the image of calm.

'And now – I don't know what will come of it but it feels right to try and help her.'

'What does she want?'

'Nothing. Not material things anyway. She lives on her own with Jackson; she seems quite sorted. Do you want to meet them?'

'No, of course I don't. What would I want to meet them for?'

'I don't know, Steve.' She shrugged, shook her head. Kept her eyes on his as she implored him to see beneath, to help, just for once ... 'You know, she's a nice girl. He's a really sweet little lad. He's got Down's syndrome.'

'What?' Steve shook his head slowly and tutted under his breath.

Tracy looked at him, looked at his profile. She felt something so sad inside that it made her jump up and cover her mouth in case it escaped. She went into the kitchen and wiped the clean work surface again. She pulled out the mop and began washing the floor. She listened to Steve shout at the screen as his side conceded another goal.

Chapter 7

Tracy walked through the park entrance and saw
Danielle standing just inside the gates and texting on
her phone. Jackson gave her a smile. Tracy bent down
to talk him.

'Hello, Jackson. Are you warm enough?' His eyes
were watering from the cold. A dog came around
from the other side of the buggy and pushed into her.
She saved herself from falling backwards by reaching
out to put a gloved hand on the railing.

Danielle yanked the dog's lead. 'Scruffy, off!'

Tracy stood and smoothed the creases out of her
coat whilst Danielle finished her text. Tracy was
dressed in a navy double-breasted coat, a red pashmina
scarf around her neck. She looked like an air hostess.

'Sorry, he's a rescue dog,' explained Danielle as she
put her phone back in her pocket. 'He wants a lot of
attention.'

'Ah, shame ...' Tracy gave him three pats on the
head at arm's length.

Danielle pulled his lead back around. 'Scruffy, heel!'

'How's Jackson?'

'Ask him yourself. He's not stupid.' Danielle turned

the buggy into the park and they walked along the central pathway towards the kids' playground.

'Of course. I didn't mean it like that.' Tracy was taken aback. They stopped at the lake and Danielle untangled a bag from where it was looped on the top of the buggy.

'Wait, Jackson.' He was arching in his seat, trying to get out of the buggy.

'Undo him for me?' she said as she untied the bag.

Tracy bent down and fiddled with the clasp holding Jackson in his seat. She finally managed to open it and Jackson rushed forward.

'Grab him. Before he ends up in the water!' shouted Danielle.

Tracy made a lunge for Jackson and gripped his hand as they walked towards the edge of the pond. Danielle followed them and gave Jackson a chunk of bread to hold before handing the rest of the bag to Tracy. They hovered near the edge of the pond and ducks descended on them thick and fast in a noisy squabble. Tracy leant over Jackson and held on to him tightly as he shrieked for joy and threw handfuls of bread at the ducks. She laughed at his delight. She turned to see Danielle watching them.

'What do you want him to call you?'

'What do you mean?' Tracy looked at her blankly.

'Grandma? Granny? What?'

'Uh ... oh ... I don't know,' she said, shaking her head, shrugging, burying her neck in her pashmina. 'Tracy will be fine.'

"No it won't. He wants a granny, not a friend.' Danielle called Jackson's name three times to get his attention back to her. He reluctantly turned away from feeding the ducks.

'Who's that?' She pointed to Tracy.

Jackson looked bashful and said: 'Nanny.' He gave Danielle a look that betrayed the fact that she had told him to say it.

'Nanny ...?' Tracy tried not to look offended. 'As in goat?'

'Just an idea.'

Danielle answered, hiding a smile as she pushed the empty buggy nearer to them. Tracy tried not to be annoyed or show she was bothered. 'Shall we take him to the swings?' she said as she looked down the length of the lake to the playground beyond.

'Ask him if he wants to go.' The flash of annoyance came quickly again to Danielle's face.

Tracy closed her eyes with a sigh. Then she leant down in front of Jackson's face – eyes wide and smile in place.

'Jackson? How would you like Tracy – *Nanny* – to push you on the swings?'

Jackson nodded.

'Okay then, let's go.' Tracy took his hand and they started to walk along beside the lake. Danielle followed, pushing the empty buggy.

Jackson laughed as he skipped and hung on to Tracy's arm.

'You're a heavy little thing.' She laughed as she did her best to lift him from the floor by his arm.

There were a handful of kids in the playground. Jackson ran excitedly from one apparatus to the other, unable to make up his mind which to go on first. He was followed hotly by Tracy. Finally he settled on his first choice, the swing, and Tracy pushed him while Danielle sat on a bench nearby.

Tracy looked across at Danielle between making *woo, woo* noises for Jackson to accompany every push of the swing. Danielle was texting. She'd been texting for the last ten minutes.

'Who's that? A sweetheart?' Tracy called over to her.

Danielle looked up from her phone, shook her head and smiled.

'Just someone on my course.'

'What course is that?'

'I'm taking an Access to primary education course so that I can go into teaching. I'm learning about computers as well at the moment. I want to become a special needs teacher. I want to be there for Jackson. I want to give him everything he needs.'

Tracy turned back to push Jackson, who had grown quietly content as he swung back and forth in the air.

'What about you, Tracy? Any ambitions? Any things you really want to achieve?'

'Oh, you know ... the usual – see the world, first class of course: I'm a bit old to go backpacking now.'

'No you're not. I read about it – it's all the rage, Tracy. Women going off in their forties and fifties to find themselves. Going to Thailand on treks or taking a year to work their way around Asia.'

'Well I'll have to wait a few more years then,' Tracy said.

Danielle laughed. 'Yeah, I forget you're just fifteen years older than me. We could be sisters.'

Tracy smiled as she continued pushing Jackson, pleased with the compliment. She had expected a snipe about her ageing looks but was pleasantly surprised when one didn't materialize.

'I'd love to go on a cruise,' she said. 'That's more me really than backpacking.'

'I would love to take Jackson on holiday, anywhere – I don't mind,' said Danielle, her face softening, and Tracy thought how pretty she looked today. If only she would make more of herself.

'Plenty of time yet for that, isn't there?' Tracy smiled at her. Danielle nodded, her eyes still focused on some distant dream.

'Yeah. I suppose he's young. I'd like to take him places when he's older. I haven't done much travelling. The last time I went on holiday was with Mum and Dad; that was the time we began falling out. That's when the rot set in. Gerald was jealous of the time Mum and I spent just talking; he always wanted to know what we were talking about – as if we were keeping secrets from him – just bollocks really – paranoid, controlling. That holiday marked the beginning of the end for us. What about you?'

'Oh – I always seem to be busy working and we haven't really had the money in the last few years. Before that we went to Spain usually, Majorca sometimes.

'What about work-wise? What about your career?'

'I pootle along. I've always been in the beauty industry one way or another. I used to have my own beauty salon; saw several clients a day – always had my regulars for a wax, for a facial. I like that, looking after people – but, well, it didn't work out.' Tracy finished off her sentence with a tight smile. Danielle didn't ask why. Tracy went back to pushing Jackson. 'Do you get help from Jackson's father financially?'

'Ha! I wouldn't take it. We're better off without him.'

'Still … it's a lot to manage on your own.'

Danielle didn't reply to this. She came over and lifted Jackson down from the swing. 'We have to go now. I'm going to be late for my class otherwise. Jackson's booked in at the crèche there. He likes it. But I need to give him lunch first.'

'Oh. Okay. Is it far to go?'

'No, we'll go home first. We live just over there.' Danielle pointed to tower blocks on the edge of the park.

'Oh … that's handy. I live in Hornsey.'

'Yes I know. I looked you up in the phone book. You can come and have a cup of tea with us, Tracy, if you want.'

'Yes. I'd like that.' Tracy smiled. 'Maybe I could look after Jackson for you sometime if you'd like to go out?' Danielle looked at Tracy. 'I could do your make-up for you. Style you. I'd like that.' Danielle didn't answer. She rolled her eyes and looked away. 'I don't mean you're not a pretty girl,' Tracy said hurriedly. 'It's just something I could do; it's what I do every day. I make people up. I expect you don't get out much? I bet you don't have much chance to find yourself a boyfriend.'

'So the women you make up – they all look like Barbie dolls?'

'No, no. Of course I wouldn't make *you* look like that.'

'Like you?' Danielle smiled at Tracy but she meant to be hurtful.

'No. As I said—' Tracy's tone turned frosty – 'this look is not for everyone.' Tracy stared at Danielle as she watched her strap Jackson back into his buggy. She didn't know her daughter well enough yet to know what to make of her swings between liking and loathing Tracy. She seemed to be still so young, so unforgiving. They would have an uphill battle on their hands if Danielle was determined to harbour so many grudges.

'Maybe not then. It was just a thought.' Tracy said sighing.

Danielle glanced up at Tracy apologetically. 'Sorry – I didn't mean it. I'm just tired. I would appreciate it if you could babysit for me though, just once in a while. I wouldn't take the piss.'

'Of course.' Tracy recovered her composure. She was used to people talking about her looks when she was behind the counter – especially the young girls that came in. One of them had said she looked like an ageing porn star. Tracy looked on it as her job to wear make-up. They could criticize it all they liked. 'I'd love to babysit. You'll have to show me what to do. I've never had children.'

'No. You gave yours away.' Tracy just looked at Danielle; she didn't know what to say. Danielle turned away. 'Come on, Jackson. Let's show Nanny where we live.'

Tracy was too flustered to know what to reply.

'What, now?'

She stayed where she was as Danielle started walking away.

'Yes. You coming, Nanny?' Danielle pushed Jackson towards the crossing at the traffic lights on Seven Sisters Road.

Tracy looked at her watch as she caught them up.

'Just for ten minutes then. A quick cup of tea. That will be lovely.'

It was short walk to the block of flats with a parade of shabby shops with reinforced shutters on their windows that made them look shut when they weren't. Tracy had never been inside a tower block before. She's been to high-rise hotels in Spain. This was nothing like that.

The lift was out of order, so Tracy helped Danielle with the buggy up the flights of stairs. Jackson got out and walked, holding Tracy's hand.

'I must be so unfit.' Despite the cold Tracy felt herself beginning to perspire beneath her coat. 'I need to get to the gym. I can't remember the last time I did any exercise. We used to go regularly, me and Steve. We couldn't keep up with the membership in the end. Still, no excuse. Back to the gym for me. I'll have to get fit if I'm going to chase after Jackson. Hey, scallywag?' Tracy smoothed Jackson's hair to one side.

'Here we are.' Danielle ruffled his hair back into peaks.

Leaving the stairwell at the third floor they walked along the landing until they came to a pink door. Number 372. It would be easy for Tracy to remember. She was good with numbers. She could always remember exactly how much stock was left of every product on the counter. She knew the serial numbers of each product. She knew the lipstick colours by their codes.

'What's happened here?' she asked, looking at the dents in the metal plate that was put on to reinforce the door.

'Someone tried to break in,' Danielle said. Tracy opened her mouth to say something but then shut it and didn't say anything. She waited while Danielle found her key and unlocked locks top and bottom, then pushed the door back until it jammed on the wood laminate flooring. Jackson ran in, excited. Scruffy followed.

Danielle folded and rested the buggy against the wall in the hallway and walked through to the kitchen on the right.

'What a lovely place. You've done a good job with the decoration,' said Tracy. Danielle's place looked like it had come out of a back issue of the Ikea catalogue.

'Thanks. Tea or coffee?'

'Tea will be fine.'

Tracy took off her coat and put it over the buggy – she couldn't see where else she should put it – then she stood in the kitchen doorway. Jackson's drawings were everywhere. Danielle saw Tracy looking at them.

'It's hard to throw any of them away.' She smiled, embarrassed but proud as well.

'They're lovely colours. Can you tell what they are?'

'Of course!'

'Can you really?' Tracy peered at the pictures.

Danielle pointed to a long shape with four sticks coming from it. 'Look, there's Scruffy. That's me, you can see by the hair,' she added, pointing to a blob with brown on top. Tracy peered in to get a closer look at the picture.

'Oh yes, I see it now.'

'I know.' Danielle laughed. 'It's an acquired skill. He's very good for his age actually. He's able to go to an ordinary school ... for now anyway. Does anyone else in the family have Down's syndrome?'

Tracy was taken aback. She shook her head. 'I don't think so.'

'What family have I got anyway?'

Tracy couldn't hide it as a look of panic took hold. She hadn't thought of that – the implications of meeting up with her daughter and the fact that it affected more than just her. What if Danielle made a nuisance of herself?

'It's all right – I don't intend to contact people.' Danielle turned away and finished making the tea. Tracy instantly regretted her reaction. It was as if Danielle had read her mind.

'No. I mean I am sure that, given time, everyone will want to meet you.' She could see by Danielle's demeanour that she was brittle and trying not to show how much Tracy's negative reactions mattered as she poured away a little of the hot tea from each cup and topped up with cold water. Tracy watched her, mesmerized. She wanted to say: 'I always do that. I always top up the tea with cold.'

'Um – you have an aunt. My sister Julie and her husband Nigel. They live in Manchester. They have

three children all older than you. They have five kids
between them. So Jackson has a few cousins.' Tracy
smiled broadly, trying to make things better.

'My first cousins. They are his second cousins,'
Danielle corrected.

'Yes.' Tracy stood corrected.

'Do they look like me?'

Tracy thought about it and shrugged 'Maybe ... I'm
not sure. Oh, I forgot.' She went out to her bag by her
coat and came back into the kitchen with an envelope.
'I brought you a photo of me to show you.'

She took out a small handful of different-sized
photos and came to stand next to Danielle. With the
photos was a small box.

'Before I show you the photos I want to give you
this.' She opened the box to show Danielle. 'This is
for you. I got it when I was ten.' She took out a silver
charm bracelet from the box. 'I added to it every year.
I would like you to have it.' She held it out for Danielle
to take it. 'Charm bracelets have come back in, haven't
they? Each one of those charms means something
to me.' Danielle held the tiny charms between finger
and thumb as she examined each one. 'That London
bus I got when I passed my driving licence so I
wouldn't need to take a bus again – that's when I was
seventeen. The ballet shoe I got when I passed my
exams at eleven. This Mickey Mouse my parents got
me when I was twelve. Oh, my whole life is here.' She
smiled, delighted to see Danielle's reaction. 'You are
here too. I bought this silver heart when I became
pregnant with you.' Danielle couldn't look at Tracy.
'I don't have much else to pass on to you.'

'Tracy. I'm so ... well, I'm touched. Thank you. I'll wear it now.' Danielle put it round her wrist. Tracy did it up for her.

'Don't lose it, mind.' Tracy smiled. She wanted to kiss Danielle's cheek but she didn't. Instead she passed her the first photo. 'I've just got a few I thought you might like to see. I don't want to bore you. This was the year I fell pregnant with you.'

Danielle held the photo closely. 'Oh my God – you were a child.'

'Yes – I suppose I was.'

'You look so young.' She looked at the photo of Tracy in her school uniform.

'I was fifteen – I guess that's young. I didn't feel it at the time.' Danielle didn't look at Tracy and she took out the next photo. 'Here's a photo of me and my parents, your grandparents and there's Julie.'

Danielle laughed. 'You can see you're the rebel. Look at Julie. Her socks are pulled up, her skirt is under her knee and look at you!'

Tracy laughed too. 'I was always in trouble for hitching my skirt up, rolling it up at the waist. Those were the days.'

'You're not old, Tracy. You could still wear a miniskirt if you wanted.'

'I suppose not but I could do with getting back into shape.' She passed another photo over. It was of a school football team. 'Which one do you think he is?' Tracy beamed as she watched Danielle's face light up.

'What do you mean? Is my dad in this photo?'

Tracy nodded; she could hear the excitement in Danielle's voice as she held it close.

'Him.'

She pointed to a boy on the left of centre. Tracy nodded again. 'That's who you look like, isn't it?'

She could see Danielle's eyes welling up. Danielle turned away and wiped her eyes with her sleeve as she took a sip of her tea.

'Where is he now?'

Tracy shook her head. 'I haven't seen him since I was about your age. He married someone and they moved away. You could probably find him as well if you wanted.'

Danielle thought about it.

'Maybe. But I think you're enough for now.'

She stared blankly at Tracy, who was frowning and obviously trying to understand what she meant by that; Danielle grinned. Tracy laughed then smiled.

'It's funny how you remind me of him. It's the way you smile.' She picked up the football team photo and her eyes focused in and melted as her mind spiralled back to that summer of love.

'So I ruined your life.' Danielle watched Tracy.

Tracy looked up from her memories and shook her head. 'No. You could have been the making of me. Of him, maybe. I should have kept you. I should have followed my heart. I nursed you for a few days before I gave you up. I was so tired and there was so much pressure, but when you'd gone, my whole body yearned for you. I couldn't hear a baby cry in the street without my milk rushing into my breasts. I couldn't pass a little girl in the street without wondering if it was you. On your birthday, March the twenty-seventh, I always have a little cry. So many regrets, Danielle. Now, to find out that my sacrifice wasn't worth it, that the couple who I gave you to didn't deserve you – it breaks my heart.' Tracy turned away as she felt herself crumble. 'Oh God,' she said, 'how pathetic I am. Sorry I didn't mean to get upset.'

Danielle shook her head. 'It's all right, Tracy. You did what you thought was best, what others thought was best for you.'

Tracy dabbed at her eyes and the tissue was streaked with make-up. 'What was it really like, living with them – the Fosters?'

'The early years were wonderful. It was when I hit adolescence that everything went wrong. Gerald, especially, just couldn't have found it more difficult. I think he hadn't thought it through. He wanted me to be a child for ever. He never bought into the whole teenage girl thing.'

Tracy shook her head, still trying to stop her make-up from melting. 'What do you mean?'

'He got nasty with me. He just couldn't hack the hormones. I was moody, difficult – typical teenage girl, I suppose. I think my self-esteem hit rock bottom. I rebelled against everything and anything. I thought I was being clever but looking back – it was stupid. I started missing school, hung about with the wrong types. Before long I had gone too far to recover. I had thought that I would still be able to pass my exams even though I didn't work. People had always told me how bright I was. But I didn't go to the lessons and I failed. I started taking stuff. I met Jackson's father that way. I thought he was really cool, but he was a real loser. He sold drugs to kids. He hit me when he felt in a bad mood, plus he was never faithful. My mum got ill and my dad wouldn't let me help. I was so angry and I hated him. He tried to keep me away from her. When I got pregnant at seventeen it was the perfect excuse to chuck me out.'

'Didn't Marion stop him?'

'She tried. I remember her crying and pleading but he just stood there glaring at me; he really hated me by that time. Social Services became involved. They said I was better off moving out. They fixed me up with a flat and I moved in with Jackson's dad, Niall. But Niall didn't want us. He just wanted the flat so he could do his deals from it. I didn't really care until Jackson was born and then I saw Niall was never going to change and suddenly everything became clear to me and nothing mattered but Jackson.'

'Is that why you got in touch with me?'

'I suppose it is.'

'What do you want to happen between us? What do you want from me?' Tracy had rehearsed what she was going to say many times in the last week. None of those times had it come out like that.

Danielle shook her head. She looked up, angry. 'I don't want anything.'

'You must have had something in mind?' Tracy replied, trying to keep her voice soft, low. She knew it would rise and become panicky if she didn't watch it.

'I just need you to promise something.' Tracy waited. Danielle's eyes softened. 'I need you to promise to take care of Jackson if anything happens to me. I haven't got anyone else. You're his granny. You have to do it.' Tracy stood blinking at Danielle, her shoulders raised, her eyes frightened. She didn't answer.

'My friend went missing from my course. She just disappeared; flipped, I suppose. She left a child alone, a little girl called Sky, but she had her parents to rely on. They're looking after Sky now. I thought, who has Jackson got? I know it sounds silly. I know it sounds like I'm thinking too hard about some stuff but I reckon if you put a Plan B in place hopefully you'll never have to use it.' She turned to Tracy. 'You are my Plan B, Tracy.'

The man made his way along the busy streets and hurried to his home. Fumbling with the keys he closed the door behind him and stood listening. In the gloom his eyes shone and his heart quickened. His senses heightened. He walked slowly down the hallway, tilting his head to listen as he did so, and then up the stairs to the top landing. At the end of the landing, he stopped by a door on his left and smiled as he closed his eyes and breathed in the smell deeply through his nose. A buzzing fly interrupted his thoughts as he opened his eyes just a fraction and watched it. It landed on the doorframe and his hand, fast as a chameleon's tongue, squashed it flat. He looked at the mess on his hand.

From behind the door someone groaned. He wiped his hand on his chest then he squeezed and turned the doorknob. He flicked on a light switch and an old chandelier flickered into meagre life. The room was filled with more shadows than light. The smell of decay hit him. It was a sweet perfume to his nose. Music started as he opened the door. A violin solo, melancholy at first and then growing in tempo. The woman's crying just audible with the violin. He spun and danced as he waltzed his way towards her. She turned her body from him, her knees tucked up against her chest, whimpering. She was skeletal. Around the room were photos of emaciated women in bikinis. He pulled her up from the floor as she cried in pain and he held her to him as he twirled her round the room. He danced as she cried in his arms.

Chapter 8

'*It is the still and silent sea that drowns a man.* That's the literal translation of the tattoo. Doctor Harding was right about the language.' Carter and Willis were in the crime analyst's office.

'The tattoo on the mermaid's ankle is a Norse saying.' Robbo placed a file in front of them. 'This is her.'

Crime Analyst Robbo worked in an office which he shared with one full-time civilian worker, Pam, and two researchers, available when the investigation warranted more help. Robbo had been a long-serving detective in the murder squad and had retrained as an analyst when he retired.

Operation Sparrowhawk was written up on the board behind his desk.

On the front of the file was a picture of a smiling woman in her early twenties with a bottle of beer in her hand. She was dressed in frayed denim shorts, a bikini top, big floppy hat and pink Wellington boots. She had long auburn hair flowing over her shoulders.

'This is twenty-three-year-old Emily Styles – went

missing on June the fifth. This picture was taken at a festival a couple of weeks before she disappeared. She lived in Camden with her parents and her two-year-old daughter Sky.'

'Christ almighty.' Carter picked up the photo and studied it. 'Not what I was expecting.'

'I remember her disappearance,' said Willis. 'MIT 15 were dealing with it. Jeanie was loaned to them for the case; she was their Family Liaison Officer.'

'Ask Jeanie to come,' said Carter. 'And tell her to bring anything she has on it.'

Ebony was already on her feet and half-way out of the door. She found Jeanie back at her desk in the Enquiry Team Office.

'Yeah, I went round there when she first went missing,' said Jeanie when she got to Robbo's office.

'What were her circumstances?' asked Carter. 'Did the initial investigation throw up any suspects, Jeanie?'

'Very few. It was handled by MIT 15. I was loaned to them when they were overstretched back in the summer. Emily went missing one afternoon and no one seemed to think it was that out of the ordinary. Her parents didn't even think to report her missing for five days.' Jeanie perched on the edge of the vacant researcher's desk.

'But she left her belongings?'

'Yeah, everything except what was in her handbag – phone, purse, what-have-you.'

'She never turned up to collect her child from nursery. That must have been the biggest cause for alarm bells to start ringing?'

'You'd think so – but, according to her mum, they pretty much look after the little girl anyway. They said Emily was a bit wild. I got the impression she was a good mum but she was taking time to tame; still took the odd pill and used to stay away for a night without letting anyone know a few times. She'd been travelling and found it hard to settle. It seemed to me that her parents thought she'd just gone off more than disappeared. They seemed to be apologetic about Emily and resigned to bringing up the little girl themselves. It was as if they blamed themselves for the fact that Emily wasn't that keen on settling into motherhood. They thought they'd tried to make her into something she couldn't be.'

'She still lived with them?'

'She was planning to move out and had been offered a flat. Even though she'd officially taken on the tenancy. She wasn't in any hurry to leave; she had a good set-up there.'

'What about the father of the child?'

'She'd split from the father. He's part of the Romany community.'

'Could it be some sort of retaliation for ending the relationship?' asked Robbo.

Jeanie shook her head. 'The father was interviewed when Emily first went missing. He was counted out of the equation; he was in prison. His family was cleared as well.'

'And there was no one new in her life?' asked Carter.

Jeanie shook her head. 'Her parents didn't know if

she was seeing anyone special but she hadn't gone so far as to bring anyone home.'

'And what about her friends?'

'The morning of the day she disappeared,' answered Jeanie, 'she phoned a friend at ten in the morning, and they met for coffee in Camden where she did a bit of shopping, hung around Camden Market for a couple of hours. Her friend left her there and she was picked up by cameras walking back towards Camden Town Tube.'

'Was the person she went with a friend?' said Robbo.

'Maybe he was a potential boyfriend, under the radar,' said Carter. 'We need to open the investigation wider and we'll take it over from MIT 15. Were her phone records requested at the time?'

Robbo shook his head. 'This was a Mispers, not a murder investigation.'

'We'll do it now then. Get all her phone records from the last five years,' said Carter.

'What about any other social media?' said Ebony.

'I'll put in a request.' Robbo made notes as Carter talked.

'Did she take a passport?'

'No,' answered Jeanie. 'But she had a driving licence and she'd run away with the Romany community before. That's how she ended up pregnant in the first place. She had a wandering heart. I guess that's why her parents just accepted it.'

'What are they like?'

'Ordinary middle-class people. They brought her up in a good home but she rebelled from an early age.

She was an arty child, a bohemian type. Her parents rode it all out in the hope that she would come home. When they finally persuaded her to come back, go to college, get a life, they offered her full support for her and Sky. It worked, but they thought she'd had enough of the struggle. They thought Emily had just decided to leave it all behind.'

'What was her normal routine, Jeanie?'

'She was in between jobs. Her parents supported her. In many ways she was quite privileged, spoilt even,' answered Jeanie. 'She took Sky to nursery most days, paid for by her parents. Otherwise she went to college. She met friends, went shopping. She hung out at home – normal stuff really.'

'We'll go and see the parents, prepare them for the worst, said Carter.

'I'll come too,' said Jeanie. 'It's going to be a shock for them. I still think they were expecting her to walk back through their front door when she felt like it.'

Carter looked at the photo of Emily Styles.

'What do we know about her lifestyle?' Carter asked. 'Could she have been moonlighting as an escort? Prostitute perhaps?'

Jeanie shook her head; 'Unlikely but not impossible.'

Carter continued: 'Murdered by a pimp and she was put in the Regents Canal as a warning to others? A place so that she would be seen? Otherwise, why not dump her in the countryside?'

Ebony had a map of the canal and the surrounding area on the screen.

'He chose a place where there aren't many cameras but you can see it from several vantage points, the bridges, the park.'

'Hawk is a watcher,' said Robbo.

Chapter 9

After Jeanie rang the doorbell they heard the soft shuf-
fle of feet approach from the other side of the door.
They waited on the step. The small front garden was
occupied by a large magnolia tree that had been
allowed to get leggy and was desperate for light.

'Jeanie?' A long-faced man in a grey V-neck sweater
almost smiled at Jeanie until he saw that she was not
alone and, judging by the look on the faces of the
three people on his doorstep, had gauged that their
visit was not going to make him happy.

'Can we come in, Trevor? These detectives want to
have a chat.'

Carter held up his warrant card. 'Hello, Mr Styles.
My name is Detective Inspector Dan Carter and this
is Detective Constable Ebony Willis.'

Trevor Styles nodded slowly and stood back to
allow them inside. The last of the colour was
already draining from his face. He looked down the
corridor to where his wife Elaine had stepped out of
the kitchen, tea towel in one hand and plate in the
other.

'Hello, Elaine.' Jeanie smiled at Mrs Styles; she

nodded back, her eyes flitting worriedly from one detective to the other. 'Will you come here please?'

Elaine Styles walked mechanically forward, clutching the plate in her hand.

Carter spoke: 'Mr and Mrs Styles. A young woman's body has been found that we believe to be Emily's.'

The Styles stood apart from one another, each lonely in the grief, unable to stand it alone or together. Mr Styles nodded and turned to look at his wife as she stood in the hallway. Swaying, still clutching the tea towel, she dropped the plate. Jeanie went over, and knelt to pick up the pieces.

'Have you got a dustpan?' she asked Trevor, who nodded and went past his wife. She was still staring at Carter.

'Are you sure it's Emily?' Elaine said as she wrapped her hands in the tea towel.

Carter nodded. 'We are pretty sure. I'm so sorry, Mrs Styles.'

Trevor Styles returned with the dustpan and began sweeping up the last of the crockery shards.

Jeanie put her arm around Elaine. 'I'm so sorry.' She guided her in to sit down on the sofa in the lounge.

'We just need to ask you a couple of questions,' said Carter. 'Did Emily wear an antique ring on a chain around her neck like this one?' He showed her a photo of the ring.

Elaine looked hard at Carter, her mind revisiting painful images. She shook her head.

'I've never seen it before.' She looked at her husband, her eyes wide as he returned from the kitchen having disposed of the broken crockery. 'Maybe it's not her,' she said as she shook her head, her face beginning to crumple.

'Are you sure, Mrs Styles?' asked Ebony. 'About the jewellery?'

'Yes, we're sure,' answered Trevor, looking at the photo whilst his wife fought to stop herself dissolving with the pain of grief.

'Emily's tattoo – the one on her ankle – can you tell us about that?'

Trevor shook his head sadly; his eyes were distant. 'It's an ancient Norse saying about the sea. We lost our son, Emily's younger brother, when she was ten. He drowned off the beach in Cornwall. They were playing at the water's edge. The next minute there was just Emily and he was gone. It was a calm day. He was only up to his knees. We will never know how it happened. They told us the current took him.' Trevor shook his head again, his eyes misted as he still tried to understand what had happened. He looked up at them. 'It looked so calm on the surface; we never knew there was a rip tide. Emily never got over it. She never went near the sea again. She was not the same girl afterwards. None of us were. You never get over something like that. Makes you feel like nothing you have is for ever.'

Elaine held the tea towel against her face, smothering her cries.

Ebony looked at Carter and he nodded; his eyes went to Jeanie and then flicked towards the door.

Jeanie stepped forward to hug Elaine Styles.

'I think the best thing is if you come with me now and we go and see if it's Emily.'

Mr Styles looked up and nodded. He looked at his wife.

She nodded.

'Will you lock up? Elaine asked him.

The couple sat in the back of Carter's car with Jeanie. Ebony looked across at Carter, who was driving. In the year she had worked with him she was still learning about his character. Things affected him that she didn't think would. He was feeling it today. He kept his eyes on the road. He was saying the bare minimum. It was a Sunday morning. Shoppers were beginning to feel the Christmas lure. The sun had come out to start melting the snow. The car was silent until Trevor Styles asked:

'Where did you find her?'

Carter looked in the mirror as he answered.

'She was found in King's Cross, Mr Styles, in the Regent's Canal.'

'Did she drown?'

'No. We think she was strangled.'

Elaine turned her head away and sobbed quietly.

Ebony waited outside the mortuary with Mrs Styles whilst Carter and Jeanie took Mr Styles into the viewing room.

'I think it's better that we stand here, Trevor.' Jeanie led him to stand before a large window in the viewing room. They looked onto the body, laid out beneath a shroud. Only her face was showing. Mark had done a good job on her. They stood behind the glass.

'Yes.' He nodded. 'It's my daughter.'

Carter felt Mr Styles sway next to him. He turned to look at his reaction.

'Her face looks so strange.'

Carter nodded. 'The water.' Trevor Styles was staring at Carter as if at any moment he might make a run for it. 'But are you sure it's her, Mr Styles?'

Trevor Styles' face had lost all colour. 'Yes.' Words caught in his throat in a mixture of anguish and catarrh. 'I'm sure. It's my daughter Emily.'

Carter placed his hand on Mr Styles' shoulder.

'I'm sorry for your loss.'

Trevor Styles bowed his head and nodded. Carter led him back out to the reception area where he hugged his wife as she cried openly. His eyes stayed on Carter.

'Will you find whoever did this?'

Carter nodded. 'I give you my word.' He waited until Mrs Styles drew back from her husband. 'Is it okay if we take you home and ask you some questions? We will try to keep it as brief as possible,' he asked.

Elaine was about to object but Trevor Styles answered.

'Yes. The sooner we find out who did this and bring them to justice the sooner my wife and I can rebuild our lives – and there's Sky to think of. Life has to go on now. We have to make the best of it for Sky.'

Back at their home Jeanie went into the kitchen and helped Elaine make tea for them all. Willis and Carter went into the lounge with Trevor.

Ebony watched him as he went to stand and look

out of the window; outside the sky had clouded and the daylight was fast slipping away. It was three in the afternoon but already streetlamps were coming on.

Trevor stood in silence in the dark room, looking into the space beyond the net curtains. People passed as they walked home. The lights of cars lit up his face as they passed. Ebony was a good waiter and watcher. Life had taught her to be an observer. Life had taught her to wait for emotions and not to drag them out of people – they had a habit of coming out whether it was a good time or not. But then life had given her a bipolar mother who had ultimately killed someone. In between, Ebony had watched the kettle stay at boiling point her whole life. She saw no reason in agitating water that was already boiling, even if you couldn't see it. It could still explode in your face.

Carter was always in a hurry. Always wanting to fill the silence. He looked over at Willis, wanting Ebony to be the first to break the silence, but she didn't.

'Once again.' said Carter. 'I am sorry for your loss, Mr Styles.'

Trevor Styles turned from the window and nodded his thanks. Styles looked across at Ebony.

'Mr Styles,' began Carter, 'I'm going to get a few questions out of the way, if you don't mind? I apologize if they sound offensive or cause distress but you will understand I'm only doing what I have to so that we can find who did this to Emily.'

'I understand. Ask whatever you need to. I'll answer if I can.'

'You have a lot on your plate with little Sky?' Carter asked.

He looked towards Carter and sighed out loud as he shook his head.

'We will manage.' Already his face was turning from the look of grief to a deep residue of anger. 'We've looked after her all her life. I'm sure Jeanie's told you – my daughter relied on us to look after Sky.'

'Did you have a good relationship with Emily – were you close?'

He turned back to the window. The shadow from the net curtain chequered his face.

'I regret being a little too easy on her.' He sighed heavily. 'Sometimes I think I could have been tougher on her; but with her brother gone ... well, it was hard to get the balance right. We were so busy grieving we didn't notice she wasn't going to school. She got into trouble – drugs and a bad lot of friends – and then she left home for three years, we didn't see her and then she came back pregnant. When she went missing I thought she'd slipped back to her old ways. Yes, we spoilt her, I know. But, who wouldn't? After what happened to her brother we felt we had to treasure her. Maybe we allowed her to get away with too much. But, inside, in her heart, she was a lovely person. She would never intentionally hurt anyone. We had our rows but in the past year she seemed to really be making a go of it. I can't understand why anyone would want to harm her, she was so lovely. She was an honest person – direct.' He smiled and looked across at Ebony. 'Very direct, almost in a child-like way. She never hesitated to say what ever came into her head. But she didn't always understand people. She didn't always have the skills you need to understand.' A wash of confusion crossed his face and then sorrow replaced it. 'But she was beautiful, inside and out – trusting, a free spirit and she had guts, determination. She knew she had a lot to learn; she held her hands up ... but she did something about it. I failed her – didn't give her credit. I should have trusted her to stick by Sky, to honour the promises she made to us.'

He shook his head. He looked at Ebony and waited for her to give him some reassurance but she couldn't. Ebony stared back at him. He turned back to the window.

'I guess that's just something I have to carry with me.'

'I'm sure you did what any parent would have done, Mr Styles.' Carter smiled sympathetically. 'She obviously loved living here and she trusted you to look after Sky. Why was she going to move out?'

'It was time, the next part in her journey in life. She was taking small steps and we didn't mind how small they were. We loved having her back here and we adore Sky. She was really pleased with the flat. Her mum helped her buy all the bits for it. It's just around the corner from here. Still we thought maybe that's why she ran away, the thought of having to cope alone. But she didn't run away. We did her an injustice. We should have known she wouldn't.'

'Did she have a boyfriend?' asked Carter, trying to seem sympathetic but also trying to push the conversation along.

'Not that we'd seen. Nobody serious anyway.'

'She must have had some male friends?' Carter persisted.

Mr Styles wrapped his arms around himself and his face was lit with the lights from the passing traffic.

'Yes, she had some.' He shrugged. 'There are ones she's known since she was young; she grew up around here. She spent her childhood in this house.'

'But no one special?'

'She was at college, she'd made some new friends through that. I think she'd had a few dates with the same person. But nothing you'd call a relationship.'

'Did you hear a name being talked about?'

'No. Emily was quite a private person, especially where we were concerned. We were on a "need to know" basis. Plus, if she had been seeing someone she wouldn't have brought them back here. She had spent a few nights on and off in her new flat. She would have taken them there.'

'What was she studying?' asked Ebony.

'She was taking basic qualifications, hoping to train as a veterinary nurse, first rung of the ladder type of thing.'

'What about Sky's father's family? Do any of them ever come around?' asked Carter.

'Occasionally Bo used to show up with a present for Sky. He doesn't give any money, that's for sure. When he went back inside, Emily got the odd phone call from him, that was all. She'd definitely moved on.' He shook his head. 'She was so busy, so excited about college, that's all she talked about. She had a new set of friends.'

'How did she manage for money?'

'She didn't really.' Styles smiled, shook his head. 'She was always broke. We helped her out.' He smiled. 'We didn't mind.' His voice was barely audible as he addressed no one in particular. 'It doesn't seem right that it happened to her – just when she was getting somewhere and things were going right.'

'I understand. I am sorry. It's very tough for you. One more thing – I think I know the answer to this but please understand I have to ask. Was there any chance Emily was injecting any kind of drug?'

Trevor Styles shook his head, saddened that the question had been asked. He looked across at Ebony. She didn't flinch from his gaze. He shook his head.

'Absolutely not heroin or anything that involved needles. Emily has a real phobia about needles.'

Chapter 10

'What are your thoughts, Ebb?' Carter pulled away from outside the Styles' house. 'Do you think she could have hidden a lot from her parents? Could she have had a whole life they didn't know about? They didn't seem to worry when she didn't come home at night. She could have been someone's regular escort? Hawk might be someone who paid her for sex.'

'Not likely, Guv, if she was always broke. Jeanie said they spoke to her friends at the time – I think it would have come out then. Plus, a rich punter is unlikely to want to draw attention to his crime by dumping her in the canal – much more likely to dispose of her in the countryside or the sea.'

'I agree. He's definitely made a point with location and method. Why? For notoriety?'

'Think it's fame, Guv.' Ebony looked across at Carter as he drove. They were caught in a traffic jam.

'Yeah.' Carter nodded his agreement. 'Everyone remembers the body found in the canal; no one remembers the one found in the woods. And, sometimes that body isn't even found. Somehow Hawk doesn't seem the type to want to waste the kill. He wants everyone to see it.'

'I think he wanted to be able to see her when she came back up,' said Ebony. 'And he wanted us to find her exactly as he intended: face, body, make-up, everything.'

'Maybe he even guessed when her body would float to the surface? Is that possible Ebb?'

She nodded. 'He could take a guess. He could work it out to the nearest two weeks, maybe. All he would need to do was to be sure of the temperature of the water, the weight of the body, the amount of fat, the food in her stomach even. But the temperature of the water dropping like it did would have been difficult to calculate.'

'The freezing? Yes. That's something he couldn't control,' said Carter.

'That and the subsequent lack of oxygen in the water would have slowed the whole process down.' Ebony said.

'Then we need to examine all CCTV footage of the area and look for someone who couldn't stay away. Someone who's been visiting that area for the past three weeks, every day.'

On the way back to Fletcher House they stopped off at the Whittington to see Doctor Harding. They found her in her office. She had just finished cutting what was left of Emily Styles' liver into centimetre slices to create slides for the laboratory.

'I can spare you half an hour,' she said.

'Thirty minutes will be all I need,' answered Carter.

'Shoot.' Harding indicated that they should pull up chairs.

'Now we know who Emily Styles was,' said Carter, 'I'd like to run through some of the post mortem findings again with you, Doctor Harding. I want to try and get an idea of what was happening to Emily in the last months of her life and get a sense of where she might have been and what she's been through.'

'You mean now we know she wasn't a sex worker on her way to a fancy dress party?' Harding fixed Carter with a look that betrayed a hint of mockery.

Ebony tried not to smile as she studied the notes in her lap as she shuffled in her chair. She liked Harding. She might be the only woman in the department who did. But then, Ebony didn't have a husband to lose and she had everything to learn from Harding.

Carter put his hands up in surrender mode.

'I agree I might have jumped to conclusions but everything pointed to someone who had a drug habit and lived a dangerous life right up until the day she died. Not a single mum on the way to collect her child from nursery and held hostage for months. That came out of nowhere.' Harding scrolled through the results on her screen whilst tapping her forefinger on the desktop as she waited impatiently.

Carter looked across at Ebony and rolled his eyes; she responded with a raised eyebrow and a sideways smile. Carter gave a look that said he might have guessed whose side she'd be on.

'We can be pretty sure she was held somewhere against her will: starved and abused. We need to get an idea of how she was kept in order to find out where that might have been. Could the marks on her ankles and wrists have been caused by being restrained?'

Harding opened Emily Styles' post mortem notes on the desk. 'Yes. I would say so. There are variations in the depth of the wounds, where the weight of her body could have rested for long periods of time. The injuries to her wrists and ankles indicate that she was restrained and suspended by the arms primarily: hoisted up by her arms, at the wrists were where the wounds are deep. We will never know by what because the flesh has been destroyed by the pond elements.' She pulled a piece of paper out from the drawer under her desk and began drawing a diagram of a sophisticated hangman's noose.

'So ...' Carter tapped his pencil on the hangman diagram. 'She was suspended somehow and her ankles were bound.'

Harding nodded her agreement. 'Yes. I would have no trouble testifying to that in court.'

'He raped her, he assaulted her. He starved her, we know *that*,' added Carter. 'He could have killed her within moments of kidnapping her but he enjoys the wait. He enjoys watching her suffer. Three months is a long time to keep someone alive – someone so sick.'

'There's no doubt that her organs were shot,' said Harding. 'I've just finished slicing them up for examination and I can tell you now that the liver was beyond repair and so were her kidneys. The infection had poisoned her whole system.'

'Emily Styles' parents say she had a phobia about needles – can't see her "popping",' said Carter.

'There's no heroin in her system.'

'Well, if it's not contaminated heroin what is it?' asked Carter.

'Could be many types of bacteria,' Harding answered. 'I told you it takes time for the lab to get results.'

'If he was looking after her, holding her, then he was also nursing her.' Ebony was looking at Harding's hanging woman diagram. 'He seems to want to preserve her face so that he can mock her with the make-up, whilst destroying her body.'

'Yes, she would have been a walking gangrenous site,' said Harding.

Ebony began drawing a make-up mask onto Harding's hanging woman. 'That's what he likes.'

Chapter 11

It was Monday morning and Tracy was anxious for Steve to leave for work but he didn't seem to want to go. She looked at the clock. He should have left ten minutes earlier. She didn't understand what was keeping him.

'You'll be late for work, love.' She stated the obvious. He didn't answer. He was making heavy weather of the last few things he always did: check his briefcase, check he had his phone, check for any specks on his shoulders and give his shoes a little polish with the cloth that Tracy kept just by them for that very purpose. Tracy believed in taking pride in your appearance and always making sure you looked immaculate for work. She had tried to instil the routine into him, to make his life easier.

'Will you miss your train?'

'There'll be another one,' he growled.

She watched him from the corner of her eye; he looked like he was itching to get something off his chest. But Tracy knew when he was spoiling for a fight and right now she didn't need it. Tracy wasn't prepared for an argument about Danielle and

Jackson again. She said nothing and waited patiently.

'What are you going to do today? It's your day off, isn't it?' he mumbled.

'I've got plenty to do; don't worry about me,' she replied in short sharp fashion.

He responded with an irritable snatch-up of his briefcase and grunted a goodbye as he left.

Tracy breathed a sigh of relief as she watched from the lounge window and saw him walk away down the street; he was walking on the road as the pavement was icy. She thought how sad he looked – something about his demeanour had changed recently, his shoulders had dropped, eyes on the ground. If he didn't get a move on he'd miss another train, thought Tracy.

Alone at last, she spent the day tidying and sorting out old photos. She couldn't help but spend some time looking online for Christmas presents for Jackson. She also rang a few gyms in the area to see how much it would cost her to join after Christmas. They would all have offers on in the New Year. *New Year, New You*, they promised her. She liked the sound of that. At six in the evening Tracy got ready to go to Danielle's. She left a meal for Steve in the fridge and an apology for not being there. She drove to Danielle's estate and parked her immaculate old yellow Fiat as far away as she could get from the abandoned-looking car that seemed to have a party going on in it. The entrance was off a side street and the five tower blocks were laid out around a courtyard. It was already pitch dark outside but the landings were lit by security lights all night.

'Thanks for coming, Tracy. I'll just be gone for a few hours,' Danielle greeted her as she opened door.

'That's no problem,' Tracy said as she stepped inside the flat. 'Are you going anywhere nice?' She took her coat off.

'Just meeting a friend for a few drinks, that's all. I'll be back by eleven.'

'You enjoy yourself. I'll be okay. I've got my car outside so I can get home, and the roads are gritted from door to door so don't you worry.'

Tracy went into the lounge to sit with Jackson whilst Danielle got ready to go out. Tracy resisted the temptation to ask to help with her daughter's make-up. She was still smarting from the last time she'd offered. Jackson was excited to see her and got all of his toys out to show her. She sat on the floor and helped him build a pretend beauty salon with his Duplo.

Danielle came into the lounge whilst the news was on. Reporters stood next to the Regent's Canal; behind them the crime scene tent had gone but the canal boats were still stuck in the frozen water. The area was still taped off.

Danielle turned the television off.

'I'm almost ready to go now. Will you be all right to give him a bath and put him to bed? I don't like him watching too much television before he goes to bed. He likes you to read to him. He'll choose a book.'

Tracy jumped up and followed Danielle out into the hall. 'Can you just run through exactly what he has and when? And where everything is? I want to get it right.'

Danielle laughed. 'You can't get it wrong. There is no wrong way. Ask Jackson and he'll tell you where things are.'

'But he must have routines, things he always likes doing a certain way.'

Danielle smiled. 'You can make it up as you go along, Tracy, honestly. Jackson is usually in bed by seven-thirty but just do your best.' Tracy nodded. 'Don't look so worried – honestly, he's an easy kid.' Danielle went in to kiss Jackson and give him a hug before coming back to Tracy. 'Double-lock the door and put the chain across when I've gone,' she said and then she raced out of the door.

'Mummy?' Jackson looked ready to cry. His eyes were on Tracy as she came back into the lounge. Tracy smiled and tried to look confident.

'Mummy will be back in a little while, Jackson. She's gone out to see some friends; that's nice, isn't it? We are going to have such fun, aren't we?' He nodded but his eyes were wide and full of fast-forming tears. 'Come and show Nanny what else you can make with your Duplo.' Once she felt he'd settled she left him and went into the bathroom and began running a bath. She was running it through in her head: anything she'd ever heard about small children and bath and bedtime routines. She finished running the bath and was on her way in to get Jackson when a banging on the door stopped her in her tracks.

Someone's flat hand began thumping hard against the front door.

'Hello?' Tracy called out. There was a glance

between Tracy and Jackson. He watched her from his seat on the lounge floor. She stood, frozen in the hallway. Her heart was racing.

'Danielle? Open the door!' someone shouted.

'What do you want? Danielle's not here.'

Tracy edged forward towards the door to double-lock it. She'd been so keen to distract Jackson when Danielle had first left that she'd not done it. She didn't want to panic. She didn't want to scare Jackson.

'Tell Manson to get out here.'

'I don't know who you're talking about.'

'We only want to talk to Manson. Open the door.'

'Go away; there's no one here by that name.' Tracy watched as Jackson put down his Duplo and crept towards her. She held up her hand to make him stay where he was. 'I'll call the police if you don't go.'

Tracy screamed as the door flew open and crashed against the hallway wall and she was pushed backwards. Three men burst through. She rushed to pick up Jackson.

'Get out! Who do you think you are? Get out now . . .!'

One of them came to stand in front of her as she held tightly onto Jackson.

'Where is he?'

Tracy tried to stay back from him but he was in her face and shouting. She was trying to stay calm as Jackson began crying and clinging to her so tightly that his fingers were like needles in her arms. Tracy shook her head.

'Who? Who is it you want?'

'Manson? Where is he?'

'I don't know who you're talking about. I don't know anybody called Manson.'

'Where's Danielle?'

'She's out. I told you.'

Tracy shrieked as she was pushed into the lounge and then she and Jackson were forced backwards onto the sofa where they were ordered to stay. Tracy pulled Jackson onto her lap and they sat and listened to the flat being ransacked.

I can't sit here and do nothing ... thought Tracy. Her bag was the other side of the sofa where she'd put it when she was going to bath Jackson. Tracy kept one eye on the door to the lounge as she edged closer to it, still managing to hold on tightly to Jackson. She slid her hand over the side of the sofa and reached inside the bag for her phone. In one movement one of the men leapt into the lounge and snatched it out of her hands and threw it to the floor. She heard it crack as it landed on the wood veneer. He kicked it across the room and it slid beneath the television stand. She tried to shrink back into the sofa as he pushed Jackson to one side and pulled her up by the arm and shouted in her face.

'Tell Manson he has two days. We hear nothing? We're coming back. You listening?' He breathed an inch away from Tracy's face. 'You tell the police? Then ... we're coming for *you* and *him*.' He pointed to Jackson then jabbed Tracy's chest hard to make sure she understood. After that the men left as dramatically as they had arrived.

Tracy rushed to the door to lock it with the remaining locks and she slipped the safety chain across and came back to Jackson, who was looking just about ready to start howling. Tracy couldn't stop herself shaking.

'Okay. Okay.' She repeated the word to reassure herself and see how it sounded. She tried it on Jackson. 'It's okay, Jackson. We're not hurt, are we? It could have been a lot worse, couldn't it? We're okay now. She sat beside him on the sofa and hugged him to her while at the same time looking at the mess and wondering if it had all really happened. Should she ring the police now? She kept thinking about what the man had threatened. Would he come for her and Jackson? He didn't look like he'd think twice about slitting their throats. No – she wouldn't be calling anyone, not just yet. They were gone, a few things broken in the flat probably – but she and Jackson were okay. She needed to ask Danielle first before doing anything. What did she know about this world? What did she know about any of it? All she knew was that Jackson was a little boy who was very scared right now and he depended on her as the adult to look after him. She would stay calm and talk to Danielle when she got back. Yes, she told herself, that was what she'd do – tidy up and wait for Danielle to come home and then tell her what had happened and let her deal with it.

'Nanny needs you to be a good boy now while I tidy up a little bit.' She found Jackson something to watch on the television and a plate of snacks he wasn't really supposed to have. She put the furniture back where they'd pulled it out and tipped it over. She retrieved her phone from where it had ended up under the telly – the screen was cracked but it still worked. Tracy was momentarily sad. She wouldn't be able to get a new phone for months; she'd have to make do with it, put some tape over it.

After an hour of doing her best to restore order in the flat she gave Jackson his bath and read him a bedtime story and tucked him up with his Peppa Pig toy. She sat on his bed and listened to his breathing grow deep and when she was sure he was asleep she came back into the lounge and turned the telly off. She sat in silence and listened to the echoes of footsteps outside in the hallway and felt her heart race every time it seemed like someone was stopping at the door. When she finally heard a light knock at the door she jumped and almost scalded herself with her hot cup of tea.

She crept into the hallway and stood at the other side of the locked door.

'Who is it?'

'Me.'

Tracy unlocked the chain and Danielle looked at the broken lock on the door. As the realization that there'd been trouble crossed her face she rushed past Tracy towards Jackson's room.

'He's fine. He's fast asleep.'

Danielle stopped and rested against the wall.

'What happened?'

'I don't know. Three men burst in here and turned the place upside down looking for someone called Manson or something and then they threatened us.'

'Did you call the police?'

Tracy shook her head. 'They said they'd hurt Jackson if I did. I wanted to wait and ask you. I didn't know what to do. I'm sorry if I didn't do the right thing.'

'Bastards.' Danielle went into the kitchen and put the kettle on.

Tracy followed her into the kitchen. 'Who were they?' Danielle opened a cupboard and got a mug and took tea from a container. She was taking her time answering. Tracy stood in the doorway waiting. 'Do you know them? Do you know who they were talking about, this person called Manson?'

Danielle nodded, turned back and made herself some tea. When she was done she turned to face Tracy: 'That's Jackson's dad, Niall. My ex. Can we go and sit in the lounge; I've had a few drinks. I'm not used to it any more. I feel a bit pissed.'

'What did they want? What do you think they were looking for?'

'He must have been dealing. He must have given this address.'

'Dealing? As in drugs? From here? With Jackson here?'

'I told you – that's why I left him.'

'I didn't know whether to phone the police or not but they said they'd come back for me and Jackson if I did.' Tracy's voice was getting shriller. Danielle slumped in the sofa. She reached inside her bag and took out tobacco and began rolling a cigarette. Tracy looked at her as if she were about to shoot heroin into her arm.

'What's that?'

'Tobacco,' she snapped. 'What do you think it is?'

Tracy stared, wide-eyed, as Danielle rolled and lit the cigarette and then sat back on the sofa and smoked it as she stared straight ahead; they sat in silence.

'What are you going to do?' Tracy waved the smoke away from her face.

'Nothing. They found nothing. They can see he's not living here. They'll know he lied. They'll leave us alone now.'

'How do you know it won't happen again?'

'I'll get hold of him and make sure he doesn't use this address again. I'm not going to make any trouble for myself.'

'Will you let him see Jackson?'

'I told you. I don't. He doesn't see him anyway. I wouldn't allow him and he's not interested.'

Tracy stood and picked up her bag.

'I can't put up with things like this happening. I mean – I've never seen anything like that. No one's ever been so aggressive towards me – and to threaten Jackson. What kind of people do you know, Danielle?'

'They are people I *used* to know. Not any more. Now it's just me and Jackson and I hoped it would be you but if it's all too much for you then you better go. Because, you know what? I won't take any fucking criticism from you, Tracy. You've no right. You're either on our side or you're out for good. We don't need it.'

'I didn't say that. It's just . . .' Tracy shook her head.

'You seem to think it's nothing, but it terrified me.'

Danielle switched the telly on as she kicked off her shoes and sat back in the sofa.

'You'd better go.'

Chapter 12

Pam was just leaving. She'd already stayed beyond ten and Robbo thanked her. Pam and Robbo had worked together for many years in his former life as a detective and although both had long marriages at home, Pam was Robbo's 'work wife'. They had worked together in the Major Incident Room, manning the telephones, and feeding all incoming information into HOLMES.

Robbo was agoraphobic. He had battled against it all his adult life. Sometimes he had to face his demons like in the court room. Then he'd learnt the technique of finding security within a comfort zone he concocted for himself. When Robbo retrained and moved to a new office he'd had to spend time adjusting. Moving the desks around and reshuffling the cabinets to make it seem familiar, he had finally settled on an arrangement where he was slightly backed into the corner of the room, with white boards behind him. From there he could see the corridor and he felt cocooned and not trapped. He didn't like germs. He liked things to be in order and precise. He liked to see the same people every day but only ever liked a few people in the office at one time. The door to his office was always open and he knew where the exits were in case of panic attacks.

Many times he thought the daily struggle was too hard but he also knew that he loved his job and would battle against anything to do it well. He also knew that if he didn't fight it he would lose the battle.

'Night, Pam. See you tomorrow.'

'Are you going to get some sleep?' she asked. He nodded vigorously. She gave Carter a look that said 'That's what he always says'.

Carter winked at her. 'We'll take care of him. See you tomorrow.'

'Night, Pam,' Ebony called out as she was coming down the corridor to Robbo's office.

'Doctor Harding's sent over some results on the flaps of skin taken from Emily Styles' back.' She read out the results to Robbo and Carter. 'They contained splinters of wood – it's a soft wood, possibly pine.' Robbo rocked in his chair as he listened. 'Doctor Harding says that the skin had closed over the splinters – that would indicate she was lying on something wooden, rubbing against its surface.' Ebony finished reading and looked at Carter. 'A pine box – like a coffin.'

'Not *like* a coffin,' corrected Carter. 'It was one.'

'And she was there for some time – must have been to allow the skin to grow over,' said Robbo.

'Three months would do it.' Carter pulled his chair closer to the desk and typed a search onto the PC.

'Jesus, you can't keep someone in a box for three months,' said Robbo.

'Gets her out to abuse her. Puts her back in,' said Carter as he typed on the keyboard and scrolled down to read the information on the screen.

'Just adding this to what we know about Hawk,' he said. 'All the men on file for false imprisonment in a box of some kind are serving life several times over. All of them killed. Two out of the three demanded ransoms. One of the victims got away when she fooled her captor into thinking she was emotionally involved with him. He thought it was the start of a beautiful relationship and let her go. Most of the time the victim was threatened with death if she tried to leave the box, thought it was wired to explode if she moved, that kind of thing. The men who kept their victims like this were undoubtedly some of our worst, most sadistic killers.'

'Now there's a new kid on the block,' said Robbo.

'Could Hawk have modelled himself on one of these men?' asked Ebony.

'It's always possible,' said Robbo. 'We'll look into it.'

'But he's not asking for a ransom so it's all about the killing and the torture.' Carter was absorbed with reading the profiles of the murderers on his screen.

'And he's bringing his own style to it. He is making sure his MO is unique: the make-up and the jewellery,' Ebony picked up the antique ring from Robbo's desk and held it in the palm of her hand. 'The Styles were adamant they'd never seen it before when we showed them a photo.'

'It hasn't been reported stolen or lost,' Robbo said, looking at the screen in front of him.

'Did he give it to her and does that mean it holds a special significance to him? Or the symbolism?' asked Carter.

'It's really pretty.' Ebony held the ring up to the light. 'Is it an antique engagement ring or maybe an eternity ring?'

Robbo tapped on his keyboard and brought up photos of similar ones on his PC. He turned the screen round to show them. 'One central diamond surrounded by small clusters in the shape of a flower – engagement. Eternity rings all tend to be a band with stones set inside, like a fancy wedding band.'

Ebony swung it in the air by the chain as she looked at it. 'The two rings don't go together. The other ring could be out of a cracker, it's the kind young girls wear – like you get free in teenagers' comics. I think it was pink in the beginning but the metallic finish has washed off.'

'If we know it wasn't Emily's then did Hawk put the two together and put it on her? Did Hawk want it to be found on her?' Ebony felt the weight of the chain in her hands.

Robbo took a sip of coffee. He was nodding without realizing as he rocked in his chair; and it creaked beneath his bulk. 'Yes. Definitely. He knew it would be lost in the canal if he didn't tie it on to her so he put it on a sturdy chain and put it around her neck before taping it under the bag.'

Carter took the chain from Ebony and allowed it to snake down onto the desk where it lay coiled. 'We need to talk to all her friends again, re-examine all the evidence. Look at CCTV from the Tube station when she disappeared to see if we can find a match with anyone hanging about the canal,' said Carter, who was mulling things over and still playing with the chain. 'You compiled the list of friends we need to talk to, Robbo?

'Yes.' Robbo tapped on his keyboard and the printer started up. He pulled out a sheet and then handed it across the desk to Carter. 'The top five names on the list are her closest friends.'

'What did they say at the time?' asked Carter.

'They all told the same story,' answered Ebony, staring at the photo of Emily Styles on the front page of the file. 'That Emily was a bit unpredictable, that she liked to party but that she was a good mother. This photo was taken by the third friend on the list Danielle Foster.'

'We need to re-interview them now,' said Carter. 'Get hold of them and get them in for an interview. We can't keep Emily Styles' identity a secret any more. It's time to give the press a name. Perhaps then Hawk will come out of hiding.'

Chapter 13

Tracy had a hard job making out who was phoning her through the fractured glass on her screen. It upset her every time she looked at her phone but she couldn't afford to get a new one till at least February. She heard Danielle's voice on the other end.

'I'm sorry, Tracy.'

Tracy moved into the bedroom to have privacy away from Steve. It was nine in the evening and she was so tired she was already getting ready for bed. Tracy had been working long hours since she babysat for Danielle. She hadn't heard a thing for three days.

'Okay, well I probably overreacted.'

Danielle sighed at the other end of the phone. 'No, you probably didn't. It was an awful thing to happen. I know you weren't glad, but I was really grateful it was you there with Jackson. You coped when most other people would have flipped. I couldn't have wanted anyone else but you, Tracy.'

Tracy felt a sob come into her throat. She coughed.

'That's very nice of you to say, Danielle. I hope Jackson is okay?'

'Yes. He asked where Nanny had gone when he got

up the next day. He seems to be all right about the break-in. '

'Did you have the door fixed?'

'Not yet but I will. I was ringing to ask if you would like to come to a Christmas school fête the day after tomorrow? We are raising funds to make costumes for our Nativity play. Jackson's playing a bunny.'

'A bunny?' Tracy laughed. 'I don't remember there being a bunny in the Christmas story!'

'Yeah. He's one of the animals in the stable. He looks really cute. You'll have to come and see it when it's on.'

'I'd love to.'

'So you'll come then, on Saturday? I'll see you at the park, children's playground at half ten?'

'Yes.' Tracy ended the call and sat on her bed thinking. She couldn't hear Steve moving about in the next room. He was in the lounge; she was sure of that. She could hear the news on the television. He was in a funny mood tonight, sort of hovering. He was bound to guess the call was from Danielle – she never got a call at that time in the evening. Tracy thought she should push for him to meet Danielle and Jackson now. She was sure she was meant to have them in her life. Now that she saw how vulnerable Jackson was and how much Danielle needed all her support, and especially now that Danielle had apologized. She knew that they'd taken a big step forward and Tracy felt a commitment growing. If they were her life – they were in Steve's.

Steve turned as Tracy came back into the lounge; he was jumpy. He turned off the telly and picked up the car keys.

'Are you going out?' Tracy asked, surprised but also slightly relieved that she didn't have to talk to him about Danielle and Jackson. Not right at that moment.

'Yep. Work just called – seems there are some deliveries need sorting out before tomorrow. You can't object surely? You're hardly here at the moment.'

Tracy smiled. It was her 'I'm smiling but inside I am bloody angry' look. 'Of course, love. If you're needed then you have to go. I understand. I wouldn't want it any other way – my man the manager.'

She kissed his cheek and went to turn the television back on. Steve hovered by the door. The news came back on the telly. The photo of Emily Styles, taken by Danielle at the festival, was on the screen. She looked across at Steve; he seemed to be waiting, to be building up to saying something. Tracy couldn't face it. She didn't want the criticism, the anger. 'Oh look.' She diverted his attention. 'They've found out the identity of that woman those boys found in the Regent's Canal. What a shame – what a beautiful girl.' Steve came to stand in front of the television. 'Steve? I want to see the news. Can you move please, love?'

'There's no need to get cross just because I have to go to work.'

'I'm not cross.' Tracy blinked at him, even more confused than before.

'You're either at work or you're with *that* woman and her son.'

'Danielle and Jackson?' Tracy felt panic grip her chest as she tried so hard to look in control and to stay calm and happy. 'I'm not seeing a lot of them, Steve. But ... you know? I think it's time we talked about the fact that they have come into our lives and we have to accept it. I would like you to meet them.' Tracy looked at his face. 'Not now maybe ...' He seemed so upset that Tracy decided she'd been right that now was not such a good time to discuss it. She'd made a start at least. 'Shall we have a proper chat about this when you're home and you're free?'

'Oh I'm home a lot – sat here on my own,' he said accusingly.

'Sorry, love.' Something wasn't right but Tracy couldn't work out what was at the heart of it with Steve. He seemed to be doing his best to start an argument. 'I've been working long hours at Simmons; I asked for extra shifts – but then we could do with the money.'

'Oh, I know. It's all my fault, isn't it? I am always going to be blamed for everything in this house. Well I've had enough of it. You go and spend as much time as you like with your new-found daughter and I'll make my own life.'

Tracy was stunned into silence. She heard the front door slam. She couldn't remember the last time Steve had thrown a wobbly like that; she had no idea what it was all about. She had to admit she hadn't really wanted to discuss things with Steve because she knew he always reacted badly to stress. Tracy's attention was back on the television – the tall, sickly-looking blond Detective Chief Inspector Bowie was appealing for the public's help; they had to phone a number if anyone had any information about the dead woman in the canal. The photo of Emily Styles stayed on the screen.

Danielle was about to switch the news off and look for a film to watch when she froze as she looked at her friend's face. Emily Styles with her distinctive auburn hair was smiling out of the screen just the way she was the last time Danielle had seen her at the festival. Danielle edged closer to the television and listened to the news report; everything else in the room disappeared as her brain tried to make sense of what she was looking at. She stared at Emily's photo on the screen and saw the film of the officers searching the towpath in the background. Detective Chief Inspector Bowie was giving a press conference, recorded earlier in the day.

'We need anyone with any information about Emily to come forward. We believe she was held somewhere for a number of weeks prior to being murdered and her body disposed of in the Regent's Canal. We believe someone must have information about what happened to Emily. She was a gregarious young woman and a devoted mother to her daughter Sky. She disappeared on the fifth of June in between meeting her friend in Camden and collecting Sky from nursery. Someone somewhere knows what happened to her; if you have any information please ring the number on the screen.'

Danielle reached for her phone.

Chapter 14

Saturday arrived with a warmth to the sunshine.

Great day for it, thought Tracy as she checked her watch – it was nearly eleven o'clock. She had been inside the park for forty minutes. Where was Danielle? The kids' park was busy with children dressed as Santa's helpers and elves and fairies. Girls running around in princess dresses that still filled Tracy with a sense of longing. When she was their age she would have gone on and on at her mother to make her the best, the most beautiful dress in the world; and she would have got it too. Things were never the same after she got pregnant. Tracy walked across to a young woman with caramel-coloured dreadlocks, massive freckles over her face and a baby tied onto her back. She was running a stall selling non-alcoholic mulled wine and vegan mince pies.

'Excuse me. I wonder if you know Danielle, Jackson's mum?'

'Of course.' The woman was briefly distracted serving mince pies then she came over.

'Yeah. I know Danielle well.' She smiled. 'She

should be here by now. We were going to run this stall together. She should have been here two hours ago to help set up.' The woman poured out a mulled wine for a customer. 'Must have overslept. I'm surprised Jackson let it happen though, he was so keen. One of my friends is dressing up as Santa and we've all bought our kids a gift for him to hand out. I can't believe Jackson's not first in the queue. He was so excited about it yesterday.'

Tracy looked in the direction of Danielle's estate.

'Maybe I should go and see if she needs a hand.'

'Do you know where she lives?'

'Yes, I know. I've been there before. I'm going to go and knock on her door. If I miss her, tell her I'll come back. My name's Tracy.'

'No problem.' The woman went back to pouring mulled wine.

Tracy crossed over Seven Sisters Road and walked towards the high-rise blocks. A growing feeling of anxiety was making her walk quickly. What if the three men had come back? What if Danielle or Jackson was hurt? Tracy would never forgive herself. She knew she should have phoned the police. She sprinted up to Danielle's landing and ran along to the pink door. She could barely breathe. When she knocked she heard a low growl in response. She knocked louder and waited. This time Scruffy answered with a bark. Tracy bent low and looked through the letterbox. Jackson was looking back at her.

'Hello, Jackson, is Mummy there?' Tracy looked past him. She was relieved to see him safe but was now feeling slightly cross with Danielle for letting everyone down. 'Danielle? Danielle, they're waiting for you at the park.' She listened and heard nothing.

Scruffy came and tried to lick Tracy through the letterbox, knocking Jackson off his feet.

'Scruffy, NO! Jackson? Jackson?' Jackson came back into her vision; his little fingers clasping hers through the open letterbox. 'Get Mummy for me.'

'Nanny?' There was dried blood over his hand. It was ice cold.

'Are you hurt, Jackson?' He started to cry.

'It's all right. There's a good boy. Don't cry. It'll be all right. Nanny's here, darling. Where's Mummy, Jackson? *Danielle?* Is she in bed? *Danielle?*' She looked past him and called through the letterbox. '*Danielle, are you okay?*' Beyond Jackson she could see an upturned table in the hall, and she became aware of a long whine coming from the phone receiver, which was off the hook.' Jackson, is Mummy in the flat somewhere? Is she sleeping?' She called out again. 'Go and get Mummy, Jackson.' Jackson didn't move. He held on to Tracy's fingers. Tracy jammed the letterbox open as wide as it would go with one hand to stop it closing on Jackson's fingers. With the other hand she scrabbled in her bag for her phone and managed to call Danielle's number. She listened. She heard nothing. *Oh God.*

She knelt down again and looked at Jackson's face.

Jackson's fat little hand was wedged into the letterbox further. She looked at his face. He looked like he'd been crying a long time, thought Tracy. He was still in his pyjamas. Tracy kept her hand on his as she stood up and looked along the landing to see if anyone could help, but there was no one about.

'Oh God,' muttered Tracy. 'Something's definitely not right. I should have called the police then and I'm definitely calling them now.' She started dialling 999 at the same time as Scruffy began non-stop barking.

Chapter 15

Robbo was on the way to see Bowie when he passed his old office. The man in charge there now was Griff, a softly spoken police officer who had come over from Organized Crime six months ago and was still learning the ropes. Robbo had taken him under his wing.

Griff was on the phone as Robbo passed. He was concentrating hard on a call. Robbo lifted his chin in a 'I won't disturb you – I'm just passing' gesture when Griff's hand went in the air to beckon him over. Griff finished up the call.

'What's the problem?' asked Robbo.

'Just got a call about a missing person. Thought you might be interested. It came via the police station next door. One of the officers was called to help break into a flat where a young mum wasn't responding and her child was inside alone. When they got inside they found that the mum was missing. There were signs of a struggle. The name came up on the system – Danielle Foster, a friend of Emily Styles, but she is also one of the people who phoned in after the appeal on Thursday.'

'Can I listen to her call?'

'Yes, it's just been sent to me.' He turned back to his PC and opened a link. They listened to Danielle's call.

Hello – thanks for calling our appeal line. Do you have information on Emily Styles?

Yes . . . well I don't know. I am a friend of hers – was . . . I had no idea. I thought she'd just gone off for a while.

Have you made a statement already?

I did, at the time.

What did you want to add?

It's just that I was out a couple of nights ago and one of the men who knows Emily was making jokes about what if it was her in the canal and wouldn't she have hated getting her hair wet, spoiling her make-up, that kind of thing. It just seems much too big a coincidence to me. These are people I am very close to. Now I'm really worried.

Okay, Danielle, I understand. Would you like to come into Archway Police Station or if you prefer we can get one of our officers to come around and interview you?

I don't want any police coming here. I'll come in the next day or so and I'll talk it through.

When you come in, ask for an officer from MIT 17. They are connected to Archway Police Station. I will leave a note and you will be expected. Thank you for your call.

Griff pressed the stop button. 'She didn't come in, but that's not to say she wouldn't have. What do you want to do?'

'Good work, Griff. I'll inform Inspector Carter and Willis so they can go round there now and decide whether we need SOCOs. Tell the first responder to stay put until someone gets there.'

Ebony and Carter arrived to a gathering of onlookers on the landing and people on the stairwell leading up to Danielle's apartment. An officer was waiting for them.

Carter took him to one side. 'You the first responder?'

'Yes, Sir. My colleague and I.' He turned to point out another officer further down the landing who was talking to neighbours.

'What did it look like when you got here?'

'We had to break in to gain access but the door was already damaged. It hadn't been bolted from inside. The little boy was inside on his own with the dog. There's definitely some kind of scuffle gone on in there. The lights were all off, curtains drawn. Looks like she'd been gone all night. The little boy was still in his pyjamas. Furniture's not ransacked but a few things are knocked about. Enough to indicate she put up a struggle. There are also some blood splatters on the wall in the hallway, Sir.'

Carter looked inside the flat from the doorway. He turned to Ebony.

'Let's get Sandford and the SOCO team over.' Then he turned back to the officer. 'Make sure no one goes inside until they arrive and take over from you.' Ebony took out her phone and called Robbo.

'Robbo, we need SOCOs.'

'How's it looking?' he asked.

'She left a small child alone all night possibly and there are signs of a struggle. Beyond that, not sure – too early to tell.'

'Okay, Sandford's on his way.' Ebony hung up. She looked over at the woman struggling to get a little boy into his all-in-one suit and then at the officer still talking to Carter.

'Who's that?'

'This is Mrs Collins. She made the 999 call. It's her daughter's flat.'

'She's the boy's grandmother?'

'Yes.'

Ebony waited as Tracy finished getting Jackson's suit on and zipped up.

'Mrs Collins?' Tracy nodded. 'I am Detective Constable Willis and that's Detective Inspector Carter.' Ebony nodded towards Carter who was standing at the entrance to the flat, still in conversation with the officer there. 'You made the 999 call?'

'Yes. I think something's happened to her. I know she wouldn't leave Jackson on his own. And on Monday, when I babysat for her, three men broke in.'

'Did they do that?' Carter pointed to the door.

'No. Someone else had already done that damage. The men broke the lock. They ransacked the place and frightened the life out of me and Jackson.'

'Who did Danielle say they were?'

'Friends of her ex-boyfriend, Jackson's father. Jackson is so upset – he's really cold . . .' Tracy shook her head. 'I knew I should have called the police but Danielle wasn't keen. She didn't want any trouble, she said.'

'Trouble from her ex-boyfriend?'

'No, from the men, whoever they were.'

'Okay, Mrs Collins. You did the right thing to call us. Do you live near?'

'Not very. Hornsey. I was coming here today to go to the Christmas fête with them. That's why is seems odd that she's not here.' Ebony nodded. She was looking at the streak of congealed blood in Jackson's hair.

'We'll need to take you and the boy somewhere while we examine your daughter's flat.'

'Can't I just go in and get some more clothes for Jackson?' Tracy asked. 'I only managed to get this suit for him because it was on top of the buggy.'

'Sorry, Mrs Collins.' Ebony stopped her. 'It's not possible at the moment.' Tracy took out a tissue from her bag to wipe Jackson's face. He squirmed from her as she tried to tidy him up.

'I wouldn't worry about that, Mrs Collins. Take him as he is and we'll arrange things later. We'll tidy him up when we get him back to yours.' Ebony was making a mental note to take Tracy's fingerprints as she'd obviously been in as far as the hallway. She'd need to send her clothes away for analysis as well.

'Oh ... yes.' She looked a little confused but then looked down at Jackson and smiled reassuringly. 'But how long before we can go in and get his things? Obviously we can't manage without them?'

Ebony shook her head apologetically.

'Sorry but we're going to have stay out of the flat while the forensic team look at everything. We're doing everything we can to find out what's happened, Mrs Collins. We'll give you and your grandson a lift home. I presume you will be looking after him? We'll take a full statement from you then.' Tracy blinked at Ebony for a few seconds. Jackson stood patiently watching Tracy's face.

'It will be all right, Jackson. Nanny will look after you till Mummy comes back.'

Ebony whispered to Carter: 'There's blood in the boy's hair.'

Carter glanced across at Jackson. 'When we get to her place, bring in the forensics kit from the car and take a sample. Shall we go, Mrs Collins?' He turned to Tracy, who looked like she was waiting for someone to wake her up from a nightmare.

'Thanks for your help.' Carter addressed the half a dozen neighbours who had come out to take part in the drama. 'Please wait here for a few more minutes while your statements are taken.' Carter turned to the two police officers. 'Then you're finished here.'

Tracy led Jackson away by the hand and followed Carter past the neighbours and down the stairs.

'Mrs Collins? The dog?' one of the officers called out to them as they walked away.

Tracy stopped. 'What about the dog?'

She was about to say: *I don't think so*, when she looked at Jackson's face and realized she had no choice. She turned back to pick up Scruffy's lead.

'Of course. Come on, Scruffy.'

As they drove to Tracy's house, Tracy sat in the back seat with Jackson and Scruffy. She stared out at the traffic and Jackson held on to her hand. It took them forty minutes to get through the traffic and pull up outside Tracy's flat; it was the bottom half of a town house in a residential street in Hornsey near a busy main road.

'Please take your shoes off at the door.'

Tracy turned to them as she unlocked the front door, stepped inside and set Jackson down. She looked exasperated as she watched Scruffy saunter in past her as if he owned the place.

Ebony took off her shoes reluctantly; she had odd socks on and one of the socks was missing a big toe. She looked at Carter's feet – there were polo ponies galloping across his socks. Ebony tried to hide her feet with the hem of her trousers. She would put socks onto her Christmas list if she had one.

Ebony had in her hands the forensics kit that she'd brought with her from the car.

Tracy led the way into the flat. The place was over-done, fussy, with dried flowers and photo frames. Lots of white-painted French-style bric-a-brac.

Carter steered Tracy into the lounge and lowered his voice out of earshot of Jackson. 'Did you see your daughter regularly, Mrs Collins?

Tracy shook her head. 'I had only met her a few times. I hadn't seen her for a few days. We were just beginning to build up a relationship. You see, I gave her up for adoption when she was born. I was fifteen at the time.'

'When was the last time you saw her?'

'I was babysitting for her on Monday when those three men burst in and threatened me and Jackson. Do you think they came back?'

'Do you know what they wanted?'

'No. They turned the place upside down

searching for something, I don't know what. Didn't find out.'

'Were they looking for Danielle?'

'No. Manson. Someone called Manson. Danielle said it was Niall Manson, Jackson's dad. She said that he must have given her address. He's a – you know ...?' She whispered. 'A drug dealer ... and *that's* why she'd left him in the first place.'

'Did she seem very worried about it?'

'No. If I'm honest, that's what shocked me. I thought to myself – she just thinks that's normal. She said she'd speak to him. She didn't seem that bothered, or maybe she wasn't showing it. She didn't like me knowing about that side of her life. But she phoned and apologized a few days later and asked me to come to the Christmas fête in the park today.'

'Would you recognize the three men again, Mrs Collins?'

'Yes I would – they were covered in tattoos and piercings. Terrible teeth. It was awful.' Tracy shook her head. She was looking at him wide-eyed. 'I seriously wondered whether I should see Danielle again. I thought about it, you know ... it's not a world I know about – drug dealers and gangs. They pushed me against the wall, frightened the life out of poor little Jackson.'

Ebony went into the kitchen with Jackson and opened up the forensics kit on the kitchen worktop. She looked around the immaculate room with its colour scheme of black and white with bold red kettle and toaster.

Jackson was watching everything Tracy did. Scruffy

had come into the kitchen too and he was sniffing out the corners of the room in search of crumbs.

Carter looked at the photos on the wall of the lounge. Tracy looked young in them, she was getting married, on holiday. She was happy and smiling. There were no recent ones.

'I think he wants water,' Ebony called from the kitchen, looking at Scruffy. 'He's panting a lot. Shall I find a container from the cupboard?'

'I'm coming,' answered Tracy. 'I'll find one.'

Tracy came in and stopped as she looked at Ebony and the forensics kit being opened on her worktop.

'I hope you don't mind,' said Ebony, seeing the scowl again. 'I need to take your fingerprints and a couple of swabs from you and Jackson and then I'll need the clothes you're wearing please.' Tracy shook her head although she kept the worried expression as she pulled open cupboards and began looking for a bowl for Scruffy.

'What for?'

'Just to check for fibres and things that might help us understand what happened in the flat. And, as you have handled Jackson, we need yours too. I'll get someone to bring some clothes over for Jackson. Maybe you've got a T-shirt and jumper he can wear for now?'

'Yes. Yes, of course.'

Tracy pulled out a stack of freezer containers, pulled one off the top and filled it. Scruffy splashed water on the tiles as he drank. She lifted the bowl and placed kitchen paper beneath it. Carter was in the other room talking to Jackson, who had wandered from the kitchen. He flicked through the TV channels and found something that seemed to settle him. Then he rang Sandford out of earshot.

'What?' He had his usual *what the hell do you want now?* tone. Sandford, head of the SOCOs, always had the sound and look of a man dying to be elsewhere and begrudging the time spent talking to Carter. 'There were definite signs of a scuffle in the flat and a sign of forced entry at the door but it looks like it's been cleaned up. It could have happened a few days ago.'

'Yeah, it did. The place was broken into then. We think the father of the little boy may have been involved in that.'

'I've found some documents about him, the boy's birth certificate and child support stuff. I'll send them over to Robbo to trace.' Sandford continued his report. 'There's recent blood, last twenty-four hours. Not a massive amount, but enough to be unusual. It's in several sites around the flat. The heaviest flow of blood, a pattern of ten heavy drips, starts in the kitchen.'

'Any weapon? Anything that could have caused it?'

'Not so far. The bleeding continues from the kitchen out into the bathroom and there is blood around the basin.'

'Maybe she was trying to clean up the wound?'

'Maybe. There is also a smear on the bathroom cabinet. It may have been a defensive wound. There is a cast-off splatter pattern by the door in the hallway, halfway down the wall. Blood came down from a height and the droplets dispersed.'

'There is dried blood in the boy's hair – at the top of his head, so if the blood is hers then he was definitely there when she left the house?'

'Yes. He would have seen what happened.'

'Thanks. We'll photograph it and take a sample.'

Sandford hung up. Next Carter rang Robbo.

'We're back at the grandmother's house. Just talked to Sandford, who confirms that it looks like she was taken by force. Mrs Collins, the grandmother, was there on Monday, when she was threatened by three white males who broke in. They are connected to Danielle Foster's ex, Niall Manson. Find him for me, Robbo. Sandford's found some details on the father.'

'He sent them over to you.'

'We got them. I've been looking at his file.'

'What do we know about him?'

'He has been inside for burglary with intent,' answered Robbo. 'Possession of a weapon, assault, grievous, supplying of a class B drug. You name it, he's been done for it; been inside three times but nothing that got him more than a two-year stretch.'

'Have him picked up. I need Jeanie over here. There's a four-year-old child who we are pretty sure saw who took his mum – he's got blood in his hair.'

Carter got off the phone to Robbo and rang Jeanie, explained the situation to her.

'We need your help over here.'

'I want to stay with Mr and Mrs Styles until they say they don't need me any more. They have a lot to cope with.'

'Jeanie, you have experience in victim support and

child abuse. He'll need careful handling. I'm asking you for a favour.'

'Okay. I'll come over now to start the process off but I would prefer if you handed it over to someone else afterwards.'

'I'm grateful, and can you pick the child up something to wear. I would say he's a big four-year-old.'

In the kitchen Ebony handed Tracy a DNA test. 'Rub the end against the inside of your cheek for a minute please, turning the tip the whole time.'

Tracy looked at it with suspicion. 'I'm sorry. It's so strange for me. I'm not used to having anything like this happen.' She had her business face on, the one she gave to difficult customers.

Ebony smiled. 'I understand. It's nothing to worry about – it doesn't hurt.'

Tracy did as she was told. When she was done, she handed the test back to Ebony to pack away.

'Is this the kind of thing you deal with every day?'

'Missing persons, you mean?' Tracy nodded. Ebony looked back at her forensics box and tidied it. 'Every day is different. Same type of things though.'

'But is it always missing persons?'

'Not always.' She looked up at Tracy. 'I'm a member of a Major Incident Team, Mrs Collins.' Ebony didn't add that she was part of the Murder Squad.

'Is that what this is? A major incident?'

Ebony nodded. 'We are treating it as *potentially* that. I hope it turns out not to be that, but it's better that we get resources directed straight away to finding Danielle.' Ebony looked at Tracy. 'Have you got someone to come and give you some support?' Tracy didn't seem to understand what Ebony was saying; she first started shaking her head and then seemed to change her mind. 'I mean are you married, Mrs Collins, or do you live here on your own?' Ebony began searching through the box to find what she needed to take a sample of the blood in Jackson's hair.

'Sorry – yes – I'm married. My husband Steve is an area manager,' she said, smiling proudly. 'It's for a storage facility company.'

'And do you work?'

Tracy gave a sharp intake of breath.

'Oh God. Yes. I have to be in work today at two.' She looked at her watch. It was ten minutes to two.

'You'd better call work and tell them you won't be coming in. Just tell them there is a family situation.'

Tracy snatched up her phone and began searching for Jazmina's number.

She found it and turned her back to Ebony as she stood facing the back door to make the call. Ebony watched Tracy's shoulders rise and fall as she listened to the person on the other end of the phone, who seemed to be trying their best to calm and reassure her. She finished talking and ended the call.

'She says not to worry.' Tracy rolled her eyes. 'Not to worry and it's the busiest time of year!' She began furiously wiping the work surface where water had splashed from filling Scruffy's bowl.

'Did you explain?'

'Yes, but it's no good, you know? I work on the beauty counter at Simmons on Holloway Road.

There's just me and Jazmina.' Tracy stared at Ebony, her eyes wide. Ebony had an odd reminder of the make-up on Emily Styles. 'How is she going to cope? Look … this is all turning into a nightmare. I have my own life here. I can't just drop everything.'

'Do you think you should ring your husband now? He needs to know what's happening here so that he comes home prepared.'

Tracy looked at the kitchen clock and shook her head.

'He'll be busy at work. I'll try him later. Where is Danielle? Do you think something's happened to her?' She stopped as she saw Jackson standing at the kitchen door looking lost. She rushed over to him. 'Come with Nanny, darling, we need to clean you up. We'll find something on the telly for you as well. Ebony gave a small shake of the head and reached out a hand to stop Tracy taking Jackson away. She couldn't risk her wiping away evidence.

'Can I have him over here for a minute?'

Tracy followed Ebony's gaze to the forensics kit.

'Oh yes. Of course. Let's have a look what Ebony's got, shall we, Jackson?'

She led him over to the kit.

Ebony smiled reassuringly at Jackson as she knelt to his eye level. She looked up at Tracy.

'And can you go now and change and at the same time find something for Jackson to put on? Here's a bag.' She stood and unpacked a large brown paper bag from her kit, handed it to Tracy. 'Please strip carefully down to your underwear and place all your clothes in this bag.' Tracy looked as though she was going to say something but changed her mind; she took the bag from Ebony and left.

'Okay, big man?' Ebony knelt back down with Jackson. 'Can I take a photo of you?' He stared at her curiously and didn't answer. Ebony took photos of the top of Jackson's head and his hair. She took out a swab and took a sample of the blood in his hair. His eyes followed her. He stood absolutely still as she wiped his hands and face to pick up the tiniest traces of foreign DNA. She finished and placed the samples in labelled, brown paper specimen bags. She filled in the crime log and entered the codes from the bags and a description of what and where and then she knelt in front of him again She made a face at him and he almost smiled.

'You're such a good boy, Jackson. Have you got any sore bits anywhere? Does anything hurt?' He shook his head.

Tracy came back in, changed; she handed the bag to Ebony and had one of her sweatshirts in her hand for Jackson.

'We'll need to roll up the sleeves.'

'That's fine, thanks. Can you give me a hand to undress him?' They stood Jackson on a towel and took off his things.

Ebony smiled at him. 'Look, Jackson's wearing Nanny's clothes.' He didn't look happy about it. Scruffy came into the kitchen and barged into him. Jackson held onto him, put his thumb in his mouth and rested his head on Scruffy's back as he worked his fingers into the dog's fur and sucked his thumb.

They finished and Ebony closed up the kit and

packed it away. Tracy took Jackson into the lounge and Carter came off the phone and went to sit with him. Tracy left him flicking through the channels. Ebony was waiting to speak to her again back in the kitchen but Tracy had something she wanted to ask first.

'Do you think something awful has happened to my daughter?' Tracy asked as she walked in and pulled the door halfway closed.

'We don't know any more than you at this stage, Mrs Collins. But we are working fast to find out. You say you've met her just a few times before?' Tracy nodded. 'What did she tell you about her life?'

'She was trying to make a real go of it for her and Jackson. She was taking classes to get into teacher training.' She looked at Ebony, her eyes hopeful. Ebony nodded encouragingly. In her head she was going through similarities to Emily Styles: one small child, going back to school to better herself. 'She's doing it all for Jackson really,' said Tracy. Ebony thought how Tracy was looking shell-shocked. She seemed to be in a daze. 'She's a good mum. Definitely. She loves him to bits. She's had difficult times though, I know that.'

'Did she talk about anything specifically?'

'She said she had problems with the couple who adopted her. Her mum Marion is dead. She told me that she died of cancer not that long ago. I think whatever relationship she had with Gerald, the father, evaporated then.' Ebony made a note to find out more about the Fosters.

'What about the little boy's father?'

'She didn't seem very keen on him. They'd fallen out. I don't know how much involvement he has in Jackson's life now.'

They could hear the television on in the other room and the high-pitched voice of a character on children's television.

'I don't know how you're going to find him.'

'Don't worry about things like that, Mrs Collins. I'm sure the forensic officers will find out what we need to know. What about a boyfriend? Did she talk about her private life?'

Tracy shook her head as she spoke. 'Not really. We'd just begun ... as I said.' Tracy thought for a few seconds. 'I did get the impression there was someone – you know – there were a lot of texts. She came back quite merry the night I babysat. Seemed like she'd had a good time. I just don't know. I'm so sorry – I know so little to help you.' The doorbell rang.

'I'll get it,' Carter called out, opening the door. Jeanie stood in the doorway, blowing into her hands with the cold. She smiled across at Jackson.

'Thanks, Jeanie, I appreciate you coming,' Carter said as he led Jeanie into the kitchen. 'Come and meet Mrs Collins, Danielle Foster's mother.'

'Mrs Collins, this is Jeanie. She is a Family Liaison Officer, which means that she'll be the one to explain things to you and help you through all this.' Jeanie gave Carter a look that said, 'That wasn't what I said and you know it.'

Tracy shook Jeanie's hand. 'Pleased to meet you,' she said, her eyes going from one detective to another. 'Everyone – please call me Tracy.'

Jeanie smiled. 'Hello, Tracy. I know it's all a bit overwhelming, but we'll take things one step at a time. What I'd like us to do now is leave the officers to find Danielle and you and I will concentrate on looking after Jackson.' Tracy smiled, relieved. 'I need to make a list of the practical things we need for Jackson and we'll start putting it together for you, just in case he's here for a couple of days. I've brought over some crayons and some paper for Jackson. It's important that we get him settled and secure and, at the same time, we encourage him to open up about what he saw. Drawings are a great way for us unlock things in his head. I also picked up a pair of pyjamas and a tracksuit for him on my way over. I hope it's the right size.' Tracy didn't answer. She took the packets from Jeanie and stared at the label. It didn't mean anything to her. Jeanie took them back from her and put them on the worktop. 'But I'm not just here for Jackson. I'm here to help you, Tracy.'

Tracy smiled and nodded but she continued to look overwhelmed. 'Thank you.'

'Does he sleep in a normal bed or one with a side to it?'

'I know he sleeps in a bed not a cot. I don't know much about his routine, what he eats or what he likes doing really.' She held up her hands in an *it's hopeless* gesture. 'I can bath him. That's about it. I'm sorry.'

'It's no problem, Tracy. Maybe he can sleep with you tonight?' She nodded. 'We'll see what tomorrow brings. Maybe then we'll know what we're faced with.'

'You must think this is serious to be all here like

this? Taking tests and talking about unlocking things in Jackson's head?' Her eyes settled on Carter as the man in charge.

'We are concerned,' he said. 'I won't lie to you. She left without locking the Chubb. She left with her phone, but not her bag. And most of all she left her little boy behind. Do you think she's the kind to leave Jackson and go willingly like that?'

Tracy shook her head slowly. 'No. I really don't think so. She's very protective of him. It's her and Jackson against the world really. If she left him then she must have thought he was safer that way. *Oh God . . .*' Her eyes went from one officer to the other.

'When did you last speak to her, Tracy?'

'I was here at home, it was Thursday evening.'

'Did you speak about anything in particular?' Carter asked. He was trying to stop Scruffy from covering his legs in dog hairs as Scruffy clearly saw Carter as a potential playmate and kept jumping up on him.

'She called to sort of apologize, I suppose, for the other night when I babysat? She said she was ringing to ask me to come to the fête. That's where I was supposed to see her and Jackson today.'

'Did she seem anxious? Did she say something was bothering her?'

'No. She seemed fine – sounded good. I could hear it in her voice. She was upbeat.'

Tracy's phone lit up on the worktop. She looked at the caller ID.

'It's my husband Steve. Do you mind?'

'Go ahead,' said Carter and the three officers left her to talk in the kitchen. Jeanie went in to sit on the sofa next to Jackson. Carter called Ebony over to him out of Tracy's earshot.

'We'll leave Jeanie to take Tracy's statement and we'll go back to the flat now and see what Sandford's found. By that time we might know something about Manson and about the three men who paid Danielle's flat a visit the other night.'

Tracy came off the phone. She hadn't told Steve about Danielle. She was hoping she wouldn't have to; hoping that Danielle would be back. Luckily Steve had just said he wasn't coming home that night anyway.

'My husband's staying at work tonight,' she told Carter. 'He sometimes does when he has a lot on. He's got a camp bed there and a telly. He won't mind for one night and then I can concentrate on Jackson.'

Carter nodded. 'We'll leave you and Jeanie to settle Jackson in and Jeanie will take your statement as well.'

'I thought I'd done that already.'

'We need it written down if you don't mind, Tracy.' Carter called Jeanie outside the front door to speak with her.

'You think this is linked to Emily Styles' death?'

'My gut instinct says it. She even phoned the help-line. Maybe someone didn't want her to talk. Yeah. I think we have to assume it until we know otherwise. If she turns out to have nipped out to buy an Elastoplast after cutting herself then I'll be pleased as punch but somehow it's all a bit wrong. If Hawk has her, Emily was held over a period of months. That means that if it is our man, we have time to find her.'

Carter left Jeanie to go back inside and Ebony came out and closed the door behind her.

Her breath came out in a white cloud as their feet crunched across the frozen pavement. It was five p.m.

Ebony paused by the car and looked across the car roof at Carter. She could see by his face that he'd had enough of Tracy's house. He was a doer rather than a thinker. He'd only stayed long enough to know what action should come next. There was another reason he had had enough of Tracy's home. Ebony understood it. He pulled hard on the frozen handle, wrenched open the door. Once inside, he leant over to push Ebony's door open from the inside.

Ebony kept silent for a few minutes, busying herself with pulling on her seat belt and getting out her notebook. Jeanie had the effect of making Carter unsettled, claustrophobic. Ebony waited for him to relax again.

Carter switched on the engine. He sat thinking whilst it warmed up and de-misted the windscreen. Ebony began writing up the last few minutes of their time in Tracy's flat and recorded the actual time of leaving. She wrote: *DI Jeanie Vincent to begin questioning the victim's son, Jackson. Returning to Fletcher House with samples of clothing. Includes bloodstained child's pyjamas.*

When she'd finished, Carter flicked off the light switch.

'What do you think, Ebb?'

She looked back at the house. The security light above the door was still on.

'I think that if she doesn't show up in the next

twenty-four hours, Guv, then Tracy's and Jackson's lives are never going to be the same.'

He sighed. 'Yeah. Twenty-four hours and then we'll know for sure. This is what we asked for, Ebb. We were supposed to flush him out when we revealed her identity.' Carter put the car into gear and pulled away. 'Not make him do it again.'

Chapter 16

After Jeanie had finished taking Tracy's statement she packed it away in her bag and took out some things she'd brought especially for Jackson's interview. She laid out paper and crayons onto Tracy's kitchen table. She placed a bag on the table.

Jackson was watching the children's programmes on television in the lounge.

'Do you think Jackson saw what happened?' asked Tracy. She sighed; suddenly she looked exhausted.

'I don't know; but the quicker we question him about the event the more chance we have of getting all the small details. I'd like to make a start now if that's okay? I would like to establish who was in the flat at the time his mum left. Can you start with drawing me a rough plan of Danielle's flat? It's mainly for me to use.'

'I'll try.'

'The main thing is that you put in the things you think Jackson will remember in his flat – anything distinctive that you think he'll relate to, like where the telly is, what colour his front door is, that kind of thing.'

Tracy nodded. She sat at the table and sketched an outline of the flat, then handed it to Jeanie.

'It's pretty good. You have a good memory for detail.' Jeanie smiled. 'Okay, you ready?'

Tracy nodded. 'I'll get Jackson.' She went into the lounge to fetch him.

'Sit on Nanny's lap, Jackson,' Tracy said as she led him to the table and helped him climb up.

'Jackson. Shall we do some drawing?'

He looked interested when he saw the crayons.

'Jackson?' Jeanie got his attention. 'Shall we draw your house? Tell me about your house.'

Jackson began drawing a front door and a window next to it.

'What colour is your front door, Jackson? Choose a crayon that colour.'

'Pink.' Jackson was colouring, concentrating with his tongue sticking out. He coloured inside the lines of the door he'd drawn.

'How many bedrooms are there, Jackson?'

'Mummy's room and Jackson's.'

'How many is that?'

He held up a thumb and finger. 'Two.'

'What's Jackson's room like? Can you draw it?' Jeanie gave him a new piece of paper.

Jackson chose a blue and a yellow crayon. 'Fireman Sam bed.' He scribbled slashes of blue and yellow.

'Anything else?' Jeanie was writing notes. He slowly shook his head. 'What about Mummy's room?'

'Photos of Jackson and Mummy in the park.'

'Are there? Did you have a nice time?'

Jackson nodded. 'We give bread to the ducks.'

Jeanie looked around the room. Jackson did the same. 'Whose house is this, Jackson?'

He answered: 'Nanny's house.'

'Yes that's right, this is where Nanny lives, isn't it? Can you draw Nanny for me?' She gave him a fresh piece of paper.

Jackson drew a round head and inside he drew eyes.

'What a clever boy. What about Nanny's hair, Jackson?' He chose a yellow crayon and scribbled a yellow streak on the top of the circle. Jeanie smiled at him. 'I can see Nanny's arms and legs and she's got eyes. Lovely blonde hair. Can you draw Mummy and Jackson?' Jackson drew a small face with legs and the tallest figure with long dark hair. 'Is that Mummy?' He nodded.

'When you saw Mummy last, what was she doing, Jackson?'

Jackson's eyes moved around as he thought hard. He began moving his head from side to side.

'Was Mummy happy? Did she have a happy face, Jackson?' He continued shaking his head.

'Mummy said *Leave me alone*.'

'Was Mummy cross?' He nodded. Where were you standing then, Jackson?' Jeanie had the plan that Tracy had drawn in her hands. 'Were you in the kitchen?' He shook his head. 'Were you standing next to anything, Jackson?'

'My buggy fell *bang* on the floor.'

Tracy had drawn the buggy resting against the wall in the hallway.

'Were you standing next to your buggy when it fell over?'

He nodded.

'Did Mummy say anything to you, Jackson?'

He looked at Tracy as he answered. 'Mummy said *go back in your bedroom.*'

'Was there anyone else in Jackson's house?' He nodded again.

'Jackson, how many other people were in the flat with you and Mummy and Scruffy?'

Jeanie pulled out some puppets from the bag. The first one was a woman. 'Was there someone like this? A lady there in the flat?' He thought hard and shook his head. 'A man?' asked Jeanie as she pulled a male puppet from the bag. Jackson nodded his head. He was concentrating hard. 'Show me how you can count, Jackson. Where are your fingers?' Tracy smiled encouragement. Jackson lifted both his hands in the air. 'How many fingers have you got on your hand, Jackson?'

Tracy touched each finger as he counted them. 'One, two, three, four, five.'

'Good boy. Very good.'

Jeanie took out two more male puppets. 'Was there more than one man, Jackson? How many men were there in the flat, Jackson?' He held up one finger in the air.

'Where is Mummy now, do you know?' He shook his head; his eyes focused ahead, his face confused and sad. 'When you last saw Mummy, where was she standing Jackson?'

He didn't reply. His face was clouded with thought.

'Was there someone else there with Mummy?'

He nodded. 'Mummy said *don't hurt my son.*

Mummy said *you bastard*. Poor Mummy ...' Jackson looked at his hands; he turned the palms over and shook his head. 'Poor Mummy hurt her hand. *Get out. Get out.*' Jackson looked up and shouted across the room towards the lounge door. '*Bastard*!'

Jeanie reached out and soothed him.

'Can you draw that other person for me, Jackson?'

Jackson picked up a brown crayon and begun to draw a head but he stopped and picked up a red crayon and began to scribble.

'Mummy loves Jackson.' Jackson tore the paper as he held the crayon in his fist and scoured the paper. 'Leave Mummy alone. Get out. Get out.'

Jeanie reached inside a bag she'd brought with her and pulled out another doll. 'Does this look like Nanny?' He nodded. 'Hello, Nanny.' Jeanie talked to the puppet and set it down on the table.

'Who is this one do you think, Jackson?' Jeanie handed a dog puppet to Jackson. He held it in both hands and wiped his nose on it.

'Doggy.'

'Yes. Do you think this doggy is like Scruffy?'

'Yes. Scruffy.'

'And who is this then?' Jeanie held up a little boy doll with short blond hair. Jackson shook his head.

'This is Jackson.' Jeanie galloped along with a toy in each hand. She pretended to have the dog jump all over the little boy and lick him furiously. Jackson laughed and said:

'*No, Scruffy. Don't even think about it.*'

Jeanie smiled at him.

'Is that what Mummy says to Scruffy? "*Don't even*

think about it?"' Jackson nodded. Jackson picked up the dog toy and galloped across the table with it in the same way Jeanie had.

'Clever boy. That's right. Now, Jackson ...' Jeanie pulled out another doll from the bag and she held it up. 'Who do you think this is?'

He looked at the blue-eyed doll with its brown hair: 'Mummy.'

'So this is Jackson and Mummy and Scruffy.' Jeanie held the three puppets and placed them on the table in front of Jackson.

Jeanie pulled out two different puppets. One was black, one was white.

'Which one of these looks like the man with Mummy, Jackson?' He took a good look at the puppets and touched the white one.

'What colour hair has this man got?' She took out a bald puppet, one with black, one with brown and one with blond hair and held them out one by one and then laid them in a row on the table. Jackson picked up the brown-haired puppet. Then he picked up the puppet representing himself and held it up to show it to Tracy.

'Yes, that's Jackson, isn't it?' He was losing concentration; Jeanie knew the session was coming to a close.

'Shall we find the one of Nanny?' Jeanie looked back inside the bag and pulled out the Nanny puppet again.

'There, Jackson, this one is Nanny, isn't it?'

Jeanie packed away the puppets.

'All right, Jackson. I think that's enough for today.

He's getting tired. We'll do some more tomorrow.'
Jeanie started packing the crayons away; she left them
in a tub on the corner of the table. 'It's a good start
though.' Tracy didn't say anything. She was in shock.
'Tracy, let's get Jackson some tea and the bath and
bed. Tracy?'

Tracy nodded.

'Yes.' Jackson looked up at her. He looked as if he
were about to cry.

'Jackson needs a cuddle, Tracy.'

'Of course. Come here, Jackson. Nanny loves you
such a lot. Shall we see what Scruffy's doing?' She led
him into the kitchen. Jeanie gathered up the drawings
and numbered them. She finished up her notes and
closed her pad.

Tracy gave Jackson his tea and bathed him and left
Jeanie reading a book about Spot the Dog to him
whilst she went into the kitchen to tidy.

'It's late, Jackson.' Tracy heard Jeanie's words as she
stood in the kitchen staring out at the dark. She was
wondering what she'd say to Steve. Jeanie checked her
watch; she'd promised Peter she'd be back an hour
ago. She had lost all track of the time. It was gone
eight o'clock. She had promised to make it home in
time to read to her own daughter Christa. She would
have missed bathtime now. She'd have missed playing
with Christa. She must try and get back to put her to
bed. 'Spot is getting very tired. I think it's time for
Spot and Jackson to go to bed.' Jackson watched
Jeanie's face for a few seconds before he nodded and
jumped down off the sofa. Jeanie looked up at Tracy
as she came in from the kitchen. Tracy nodded.

'Come with Nanny and I'll tuck you in.'

Tracy took his hand. 'Say goodnight to Jeanie.' Jeanie bent down for him to give her a kiss.

Jackson went across to Scruffy and hugged his neck. He kissed him and wiped his face in Scruffy's fur. 'Night night.' Jackson was looking for something. He went to the table where he'd sat with Jeanie and the puppets and he climbed up on the chair and leant his weight across the table.

'Careful Jackson.' Tracy rushed towards him.

Jeanie held up her hand for her to take her time. Jackson looked back from Tracy to the table and he found what he was looking for, he kissed the Mummy puppet. Then he got down from the chair and came towards Tracy.

'Night. See you in the morning.' She looked up at Tracy as she came back out of the bedroom having settled Jackson down.

'I'm going home now, Tracy.' Tracy nodded and smiled. She sympathized with Jeanie – she could see she wanted to be going – but she needed to clarify something first:

'What Jackson said about there only being one man in the flat when Danielle left, could that be his dad?'

'I think he would have said so if it was,' Jeanie answered.

'But I know it's been a long time since he saw him.'

Jeanie shook her head. 'Nothing is certain, Tracy.' She smiled kindly. 'We're bringing in Niall Manson and we'll start from there. You must be shattered.'

'Yes, I am.'

'Please get some sleep and let's hope it all gets

resolved in the morning. I've left my number on the kitchen worktop. You call me if you need anything and I'll bring more things for Jackson tomorrow.'

Tracy watched through the lounge window and saw Jeanie's car tail-lights disappear down the road.

Jeanie tried Carter's phone but it was busy. She rang Robbo.

'The child has Down's syndrome, right?' asked Robbo.

'Yes, but I think we have a bright child, despite that. He is perfectly able to count, to recognize colours. He draws to a good ability for his years.'

'Have you been able to interview him?'

'I've made a start. I think we can be sure that someone took her out of that flat in full view of her little boy. From what Jackson has said, I feel that she must have known her abductor. She must have known enough to trust that if he said he wouldn't harm Jackson then he wouldn't. She felt secure enough to think the best option was to go. Seems like there was just one man in the flat with him and his mother. I have a description of sorts: white, brown hair. I'll keep chipping away.'

Tracy went to lie in bed next to Jackson and listened to his breathing.

She had given him a penguin toy she had got from the women working on the nail bar. It was being given away free with a Christmas manicure. She lay there listening to him and felt such a deep panic that she couldn't have closed her eyes if she wanted.

Only the sound of his rhythmical breathing calmed her.

She went over what Jeanie had said and what had happened with the puppets and drawings. If it was Niall Manson who was in that flat then Tracy felt sure things would be sorted out and he wouldn't harm the mother of his child. Fingers crossed, Danielle would come back tomorrow. Jackson's face was turned towards her. With Jeanie's help she'd pushed her bed up against the wall to make sure he couldn't fall out and she'd put a rubber sheet beneath his side of the bed. She'd found it in the spare-room cupboard, kept from when Steve's niece and nephew used to come and stay when they were young.

Tracy watched Jackson as he slept, his eyelids pink and paper-thin. He was dreaming. She dreaded what he might say when he woke up. What questions would he ask her? He'd never said a whole sentence to her yet. She had no idea what he was capable of. All she could think was that something awful must have happened to Danielle for her to leave her little boy.

She didn't remember falling asleep but she awoke when she heard people outside on the street warming their car engines ready to go to work. She heard a whine coming from the kitchen. She got up, agitated; she'd forgotten all about Scruffy, who she'd bedded down on an old duvet on the kitchen floor and now he was whining for something. She thought about calling Steve – he'd be getting ready for work now – but decided against it. She would get everything organized so that when he came home later he wouldn't notice a thing out of place. If she told him the truth about what was happening she would have one more problem to deal with. She'd tell him when and if she had to. After all, Danielle might appear at any moment.

She pulled on her dressing gown over her pyjamas and opened the bedroom door, leaving it slightly ajar as she padded softly out into the kitchen. As she opened the kitchen door Scruffy went ballistic with happiness.

Tracy unlocked the back door to their patio garden, which had half a dozen tubs, a gazebo and a barbecue. The patio furniture was all covered up for the winter outside. There was no lawn, just pots, mostly emptied now till spring when they would be planted up with geraniums. But some of her pots had herbs in all year. She had brushed the snow from them. The purple sage was still usable, the rosemary a great asset to her culinary skills.

Scruffy went bounding outside and cocked his leg against the herbs.

'*Oh God*,' Tracy moaned.

She watched him nose around the rest of the garden until he was satisfied that he was master of the territory and then he leapt up onto the shrubs in a small bed at the end of the garden and crapped.

She let Scruffy back in and then crept back into the bedroom. Jackson was still asleep but he looked like he'd moved slightly. He was frowning, cross. He was fighting something in his sleep.

She tried hard not to feel despondent when she walked out of the bedroom and back into the lounge and saw Scruffy on the couch.

'Down. Get down,' she hissed. Scruffy didn't move. Tracy marched over and pushed him off the sofa. She heard her phone ring from the kitchen. A sense of relief came over her. It would be Danielle. She would be phoning to tell Tracy she was all right, she was coming home. She walked towards the phone with a calm breathy smile on her face. *Stay calm. If I'm calm then so will everyone else be.* She answered it before she realized it was a withheld number. She heard the delay between her answering the phone and someone speaking and knew what that meant. Oh God! Even on a day like today, even with every trouble in the world heaped on her shoulders, they were going to ring her about double-glazing or accident compensation.

'Tracy Collins?'

Tracy was instantly annoyed. They didn't usually get her name right. They usually called her Mrs Smith or Mrs Jones. They just picked any common name and pretended they weren't cold-calling She listened hard. The line wasn't good. Now she was doubly irritated: not only was it an unwanted call but she could hardly make out what the person was saying, it was so quiet and muffled.

'Yes. Who's calling? What's it about?'

The voice, so dark and low, rolled out the words: 'It's about your daughter.'

Chapter 17

'Niall Manson's in the police cells next door, Guv.' Ebony came into Carter's office. She'd been at work since seven. Carter had arrived a short time later. He had managed to get home for a few hours' sleep after they left Sandford. He had a feeling they had better grab sleep whilst they could.

'Where's he living at the moment?'

'No fixed abode. He was picked up at a friend's home last night.'

Carter and Ebony crossed over from 'The Dark Side' into Archway Police Station next door – a door was all that separated them.

'I'll catch you up, Ebb.'

Carter went to talk to another inspector for a few minutes. Ebony's friend Zoe was waiting outside the interview room.

'Hi, Ebb.'

'How's he been, Zoe?'

'He's calm; the lawyer's arrived now. Don't think Manson knows what he's been brought in for.'

Carter joined them and Zoe blushed. Carter was the station's pin-up boy.

'Can we go in, Detective?' Zoe smiled, standing tall. 'Just taken my detective exams, Sir, not sure if I've passed yet.'

'You'll be fine.' He winked at her; his hand was on the door. Ebony followed him inside the interview room and sat down across from Niall Manson. Carter sat next to her, opposite the lawyer.

Manson sat back arrogantly and stared at them. He played with the fingers of his left hand: tapping the tip of his index finger against the pad on his thumb. A nervous habit like someone playing with a rosary. His lawyer sat beside him, tired, yawning.

Carter switched on the recording machine and read Manson his rights. Then he sat back a little in his chair and studied Manson. Carter was good at interviewing. He was good at establishing a base-line. Seeing what was normal for the person and then knowing when something he said created a reaction in their habits, in their voice pitch, control, in the way they breathed – the tell-tale signs that the answer they had just given had been a lie.

'Can you confirm your name and address for me please?'

Manson sat back and stared around the room.

'Could you answer please.'

Manson looked across at his lawyer, who nodded, more irritated by his client than Carter was.

Manson's voice was deep. He had a habit of nodding, breathing in through his nose loudly as if he were bored.

'Niall Manson.'

'Address?'

'Don't have one.'

Carter spoke into the machine. 'Address given as "No fixed abode". Mr Manson, do you understand why we've asked you to come in today?'

Manson blew out his cheeks, breathed in, answered,

'No.'

'It's concerning the disappearance of Danielle Foster.'

'Where's the bitch run off to?'

Carter smiled; he made sure his eyes stayed on Manson. 'When was the last time you saw Danielle?'

'Three weeks ago.'

'Can you tell me about that time?'

'It was Jackson's birthday. She wanted money. If she's gone missing you better ask one of her dyke friends.'

'What about when you sent some of your mates around to her flat on Monday night?' Manson looked at his lawyer, who was busy making notes.

Manson looked disgusted. 'Yeah – that's really my style?' His voice had risen a little.

'Who were they? They asked for you by name. They definitely knew who you were.'

'Business acquaintances. I owed them some money is all it is. Nothing more.'

'You used Danielle's address to make your deals?' He shrugged his answer. The finger-tapping had disappeared. 'How do we know they didn't just come back and decide to take things further for themselves?'

'Because I've seen to it.'

'How?'

'I've settled it. They don't have no reason.'

'I want their names.'

Manson thought it through; he looked around the room for a few minutes. He shook his head. 'I won't cause unnecessary trouble. I will ask around about Danielle. Although it's no skin of my nose if she's in a skip somewhere.'

'I take it you two don't get on very well?'

'Could say.'

'But you have a child together.'

'Havin' a kid was the worst thing we ever did.'

'Jackson's not easy?'

'Oh he's easy all right but then you're never going to get much back from him. He's never gonna to be playin' football for England, is he?'

Carter didn't answer this.

'You still feel something for Danielle, Niall?'

He shrugged. 'Sure. But most of it is hate. She looks at me like I'm shit on her shoe. I ain't good enough for her any more.' Manson sniffed and turned away and pretended to be looking at the décor in the small inter-view room. There was nothing for him to look at except the sheen of the grey paint.

'You think she got ideas above her station? She wants to be a teacher now, doesn't she? She's going to classes, isn't she? And it feels like she doesn't want to know you any more. I sympathize. I have a kid, Niall. I understand how tough it is.'

Niall turned back and sneered. 'Yeah well, she's got a new set of friends. Go and talk to them. What you botherin' me for?'

'Who are they?'

'All those single women she meets in the school. Bunch of dykes. Plus – she denies it but I know she's seeing someone else.'

'That's tough.' Carter sat back in his chair, nodded sympathetically.

Manson watched Carter closely. Then he mirrored Carter's actions. He relaxed, sat back.

'How do you know?' Carter continued.

Manson shook his head slowly, screwed up his face. 'I can tell. You can, can't you? When they're cheating on you?'

'You been together long then?'

'Long enough.'

'A few years?'

'Since we was teenagers. You'd think she'd feel some fucking loyalty – bitch.'

'You ever feel the need to put her in her place? You ever slap her, Niall?'

'Once or twice. Nuthin' bad. Nuthin' she didn't deserve.'

'Where were you yesterday evening?'

'Round my mate's house.'

'Address?'

'Concord Square, Lewisham.'

'Can you prove it?'

'Yeah. We had a visit from friends of yours. Thought there was some chance of finding a cannabis farm; turned out to be next door. No apology – nuthin'. Just smash the fucking door down and leave.'

'Make a complaint.'

'Tsss.' He turned away, disgusted. 'Fucking filth. What about my son? What about Jackson? Who's got him?'

'He's being looked after by family.'

'I hope it ain't Danielle's dad?'

'Why do you say that?'

'Because he's a weird fucker. Never liked me. Never wanted nothing for Danielle. Kicked her out when she got pregnant. Who's got my son?'

'He's with Danielle's mother.'

He shook his head, confused. 'She's dead.'

'Her birth mother.'

'What? What is that shit? Where did she crawl out from? She never tried to find Danielle before. Why did she bother now?'

'Apparently it was Danielle who made the contact. Does that seem strange to you?'

'Yeah. The way she talked about her real mum I'm surprised but ... Danielle was full of surprises lately.'

'I know that things didn't work out for you and Danielle but this is the mother of your child and she's disappeared. You think of anything she may have said to you?'

'The last thing she said was that she hopes I die slowly. Oh yeah, and if I didn't want her contacting the filth I better sort out my affairs fast. I want to see Jackson.'

'You're not allowed, are you? The court order says you are refused permission to see your son ever since you put him in danger with your drug dealing ways. You can reapply to the courts to have the injunction lifted. If you help us we'll certainly put in a word for you.'

Niall's face took on an indifferent expression.

Tracy watched Jackson waddling out of the bedroom, his eyes full of tears.

'What? Pardon? Sorry?' Tracy still hadn't really understood what the person on the other end of the phone was saying.

Jackson came to stand in the kitchen doorway. 'Mummy ... Mummy?' He stood rubbing his eyes, still half asleep.

The voice, deeply distorted, now became loud in her ear. 'Tracy? You listening? I have your daughter here.'

Tracy turned away from Jackson and the phone became part of her head, clamped to her ear. The clock stopped. Her eyes saw nothing. Every sense was tuned into her ear, listening.

'What do you mean? Where is she?'

'Right now? She's somewhere dark.'

'Who are you?' Tracy struggled to understand what the man was saying. His voice was so deep and each word rolled into the next. 'Let me talk to her. Danielle?' Tracy listened hard as she pinched her free ear shut with her forefinger and Jackson gripped her leg, whimpering. Tracy called into the phone. She strained to hear. There was a background noise, persistent but erratic.

'You hear that noise, Tracy?' He breathed down the phone. Beneath the knocking Tracy could hear another noise: it was the sound of scraping. He started laughing and then Tracy heard muffled sounds of someone screaming. 'That's the sound of your daughter trying to get out of her coffin.'

The line went dead.

Tracy stared at the phone in her hand and looked at Jackson. He was looking up at her with Scruffy behind him. All three of them were frozen. Tracy looked back at the phone; her hand was shaking so much that she thought she was about to drop it but it was stuck to her hand like tar. It was burning in her hand. She gasped, clasping her hand over her mouth to try and halt the scream that was about to escape. The image of Danielle buried alive made her want to vomit. She turned and ran for the bathroom and clung to the cold porcelain of the toilet seat as she retched. Jackson came to stand in the bathroom. She washed her face and rinsed her mouth and stooped to see if Jackson was okay. When the doorbell rang Tracy squealed in fright. Jackson started crying.

'Sorry. Sorry. It's okay, Jackson. Nanny's sorry.'

She went to look out of her lounge window and saw Jeanie's white Renault. Tracy rushed towards the door with a sense of relief, picking up Jackson on the way. She opened the door to Jeanie, who took one look at Tracy's face – white as a sheet.

'What is it?'

Tracy shook her head as if to say she couldn't tell her in front of Jackson. Jackson was watching her. Tracy stepped back to allow Jeanie in.

'Come on, Jackson, show me how you can build a house out of your bricks. Jeanie led the way across the lounge with the box of toys she'd brought over from her house, borrowed from Christa. She ushered Tracy into the kitchen.

'What is it?'

Tracy held the phone up and looked at it as if it were alive.

'Someone rang me.'

'Who?'

She stood there shaking her head, looking like she was still trying to work out what happened. She looked at Jeanie, panic in her eyes.

'He knew my name. He says he has Danielle. I could hear her ...'

'What did he say to you? Try and remember the exact words.'

'At first I couldn't understand what the person was saying. It was muffled, didn't sound right.'

'So it was a man?'

'It sounded like a man. He had a really deep voice but it was slowed down, distorted like one of those kids' toys that makes voices sound strange.'

'What did he say?'

'He asked if I could hear a noise.' Tracy's face paled again. She had started to shake. Her eyes lost their focus. Jeanie was beginning to think she'd have to get ready to catch her if she fainted. 'It was a knocking sound.' Tracy took some deep breaths. 'He said it was the sound of Danielle trying to get out of her coffin.'

She turned away and clutched the edge of the kitchen sink and her face crumpled.

'It's all right, Tracy. You're doing okay. Tell me, did you hear Danielle's voice?'

Tracy began to slowly move her head, nodding as her eyes focused on some horror that was locked in her mind. She turned to Jeanie. 'I heard someone scratching, someone screaming. I don't know if it was her.'

Ebony looked around as the door to the interview room opened and Robbo called her outside into the hallway. She closed the door behind her.

'What is it?'

'Just got a call from Jeanie: It's Hawk, he's made contact. It seems he's got Danielle Foster.'

'Guv – a word?'

Ebony called Carter out of the interview.

'Tracy Collins has had a phone call from Hawk. He told her he has her daughter. She heard the sound of someone knocking on wood.'

Carter turned to Zoe. 'Have you got an office we can use? We need to talk.'

'Sir – the interview room across the corridor is free?'

Robbo sat; Willis stood and Carter paced.

'The only way Manson could be involved is if he's Hawk's accomplice. I don't see it, do you?'

Ebony answered with a shake of the head. 'He's not the sharpest knife in the rack, Guv. Plus – you know what he cares about in life? His wallet. He's still got a habit by the look of him and he sells drugs to feed it. No way is he into something this big without a payoff of some kind.'

Robbo crossed his arms around himself and his foot tapped. He was uncomfortable with the closed door but was too preoccupied to give into it.

'You're right – if he was going into the kidnap business it would be for a big ransom. Could Hawk have manipulated him somehow?

'How?' asked Carter. He stopped and looked at Robbo.

'He could have used Manson to draw Danielle Foster out. We need to ask him about Emily Styles.'

'The lawyer won't like it,' said Ebony.

'No, but we may not get another chance to ask him,' Carter replied as he stood to open the door. Robbo wiped the sweat from his face.

Willis and Carter went back into the interview room and Carter sat and leaned across closer to Niall.

'Do you know a friend of Danielle's called Emily Styles?' Carter showed him her photo.

'My client chooses not to answer that.' Manson looked across at his lawyer. 'My client has come in here to help with the disappearance of Danielle Foster, not to answer questions in a murder case.'

'That's the girl who was fished out of the canal?' asked Manson.

'Yes.' The atmosphere in the room changed. Carter's eyes hardened on Manson.

'Never heard of or seen her before.' Manson stiffened. He began looking nervous again.

Carter watched Manson as he displayed all the attributes of someone who was lying. His breathing pattern had changed; he was sweating.

'You better start telling me the truth, Niall, because I got witnesses that say they saw you and Danielle arguing. They heard you rowing and you turned up outside the college where she's studying. Did you see this woman there?'

Niall sat back in his chair and stared at the wall defiantly.

'CCTV footage will confirm it, Niall. You want to save me the time, time that could cost your Danielle's life?'

Niall rocked on his chair and then sat forward, elbows on his knees.

'All right. I went there. So what? I went there to see the bloke she's seeing.'

'What for? You said you didn't care.'

'She's still mine. My property,' Manson corrected himself. He sucked air in behind his front teeth. 'Tsss. I wanted to frighten him a bit.'

'Did you see her?'

'Yeah. I saw her.'

'And him? Who was she with?'

'Some weedy fucker.'

'Describe him to me.'

He shrugged.

'Was he white, black?'

'White, six foot, average.'

'Colour of his hair?'

'Brown.'

'What did you do? Did you follow them?'

'Yeah. I wanted to see; make sure.'

'Did you?'

Niall shrugged. 'I saw enough. That dead woman – Emily Styles – that's the only time I've seen her. They went their separate ways at the station. I'm not saying it was definitely something going on but there could have been. You know what I mean?'

'So you went to her flat to talk about it? Yeah, and?'

'We rowed, sure. She told me to fuck off.'

'Did she admit to seeing someone from the college?'

'She didn't deny it.'

Carter watched Manson – he was telling the truth.

Chapter 18

Jeanie watched Carter arrive and park up before she left Tracy, and went out to talk to him in private. She waved for him to stay where he was and got into the passenger seat.

'How is she?' he asked.

'She's very shaken,' said Jeanie.

'Did he demand a ransom?'

'No. Do you think he will?'

'I don't know,' said Carter. 'He had months to make contact in Emily's case but the Styles were never contacted either to ask for money for her release or to taunt them like this. And yet we know she was alive all that time.' Jeanie looked back at the house as she thought. The lounge was lit up. She saw Tracy hugging Jackson as they walked past the lounge window.

Jeanie looked across at Carter. His face was dark. The sky outside was grey. Overhead the clouds were full of snow.

'He phoned Tracy to tell her he had her daughter and to involve her in her daughter's suffering. If she's in the loop we could use it.'

'In the loop?' Jeanie looked at him incredulously. 'So we feed him Tracy to heighten his pleasure?'

'I was thinking more that we could work on her being a human side to this. A mother figure, someone he might build a rapport with.'

'We are talking Tracy – who gave away her only child for adoption and has more make-up than Boots the chemist?'

Carter smiled. 'You're a miracle worker, Jeanie – think about it for me at least.'

'Yeah. I'll file it under "more stupid ideas from Dan".'

They watched Tracy come to stand at the window.

'I'm going to have to tell her everything we know now,' Jeanie said. 'It's only fair she is told about Emily Styles.'

Carter was nodding, thinking. He leaned forward and studied the other houses around. The curtain in a house across the road moved in the front window.

'Do you think he might be watching the house?' Jeanie asked.

'I don't think so.' They sat in silence for a few minutes: both deep in thought.

'I want you to push hard interviewing this little boy – Jackson. It's a difficult process,' said Carter, shrugging. 'I understand it's not going to be easy. But we can't underestimate the importance of that little boy's memory and we can't afford to lose it.'

'I don't know much about Down's, to be honest, or what his limitations are.'

'You'll have to work it out. Research it. Do it on the job. Use your intuition.'

Jeanie shook her head. 'I don't feel qualified to handle it. Have you talked to Child Protection?'

'Yes, but I think you should handle the whole thing. You're Family Liaison and you've been in Child Protection. Too many people in the house might just make him more worried and freaked out. We have a woman in the morgue, and one missing, and he's the nearest thing we have had to a witness. What has he said so far?'

'One man was in the flat that night. He was white with brown hair. Danielle tried to make him leave but he wouldn't go.'

'Anything else?'

Jeanie looked at him accusingly, then she turned away, shaking her head.

'Look, Jeanie – bottom line, I have faith in you but if it gets too much we can pull you off it. Just remember we're a team. We're all in this twenty-four seven till it's over.'

She turned on him: 'I can't stay round here twenty-four seven. I have Christa to consider. I have a life beyond the job.' She looked across at Carter who was watching her. The old affection they had once had for each other gave them an intimacy. He studied her profile. It was hard not to remember what she looked like lying next to him. His eyes went past her to the large snowflakes that had started to fall, drifting so slowly down to earth.

Her eyes searched his. 'Maybe I shouldn't have come back after I had Christa. It's been an uphill struggle since then. Then I left myself open to the mistake that nearly cost me my life. It's a year ago I was stabbed. Maybe I should have called it a day then.'

'No, Jeanie. You were meant to work in this field. It's not a job for you, it's a vocation.'

She rolled her eyes and groaned. 'Don't give me that crap please.'

But he could see she knew what he was saying was right.

'You have to juggle life.' She didn't answer but stared out at the snow. 'Look,' Carter continued. 'I understand. I don't want to lose you. Just be here in the day to talk to the boy and someone else can take over the evening shifts *if* she needs someone to stay the night. She probably won't. How's that?'

Jeanie sighed, rested her head back on the headrest. She closed her eyes, exasperated. 'It's bound to entail more than that. I'll think about it. I have to talk to Peter.'

'Peter knows it's your job, Jeanie. He married a copper.' Carter got out of the car. Jeanie caught him up. She was cross and she held him back by his arm.

'Don't be a tosser, Dan. Last year, almost to the day, I nearly bled to death on the job you say I was born to do – I nearly died doing it. There's not a moment I don't feel vulnerable. I have a hard job coping with the anxiety. You don't understand what it's like.'

He stopped and turned to face her.

'I'm sorry ... I do understand because I understand you. I know what you are capable of and how certain things are important to you. I know you can be very tough and still be your sweet, warm, loving, intuitive, wise-beyond-your-years, if not a little self-deprecating self.'

He could see a smile appearing – despite everything he'd managed to work his charm. He was pleased with himself as he turned and started walking towards the house.

She caught him up. 'Smug bastard.'

'We'll get the phones fixed. Every call that comes into Tracy's phone will go via us. Hello, Tracy.' Carter stepped inside the house and Jeanie followed, closing the door behind her. 'I hear you've had a phone call?'

She nodded: her eyes wide. Still reeling. 'Is it Jackson's dad?' Tracy was whispering. Jackson was preoccupied with the new toys that Jeanie had brought over for him. Scruffy was lying beside him on the floor, in the corner of the lounge. Tracy had laid out a blanket for Jackson to keep his toys on.

'No it isn't him. He was in custody at the time of the call, Tracy.'

'Who is it then? Who phoned me?'

'Please, Tracy, keep calm. I know this is something you never imagined you'd have to cope with but you *are* coping with it,' said Jeanie. She looked to Carter to continue.

'We believe that the person who has taken your daughter was also responsible for the death of a friend of Danielle's – a woman called Emily Styles. Do you know that name?'

'She was the woman pulled out of the canal.'

'Yes. She was.' Tracy sat on the sofa, staring straight ahead. 'What does he want with Danielle or me?'

Carter glanced at Jeanie. Tracy lifted her eyes. Jeanie shook her head.

'I can't answer that, Tracy. He didn't contact Emily Styles' family.'

'Is he going to kill her?'

'No,' answered Carter. 'Nothing is certain, Tracy. He kept Emily captive for months before he killed her. We still have time to find Danielle.

'He knows who I am. Will he come here? What about Jackson?'

'Someone can stay with you all the time. Or we can move you to a safe house but, for now, I'd rather you stay here because Jackson needs stability. It's paramount we handle this right, this is now between you, your daughter and the person who has her.' Jeanie reached out to try and reassure Tracy with a touch. Tracy had paled, her eyes wide. Jeanie sat beside her and placed her hand on her arm.

'The phone call was distressing for you, I know, but it means she's still alive and there's hope.'

Tracy shook her head, uncertain. She was in a place of panic, fear, a trapped place that Jeanie often saw. It was her job to comfort and to guide families through the trauma of waiting for news about a missing child, of holding on to any hope, of facing facts in the new world they had been dropped into.

Carter tried to reassure her.

'There is still hope that you will get your life back, Tracy, and Danielle will come back to Jackson, but we have to get it right. Let's not scare this man off. He contacted you for a reason. We need to leave the door open for him to contact you again.'

'Why is he phoning?'

Carter shook his head. 'Could be a number of reasons.'

Tracy looked at Jeanie's face. So far Jeanie had read Tracy as a no-nonsense, tell-it-straight type. That was the way she'd deliver news to her, she'd decided. Of course, as the days and sleepless nights passed Jeanie might have to change her tactics.

'We are doing our best to put together a profile on him, Tracy,' she said.

'Yes.' Carter kept his eyes firmly on Tracy.

Tracy held on to the sides of the sofa. 'Is he going to kill her?' she repeated.

'I'm not going to lie to you, Tracy – we don't know.' Jeanie put her arm around Tracy's shoulders. 'The last call you had with Danielle, did she mention that it was Emily's body that was pulled out of Regent's Canal?'

Tracy shook her head.

'She told me that someone on her course had gone missing when I first went round to her flat for tea. She said that was really why she contacted me. She wanted a Plan B just in case anything happened to her. She wanted some assurance from me that I would look after Jackson. *Oh God . . .*' Tracy hid her face in hands. 'How terrible. Did she know then? Did she know that she would be taken like this?'

'She phoned you on Thursday, on the day that the news about Emily Styles' identity was released?'

'Yes that's right, in the evening. I was standing here watching the news with Steve. The identity of that young woman from the canal hadn't come on the news at that time. It came on after I talked to her when I went back into the lounge – Danielle didn't mention it at all. If she'd have known that it was her friend she would have told me.'

'She must have seen the same news bulletin as you then, Tracy. Then the records show she phoned you back.'

Tracy shook her head. 'I didn't hear anything from her. I need to get my phone sorted. It hasn't been working right since that thug threw it across the floor.'

'We checked Danielle's phone records. She phoned you here on your landline about twenty minutes after she'd spoken to you on your mobile. Did you check your messages on your landline?'

Tracy shook her head. 'Steve told me the other day that the landline wasn't working. I need to ring the company. She couldn't get through, I suppose. Oh God, maybe I could have prevented this somehow?'

'Tracy, don't for one minute think anything like that. We are just piecing together everything we know about Danielle's last known movements, that's all.' Jeanie gave Carter a look that told him to mind how he put things.

Tracy turned and watched Jackson playing with his toys on the floor by the telly. 'Do you think he can help?'

'I think so, but we need to do our best to keep things calm here. I will stay here with you,' said Jeanie. 'I'm going to be here for you and Jackson and I'll continue our interviews with him and try to find out what he saw.'

'It will be good for you to have you husband back here to help in the evenings,' said Carter. 'We'll talk things through with him when he gets here. Tell him what he can do to help.'

'I'd better phone him now.'

Tracy went into the kitchen, picked up her phone, and dialled Steve's number. He answered at once.

'What is it?' She could hear the irritation in his voice already.

'Sorry, love. Something's happened. I just wondered whether you could come home now.'

'What is it?' Steve had that same disapproving tone in his voice that always made Tracy take a deep breath and talk slowly, precisely – wish she didn't have to tell him anything.

'Danielle has gone missing.'

'Christ almighty . . . I knew she'd bring nothing but trouble. Where's she gone? Run off to find herself? As long as she hasn't dumped you with the kid . . . Tracy? She hasn't, has she? For Christ's sake, tell me she hasn't?'

Tracy's eyes were shut tight.

'Please, Steve, it's only for a while; just until things are cleared up. I had no choice. Jackson doesn't have anyone else. It's serious. The police are very concerned.'

'Police?'

'Yes. There was blood. Jackson was all alone overnight. She would never have left him like that. They are here now. They would like to explain things to you. I've been contacted – by the person who has Danielle.'

There was a silence on the other end of the phone. Tracy tried to keep her voice calm. She tried to make it sound like it was all going to be fine, even though she knew in her heart it wasn't. 'It's all very difficult, Steve love. The police are going to tap my mobile. They don't know what he wants yet. That's why they need to brief you, talk to you. It won't take long.'

'Brief me? What do you want me to do about it? Christ almighty, Tracy. I knew she'd be nothing but trouble.'

'It's not Danielle's fault.'

He sighed. 'Okay, okay, but I'm not going to be part of it. I've got enough on my plate. I'll find a hotel.' Tracy didn't answer straight away. Part of her was relieved not to have to deal with him as well as everything else.

'Okay,' she said. 'Find a hotel and once you've booked in I'll send along a case with your things in it, enough to last a few days. You can sit and watch football all evening. It won't be so bad.'

'I suppose.'

'I'm sorry, love.'

He grunted something and hung up.

Tracy went back to see Jeanie sitting on the sofa with Jackson on her lap. She was reading him the Spot the Dog book. He looked very tired, thought Tracy as she saw him rub his face into Jeanie's fleece. Carter had his keys in his hand. Jeanie looked at Tracy questioningly. Tracy shook her head, then smiled.

'He's going to stay in a hotel. He feels more comfortable with that.'

Jeanie nodded. 'We'll get some extra help for you for the evenings when I leave.'

Tracy shook her head. 'We'll be okay.'

'Okay, you can change your mind whenever you like,' said Carter. 'The Technical Support Unit will set the phone surveillance up so you don't need to worry about doing anything this end. I'll leave this phone for you to ring family and friends on, use it for all your usual calls and ask people to call you on it instead. If he telephones you just keep him talking on the phone for as long as you can so we have a chance of tracing the call.'

'What shall I say? I'm frightened to say the wrong thing.'

'Ask for proof that he has Danielle. Ask to talk to her. Try and sound soft on the phone. Try and stay calm. The more upset you get the more he's going to enjoy it. Let's take some of the rules away from his control. I am pretty sure he'll ring again. When he does, remember – stay calm. Deep breaths and be business-like.' Tracy nodded but her eyes were panic-stricken.

Carter left and Tracy took Jackson in to lie down in the spare room on a bed that Jeanie had brought for him. Jeanie could hear her talking to him. It was her job as a Family Liaison Officer to be the bridge between the police force and the victim's family. It was her role to offer support, to gain trust and to keep the family informed of the investigation. Most of all, she could gain information that might prove vital to the enquiry. Today she would spend the time gaining Tracy's friendship. Jeanie looked about at Tracy's possessions. The place was super-tidy and fussy. It was a woman's choice of décor; a woman's furnishings. That told her that Steve and Tracy had been together a long time and that he wasn't the driving force in the relationship. The only evidence of him in the flat was the massive television set with an armchair facing it. Jeanie looked at the wedding photos on the walls. Tracy didn't look much different now than she had done then. She just looked a little fuller in the face now. Steve had a handsome-looking face, an attractive smile – quite a catch. They looked an attractive couple. Jeanie looked around the rest of the lounge and was thinking how she couldn't bear to live in this flat with its French-style white bric-a-brac and satin cushions everywhere. She wondered how long it would be before Jackson started wrecking everything. Christa would have already done it by now – gotten her grubby little hands all over the furnishings. Jackson was much more reserved. Jeanie reflected on her own life. Even before Christa, Jeanie would never have had a fussy flat. Looking around the lounge, it struck Jeanie that if she didn't watch it, if she let her guard down, Pete would be straight in there with the French bric-a-brac. She smiled to herself. Dan and clutter – no way, thought Jeanie. Archie must have the most washed hands on the planet.

Tracy came back from settling Jackson down for a nap. She closed the bedroom door and stepped back out from the hall into the lounge.

'Jackson's so tired. Is it normal for him to want to sleep like this?'

Jeanie nodded. 'He's going into shut-down mode because he's in shock.'

'I'll pack a bag for Steve while things are quiet.'

'Okay, I'll join you.'

Tracy led the way through to her bedroom. She pulled down a suitcase from the top of the wardrobe and unzipped it, started to fill it. Steve's neatly ironed pyjamas went in first. Then T-shirts, then she took his shirts from the hangers in the wardrobe and zipped them into a suit bag. Jeanie was impressed by her methodical packing.

'You been together a long time, Tracy?'

She stopped mid folding a T-shirt into the bag. 'Seems like forever.' She looked up and smiled. 'In a nice way, of course.' Jeanie smiled, waited. Tracy busied herself with repacking the case. 'We've known each other since college. That's what I mean.'

Jeanie watched Tracy as she smoothed out creases and folded into perfect neat squares. It struck her that Tracy would have a hard job maintaining her level of perfection with Jackson running around. For now, she was still clinging to her lifestyle and making him fit into it but it was like trying to fit a square peg into a round hole.

'You've done that before.' Jeanie stood beside Tracy and looked into the perfectly packed suitcase.

'One of the many jobs I've done in my life – worked in retail. You learn how to fold a shirt. It's funny how you collect skills. But I don't have a clue how to look after Jackson.'

'You're doing a good job, Tracy. No one gives you a rule book. You just learn along the way.'

'That's what Danielle said to me. There isn't a right way of doing things.'

'She's right. Has Steve got any kids?'

'God no.'

'Not keen, huh?' Jeanie smiled.

'You know what? We've never really sat down and said, shall we?'

'Did he know about Danielle?'

'Yes – well he knew I had a baby but we didn't talk about it much.'

'What was it like when you gave her up? You were very young?'

'I was fifteen.' Tracy's voice came out shrill. She took a breath, closed the suitcase and sat on the bed. 'It was very difficult. I came from an ordinary family; I was one of two kids. My sister never did anything wrong.' Tracy sat on the edge of the bed and tucked her hands beneath her thighs. Jeanie could see Tracy didn't have a lot of practice when it came to talking about her past. Tracy looked up at Jeanie. Her eyes distant, sad. Gone was the super-efficient Tracy, in control. The fifteen-year-old, caught out and cracking up, sat before her on the edge of her girly white satin bed. 'I was just unlucky, I guess. The first boy I felt deeply for and I ended up "up the spout". I left it too late for an abortion; I had no idea what was happening to my body. My parents had never really told me much. I'd have done that if I'd had the choice – got rid of it – I mean, I was just a girl. I knew nothing about parenting. I lost so much schooling. My academic side just came to a standstill. I suppose … if I'd been really bright, really keen, I might have made it to uni but …' She shrugged. 'It wasn't really talked about. It wasn't on the cards.'

'It must have been a difficult time.'

She didn't look at Jeanie.

'Devastating. My mum and dad were so upset. They couldn't look me in the eyes after that.' Tracy's hands spread out along the satin bedspread as if she looked for comfort in its silky touch. 'No more *princess* for me!'

'They helped you in making the decision to give Danielle away?'

'She wasn't called that then. I named her Clare.' Tracy flashed a look Jeanie's way then smiled, embarrassed. 'Yes they decided, with me, that I was too young. I couldn't have coped. They decided it was best.'

'Did you think it was?'

She shook her head. 'I did at the time, or rather I didn't know what to think.'

'But you picked yourself up afterwards and went back to college?'

'Yes, sort of – we papered over the cracks. We tried to behave like it never happened. I went to do a course in beauty therapy and I met Steve. He was doing a mechanics course. My parents were really anti him in the beginning but he was a friend more than anything else and I needed that.'

'Is he still?'

'What?'

'A friend? The love of your life?'

Tracy gave a half smile but didn't answer.

'Marriage is hard work, isn't it, Tracy?'

'Yes. You need to do it when you're young, that's for sure. You compromise then, don't you? You're willing to bend an awful lot to accommodate someone. Too much, really. Then, before you know it you've lost yourself and you kind of hate them as much as love them.' She turned her face away. 'But you can't imagine life without them, that's the trouble. You get caught in a love trap.'

Jeanie could see Tracy's reflection in the window, she could see that she was thinking hard what to say; her expression was a sad one.

'Love loses something along the way, doesn't it?'

Tracy shut the case and looked earnestly at Jeanie. 'I certainly wouldn't do it again.' Jeanie smiled. They looked out at the street outside. 'Is Jackson safe?'

'Yes. I don't think he'd come near Jackson here.' Jeanie smiled. 'You're doing a good job, Tracy.'

Chapter 19

It was midday when Carter left Tracy's house; he drove to Camden and parked up on a quiet residential street with a smart-looking row of Victorian terrace houses. He walked along to the end of the terrace and smelt the bonfire as he turned up the driveway and walked past a battered-looking van.

He rang the doorbell and waited. No one came. He walked to the edge of the house and heard the crackle of the bonfire as flakes of soot drifted past him. Carter knocked on the side gate and tried the latch. He called out:

'Mr Foster?'

'What do you want?' came the reply.

'A word.' Carter opened his warrant card and showed it above the garden gate.

The gate opened and a man stood wiping his hands on a rag. Behind him was a long garden with a clump of trees at the end and a smoking bonfire in the middle. 'Gerald Foster?' It struck Carter that Foster was a tough-looking man. He was over six foot. His frame was still upright and strong. He would have put his age at fifty. Foster wore heavy-rimmed glasses covered in a layer of dust. They were ones that had come back into fashion, clear at the bottom, black and heavy at the top.

The man nodded but he didn't move from the gate.

'I won't keep you long, can I come in please?'

For a moment it looked as if Gerald Foster was about to say no but then he turned and walked over to the bonfire.

Carter followed.

'Funny time to be burning stuff? Isn't that ground a bit wet?' Foster shrugged. He carried on past the bonfire and through into the utility room and kitchen at the back of the house. The kitchen table was covered with newspaper and tools being cleaned. Foster unscrewed a chain-saw that was secured in a vice screwed to the edge of a worktop and blew onto the newly sharpened chain blade. Christ, thought Carter – this is what happened to some men when there was no woman around. Foster had turned his house into a tool shed. 'You're having a tidy-up?' Carter looked around the kitchen. There were large pieces of antique-looking mechanical equipment on newspaper. There was a wooden box under repair, its hinges hanging out, its broken lid resting on top of it.

Foster shrugged and turned his back to Carter while he washed his hands in the kitchen sink.

'I'm very busy as you can see.' He picked up a dirty towel from beside the sink and wiped his hands.

'What's all this stuff? You repair antiques? Looks like you have a lot on here.' Carter knelt down to look at a piece of old machinery that looked like a pump.

'It's a hobby.' Foster glared at Carter. 'What's this

about?' Foster's voice was surprisingly soft for such a gruff-looking man, thought Carter. He looked nervous. He definitely wasn't comfortable with visitors.

'It's about your daughter Danielle. She's gone missing.' Foster stared blankly at Carter for a few seconds then he shook his head and turned away, irritated. 'We're very concerned about her welfare. We think she's been abducted.'

'Whatever trouble she's in she brought it on herself.' Foster picked up a pair of shears from the kitchen table and began sharpening one of the blades on an oiled stone. 'I haven't seen her in two years. Don't want to either. I'm finished with her – I've done my bit. Brought her up as best I could.'

'Bit if a handful, was she?' Carter nodded sympathetically at Foster. He didn't answer; he continued sharpening the blade.

'You could say that. She caused my wife's death; she brought it on with all her shenanigans.' He turned to look at Carter and make sure he understood. 'She was never any good. I could see it as she grew. She had that look about her. Nothing but trouble and then she got herself pregnant and I told my wife not to have anything to do with her but she felt sorry for the little boy. Poor blighter.' Foster lifted his eyes and looked at Carter.

'I don't know what he's capable of. Not much, I don't expect. He's disabled. You seen him?'

'Yes I saw him. He's a sweet little kid. He's in shock. He was left alone overnight.'

'He'll soon forget. He's going to be better off without her, that's for sure.' He picked up some bits of debris and threw them angrily into the bin. Then he turned back to Carter. 'Marion saw them despite my wishes. I told her not to but she disobeyed me and look where it got her. It put her in an early grave. If someone has taken that girl, good luck to them. They've done the world a favour. She's never been any good to anyone.' He paused and looked up from his sharpening. 'The boy's better off without her. What's happened to him now?'

'He's with Danielle's birth mother, Tracy.'

Foster looked away and shook his head with a cynical smile on his face. 'What's she like, Danielle's birth mother? Rough, I expect?'

Carter shook his head. 'Not at all – she's a nice woman: hard-working, respectable. So you haven't seen Danielle for some time?'

'Not since the funeral. I didn't want her at that but she turned up and I didn't want to make a scene. Marion wouldn't have wanted that. Marion was nothing but goodness. A saint to put up with the things she did. A wonderful woman who deserved better than the treatment she got from her own daughter. Well, adopted daughter. I never used to think there was a difference – I do now. I think of her as a cuckoo in our nest. All she did was take – bled us dry.'

'I understand what you're saying, Mr Foster. I know it's not easy. I came from a big family – fallouts are an everyday thing, but you might want to keep the door open on Danielle and your grandson. She was trying her best to put her life in order. She had enrolled in evening classes, she was living in a new place with Jackson. She was trying to make a go of things.'

'Oh I know she was attending classes. She told me.'

'So she did contact you recently. I thought you said she hadn't?'

'I said I hadn't seen her. She rung up six months ago, said it was to see how I was. But she always has an angle. She got to it in the end. She asked me for the details about her birth mother. I gave them to her. It was no skin off my nose. Typical – now that she can't tap my wife for money she's trying to get it out of some other poor sap. Good luck to them both.'

Carter watched as Gerald started sharpening the other side of the shears.

'Do you work, Mr Foster?'

'I'm a London guide. I take people on guided walks around the city and the surrounds. I'm working this afternoon.' He looked at Carter as if to say – so hurry up.

'A tourist guide?'

'Yes. I show people round. Charles Dickens' London. Jack the Ripper's haunts. That kind of thing.'

'Interesting job.'

'It's more of a hobby really. I'm semi-retired.'

'What did you do before?'

'I'm a carpenter by trade. I still get the odd call to make something but I haven't done so much since my wife died.' He caught Carter looking around at the mess in the kitchen. 'I don't see the point in keeping up with the housework any more. Never did really. That was always Marion's domain. But I make sure I brush up well when I go to work.'

'You manage here on your own?'

'Yes. I can live very frugally. I don't need a lot of money.'

'Looks like you look after your tools. My granddad was one for making and mending, always saw him with a pair of pliers in his hand, always fixing something.'

Foster didn't reply, instead he motioned his head towards the back garden and the bonfire.

'Of course, I won't keep you.'

Foster picked up his gloves and marched outside. Carter followed him out. They passed the overgrown edges of what had once been a neat and well-cared-for garden. There was lawn in the main middle part, shrubs around the outside now looking wintry and uncared for. The lawn came to an abrupt stop at a small copse of trees.

'You've got a lot of space here. Ever thought of getting planning permission? Is that a big shed you've got at the bottom there?' Carter took a few paces towards the trees and a shed with an open door.

Foster blocked his way.

'It's a workshop. I'm giving it a tidy-out. Look – I'm busy. If you want to talk to someone go and find that worthless no-hoper Niall Manson, the boy's father. What about him? She said she'd broken away from him but I never believed it. If there's some muck to roll in he'll find it.'

'Funny,' said Carter, watching Foster work. 'He didn't seem to like you either.'

Foster stopped and looked him.

'You've talked to him? What did he say?'

'We talked about Danielle *mainly*.'

Carter watched as Foster seemed to be mulling this news over.

'Ah well.' He stamped on the growing pile of debris to burn. 'Those that live in glasshouses shouldn't throw stones.' He glared at Carter.

'Okay, thanks for your time, Mr Foster. I'll leave you to it. I'll leave a card for you in case you remember anything you think will help find her.' He held up his card for Foster to see.

Foster took it from him and stuffed it into his trouser pocket. He watched Carter leave through the side gate then waited till he heard a car start off further down the road. He walked quickly down past the bonfire and into the copse. His heartbeat quickened as he approached his shed. He wouldn't leave it unpadlocked again. That was silly of him. The policeman could have asked to look inside. Foster would have had to say no. The policeman would have been suspicious. Foster turned the handle and stepped into the shed and into a world that smelt of wood and creosote. The dust from newly cut chipboard was in the air. He walked across to the far wall and stood in front of the box he'd finished a few days ago. He pulled back a hessian curtain. Pinned to the wall behind it there were hundreds of photos of Danielle as a little girl.

Chapter 20

Carter was still out of the office when Ebony got a call from Robbo and headed down the corridor to see him. He was in there with Pam and one other researcher, a young graduate named James. The door was open as usual. Pam smiled. Robbo was sitting behind his desk, rocking his chair, and motioned for Ebony to come and sit beside him.

Robbo was giving James instructions. 'Get a list of all of Danielle Foster's contacts on Facebook, James, specifically the ones who are in the same circumstances as her – same age and with a child and keep it to North London for now. And concentrate on the ones that cross over with Emily Styles first. Hawk could have access to these women via a Facebook account. People have hundreds of friends on social media sites. Just a handful, maybe ten per cent, are real friends.'

He looked over his glasses at Pam and noted her disapproving look. Hacking into Facebook was not without its problems – getting permission from the American company was laborious at best. But then both Pam and Robbo knew there were other ways, not quite so legit.

He turned back to talk to Ebony.

'Thought we could brainstorm.'

He picked up a highlighting pen and looked at the profiles of the two women as he highlighted the common traits. Robbo was making notes by hand, on his desk.

'I want to go through the similarities between the two women and try to understand what Danielle is going through and what motivates Hawk. We can start with the info so far: age, physical type, lifestyle, family, relationship status. Emily and Danielle? What do they have in common physically?'

'Physically? Just age, as far as I can tell,' answered Ebony. 'Emily was auburn, five foot seven, size twelve, and Danielle is dark-haired, five foot eight inches and very slim.'

'So Hawk doesn't go for a particular colouring in a woman. Personality-wise?'

'We don't know how similar they are really – we only have Tracy's concept of her daughter and that's based on a few meetings,' said Ebony. 'We do know that they liked one another. They were friends so they must have been alike in many ways or in the core things like the way they were towards people, their principles.'

'Yes,' agreed Robbo. 'The core of a good friendship has to be common interests. Shared values. We have to talk to someone who really knew the women.'

'Yes. It has to be another woman,' agreed Ebony. 'A friend from college, maybe.'

Robbo nodded. 'We know that both women had been through a lot in their lives, both were starting over, trying to turn their lives around, and were tough women.' He looked at Ebony.

She nodded her agreement.

'Point is? You'd think they would have learnt not to trust?'

'Yes, but something about Hawk made them think they were safe with him.'

'He has some sort of affinity with them, with women – with children.'

'But he feels something for the child, he doesn't harm it. He didn't harm Jackson,' Ebony said. 'He empathizes with the child. He relates to children better than adults. He identifies with the child. He takes pleasure from parting the mother and child. Something happened in his own childhood.' Robbo was making notes: 'Yes. Some parting with his mother. Some unnatural separation or betrayal in his childhood left him missing a piece of the emotional puzzle.'

Pam had stopped typing. Robbo heard it. He was used to her ways. She didn't like to interrupt. But Robbo knew her silence meant she had something to add.

'What you got for us, Pam?'

'So many names – over fifty so far – women who went missing in their twenties with one child or more.'

'Any of those turn up dead? Bodies found with splinters of wood in the skin, emaciated? Asphyxiation, strangulation suspected?'

'The few that had turned up dead were too badly decomposed to know anything about how they died.' Pam handed four files across to Robbo. 'All of them dating from the last five years. I'll keep searching through Mispers.'

Robbo read off the top few names:

'Charlotte Rogers never returned from a night out, disappeared in 2011 from Finsbury Park. Her body found a year later in National Trust woodland in Bushey. She could fit the bill – so far as we can currently tell,' Robbo said as he handed a photo to Ebony. 'What month did she disappear?'

'She disappeared in June of that year. That would cross over with another woman, Sophie Vein, found decomposed in Rickmansworth in February 2012, missing nine months.' Ebony looked at the photo of the body.

'Impossible to ascertain cause of death – her body was scattered by wildlife. There was very little of her left.'

'We are going to have to get some other factors going to narrow this down.'

Ebony picked up photos passed over from Pam.

'Pauline Murphy, Jenny Smith, Mispers. The list goes on and on.' She opened her hands in the air, exasperated.

'Okay. Thanks, Pam.' Robbo passed the files over to James. 'Make a list of links between these women for me, James. I want to see how many of them share more than five similarities.'

'If Hawk is responsible for even one of these women it means he is how old?' Ebony was making notes on a sheet of paper on Robbo's desk.

'We are going back five years. Let's say he started killing when he was in his mid-twenties – hardly anyone starts before then – then he's thirtyish now. We know he's strong enough to haul Emily Styles' body down to the canal and to drop it in.'

'But she weighed no more than a child.'

'Granted. Could be a father-figure type then?'

'I don't think so,' said Ebony. 'Something tells me they would trust a man more who was their own age. There's some sort of attraction there.'

'What do we know about the geographical layout of these two crimes?' Robbo laid out a map of North London on the desk. He drew a line from Regent's Canal out to Emily Styles' parents' house in Camden, to where she was last seen and then he drew one out from Regent's Canal again but this one was to Danielle Foster's flat in Finsbury Park.

'There was also the flat that Emily was about to move into.' Ebony peered at the map. 'That's a fifteen-minute walk from her parents' house the other side of Camden towards King's Cross. There – Archer Street.' She found it on the map. Robbo lined it up. 'The nursery was in between the two.'

'Was that council-owned?' asked Robbo.

'Housing association like Danielle's,' answered Pam.

'James, add that to the list of similarities – they must be in social housing.'

'Just added that,' said Pam. 'Now we've narrowed the list to twelve.'

Robbo gave Ebony a cautious smile.

Chapter 21

Ever since he'd got out of the station Niall Manson had been chewing things over in his mind. He felt more aggrieved than sentimental about Danielle's disappearance. He felt, deep inside, that it wasn't right, and he took it as a personal injury done to himself. There had been a time when he cared about her, in his own way. If things had gone differently they would still be together now. Manson felt he was unlucky. He'd been dealt a raw deal all through his life. It had led him down a few shady paths that he probably wished he hadn't travelled but now it was his time to make a stand: change his life; take it into his own hands. It looked as if Danielle was as good as gone and Niall Manson needed to cash in. A small part of him knew it would never have worked. She was too good for him: he knew it; she knew it. But money could make Manson feel a lot better.

Gerald Foster was at work when he got the call.

He was explaining to an American tourist how the salt used to come into London and into the pit where it was stored and in the warehouses at King's Cross. He answered the third time that Manson tried his number.

'Yes?' His voice was hushed as he walked to the other side of the room to talk.

'Foster?'

'Yes.' Foster was already recognizing the voice on the other end of the phone. 'What do you want, Manson?'

'Good memory. Good recall.'

'Yeah. What do you want?'

'Danielle's gone missing.'

'I know. So?'

'So, I thought you and me might have a talk about it.'

'What is there to say?'

'I was called in to the Old Bill. They asked me all sorts of questions about her home life . . . I didn't say all I could have.'

'What do you mean by that?'

'Ha . . . I tell you what I remember – I remember you getting nasty more than once. You locked her in her room; made sure only you had the key. You get what I'm saying? Seems like fuckin' strange behaviour towards your daughter. What went on behind them locked doors? You hear what I'm saying?'

'You're a loser, Manson. Piss off – you're deranged.'

'I could tell a lot of stories about you. I could tell them how I've seen you in your van, cruising along certain streets. You know what I'm saying? Picking up women.'

Foster had difficulty getting his words out.

'I was never unfaithful to my wife.' He hissed down the phone. 'We had a good marriage. What I do now is my business.'

'But, it's not is it? I could tell the police everything I know ... make up a bit more – it will take them time to prove it. All that time you'll be banged up.'

'I've got nothing to hide.' Foster's voice was shaky. He turned to look at the clients waiting for him to return. He was desperate to get off the phone and back to the job he loved.

'You sure you want all your dirty linen washed in public? You'll lose your job for sure whilst they investigate you. Here's what I'm offering: I'll say nothing but I want compensating. You get me?' There was a silence on the other end of the phone. Manson continued. 'I'm looking at ten K. I'll give you one week to find it. By the way – I don't give a shit what you do with the bitch Danielle.'

Gerald Foster put his phone away. He went back to his clients and apologized – he would need to hand them over to a colleague as he had personal stuff come up and had to leave.

Later that day Niall Manson was on his way to meet a friend. He was helping with deliveries of weed today. The police interest had halted distribution for a few days and now people were gagging for it. There were several drop-off points around the area where people could call and meet and buy weed from him. Demand was rising with the Christmas stress. He walked along the outside of the pavement and took a call on his mobile. His first customer. He took the order and closed his phone. Today was going to be a good day. Get some money in, put a bet on the horses, have a few beers later; find himself a friendly girl who wasn't too fussy. Still, Danielle was there nagging at the back of his mind. It was all fucking weird. The more he thought about it, the more Manson was convinced that Foster could have flipped. Manson had known him for ten years. He'd seen him get stranger every year. He knew he spent all his time in the shed in his garden, banging away on some creepy project, restoring some useless old thing that came off the barges. That was another thing – the canals; Foster was obsessed with the canals and now they had pulled that friend of Danielle's out of one. Then his face lit up at a new thought — *compensation*. If she was killed by some lunatic – her father no less – would there be any money? Jackson would get the money. Simple then – he needed to get Jackson. After all, it was his son. The deal with Foster might work out, as well. No matter what any of them thought or said about him, he had rights and he intended to exercise them. Jackson was coming home with him.

Niall was so busy with his thoughts he didn't notice the dark-coloured van that had just pulled out. As he heard the screech of acceleration he turned to see a familiar face focused on him from behind the steering wheel. He felt the impact of the van's side bumper smack against his body, and pain as his legs slid beneath the front wheel and then his head disappeared under the back wheel and he felt nothing else.

Chapter 22

Tracy was taking a shower as Jeanie flicked through the TV channels to find something for Jackson to watch. They were watching *In the Night Garden* and Jackson was very intent on his programme. He got down from the sofa and sat in front of the television with Scruffy. Jeanie put a cushion on the floor for him. She was sure Tracy would have had a problem with it but pretended to be unaware. There was nothing in the house that seemed designed for use; it was all for show. Jackson's solid little frame sat hunched over as he curled his fingers in his toy penguin's fur and watched *In the Night Garden* in silence.

When it was over Jeanie flicked through the channels again and found *Peppa Pig*.

'Here is Peppa and her brother George.' George grunted and waved. 'Here is Mummy Pig and Daddy Pig.' They came onto the screen, Mummy Pig smiling serenely, Daddy Pig waving at the viewers.

Jackson sat up and began pointing and talking to the television. He turned to look at Jeanie and then looked past her, as if he were looking for someone.

'What is it, Jackson?'

He pointed to the screen. He was agitated. He got to his feet and went over to Jeanie. His face was crumpling. He was still pointing at the screen.

'What is it, Jackson?'

He came over to Jeanie and held on to her as he kept turning back to the television and pointing.

'Is it Peppa Pig?' Jeanie watched him. He seemed slightly calmer until Daddy Pig came back onto the screen. He twisted away and buried his face in Jeanie.

'No. No, Daddy Pig. NO.'

'What is it, Jackson?' Jeanie lifted him onto her lap. He clung onto her so hard that he was pinching her arms. He shouted at the telly.

'No ... no! Leave Mummy alone!'

'What is it, Jackson?' He looked at Jeanie and his eyes filled. 'It's okay, Jackson.' She switched off the telly. She cuddled him and led him across to the table. She sat him on the cushion on the chair again and she sat next to him. She picked up the crayons and hastily drew Daddy Pig's head on a piece of paper: his head flat like a hairdryer shape, a few hairs around his chin, round black glasses. She drew a picture of Daddy Pig's face and cut out the drawing and then picked up the bag containing the puppets and took some out.

Jeanie held two adult puppets near one another and placed them in front of Jackson on the table. He picked up the Mummy puppet and held it tightly in his left hand. With his right hand he pushed away roughly the male puppet onto which Jeanie had pinned Daddy Pig's face.

'No,' he repeated.

'What is Mummy puppet saying, Jackson?'

'Mummy said, "No no no. Get out. Get out."'

'Did Mummy say this man's name?' She picked up the Daddy Pig puppet and held it at arm's length for him to look at it. Jackson nodded. 'What did she call him, Jackson? What's this man's name?'

He pointed to the puppet. 'Daddy Pig.'

Tracy came out of the shower. Jeanie stood outside the bedroom door as Tracy got dressed.

'I want to try another session with Jackson when you're ready?'

'Coming.'

'We are definitely getting somewhere with him now, Tracy. I added another puppet; from the Peppa Pig cartoon. The puppet has Daddy Pig's face pinned on.'

'He loves Peppa Pig. He had a Peppa Pig toy when I first met them at the Christmas Fayre,' said Tracy from behind the closed door.

'Not any more. He just got very distressed when it came on the telly. He started shouting when the character Daddy Pig came on the screen. I think something about Daddy Pig reminds him of this man.'

'I'm ready.' Tracy came into the lounge and called to Jackson as she pulled out the chair at the table ready for him to climb into. Jeanie waited for Jackson to get settled. One by one she took three puppets: Scruffy, Jackson and Danielle. She asked the same question each time:

'Who's this, Jackson?'

'Scruffy.'

'Yes, it's Scruffy, isn't it?' Jackson nodded. 'Jackson, what colour is your front door?'

'Pink.'

'Did you see Mummy when you were standing at the front door?' Jackson didn't understand. 'Jackson, who's this?' Jeanie showed him the Mummy puppet and the Daddy Pig puppet.

'Where did you see Mummy talking to this man, Jackson?' Jackson shook his head.

'Where is Mummy now, Jackson? Do you know?'

Jackson looked around him, his eyes drifted skyward as he thought. A sad expression crept over his face. He shook his head again.

'Mummy's gone.'

'Where was Mummy standing when you saw her last time, Jackson?'

'Mummy's in Jackson's house.' He frowned. He was thinking hard.

'And what was Mummy doing?'

'Mummy shouting. Mummy was very very cross.' Jackson's movements became agitated as he wriggled on the chair and flapped his arms in the air.

'What was she shouting, Jackson?'

Jackson sat up straight in the chair and his face flushed crimson. 'Get out. Leave me alone.'

'Where were you, Jackson? Where were you when Mummy said that?' Jackson looked out into space as he thought. Tracy watched in silence. Hardly daring to make a sound as she breathed in case it stopped Jackson.

'Mummy said: "Go back to bed, Jackson. Stay in bed with Scruffy."' His eyes flashed to Tracy. '"Nanny coming."'

'Is that what Mummy said, Jackson? She said, "Nanny's coming?"' Jackson nodded. 'What happened to Mummy then, Jackson?' He tilted his head one way and the other but didn't answer. He picked up the Scruffy puppet and kissed it. 'Was Mummy on her own then, Jackson?' Jeanie asked. He shook his head. His eyes went to the puppets. He reached out deliberately and picked up the one with the Daddy Pig face. He held it near his own face.

'Leave Mummy alone. Leave her alone.'

Tracy screamed as her phone rang on the shelf. She wasn't expecting a call. She sensed who it was and looked at Jeanie.

'Quickly, Tracy. Remember, if it's him – keep him talking. Ask to speak to her.' Jeanie got up from the table. 'Come on, Jackson, let's see what Nanny's got in her bedroom.' Jeanie led Jackson quickly away.

Tracy stood up and walked over to the phone. She dreaded every step.

'Hello, Tracy.'

'Hello.' The sound of his voice made her want to drop the phone. The closeness to him was unbearable.

'Are you scared, Tracy?'

'Yes.'

Tracy could hear classical music playing in the background.

'I want to speak to Danielle.'

There was another noise in the background that she couldn't make out. It was like someone had the phone in their pocket or their bag and had rung her number by mistake. Tracy walked silently through the lounge with the phone in her hand.

She heard a shuffling. The music grew faint as she heard feet walking; then there was the sound of a door opening and the click of a switch. Somewhere at the edge of the room a woman was crying. The sounds of her cries echoed, grew louder. She heard his feet walk across a hard floor and the sound of his breathing as it rasped down the phone. Then she heard the woman crying again. Her crying was mixed with shallow breaths.

'*Please please ... I'm begging you ... I'll do any-thing ... please ... don't hurt me again.*'

Hands muffling the sound around the phone.

'Did you hear that, Tracy?'

She could hardly breathe.

He laughed. His voice was distorted like last time; it was liquid and deep and one sound rolled into another.

'Danielle? *Danielle?*' Tracy screeched down the phone.

He laughed again. Tracy heard muffled squeals of pain.

'You think this is your daughter, Tracy? You gave your daughter away. You went off and left her. You didn't really love her, did you?'

'No. No. It wasn't like that. Please. I don't under-stand what you want from me. Tell me what I can do. Where is my daughter? Danielle? *Danielle?*'

'Shussssssh,' he said, his voice vibrating in Tracy's ears. Then Tracy heard someone try to speak, but the words came out as spluttering sounds. 'She doesn't want to speak to you, Tracy.' Tracy heard the sound of squealing as if someone couldn't breathe. She could hear him working hard at something; his breath rasp-ing down the phone line. 'I'll ring you again tomorrow –

maybe she'll feel like talking then. You make sure you're by the phone, Tracy. Don't you go anywhere. Your time is coming, Tracy. Look after the boy. I saved his life. I am his saviour. Make sure he doesn't betray me.' A piercing wail drilled through Tracy's ear. 'Shhhh ... Bye, Baby Bunting. Daddy's gone a-hunting. Remember that rhyme, Tracy?' She didn't answer. Her hand was clasped across her mouth to stop herself from screaming. 'Of course you do. You know it well. Now I found a rabbit that needs skinning. Have you ever skinned an animal, Tracy? The first cut is important to get right, then you slide the knife between the skin and the muscle and, hey presto, rip it back ...' He laughed and the phone went dead.

Tracy was shaking so much that she dropped the phone as she sank to her knees, clutching her hands together and rocking. She crawled to her bedroom and sat outside, leaning with her back against the wall.

Jeanie came out and knelt beside her.

'You're okay, Tracy.'

'I can't do it. I can't do it.'

'Yes you can, Tracy. Look at me.' She looked into Tracy's eyes – her mascara was running. 'If it means going through this to get Danielle back – then I know because I've seen your strength that you can do this, Tracy.'

Chapter 23

The snow fell all night. It stopped just before dawn. Hampstead Heath was covered in a clean pure white icing of it. It looked like a country Christmas scene in the middle of London. Gerald Foster was just thinking that as he drove past it on his way back from having his van repaired – just a quick paint job. He had taken it to the Albanian garage behind Caledonian Road – they were cheap and they didn't ask questions. They didn't want to make chitchat. He didn't feel like driving straight home so he took a detour around the Heath. He watched a woman as she came alongside the passenger window. She was jogging. Her ponytail swished from side to side; her tight Lycra trousers showed every curve. Foster tutted disapprovingly – what did women expect when they wore outfits like that? He kept his eyes on her until she dodged the snow piled at the edge of the pavement and she turned into the road that led to the Heath. Foster turned into the Lido car park and watched her run past.

The jogger passed the Lido, carried on up the path and then headed right along the perimeter of the

Heath. She smiled and nodded at another jogger running the opposite way. It was funny how she saw the same people every day. The joggers were friendly to one another, just the way the dog owners were keen on anyone else with a dog but didn't like the joggers. Or rather, their dogs didn't like joggers.

Janet had had problems with dogs and their owners in the past. In the ten months she had been running on Hampstead Heath she'd been attacked three times by dogs. Now she tried not to feel anxious, tried not to give off the smell of fear.

Ahead of her a group of women was approaching, walking their dogs. The dog in front had broken away from the others and now looked like it was heading straight for her. She felt a surge of panic. She looked at the owner's face. The woman was in conversation with her friend but she was staring straight at Janet. The dog had begun a low growl and was coming across Janet's path. Janet's heart was racing. The dog owner kept eye contact and gave a half smile that said: *don't worry, he won't bite you – I think*. Janet didn't smile back. She was thinking: *she must take responsibility for her dog now ... now is a good time*. Janet turned away, defeated. She didn't want to take any risks. She stepped off the path and onto the verge. Her feet cut through the hard snow covering the ground. The cold was biting.

The dog lunged and snapped at her as she passed. The owner muttered she was sorry. Janet cursed loudly, put a spurt of speed on and powered up the hill and away from the path. Virgin snow crunched beneath her feet. She pushed hard with her thighs until she reached the copse at the summit and the trees closed around her. She had stitch now; clasping her side she slowed to a walk to catch her breath as she dragged the cold air into her burning lungs.

She moved slowly forward, stepping over the fallen branches and stopped by one of the trees to listen to the faint knocking sound of a woodpecker drilling for food or maybe it was a squirrel cracking a nut – she didn't know which. It was a knocking sound. Her breath snorted into the air, her body was steaming. She felt the chill begin as the sweat cooled her body but she stood in the perfect still beneath the pines and listened to the knocking. Her eyes searched the copse and found the slight movement responsible, the bobbing head of a crow. She walked quietly towards it, her eyes fixed on the black shiny wings of the bird. It looked up as she approached – it was feeding, working hard at something on the ground, knocking it with its beak. As she approached it stopped and stared defiantly at her but then flapped noisily off into the nearest tree and watched her approach. As Janet stepped over the fallen branch her feet moved in slow motion as her eyes made sense of what she saw. A woman's naked body surrounded by a shroud of the freshly fallen white snow. The woman's face was a scarecrow mask of make-up and the skin had been peeled up from her breasts like a crimson bra. Her black empty eye sockets stared up at the crows in the trees.

Chapter 24

Carter pulled up the hood of his forensic suit as he and Willis waited to be allowed to cross over into the crime scene. They saw the tall frame of Sandford walk across to them from where he'd been searching the far side of the trees. He climbed over the fallen tree debris; moving cautiously, picking his way amongst the branches.

'I've finished here, for now.' he said to Carter. He nodded to Ebony. 'We'll keep it taped off for a few more days yet. We'll have to wait till the snow melts to look for tracks.'

'How long's she been here, do you think?' Carter asked Sandford. Ebony was looking down over the white expanse of the Heath. In the distance, people were walking their dogs or jogging along the paths around its edge. Carter followed her gaze and then swung back to Sandford. 'She can't have been here any longer than a couple of days. This is a busy place.'

'Twenty-four hours, Doc estimates,' replied Sandford. 'Left here before last night's snowfall. She's frozen solid.' Sandford turned and led the way woods.

'Who found her?'

'A jogger named Janet Leonard. She's waiting in the squad car.'

'Does it look like it's the same man? Is it Hawk?'

Sandford stopped walking and turned to fix Carter with a gaze that told Carter that, even for a seasoned professional, it was a sight not soon forgotten. He nodded. 'Her body's a real mess.'

They came to the area beyond the fallen tree trunk and the woman's body began to come into view. Harding had brushed away the snow from around her.

Carter stopped in his tracks. 'Christ.'

Ebony took a step to his side and crouched beside her.

'It's the same as last time.'

'Yes,' said Harding.

'What happened to the bag?' Ebony was looking at the plastic shards scattered in the snow.

'A badger, fox or even someone's pet dog has been at it,' answered Harding. 'Maybe they were disturbed.'

Carter drew level. 'What about her eyes?' he asked.

Harding looked up at the pine trees around them. The crows watched them. The air hung dank and dark, trapped in the shadows of the trees. The crows shifted in the upper branches of the pines as they waited, ever hopeful of finishing their meal.

'Crows have large beaks for tearing flesh. The birds have had a go at her face. Soft entry points like the eyes were the best option; the rest of her is frozen.

Ebony watched Harding brush the last of the snow

away from the body and onto a plastic sheet she had tucked in around it. She looked down at the ulcerated sites across the body. 'She is just like Emily Styles but a lot thinner, a lot more emaciated.'

Harding paused in her work and sighed; her white breath stayed as a shroud in the air. She shook her head. 'It's hard to know how she made it to even this point. She has been like this for a *long* time.'

'She looks like a sick joke,' said Ebony. She looked at the remnants of blue eye-shadow and the few spikes of painted-on lashes visible above the empty eye sockets, the clownish circles of red stain on her cheeks.

'He must really hate women, all women – vanity, masks of make-up.'

'Absolutely,' said Carter. 'He's saying – do you still find her pretty? Folded the skin from her breasts like a bra top, exposed the flesh beneath to say: look at the woman beneath. We can rule out this being Danielle Foster,' said Carter. 'This woman's skeletal, she must have been kept somewhere a long time to get like this.' There was silence except for the slip and splash of snow from the branches. 'How did she die, Doctor?'

Harding moved the woman's head to one side as she examined her neck.

'There are signs of damage here. I can't rule out strangulation or asphyxiation. But with her being in such a poor state, any massive trauma could have been her last. I think she would have died quite fast after he began skinning her.'

'She was alive when he did that?'

Harding nodded. 'She wouldn't have bled like that otherwise ... she must have been.' The remnants of trails of blackened blood were streaked down the woman's body.

Carter looked around him, fighting back the nausea. He needed to breathe in the scent of the pines, the cold from the damp air.

'Did she die here?'

'No,' said Harding. 'She was definitely moved and placed here. Suspended from the wrists while he mutilated her. The blood has flowed in even paths down over her torso.'

'Where's the nearest car park?' Carter asked, swallowing the taste of bile that filled his mouth.

'About five hundred metres away,' answered Sandford. 'Down by the Lido.'

'I suppose someone could carry her this far but would have to be fairly fit to get her up this hill.' Carter looked at Sandford. 'How else would you get her up here – by car?'

'You can't drive a vehicle up here unless you are one of the maintenance gardeners,' replied Sandford.

'I'll see if there's anyone on their staff list who has history, any padlocks broken or interfered with,' said Ebony, taking out her radio. 'And I'll ask if there's any CCTV footage we can find in any of the car parks around this side of the park.'

Carter looked around him.

'He must have gone to a lot of trouble to put her on the Heath. He chose to place her here. He didn't even try and cover her up.'

'The snow did it for him,' said Sandford.

'But she was always going to be found. It's too public. Just to stall us then maybe?'

They were interrupted by the approach of a familiar figure climbing the steep bank up towards the copse. Robbo was sweating despite the cold.

'Any idea who she is?' asked Carter.

Robbo was taking his time to study the victim. He needed time to see beyond the horror.

'I have several people on my list I think it could be,' answered Robbo. 'I need some DNA confirmation first. Any operation scars?'

Harding ran her gloved hands down the woman's limbs. 'I'd say she'd had a few broken bones in her time.'

'He's left us a lot more clues this time,' said Carter.

'Is there evidence of sexual assault?' asked Robbo.

'Yes,' answered Harding.

'We might have a chance of getting a specimen of DNA from her then. When can you start the post mortem, Doctor?'

'We need to wait till she thaws.'

'How long will that be?' asked Robbo. He had a million things now that were zapping across his database of a brain. All the photos of all the names on his list.

'Twenty-four hours at room temperature.'

Sandford unpacked a new body bag and helped Harding wrap the body in its plastic sheet. As they lifted up her left arm a silver charm bracelet slipped to the ground, a silver heart uppermost.

Chapter 25

Tracy looked at her watch; Steve would be heading to work soon from the hotel. She ought to phone him. She prepared herself; a deep breath, a smile on her face.

He answered; she could hear the breakfast news on in the background.

'Steve? Are you okay?'

He sighed irritably. 'Is she back yet?' His tone was sarcastic.

Tracy snapped. 'It's serious.'

'Serious in what way?' He still didn't sound convinced.

'The young woman found in Regent's Canal was a friend of Danielle's. The police think that the same man has Danielle. He's keeping her hostage. It was terrible, Steve. He's been phoning me.'

'It's probably some prank – the whole thing,' he countered, not taking in what Tracy had said about the phone call. 'I knew it would end like this. I told you she'd be nothing but trouble. So let me guess. We're stuck with the kid? I'll tell you where she is. She's done a runner and left us with her disabled son to look after.' His voice rose, almost hysterical. 'Tell me he's not staying with us permanently?'

'I can't, Steve. I can't just abandon him. He's not disabled – he has learning difficulties – special needs that's all. He's a lovely little boy and quite bright.' Tracy found herself screeching back at him. As hard as she'd tried to stay calm, it hadn't worked and she was tired of staying calm. 'For God's sake, he's got no one else, Steve. It's not his fault.'

'She must have got friends, relatives of her own? She must have someone who can look after him?'

'No she hasn't. She's got me and I feel like I have to. He's my grandson – our grandson.'

'He's nothing to do with me.'

Tracy closed her eyes. Suddenly she felt exhausted by it all. She wanted to cry. Instead she put a smile back on her face.

'I know it's hard, love. I need your support right now. I'm not going to pretend it's going to be easy but it just has to be done.' Tracy reached down and began smoothing Jackson's hair whilst she talked. He had just come into the kitchen.

'Who else is there?' asked Steve irritably.

'Just Jackson right at this minute. A policewoman will be arriving any time now; she's called a Family Liaison Officer. She's here to help us in any way we need. You know, even with the cost of everything.'

'Cost?'

'Well, it will cost money to have Jackson here. Not much. But I'm not working. We will have to depend on your money and I'm not sure where it's all going to at the moment. I haven't seen much of it lately.'

'Typical – all you really care about: money ...'

'Steve ... please ... that's not fair.'

'What is fair?' Steve hit back. 'I haven't worked hard for years to end up using my cash up on a kid you had when you were fifteen – and her "special" son.' Tracy heard the phone go dead. She wanted to cry. She bit her lip instead. She ran her fingers through Jackson's baby hair. She knew Steve would be sorry by now. She was sure he'd want to call her back and apologize. She had no support from the one person she should have been able to rely on. She took a deep breath and tutted to herself. She needed to get a grip. She needed to be the strong one.

Tracy put the phone down and looked down at Jackson. He was staring up at her. She reached for a tissue to wipe his nose, which seemed to be always running. He stood still for three seconds and then he squirmed away from her.

'Okay. Okay. That will have to do. Let me look at your new clothes.' She knelt on the floor beside him. He stood back and pointed to the front of his jumper with its blue train.

'Thomas,' he said proudly.

'Yes. Thomas the Tank Engine. Shall we see if we can find anything on the telly for you to watch?' Jackson looked deep into Tracy's eyes, his expression worried. He put his arms around her neck and she had such a job to stop from crying. Scruffy came running into the kitchen at that moment and began furiously licking Tracy's face as she cuddled Jackson. Then Scruffy switched his attention to Jackson and started licking his ears. Jackson hid his head in

Tracy's neck as he giggled. Scruffy went around the other side and began licking any patch of skin he could see.

'Scruffy, for God's sake.' Tracy pushed him away but he came around the back and put his paws on her shoulders and began licking Jackson's other ear. Jackson squirmed and laughed and Tracy fell backwards onto the kitchen floor with Jackson on top of her and Scruffy on top of them both. She laughed. She held on to Jackson who was shrieking with laughter and pulled Scruffy to sit with them as she hugged them both.

'Group hug.'

Tracy couldn't remember the last time she'd laughed like that. She felt guilty that it was in such awful circumstances.

'Right!' She picked herself up from the floor and went to get Jackson's coat and Scruffy's lead.

'We're sick of staying in. We can't be prisoners, can we, Jackson, and this mad dog needs a walk, don't you, Scruffy?'

Tracy took Jackson to the park at the other end of the nearby shops and they tied Scruffy outside the children's play area whilst Jackson played. At the end of an hour she sat on the swing with Jackson on her lap. She had almost forgotten what it was like to sit on a swing. The last time she'd sat on one had been when a child was growing inside her. It had been the first time she'd felt the flutter of feet kicking inside her and she didn't know what it was. After that her life had catapulted forward and there were no more swings for her. Jackson had gone quiet, the way he always did on the swings. They soothed him. He sat heavily on Tracy's lap and she held onto him with one arm. She was thinking how lovely it was when their peace was disturbed by the sound of Scruffy barking; 'What's Scruffy barking at?' she said aloud. She looked up to see him straining on his lead and snapping at a man who was standing close to him. Jackson heard it too and went to jump down off Tracy's lap.

'Wait, Jackson, wait.' But Jackson didn't listen and he slipped from Tracy's grasp and landed face down on the concrete. He waited four seconds to gather the scream in his lungs before it erupted and Tracy had to struggle to pull him up from the ground and stand him upright. She looked at the bump above his eyebrow.

'It's okay, Jackson. Please ... please stay still so Nanny can have a look.' He squirmed from her touch, trying to get away. She couldn't make him stay still. The whole park seemed to be screaming. From the corner of her eye she saw the bright flames at the side of the park, just outside the children's play area, and she realized she actually could hear people screaming And there was a terrible sound of an animal in agony.

Tracy's legs started running before she had even made sense of what she was seeing. She shouted towards the nearest mum, ordering her to look after Jackson, and then she ran faster than she'd run since she was a girl. As she ran she unbuttoned her coat and then she leapt over the gate. Scruffy was a ball of fire; the smell of burning hair and petrol fumes rose

around him in acrid smoke. He was rearing and twisting against the leash to try and get away. Tracy tugged
at her coat as it got stuck in the sleeve. She threw it
over Scruffy as she pinned him down and smothered
the flames. The flames caught hold of her dress and
she felt the heat as she choked in the smoke. She heard
a woman shouting at her:

'You're on fire!'

Tracy patted at the flames on her dress and she felt
a blast of cold water as someone emptied a bottle of
water over her. She lay with her arm across Scruffy as
the flames disappeared and turned her face to cough
and clear her lungs.

'Nanny?' She looked up to see Jackson standing the
other side of the fence, the young mum holding him
back. His terrified eyes filled with tears.

'It's all right, Jackson' Scruffy had gone quiet and
Tracy feared that he was dead beneath her coat. Then
she heard him whimper and she had a sudden urge to
cry with relief, but she dreaded lifting her coat to see
what he looked like. Tracy made a call to Jeanie and
told her what had happened.

'What about you? Are you okay?'

'I don't know what to do about Scruffy. He's really
badly burned.'

'There's a police vet service. I'll call them for you.
I'll see you back at your house. You sure you're all
right, Tracy?'

'I don't know.'

'On second thoughts – stay there. I'll come and get
you.'

The pet ambulance came to pick up Scruffy, who had

been whimpering non-stop. He was still wrapped in Tracy's coat. She was shivering in the cold. Her hand ached. It was only when she looked at it that she realized it was burnt. Blisters had formed and burst and the peeled skin was weeping.

Tracy looked up to see Jeanie walking across to them. There was still a handful of women but most had left and taken their kids away. The smell and sight of Scruffy on fire was not easily dealt with.

'What happened – do you know?'

Tracy shook her head. 'Jackson and I were on the swing, he fell off my lap and bumped his head and then the next thing everyone was screaming and Scruffy was on fire. Who could have done a thing like that?' Jeanie shook her head.

Jeanie shook her head. 'Kids' idea of a sick joke. Or someone off their head on something.' She looked at Tracy's hand. 'We need to get that dressed.'

For once, Tracy didn't object.

Jeanie took Tracy and Jackson up to A&E and they waited for an hour in Casualty for Tracy to be seen. Jeanie went to get something for Jackson to eat whilst they hung about. She bought him a drawing book. He sat down on the floor of the waiting room and drew a picture. Jeanie could see the yellows and reds and she didn't need to ask whether that was Scruffy in the middle. Poor Jackson was going to have to get past another trauma. Jeanie wondered if it would set them back. They would have to pray Scruffy survived.

Tracy came back with her hand bandaged and instructions to come back in two days for her dressing to be changed. Jeanie drove them both home. The atmosphere in the car was pensive. Tracy had a million things on her mind – none of them nice.

'Is Jackson okay – he's very quiet?' Jeanie asked. Tracy looked behind her at Jackson on his booster seat.

'He's fast asleep.'

'I have to talk to you about something, Tracy. There's been another woman's body found.'

'Oh God.' Tracy looked across at Jeanie.

'It's not Danielle but there is something I need to show you.' Jeanie reached inside the glove compartment and pulled out a small brown crime scene bag. 'Have a look at what's inside. Do you recognize it?'

Tracy anchored the bag using her bandaged left hand and opened it with her right. Jeanie heard her gasp.

'It's my bracelet.'

'Are you sure?'

'Of course. Without a doubt. All of these charms mean something to me. I gave this bracelet to Danielle. Where did you get it?'

'We found it on the woman's body this morning.'

'Then it must be Danielle.' Tracy couldn't keep the anguish from her voice.

Jeanie replied calmly. 'No. It isn't.'

'Then why? How?'

Jeanie shook her head. 'We don't know but it's a message from Hawk. That's what we call him.'

In the gloom of the car Tracy was wide-eyed and whispering so as not to wake Jackson. 'What kind of a message? What's he saying?'

'We think you should do a television appeal. Would you be up for it, Tracy? You don't have to.'

'What would it achieve?'

'I think you're caught in this triangle that the killer has created. He's calling all the shots at the moment. If we put you on television and present him with a scenario, that's out of his control.'

'What would I say?'

'Leave that to us. Analysts are studying the phone calls and then we will decide.'

Tracy was thinking it over but she knew she had to do it. 'Okay.'

'Thanks, Tracy. I'll let you know when it will be; probably in a couple of days – it takes time to organize. You should ask Steve to come home, Tracy, give you moral support.'

She nodded. 'First I want to see how Scruffy is doing. She took out her phone and dialled the number on a card. After a brief conversation she came off the phone. 'He's going to be okay.'

Jeanie was relieved.

'He wouldn't have survived if it wasn't for you and the sacrifice of your coat,' she said.

'Oh well, I can always get another coat. I'm just worried who's going to pay the vet bills for Scruffy. I don't have any money to do it.'

'Don't worry. He'll be looked after by the police vet.'

'Thank you. They said he should be able to come home in a week or two.'

'As long as he's going to be all right in the end, that's the main thing. Jackson will be happy to have him back.'

Once they'd arrived at the house, Jeanie made tea for Jackson. Tracy was restless.

'I want to go and see Steve now and tell him that I need him to come home. Is that okay?'

'Can you drive like that?'

Tracy pulled a big mitten glove over her injured hand. 'Should be fine. It's an automatic.' She hesitated. 'But – I don't have to go if you think I should stay here, if it would be better for Jackson.'

'No – you go.'

After Tracy had left, Jeanie gave a now wide-awake Jackson a snack and decided to have another session with him. She was aware of the ticking clock for memory recall with a child his age. She also needed to ease his mind about what had happened with Scruffy. She cleared Jackson's plate and moved him in to sit at the lounge table. She took the puppet of Scruffy out of the bag.

'Who's this, Jackson?'

Jackson looked at it – his mouth turned down and quivered: 'Poor Scruffy.'

'Yes – this is Scruffy and Scruffy had an accident today, didn't he?' Jackson nodded. 'But do you know what, Jackson? He is such a strong little dog that Scruffy is doing very well and should be back here very soon.' She counted seven with him on his fingers. 'Then we'll have to look after him, won't we?'

Jackson nodded. Jeanie wiped his eyes and nose.

'Okay, Jackson you don't need to worry now. And who's this?' She pulled out the next puppet, the small blond boy.

'Jackson.'

'Good boy. Yes, it's Jackson and Scruffy. Here . . .' She put the two together on the table and put her hand back into the bag. 'See Jackson and Scruffy are playing together?' He wasn't listening. 'Jackson . . . listen to me a minute . . .' He was distracted. His face had crumpled and big tears welled up in his eyes. He tried to get down from the chair and accidentally knocked the bag of puppets out of Jeanie's hand and onto the floor. The puppet with the Daddy Pig face fell out.

'Listen, Jackson. Who's this?' She picked up the Daddy Pig puppet.

Jackson immediately screwed up his face in anger and shouted at the Daddy Pig puppet: 'NO!'

'What is it, Jackson?'

'Poor Scruffy. What's Scruffy barking at?'

'Is that what Nanny said?'

He nodded, big moves of his head. 'Scruffy doesn't like that man.'

'Which man is that?'

'The man next to Scruffy in the park. Scruffy barking.'

'Who was that man?'

'Mummy said, "Get out. Get out." Nanny said, "What's Scruffy barking at?" Leave Scruffy alone. I banged my head.' Jackson touched the bump on his forehead.

'Is that why you tried to get off Nanny's lap? Because you saw the man hurting Scruffy?' Jackson nodded. He was becoming upset.

'Do you know the man who hurt Scruffy, Jackson?'

Jackson nodded. 'Daddy Pig. No, no, NO!'

'Was it the same man who hurt Mummy?'

He nodded, kept nodding; his eyes looking far away as they filled with tears.

Chapter 26

Robbo stood next to Carter, ready to speak at the meeting in the Enquiry Team Office. The place was packed. It was the largest of the offices and always used when a meeting of the entire team was necessary. With the discovery of a new victim even Chief Inspector Bowie was present. Behind Robbo the photos of Emily Styles and Danielle Foster were pinned to one of the many boards around the walls. He pinned a new photo next to them.

'I've just got the results of the X-rays from Doctor Harding – taken while she's waiting for the body to thaw. The victim had a history of traceable injuries from when she was hit by a car as a child and we have a match with dental records. It's definitely this woman. Pauline Murphy.' It was a photo of a dark-haired woman in her twenties taken at a winter wedding. 'She went missing a year ago in December 2012.'

A murmur went around the office as the team took in the timescale being talked about. Ebony was sitting at her desk opposite Jeanie. Everyone had been called in to the meeting. Jeanie had a lot she wanted to say.

'Pauline disappeared without trace after a night out with friends. It was believed that she had started to make her way home alone when she was abducted. She was last seen leaving a bar on Upper Street at one in the morning. Like the others, Pauline was a single parent. She had a child of three who has since moved to France with the father.

'Pauline was described by those who knew her as a loyal friend; she was a sweet-natured woman who had struggled academically because she was dyslexic. She was attending an evening class once a week studying IT.'

Carter turned and looked at the map on the board behind him. 'He dumps a body in the middle of one of London's best-known open spaces. The Heath covers over seven hundred acres.' It was colour-coded for the areas. 'She was found here.' There was a red sticker placed over where they found her body.

'Who patrols the Heath? Who's responsible for it?' asked Bowie. Bowie was handed a mug of coffee. He looked like he needed it. He had large bags beneath his eyes.

'There is the twelve-man constabulary with dogs that patrol it,' answered Robbo. 'They hadn't been out in this particular section for forty-eight hours.'

Carter spoke: 'We are still working our way through the list of groundsmen who might have had access to the Heath on that day.' He shook his head. 'I don't think we'll find him that way. He could have easily impersonated a groundsman. I think if the Heath is familiar to him then he's likely to be, or have been at some time in his life: a dog walker, a jogger, or maintenance personnel. I would say most people who use the Heath live within a two-mile radius of it; it takes too long to get through the traffic to it otherwise.' Bowie was nodding.

Robbo took up where Carter left off. 'He stays within his triangle of offences in North London. His territory may be small but it's densely populated. The trouble is, I don't think we're going to get that lucky with him. He might make a small mistake. He's never going to make a big one.'

'What was the condition of the body?' asked Bowie.

Carter answered: 'We have to wait for the post mortem, but her injuries and the skeletal look of her body are the same as Emily Styles.' Carter nodded to Robbo and waited to continue while he managed to load the images on his laptop and connect with the PCs on desks around the room. The officers crowded around the shared PC screens to view the images. 'If you scroll the images that Robbo has just sent you, you will see. There are too many similarities for this not to be Hawk. A bag had been placed over her head. She has large open wounds, ulcerated, that expose the bone in some places. She has thick make-up on her face too – we believe that this is important to him.'

There was a silence in the room apart from the clicking of mice and the tapping on keyboards. A photo of the charm bracelet came up.

'What about the jewellery? Is it significant?' asked Bowie.

Carter answered: 'We know it belongs to Danielle. So it confirms that he has her. Why he's given Pauline

Murphy the bracelet we don't know but we presume it's to show how clever he thinks he is. In this case he's telling us that Danielle is still alive. We don't know whether the rings found on Emily Styles signified the same thing. We know they probably belonged to women he had killed or was about to kill. Hopefully we are going to learn a lot more about Hawk from Pauline Murphy's body.' Carter looked at Robbo's laptop and the images taken at the crime scene on Hampstead Heath. 'I am hoping that the post mortem will reveal where she's been, maybe through soil traces, particular fibres on her body, anything that can help us locate where he's been keeping her.'

'Does Pauline Murphy's body tell us anything new about him as a person, Robbo?' asked Bowie.

Robbo was resting his back on the wall beside the boards; he had wrapped his arms around himself.

'It tells us something very worrying – that not only is he capable of extreme torture and cruelty, barbaric as it all seems, but his calculated cruelty is something that requires intelligence. He has a type – a social type but not a physical type. I don't think it matters to him how tall they are, dark or fair, fat or thin. It matters to him what they are going through in their lives. They have to be single parents who are trying hard to make it on their own. None of these women were stupid. They all had a lot to lose and had a kid to stay alive for. It would take someone very special to lure them into this kind of trap.'

Bowie's face was flushed and rubbery. He took another swig of coffee and wiped the sweat from his forehead with the palm of his hand. 'So he's slick enough to fool them all. That can't have been easy. He must have some charm that they fell for. We need as complete a profile as possible of Hawk, Robbo.'

'I'm working on it, Sir.' Robbo read from his notes: 'We think he's going to seem like an honest member of society because he's likely to have gained their trust. Lives alone because he's been able to keep them for months undetected. So he's really clever, our guy, socially adept, a smooth operator but with a dark side that might have started on the internet. It has echoes of fantasy figures with the way they are made up. I wouldn't be surprised if there is an image somewhere that he has copied this look from, a film maybe. We know he engages in violent sex. The post mortem will tell us more but he's very likely to have a stash of violent pornography in his house and on his computer.'

'I think he takes particular pleasure in parting the mother and child. 'He tortures them mentally and physically by keeping them alive for such a long period of time and them knowing that they have abandoned their child. That's what's so frightening about him,' he added. 'I think he's evolving, getting cocky.'

'You say it's all about him – his ego,' said Bowie.

'Yes. Timing is important to him,' answered Robbo. 'He has to be the one to decide when someone dies. He has to play God.'

'Two bodies found in less than two weeks and another woman kidnapped.' Bowie was becoming agitated. 'He's sticking two fingers up at us. He can't have slipped through the years unnoticed. He must have practised before: rape, assault, attempted kidnap. We should be looking for a rapist that has got away in the last few years. He may have been through some psychiatric home somewhere.'

'We could be looking at several other victims here,' said Carter.

'If he's been holding Pauline Murphy all this time it must have crossed over with Emily Styles. He must be able to hold more than one woman at once.'

'Where's he been, Robbo?' said Bowie. 'Find out. Trace similar crimes and let's get a lead on him.'

'I'm pretty sure he's not in our system,' answered Robbo. 'Because he has definitely left forensic evidence on Pauline Murphy and he doesn't care; he didn't try to dispose of the body in such a way that it wouldn't surface – the opposite. Plus, this time we have a witness and he's calling the victim's family to add to his game.'

'Have we had any luck in tracing the calls?' asked Bowie.

Carter answered: 'No, Sir. I don't think we will either, not unless he calls from a different phone. It's not a contract phone. He never stays on the phone long enough.'

'Well, then at least the phone calls give us an insight into him.'

'Yes, Sir, if we listen to this . . .'

Carter pressed a button on Robbo's laptop and the deep distorted voice of Hawk filled the breathless office. 'Tracy? Are you listening to me?' Carter paused it as Hawk began reciting the nursery rhyme about Baby Bunting.

'Skin a rabbit. Hawk mentions skinning and that's what he did to Pauline Murphy.'

Carter resumed play and screams from somewhere primeval filled the office. Jeanie flinched. She wished she hadn't heard it. The sound of the woman screaming would stay in her memory banks, to be brought back on dark nights when she couldn't sleep, or even worse when she was asleep and she couldn't stop it coming. Jeanie seemed to be collecting bad memories in a nightmare scrapbook. But this would be nothing to what poor Tracy was having to deal with. It took someone with enormous strength to handle that.

'He didn't ring Emily Styles' parents,' said Carter. 'He didn't ring Pauline Murphy's. He's getting brazen, bold, reckless. He feels a connection to Tracy – I think we should use it. We have nothing to lose. I know Tracy has agreed to go on television and appeal directly to him. I think if he puts a face to Tracy, stripped bare, he might relent. He wants to play God, so we can appeal to that side of him – it's all within his control. Let her go.'

Bowie was thinking it through: 'We need to word it just right. Robbo?' He looked across at Robbo who nodded.

'I agree. It can't make it worse. It might work for us. Things are different this time. Tracy seems to be significant. This time Hawk felt secure enough to take his victim from her home, in full view of Danielle's son Jackson. Why? Maybe because Jackson has Down's syndrome and our killer doesn't think he'll be able to remember things accurately enough to help. Maybe because he's grown over-confident.'

Bowie shifted his perch on the desk, threw his coffee cup away and turned to Jeanie, who stood ready to speak.

'First of all I want to clarify the position on Jackson's abilities. He has learning difficulties but he's bright. He is on the higher ability scale. I've learnt that he can tell right from wrong. He can count. He can draw really well for his age. There is nothing stopping us getting just as much information about what happened to his mum from Jackson as from any other kid of his age. And that's the thing – he's only four.' Jeanie waited whilst Carter stepped outside to take a message from an officer from Archway police station. He apologized when he returned and said: 'Whoever else is in the frame to be Hawk, Danielle Foster's boyfriend Niall Manson is definitely out of it. He was killed yesterday afternoon. Someone dragged him down Balls Pond Road, left his head by the kebab shop and his body next to the Kenyos two-hour dry-cleaning shop. We've put up a roadblock to ask for help but I doubt his death has much to do with Danielle. He was a hit waiting to happen.'

He nodded to Jeanie to continue.

'I believe we are slowly unravelling a description of the man who took Jackson's mother and who he says his mother was shouting at and trying to get out of the house. As far as Jackson understands, the man is white, he has dark hair. But the most significant thing is that Jackson saw the same man when Scruffy the family pet was attacked. The way Jackson describes both the man who took his mummy away and the man who set the dog on fire is that he looks like the cartoon character "Daddy Pig". This is a well-known character in a cartoon called *Peppa Pig*. The thing to say about this character is that he has round, black-rimmed glasses, designer stubble. He wears a T-shirt type of thing – usually turquoise, sometimes purple. He has a small smile.'

'Do you have a picture?' asked Bowie.

'Yes.' Jeanie tapped on her keyboard and brought up an image of Daddy Pig, which was shared with the other PCs in the room.

'He has a sneaky-looking smile,' Ebony said. 'And the glasses are really fashionable now.

Jeanie looked across at Ebony and smiled gratefully. She'd worried unnecessarily about looking stupid.

Bowie stood up from his perch on the edge of the desk at the far side of the office across from Jeanie and Ebony.

'Let's presume Jackson is accurate and it is the same man. It's Hawk. What does that mean to our investigation?'

Ebony spoke up. 'If this proves to be a targeted attack on the dog then it means that Hawk has a lot more elements to his game. He might also be after Jackson or Tracy? He's getting physically close to them.'

Carter spoke: 'We'll give her twenty-four hour surveillance on the house.'

Bowie nodded. 'Why might Tracy interest him … Jeanie?'

Jeanie was reluctant to say that, ever since she'd seen the image of the make-up on Pauline Murphy's dead face, she'd been reminded of Tracy.

'Tracy's make-up was really thick when I first met

her,' she said hesitantly. 'It's getting less every day but, if Hawk was watching her when she worked in Simmons department store at the beauty counter, if he has a thing about make-up, good or bad, he would definitely have been drawn to Tracy.'

'So what we're saying is that something about Tracy has made him change his MO – or has brought out some other element in it,' said Bowie. 'Tell us more about her. What is she like?'

Jeanie thought for a few seconds before she answered: 'She is in a brittle marriage. I haven't even seen her husband; he chooses to stay away, I think. Or Tracy chooses not to have him there while this is going on. It's becoming obvious that things aren't great between them. Steve, the husband, was obviously not keen on Tracy's reunion with Danielle. She went to speak to him yesterday about coming home to support her but she returned saying he still wasn't coming back. It's a lot to cope with on her own. But ... having said all that, I'm amazed the way that she does seems to cope with whatever is thrown at her. She is in the middle of the crisis of her life but she copes with it the way she would cope with the busiest day ever on the beauty counter where she works. But then, I'm not sure Tracy realizes that this might have become personal to her. She asks if Jackson is safe. She has never asked me if *she* is safe. She has agreed to the TV appeal. I think the sooner we do it the better. We just have to hope it makes things better, not worse.'

'We'll look into every angle and have something ready for Tracy as soon as possible and for you, Sir.' Robbo addressed Bowie.

'I hope it's a good one, Robbo. The press will hound us. I don't want us to look incompetent. I want to find a definite connection between these women. How does Pauline Murphy match the lives of the other two women?' asked Bowie.

'The college, definitely,' answered Carter.

Robbo pinned up a diagram of three interlocking circles with the women's names in the centre.

'These women didn't all know one another but where the circles cross they have a possible two hundred and forty shared contacts from the college that we can identify by the social network sites.'

Bowie stood.

'We'll call a conference later today. Get it over with. One thing we know is that at this very minute Danielle Foster will be in a coffin and she will have already started dying.'

Chapter 27

'Do I look okay?' Tracy came out of the bathroom and stood in front of Jeanie.

Jeanie had asked Tracy to take off her false eyelashes, wear only a touch of mascara.

'A youthful look, you mean?' she'd asked.

'I mean a stripped-back, no-time-for-make-up, couldn't-care-less-about-make-up look.'

'I feel naked without my make-up. I feel vulnerable.'

'You don't need it and especially not today. You look really lovely, Tracy: natural, young, with shiny skin.'

'Shiny? Oh God!' Tracy turned back to look at herself again. 'The only time I get to go on television and the whole world sees me looking a fright.'

Jeanie smiled and shook her head.

'Couldn't be further from the truth. You ready?'

'I haven't learnt my lines yet.' Tracy looked panicky.

'We need to get Jackson settled before we go in. You can look at the statement then. It doesn't have to be too rehearsed, Tracy. Don't worry.'

They got Jackson into his car seat and Tracy sat in

the front with Jeanie. Jeanie could feel the tension coming from Tracy. She was nervous for her but she knew that the fresher Tracy appeared on television, the better. Sometimes it wasn't what people said, it was the way they looked when they said it.

Jeanie drew up outside the venue; Carter and Willis were waiting. Carter opened the door for Tracy whilst Ebony went around the other side and undid Jackson's seat belt.

Ebony took Jackson off to be looked after whilst Carter escorted Jeanie and Tracy down to a green room where they'd sit and wait and prepare for the conference.

Hawk switched on the television. The press conference was about to start. He was naked; the room was warm and dark. He didn't want to watch it alone. Beneath the decrepit chandelier he sat on a chair and got closer to the screen. He held his breath as he watched Tracy walk in flanked by a woman and a tall pale-eyed detective. Hawk watched them as they took their seats. He looked at the female officer's name badge pinned on her: *Jeanie Vincent*. He looked at the Chief Inspector's – *Simon Bowie* – and next to him was *Detective Inspector Dan Carter*.

His eyes focused back on Tracy.

'Ha ...' he said out loud and he laughed. 'Where's your make-up now?' His laughter petered out: inside he was angry.

Tracy began speaking. She glanced at the paper in her hand. It was shaking. Hawk squealed with delight. From the corner of the room a woman moved.

Hawk's eyes flicked her way but he didn't turn to look at her; he had no need – she wasn't going anywhere.

'I want to appeal to whoever is holding my daughter,' Tracy said, her voice quivering. 'I want to tell him he has the power to release her. He has the power to let my daughter come home now before any more harm is done. Please.' Tracy looked up into the camera. 'Please. Don't kill my daughter, she is a lovely mum – she cares deeply for her little boy Jackson who has special needs and he misses his mum terribly.' Tracy turned away as she was in danger of crumbling. The camera flashes popped all over the room as they looked for that one perfect shot.

Hawk stood and the chair fell backwards as he stamped his foot and raged at the screen.

'Where's your make-up? You're not playing fair. Why don't you show us who you really are? You've spoilt it now, Tracy. You've lied to me.' Hawk looked at Bowie and Carter and Vincent and he muttered: 'You think I'm stupid? You think I'm so arrogant as to be that easily manipulated? I know what's in your minds. You're trying to make me change my plan, to trip me up. I see through your schemes and I'll raise the stakes and I'll play a hand that you won't see coming. It's my game and my rules and I will prepare for the arrival of another player.'

Hawk switched off the TV and pressed the button on the music system. He closed his eyes as he swayed to the music. His heart lifted with the violins as they plucked at his emotions. His heart was full to bursting as his head moved, swam on a magic carpet of sensations – then stopped.

He slowly opened his eyes and turned to the sound that had disturbed him – 'Shut the fuck up.'

The woman was moaning in pain from the corner of the room.

He felt for the remote control in his pocket and switched up the volume until he could no longer hear her.

He waltzed around the room, his feet shushing on the bare floorboards. Then he moved towards her and picked her up and put her over his shoulder as his chest rose and fell. She moaned in pain as he carried her out of the room and down the corridor, down the stairs and into another room. He switched on the light and laid her on the floor as he moved like a ballet dancer, pointing his toes, flexing his feet he danced around her. He stood above her, his eyes gleaming, his breath quick. He tilted his head this way and that as he looked her over. Her body was peppered with maggot-infested holes.

'Ah, my sweet Jenny Smith . . . you and I have been on the longest journey. But now I feel your road is coming to an end. She did not answer; she stared back at him with the massive eyes of the emaciated. Her breathing was shallow, her bones so exposed that he could see every rib. She had on a red metallic bikini that was baggy and soiled. He took off his combat-style trousers and knelt beside her and undid the ties of the bikini from around her neck. He rolled her to her side to undo the string around her back. She groaned as he moved her.

'Be patient, Jenny. Be patient.' He slid the bikini bottoms down over her legs. 'You must hand this over to someone else now. We'll play our game one last time, Jenny, and I'll let you go.'

For a second her eyes filled with panic and then they filled with calm. She could no longer talk. She had not spoken for two years. Her eyes followed his movements as he pulled a long, silky woman's scarf from his trouser pocket.

'This was my mother's, as you know.'

He threaded it beneath her neck and her eyes stayed on his. He twisted the excess around his knuckles and twisted the scarf tighter. She struggled the way she always did as she fought to stay alive, but she didn't struggle for long and he kept the knot tight. This time he would take her to the end. When she was dead he hung her on a hook from the ceiling in the centre of the room.

After the conference Bowie went back to his office and called Carter and Willis in to see him.

'Please have a seat, both of you. If nothing happens from the press conference we have to be ready to try something new. We need someone to go undercover. We need to set someone up within the geographical triangle of the crimes and mirror the women's lives as closely as we can.' Carter was nodding his agreement. 'Detective Inspector Carter and I have discussed this in private, Detective Willis, and we both agree – we want it to be you.' Bowie looked at Ebony to gauge her reaction.

'How would you feel about it?'

Ebony stared back at Bowie whilst she took a minute. Her face betrayed nothing.

'You don't have to agree to it; it's only an idea, but we need someone quickly,' said Carter. 'I think you can do it Detective.' He smiled at her.

'You've done a test purchase before?' asked Bowie.

'Yes, Sir, I've done TP a few times, test purchasing stolen goods once from a shop in Fulham and I've done it twice buying drugs in Central London.'

'I've looked at the reports from those assignments. It says in them that you handled it very well.'

'Thank you, Sir. Do you think it should be someone from another force, Sir?'

'It should, in theory – if it was an organized crime syndicate we were watching I'd say definitely but this is one man and we need to catch him fast.'

'Yes, Sir.'

'Because of the need for setting up an accurate social media persona and creating it fast we need to bring Robbo and Jeanie on board. Normally I wouldn't risk any of the team knowing but Robbo is the only one able to do what we want and fast and Jeanie is close to both sets of victims' families and to you, Ebony, and this is going to involve a massive team performance.' He looked back at Ebony, who had remained impassive. 'Are you agreed with keeping them informed?'

She looked across at Carter. He nodded his agreement. 'Yes, Sir. I think it's the best option.'

'I will be Ebony's supervisor,' said Carter.

'Agreed.'

'You'll need to move into a housing association flat,' said Carter. 'We'll find you a flat in the same geographical area that Hawk is working in and register for some classes in the college. Get in quickly on the course that Danielle was doing if you can, meet her peers, get into their social networking groups.'

'What about the fact I don't have a kid?' Ebony looked at Bowie.

'Borrow mine,' said Carter.

Ebony looked at Carter as if he'd flipped. Bowie was a little more cautious.

'Why not?' Carter said. 'You'll only need him for a few hours. Take him when you go to the housing office and to college when you first go in to register, that's all. Let everyone see you with him once then make excuses why he's not there after that.' Ebony was still watching Carter's face, waiting for him to say that he would get Cabrina's permission before involving their son in a police operation. But he was not going to. 'It'll be fine, Ebb. He knows you. And you'll only be borrowing him for a few hours.' Bowie was listening. Ebony wondered if he was about to say 'absolutely not'. 'The rest of the time you can say that your aunt's looking after the baby, something like that,' continued Carter.

Bowie was weighing it up. He nodded thoughtfully. 'None of the children have been harmed so far, have they?'

Carter shook his head. 'Anyway it's not going to get that far, is it? Ebony borrows Archie just to make it look good, then we can switch to a doll. Job done.'

Bowie agreed. 'We have to put maximum effort into Ebony's cover otherwise it won't work. Stay here in the office from now on, Ebb. Get Robbo to concoct a plausible legend for you. We need this up and running ASAP.'

'Yes, Sir.'

Carter and Ebony left Bowie's office and headed towards the canteen to chat in private. Tina was clearing tables when they went to sit down with their coffees.

'Looking great, Tina. You lost weight?' Carter grinned her way. She giggled. Ebony rolled her eyes. Tina fell for it every time.

They sat down and Ebony emptied two packets of sugar into her milky coffee. Carter leaned across the table towards her and kept his voice low.

'You going to be all right with it, Ebb? Hopefully it'll be over by Christmas if we get it right.'

She nodded. 'What about Archie? You have to ask Cabrina if we can borrow him.'

'Yeah, I will ask, of course, but she's going to be okay with it.' He sipped his black coffee and screwed up his face in disgust. 'When are they ever going to get proper coffee in here?'

'You need to ask her.'

'Ebb . . . He's my son. I will take full responsibility.' She held up her hands in surrender mode. 'Now let's concentrate on the things we have to get right.'

'I need to look like the kind of person he'd be interested in,' said Ebony.

'Yes. Go around and look at Emily and Danielle's belongings – take in their lives. Take Jeanie with you. She's good at spotting things about people and she can tie up with anything Tracy might have said about Danielle's character. You will have to stay in contact me with me, Ebb. This feels like a risky situation to put you in. You're going to have to be on your own in there, exposed. You will have to be tested first. It's not a nice experience. I've known a lot of officers who just can't hack it.'

'I'll be okay, Guv.'

'I know you will. Robbo will help.'

Chapter 28

The next morning Pauline Murphy's body was waiting on a trolley in front of the steel fridge doors. She was thawed: her body had come to room temperature.

Harding watched Mark wheel the trolley next to the end dissecting table in the mortuary. He altered the height of the trolley and slid the body across and onto the table. 'We'll leave the sheet beneath her while we examine her.' Harding placed her papers on the table over the sink at the head of the dissection table. Mark nodded his understanding and then mirrored Harding's actions as he stood across from her and peeled back the sheeting section by section.

'Be careful to fold it in on itself and catch whatever debris she has around her body.' Mark didn't answer. He was looking at the body as it unfolded. Harding held her hand out to indicate where Mark's eyes *should* be looking. She wanted him to concentrate on her own hands. She wanted his whole attention. Mark obeyed for a few seconds but then his eyes slipped back to the body. Harding didn't bark, for once; she understood that he was sensitive. She knew he would be saddened, shocked by the sight of the female form so denigrated. Her eyes were a lot softer when they focused on him than her demeanour as she stood stick-straight, pencil-thin, all hard lines. For Harding this was her sweeter side.

'Mark?'

Mark looked up at her and nodded. His nod was a reminder to himself to stay focused. It was an acknowledgement to Harding that he knew what was expected of him and he could fulfil it at least over the mortuary slab if not in private. Mark was beginning to understand why this placement with one of the best pathologists in the UK was not an easy one. It might have helped if he had fancied her a bit but he didn't think so. She was a female predator. She offered herself for intimacy, fornicated, then she crunched loudly on men's bones. Mark loved to paint, figure painting – he sketched the women's bodies in the morgue sometimes, although usually just sections of them, the curve of a breast, the soft round of a stomach. The make-up, dressing side of his job was a pleasure to him. There wasn't much about his job he didn't like. It meant he earned enough to buy the materials to keep his painting going and he was a better anatomist for it. He was a make-up artist with a flare for making women look beautiful even in death. He had never seen a woman so unkindly brutalized and parodied as Pauline Murphy was. But he was a professional and he was already thinking of how he could undo some of the damage done to her. Mark had got the job, started training in it because he was good friends with Harding's last diener, Mathew. But Mathew had warned him.

'She's going to want to screw you – in every sense. Don't let her know you're gay if you can help it.'

'Bi,' Mark contradicted. 'Options are still open.'

Mathew rolled his eyes.

'Just because you were engaged once, to a woman, doesn't mean you're bi. It means you were confused. And that's what you need to leave her thinking until you're three months into your contract. That way she can't dismiss you. Keep her thinking you're playing hard to get. Keep camp down to a minimum and you might survive better than I did.'

'I'm not camp.'

'Yes you are – as Christmas, after a few drinks, and that's what she'll be buying you. She'll engineer it so you have to work late, so it's better you go to hers. She'll turn on a charm that's pretty irresistible in the bedroom. She'll have you trussed up like a turkey in no time.'

'Really? You've made it sound a lot more exciting than I could have dreamed of.'

'Believe me, been there, done that and got the T-shirt plus the bruises to show for it. She invented the term rough sex, but it's all one-way. Invent a girlfriend but not a serious one. Then she'll think she just has to wait. The main thing in all this is not whether you feel like seeing if you're really bi; it's that she gets bored very quickly and then one day you find your job's been given to another. Remember – treat 'em mean – keep 'em keen.'

'You still seeing her then? Thought it was over when it lost you your job?' Mark asked, a smile creeping across his face.

'Of course.' Mathew grinned sheepishly.

Harding almost stamped her foot as she waited irritably for Mark to finish observing and start laying out the tools of dissection on a tray. The stamp was transmuted to a series of toe taps. She had a nervous, irritable constant twitch in her demeanour – a coiled spring. She lived on her nerves. But Mathew had been right. She hadn't given up hope of bedding Mark so she kept her eyes soft as she watched him prepare for the autopsy. *Patience.*

'Ready?' He nodded. 'Ah, just in time,' she said as she saw Willis and Carter walked in, suited up in protective gear. 'Take hold of the camera please, DC Willis. I am about to start the autopsy examination of the female body found on Hampstead Heath yesterday morning. Height: five foot eight inches. Weight: five stone one pound. Colour of hair: dyed black, originally mid brown. Ethnicity: Caucasian. She was wearing a charm bracelet around her right wrist which has been removed.'

She stood back to record the general condition of the body: 'Severely malnourished. Yellowing of the skin possibly due to hepatitis B infection or liver failure. She has several gangrenous wounds on her that have maggot infestation.'

Mark went to switch on the extractor beneath the table. She held up her hand to stop him. She leaned over the body and breathed in the smell.

'Rat's urine,' she said. 'Mixed with the smell of gangrene from her infected wounds.' She nodded to Mark that he could turn it on now. Carter breathed out again as the smell was carried from below the body.

'Injuries: skin peeled up from over both breasts, done by using a scalpel or razor blade to cut the skin on the underside of the breast. It has then been pulled by hand, cut again around the nipples. The stripping of the skin has led to a feathered tearing around the edges of the flesh.'

Harding ran her gloved hand down the arm; she turned the hand over to expose the inside of the forearm and the irregular sections of missing flesh. She shone a light down and examined the injury.

'These are bite marks here from rodents; the action is one of gnawing as opposed to tearing. The scars are at many different stages of healing – these bites were inflicted on living flesh. There are other puncture wounds, pairs of fine needle punctures. The chafing in the skin around the ankle is uniform. Wounds are not deep.' She carried on as she moved up to the wrists. 'Soft tissue damage here at the wrists too, same type of wound, same width, deeper though. The damage to the flesh is angled as such: it cuts in where there was weight pulling against it.'

'So she was suspended again – same scenario as with Emily Styles, held with her arms above her head, you mean?' asked Carter.

'Yes.'

Harding moved up to Pauline Murphy's head and examined her neck. 'There are scars here, tissue still repairing. Not made with the same force as with Emily Styles. They concentrate more on the sides of the neck, over the carotid artery.' Harding looked up from her examination. Ebony held her gaze. 'Looks possible that there were previous attempts at killing her or that it wasn't the first time she'd been strangled in the weeks before she died. Maybe not with the intention of causing death.'

'Asphyxiophilia,' said Ebony.

Harding nodded. 'I agree. 'An intentional cessation of oxygen to the brain for sexual arousal.'

'And exact cause of death, Doctor, please?' asked Carter.

'The flaying of the skin on her breasts was the last injury inflicted on her. We need to examine her heart to tell whether it gave out but I think the shock, the pain killed her.'

'One of the oldest forms of torture,' said Ebony. 'In Medieval times they used to try and get the skin off in one piece.'

'He looks like he tried to make an item of clothing out of it,' Mark said.

'Yes,' agreed Carter. 'He masks and he reveals. He covers the skin in make-up as thick as a mask or he peels back the bare skin to show the raw flesh beneath.'

'The female form defaced, reviled,' said Mark.

'It seems like the actions of someone young to me. Someone finding their way through a minefield of emotions,' Harding added.

'Someone seriously mad,' Carter said. 'And getting progressively worse. He takes a step further with each woman. He's a work in progress. He wants us to see that.'

On the way back to Fletcher House Carter looked across at Willis.

'I've been thinking about it, watching that post mortem. I'm not sure I'm happy for you to go into this without knowing more about the man we're up against.' Ebony didn't answer. 'We could wait till we are further into the investigation to send you into it.' Ebony still didn't answer. 'You know, Ebb, you might understand what it's like to have a difficult childhood but it doesn't make you the best at coping with the man when you find him. You're going to have to act like these women, be sociable, flirt even – that's a first.' He joked but his eyes stayed on hers; they were full of concern.

'I understand, Guv.'

'Really ... you are going to have to lay yourself bare for this one. If you don't he'll spot you a mile off. Ebb – you've just seen what he's capable of. He shows no mercy and he eeks out every drop of pain from his victims, but something ... *something* made them trust him. He's clever, manipulative, like I've never seen before. My head and my heart says I don't want you anywhere near him.'

She looked across at Carter. 'I would agree – but I believe that Danielle is still alive and I think that from inside that coffin, she's praying we're going to find her.'

Carter shook his head and looked at her incredulously.

'Christ! I don't think I've ever heard you so emotional. You must want to do it.'

'I do and I think it's worth me trying. We know that something about his choice of victim says that he grew up either without a mother or with a mother who was a destructive influence rather than a nurturing one. I understand what that's like. Makes me a good target, Guv.'

Carter turned away for a few seconds to gather his thoughts. He looked back at her. He could see her eyes were hungry for it.

'Yes.' He turned back. 'It does.'

Chapter 29

'Her legend is going to have to be watertight,' Bowie said to Robbo, who had joined Carter in Chief Inspector Bowie's office. 'Can you do it this fast? The training alone for a UC would be two weeks normally.'

'We don't have two weeks.'

'Ebony has a ready-made legend,' Robbo said. 'She would be difficult to trace even if she used her own name.'

'Whose name will you give her? We can no longer use the names of dead infants.'

'Ebony's legend will closely follow her own life. We keep her Christian name so that anyone who might know her and see her in the street won't blow her cover.'

Carter shook his head. 'To be honest you don't have to worry about that; Ebony lives a very sheltered life: she works and then she goes home. She doesn't have any social media accounts, she doesn't even have a credit card.'

'We'll change her surname to Wilson,' continued Robbo. 'Doctor her birth records, issue a new

passport and driver's licence. We'll keep her childhood in children's homes – it suits our purposes very
well – but we have her come out of them at the age
of twelve and move to Jamaica to live with her
grandparents, returning six months ago. She
returned to get Archie into school here and because
this is her home. She's been on benefits. She's obviously bright but a bit unsettled in her life – big
potential but finds herself a bit out of her depth at
the moment. Life's changing, new prospects, going
solo.'

'When will you have everything ready?' asked
Bowie.

'Pretty much ready to go, Sir. I asked the guys in the
technical unit to design some special equipment for
her and I've been told it's ready so I'll collect that now
and we'll put the package together and get her familiar with it.'

'Okay. Carter, you'll have to keep the appearance of still being the SIO on this case, but I want
you to hand it over to me and you concentrate on
Ebony.'

'I think I can manage the two roles, Sir. It will look
less suspicious to the rest of the team.'

Bowie shook his head, his face strained. 'We'll share
the role. I want nothing to stand in our way. Make
sure you put her to the test before you send her out.
I want her fluent in her legend.'

'Yeah, I've contacted the UC course instructors and
they'll pick her up when she's least expecting it, make
sure she's a hundred per cent ready.'

*

'Can we talk in private?' Jeanie came to find Carter. They went to the canteen to get a coffee and sat well away from listening ears.

'I want to talk about Ebony. To start with – the UC work?' Jeanie said.

'Robbo's creating a profile for her at the moment. Can you fix her up with an image?'

Jeanie nodded. 'Yeah, but I'm not sure she's the right choice. Not Ebony. She's too vulnerable. She is only tough out of necessity. She has a lot to learn in life. She has the nice things to learn – she knows all about the horrible things.'

'She's had it tough; just like our victims. It makes sense.'

'Yes, but they had the love of their child, of their families, someone else on this earth to care about them when they were tricked into trusting this man. Ebony is yet to find that kind of trust and affection. She's never been loved like that.'

Carter looked across at Jeanie and shook his head. 'You're wrong. Lots of people care deeply for Ebony.'

'We all *care* deeply for her but love? Real love? Ebony has never known it. That's her Achilles' heel. She could make a mistake one day. The one thing Ebony has never had is affection. Every boyfriend she's ever had has only lasted a few months. It seems they reach a point when they're just not getting what they want from her. And I think that's because she doesn't know how to trust and give affection. She has massive abandonment issues. She's not a whole person – not yet. She has a long way to go. She doesn't know the game or how to play it.'

'I gave her the option of backing out. I even pushed her to do it, but she's determined to carry this through. We need to support her in her choice.' Carter wanted to reach out and fleetingly touch Jeanie's hand as it rested on the tabletop but he didn't, partly because it had a wedding ring on it.

Jeanie nodded.

'Okay. I'm not happy but I'm part of a team and I'll stand by Ebony every step of the way. She saved my life once and if I can, I'll do anything to save hers.'

'Thank you. I mean it. I can see how much you care and I can tell you I feel the same.'

'Okay, well to business then,' said Jeanie. 'We are a team after all. I'll take Ebony off to the shops to get a new image as soon as we've finished here.'

Jeanie left Carter and went to find Ebony at her desk. They drove to Emily Styles' house to pick up some things of Emily's that would give them a better idea of what she was like. The Styles had been warned and had a box waiting for them. Then they drove towards Brent Cross Shopping Centre.

'We'll go and get you some clothes, Ebb, and then I must get to Tracy and see how she is. What are you looking at there?'

Ebony turned the photo album to show Jeanie the page.

'That's on a caravan holiday with Elaine and Trevor. They told me about it. It was an important time to forge new bonds with Emily. I get the feeling they were just beginning to know her properly as an adult after all the years of her rebelling as a teenager.

Sky must have brought them all together. Babies do that, you know, Ebb ... broaden your view – start making you think about the big family picture. I've even had to make an effort to get along with Pete's mother and I wouldn't if I didn't have Christa. Quite frankly if I didn't have Christa I'd hire a hit man to take care of her.' Jeanie giggled.

Ebony smiled. She was listening but choosing not to comment. She knew Jeanie well enough to know that Jeanie didn't expect non-stop chatter from her. Ebony was someone who thought about what she would say. Jeanie was the opposite. She tended to open her mouth, start talking and then roll with it. Ebony often went around to Jeanie's to babysit Christa. As soon as she'd got her settled Ebony could enjoy the luxury of a warm house, a family home with food in the fridge and Jeanie's stash of chocolates. She'd settle down to read a book or watch telly. Sometimes she stayed over and Jeanie cooked her breakfast. Often she stayed the whole day then. Pete was a lovely guy: quiet and geeky and so in love with Jeanie. Ebony hoped she could find someone like Pete. But that would involve effort and maybe a bit of therapy to build her self-esteem when it came to relationships. Ebony preferred men as friends.

Jeanie glanced across at her. 'Christa mentioned you the other day.'

'What did she say?'

'She said Ebony likes chocolate *a lot*.'

'Damn – she must have caught me. Kids are so sneaky.'

'Yeah, I've been told off at the nursery for Christa's

swearing. She says *shit* when something goes wrong. You forget they suddenly become little mimics. She's very fond of you, Ebb.'

Ebony didn't answer – she knew what Jeanie was doing. Jeanie wanted Ebony to get on with finding a boyfriend. After the boyfriend would come the child. Jeanie was a bit of a surrogate mother to Ebony.

Ebony doubted that she would ever have kids. Her own fractured childhood was not a good template. If she did have them they would definitely never be meeting their grandmother. Ebony's mother was in a secure mental hospital after being convicted of murder. All Ebony's childhood had been spent watching her back, watching her mother's moods. Ebony's happiest times had been when she went to stay with foster parents. Even the children's homes were better than staying with her mum. But that brought a crushing guilt – not to love your own mother seemed to be a terrible crime.

She turned the pages of the album.

'She was really pretty,' said Jeanie, looking over Ebony's shoulder. 'Red hair. I always wanted red hair.'

'Individual-looking rather than sweet,' answered Ebony as she continued turning the pages of the album. 'Quirky almost: face like a pixie.'

'We didn't get a lot of useful info from Elaine. It's hard to see how Emily lived when it's all been boxed up. You can see her style though. I would say both girls were not that big on the new porno look for women or wearing kids' clothes.'

Ebony turned the pages in the album thoughtfully. 'Yeah, I don't know much about fashion.'

'What do you wear if you and Tina are hitting the town?'

'Jeans and a top.'

'Would you wear the kind of thing Emily's got on?'

Ebony shook her head. 'It's a dress. I never wear dresses or skirts. But I guess it was summer in this picture.' She showed Jeanie. 'It's a long sundress type of thing. It's a bit hippy maybe?'

Jeanie shook her head. 'Those long skirts were in fashion last summer.'

Ebony turned the pages. 'Fashionable hippy then?'

'Have you got Danielle's iPod?' asked Jeanie.

'Here.' Ebony took it out of the bag containing the personal items they'd taken from Danielle's flat.

'Let's put it through the system here and listen to it.'

Ebony connected it up.

'Oasis. Arctic Monkeys. Old-fashioned type of rock chick,' said Jeanie. Ebony skipped forward along the tracks. 'Neil Young, Bob Dylan, Black Keys, Florence and the Machine.' Jeanie reeled off the names of the artists whilst drumming her fingers on the steering wheel.

'How do you know so much about music?' asked Ebony.

Jeanie shrugged. 'Always loved it. All kinds. You have to be brought up with music to know about people like Bob Dylan. Danielle loves acoustic, poetical lyrics.' They parked up and walked into the centre, stopping outside H&M.

'Let's start here.'

Jeanie led the way, going around the shop collecting clothes whilst Ebony trailed behind her carrying them.

Within twenty minutes they were in the changing room.

'Try these baggy trousers with these five different tops and we'll decide a look for you.' Jeanie separated the different styles of clothes onto separate hanging space in the changing room. Ebony slipped out of her work clothes and waited to be handed the first pair of combat-style trousers. 'I reckon we go for practical, not too bright, with a hint of feminine about it. Let your hair down, Ebb.' Ebony undid the ponytail at the back of her head and untwisted the knot. Her hair ballooned out over her shoulders. 'So pretty, your hair, like soft, black candyfloss.'

'Legacy from my Jamaican dad.' She waited whilst Jeanie chose a top and took the hanger out of an embroidered peasant-style cotton blouse in green.

'Ebb, why have you got a sports bra on?'

Ebony shrugged. 'I always wear them.'

'They make you look much flatter than you are.' Ebony didn't answer. She pulled the blouse over her head. The sports bra was visible as an off-white cloth bar across the gape where the buttons did up. 'We'll have to get you a few bras. I reckon you're a thirty-four B. Christ, I wish I was that. Mine are huge since I had Christa. It's taking me forever to get my figure back. I'm going to go to the gym, Ebb. I'll have to stop making excuses and just do it.'

'Don't beat yourself up about it. Christa's a pretty good excuse, Jeanie.'

'I know but I'll have to think of something; I'm sick of not being able to get back into my clothes.'

'I wouldn't worry about it,' Ebony said as she

held out her hand, waiting to exchange another top.

'That's all right for you to say. If I had your figure I'd show it off, wear some short skirts sometimes – your legs are fab. I wouldn't worry about it either.'

'I'm shapeless.' Ebony put the clothes neatly back on their hangers.

'No you're not. Who told you that? Whoever it was is not seeing what I see in that mirror. Just jealous, I expect.'

'Yeah, right.' Ebony avoided looking at herself in the mirror. 'I've always been big-boned. My mother always tried to make me look pretty – never worked. My mum was petite but curvy. The opposite to me basically.'

'You're athletic and lean but with a proper waist and a woman's shape. Be proud, Ebb.' Jeanie could see Ebony was beginning to feel uncomfortable and snatch at the clothes. 'Okay. Torture's over, Ebb. I've decided. 'We'll take four of these tops, these two pairs of trousers, and we'll pick you up a pair of skinny jeans for the evening. Done. Oh, and some underwear: bras that fit, for Christ's sake.'

It would be evening before Jeanie could think of making it back to Tracy. She gave her a ring.

'There will be officers stationed outside from now on – just as a precaution. You know – I'm very proud of you – you're coping much better than you think.'

'Thank you, Jeanie. I feel exhausted. I can see me going to bed the same time as Jackson.'

'What about Steve – is he coming home tonight?'

'He might do. We have to talk about it.'

'Do you want me around tonight?'

'No, Jeanie. I'm exhausted and so is Jackson. We'll see you tomorrow.'

'Of course. If you need me, you call.'

'I will.'

Chapter 30

Ebony left Jeanie to drive straight home to spend some time with Christa whilst she got the bus home with her two bags of clothes. She stepped off the bus and was on her way to the local Spar shop to pick up something to eat. She'd been told by Carter to go home and make sure she had what she needed to prepare for going undercover. She had a new set of clothes, and had even had a lesson in putting on make-up from the woman in the Body Shop. Now she was going home to go over the details for the hundredth time. She was already beginning to think herself into another person's skin, trying hard to imagine the sights and smells of the Caribbean and had listened to endless newsreels from the last few years to make sure she knew enough about what had been going on in the place she was supposed to have lived in. First she'd go to the Spar and get herself some comfort food to sustain her whilst she continued her studies.

A car was parked up across the street as she left the Spar with her shopping. Two men were sitting inside who she didn't recognize. She could tell it was a police car – something about the way it was parked and where; its colour, the position of its number plate. She was mulling over what it could be: maybe a drugs bust, maybe a hit on illegal workers in the shop. She kept an eye on the men in the car as they stared straight ahead. Then, on some unseen signal, they switched on the engine and accelerated forward just as Ebony got close. Ebony turned to look behind her to see what they were headed for. She was beginning to feel like she might be accidentally about to get caught up in something. Her heart was racing – would they need her to assist? Was she in their way? The car seemed to be heading straight for her. They drew up just ahead of her and she saw the back passenger door swing open. Then her world went black as hands gripped her and she was pushed down headfirst and thrown into the car.

Ebony's eyes were wide open as she sat in the back of the car, held firm. Her hands were behind her back, tied with a plastic tie. Nobody spoke to her. She could only smell the cloth of the inside of the bag she had over her head. She could hear her heart beating.

They drove for twenty minutes, around in so many circles that Ebony lost all sense of direction. They turned into a place that echoed, as if it were underground. They kept the engine running and she heard the car door being opened, felt the rush of cold air as she was hauled from the car. She heard the car drive away.

They marched her along an open space and she felt the presence of two men. She listened to their footsteps. Ebony felt the air around them. The smell of chemicals. They stopped and Ebony heard the clank of a chain being loosened, slipped out of its hold and dropped onto the ground. She was pushed forward and she tripped over, landing on concrete. A door was closed and her hood was removed. Two men stood looking down at her. They were both thick set in their mid-thirties to early forties, one taller than the other. Both bald. They were dressed the same, almost in a uniform of dark clothes. One of the men was taking his jacket off. Ebony felt herself beginning to shake. She was trying to keep the panic down and her wits about her. She had to stay sharp. She looked around her to assess the situation. It was a windowless room with a concrete floor and bare brick walls. There was strip lighting on overhead, hanging down from the ceiling. There were shackles on the floor, bloodstains on the concrete. There was a sink in one corner. The room was icy cold. Ebony's breath was white. In another corner of the room was a metal tank up at a forty-five-degree angle from the ground. She knew what it was – a sensory deprivation tank. She had read about them. She knew that inside the tank a few hours was equal to weeks of solitary confinement in an ordinary cell.

The shorter of the two men hauled her to her feet and pinned her against the wall. He placed his hand in the middle of her chest and kicked her ankles back until she was touching the wall with her feet and then he came close to her face so that his nose was touching hers. It was many years since Ebony had been subjected to an attack like this. As a child she'd been assaulted many times in the power struggle that went on in kids' homes. She had learnt to keep her head down, to comply, to wait for it to be over. It had been many years and countless blocked memories since she had felt so vulnerable.

'What's your name?'

'Ebony Wilson.' Ebony's voice came out with a Caribbean accent. She had known that the trial would happen but even so, it felt very real to her. She had to try to stay focused and remember it was not going to last for ever. *They will not kill me,* she said to herself. A small voice in her head added: *they will try to and break you though.*

'Where've you been living for the last twelve years?'

'Jamaica.'

'Address?'

'One hundred and seventy-three Manning Street, Trench Town, Kingston.'

'Who did you live with?'

'My grandparents.'

'What was your grandfather's middle name?'

'Levi.'

'You're lying. What was the colour of your front door?'

'Blue.' Ebony heard the sound of metal grating against metal – the taller man was opening the tank in the corner of the room. The man talking to her grinned.

'You're rubbish at this. You must enjoy pain because that's what you're going to get.' Ebony looked across at the other man. He seemed softer, more human. She thought about talking to him directly but then thought against it.

Ebony looked back at the other man. He was stockier, bigger. He watched her and the expression on his face was one of contempt mixed with pleasure in her pain. He looked like the type of man who tortured kittens.

'What date did you leave there?' The short man slapped a flat hand against her abdomen. It doubled Ebony in pain and she snorted white breath as she answered.

'February the eighteenth 2012.'

'What day was it?'

'Monday.' She breathed through the pain.

'You're police, aren't you?' He slapped her again. She raised her head and looked him in the eyes.

'No.'

He kicked her feet away from the wall. She fell backwards and banged her back as she bounced off it and landed on her side on the floor. She sat up quickly and flinched as he pulled out her legs and rested a heavy boot on her kneecap as he rocked it with his weight.

'You're police – I'm going to break your leg just to start with. Tell us and I'll spare you the pain.' He ground his boot into her thigh as she squirmed to get away. The other officer came forward and breathed into her face. His voice was soft.

'Give us one good reason why we shouldn't kill you here and now?'

'Because I have a small child. A boy – Archie.'

'What's his date of birth? Which hospital was he born in?' The shorter officer took over again.

'Uh ...' Ebony couldn't think. She knew this – she must remember. 'Uhh ... Queen Mary's, Trenchtown.'

'Wrong. You're police, aren't you? Do you think we're stupid?'

'No.'

Ebony was hauled over to the tank and her legs were tied and she was lowered inside the pitch black. The lid was placed on the tank and she could see nothing, feel nothing, no sound except blood pumping. Ebony closed her eyes and breathed deeply.

I can do this. She closed her eyes just to rest them. She tried to imagine herself on a beach. She was with her friend Micky. Camber Sands: a beach that stretched forever within warm sun and clouds that filled the sky. Lying on their backs they stared up at the sky, the hot sand beneath them and the salty breeze skimming their skin; they looked for shapes in the clouds.

'There's a croc.' Micky had been right There was his tail, his eye. 'Or maybe an alligator,' Micky laughed. 'How many people know the difference, do you think, Ebb?

She didn't answer. She sighed and smiled. This was the happiest place in the world.

'If the world ended now, Micky, we could just float up to heaven from this beach.'

'Yeah, maybe a tidal wave as big as a mountain would just pick us up. We'd drown, and every single day for the rest of our lives would be like this.'

'Not for the rest of our lives – we'd be dead.'

'You know what I mean. For the rest of whatever it is afterwards.'

'We'd be together,' said Ebony, watching the world turn above her. 'But do you think we'd fall out?'

'We would, a bit. But then we could go to the other ends of the beach for a few hours and when we met again we'd be so happy to see each other.'

Two months after they visited Camber Sands Ebony was returned to her mother and she never saw Micky again.

Now in the tank she felt like she was drowning inside the tidal wave and all she could hear beneath the water was the sound of her own blood pumping around her body. Something held her in the darkness. She called out for her mother and heard her laugh and Ebony's face was pressed against a wall and someone was touching her in the darkness. Someone was hurting her, trying to get her clothes off, and she was fighting so hard.

She gasped and opened her eyes at the sound of the tank being opened above her head, squinting as light and pain flashed across her eyes and skull. A voice breathed in her ear. She recognized it as that of the officer who had interrogated her. She couldn't see him. He stood behind her with the lid still half on the tank.

'You've been in here for five hours. Did it seem like longer?' Ebony didn't answer. It felt like days. 'Want to talk to us before we go home to our families for a few days and forget all about you here? I want to explain something to you. Officially we were never here and neither were you. Eventually someone might find you – follow the stink. How does it feel to be dying in here?' Ebony tried to answer but she couldn't. The panic which had built up in the last five hours had left her speechless.

'You ready to tell us who you really are?'

'No.' Ebony's voice was barely audible.

'Do you want to stay in this tank?'

'No.'

'You want us to take you home?' He started to replace the lid of the tank.

Ebony found herself starting to scream. 'Yes! Yes!'

'Answer me truthfully and you can go – what's your name?'

She paused. 'Ebony Wilson.'

Ebony was dropped off at her home along with her shopping bags. She limped inside the house feeling like she was about to vomit. Her muscles ached from the confinement and cramp. Her stomach hurt. She stood in the hallway and listened. The house was quiet, everyone was at work. She left her food in the kitchen and then walked quickly up the stairs to her bedroom on the top floor. She threw the H&M bags down and drew the curtains and went back to lock the door. Then she got undressed quickly and got into bed, pulling the duvet over her head.

Robbo received the phone call from the undercover training team.

'The two main attributes needed to make a good UC are acting ability and arrogance. I don't see either of those in your candidate but ... Willis passed, just, but there were several issues that, if we had more time, we would have worked on. This part of the course is normally three days. We had eight hours altogether.'

'Is there one aspect we need to be particularly worried about? asked Robbo.

'Yes. She can cope with physical and verbal abuse. She can handle pain. What she can't handle is abandonment and there are some issues buried – she experienced something nasty in the isolation tank. Whatever she's been through in her life it's not finished with her yet. I can tell you, if we'd had longer, she would have cracked, definitely. And the biggest problem I can see is that she cannot read people's personalities, can't read the signs. She didn't try and talk her way out of it. She stood there and took it. She waited for it to be over.'

Robbo called Carter.

'She's not ready.'

'In what way?'

'She stood there and took it without trying to talk her way out of it.'

'If she were too slick, it wouldn't work.'

'We're not talking about slick. She is not good at judging character, the team report says.'

'As if we needed to be told that,' scoffed Carter. 'You know as well as I do that she has a lot to learn as a detective.'

'Yes but she is likely to make fundamental misjudgement of character under stress.' Robbo paused to see if Carter wanted to interrupt again but he didn't. He continued: 'She handled some things better than expected: pain, isolation. But we knew she would. Ebony has no trouble spending time on her own. She has a high pain threshold. She's used to being hurt mentally and emotionally.' He paused again. 'You listening, Carter? I don't want her put at risk like this. She was brought up to know only the barest affection from strangers, to know how to manage the mind of a madwoman like her mother.'

'Yeah. I hear you. But when and if the time comes, when she meets Hawk, she won't be with someone normal or balanced. She will be facing someone like her mother and she will be just the right person to be doing that.'

Carter gave Ebony a call.

'You did well.' She was coming around from her sleep. She took the phone from the side table and took it under the duvet with her. She smiled to herself. She knew he would lie.

'I didn't realize how hard it would be. I could have easily blown it. I forgot some key facts they asked me. My mind went blank when they asked me all about my grandparents, all about my Jamaican home, where Archie was born.'

'Bound to, Ebb. You're on a crash course here. You did fine. The boys on the undercover team said you nailed it.' Ebony rolled her eyes, smiled. She was tempted to say 'bullshit' but resisted. 'It starts tomorrow, then, Ebb. You won't be able to come back into Fletcher house until it's over. Everyone thinks you've gone off on a course to become a FLO.'

Ebony pushed the duvet away and lay on her back looking at the stained ceiling rose. She thought for a few seconds.

'Ebb? I think you can do this.'

'I hope so, Guv.'

'You can still back out, Ebb.'

Ebony breathed in loudly through her nose, shut her eyes and rested the phone on her cheek.

'No. I'm not backing out, Guv.'

When the phone rang that night Tracy heard it in her sleep. She had put it just outside the bedroom door. She leapt out of bed and ran for it, breathless, stumbling in the darkness. She saw it glow as it vibrated on the floor.

'Hello?' Tracy could not stop herself from shaking violently. She stood in the darkness of the lounge, listening. 'Hello?' she repeated.

'TRACEEEEEE.' She gasped as his voice boomed in her ear. 'This is all your fault. You betrayed me today, Tracy ... I thought we had a deal ... an understanding.' His voice, liquid and deep, was distorted by his breathing. He was breathing hard. She had to listen hard to understand what he was saying. 'Danielle's told me how you abandoned her.'

'What? I didn't. I had to give her up. I didn't want to. Please let her go. She has her little boy Jackson.'

'You make sure I don't regret leaving him alive, Tracy. You make sure he forgets his mum fast. Now you tried to make a fool of me; you're as guilty as I am for the killings. I want to play a game with you, Tracy. It's called tighten the noose. How tight is up to you.'

Tracy shook her head; she clutched the phone tight. She wanted to throw it down but she couldn't.

'You abandoned your child and then you married Steve. How did that work out for you, Tracy? I've stood outside your house. I know where you work.'

Tracy gasped. Her heart raced. She thought she would pass out. She leant on the wall for support.

'You fascinate me. You epitomize everything I hate. You plaster yourself in make-up and spend all your time talking nonsense about this and that product. It's all lies. You wear a mask to trap men. You're just a blow-up doll, Tracy – worthless. The one job you had in life – motherhood – you ran away from. The one thing nature made you for you turned your back on; not even the vilest of nature's creatures do that. You abandoned your child and created a false life for yourself. You're ugly inside. You're festering under your skin. You should strip it off, all of it, get down to the muscle and bone and see what lies inside you. Skin and bone and bare flesh. Just liars, all of you.'

Tracy could hear him wheezing. She could hear him masturbating. She wanted to put the phone down but she had to keep him talking. She had to play along with him and give the team a chance to trace him.

In the background she thought she heard the sound of squealing.

'Ahhh. There she goes. She's turning blue now. It's all your fault. Shall I describe her to you? Her eyes are starting to bulge. Her face is swelling. Her tongue is protruding. I think she's ready for me.' Tracy looked at the clock on the kitchen wall. Twenty more seconds to three minutes. 'Are you ready, Tracy?'

The line went dead.

*

Robbo shuddered as he watched the line go dead on his screen. He had listened to the call. It came from a mile radius of the Angel Islington. A mile was a lot of ground in the middle of London. Now he knew that the press conference hadn't worked and that Ebony was their only hope.

Chapter 31

When Jeanie arrived the next morning Tracy looked like she was desperate for her to get there. Jackson hadn't been washed or dressed.

'He phoned again – did they trace it?' she asked, hanging on to her emotions by a thread.

Jeanie shook her head.

'Nearly, Tracy. You did a great job.' She had listened to the recording that morning before coming to the house. Jackson was pleased to see Jeanie. She gave him a cuddle. When she could Tracy took Jeanie aside in the kitchen.

'No I didn't. I can't do it.'

'You can get through this, Tracy.'

Tracy shook her head slowly as she picked up a tea towel and began wrapping it around her hands. 'He's not ever going to let her live. He's going to kill her slowly and make me listen to it.' She stared wide-eyed at Jeanie. 'I can't do it. I can't bear to hear Danielle in pain. I can't pick up the phone again. He's torturing her for my benefit. Maybe if I didn't answer it he wouldn't hurt her?' She turned away from Jeanie and looked out of the back door. The ice had stayed on the patio for weeks now. 'He's punishing her for something that I've done. I'm killing my own daughter.'

Jeanie stepped forward and gently stopped Tracy twisting the tea towel.

'Don't think it, Tracy. He doesn't want to take responsibility for what he's doing. He wants to shift the blame on to others and you're one of them, but it's all down to him.'

'He knows things about me. He knows I gave Danielle up for adoption. How does he know that? He says he's been here, been watching me at work.'

'He might have followed Danielle in the days or weeks before he abducted her. He may well have seen you both together. Danielle could be under pressure to tell him things, Tracy.'

'Tortured, you mean?' Tracy stared at the back yard. The ice gave it a look as if all life was suspended and they were in a dream. Stuck in a cloud.

'Danielle needs all your strength now and so does Jackson. Even if she hadn't found you he would have come for her anyway. Somehow you have become part of the process for him, Tracy. If he stops calling then I think we will lose her. We need to sit this out. We need to wait. I think we should insist on Steve coming home now. You have too much to cope with. Let him bear some of the burden.'

She shook her head. 'I have to weather this storm on my own. It's me and Jackson and Danielle against this man, whoever he is. You get a sense of perspective, don't you?' She turned to look at Jeanie.

'This is a tough time for everyone, Tracy. How people react in a crisis like this doesn't always bring out the best in them. I've seen couples really struggle to stay close when something this big hits.'

'Not sure how close we were before it happened. I feel like I've got a bigger baby than Jackson to look after. At least with Jackson you get a cuddle now and again.'

Jeanie smiled. 'Why didn't you have any more kids, Tracy?'

'I don't know. We just never reached a time when we thought it was a good idea. We've become stuck in a rut now, me and Steve; sometimes I wonder what's left for us. We don't even own our own home; this place is rented.'

'Steve must earn good money as a manager?'

'Not bad but we have a lot of debts; we struggle to pay them.'

'Debts? From what?'

'Credit cards mainly – a few loans. Steve got in trouble with them. We owe sixty thousand pounds still. It cost us our house. I thought Steve was paying the mortgage but he wasn't. I don't even know what he was doing with all the money. He says he can't remember, that the debts just mounted and he used one card to pay off another. I had a beauty salon until it all happened. I had the garage converted into a treatment room. It was so beautiful: candles, potted palms, lovely and relaxing. I had hoped to expand – get a proper premises. I lost my studio and my clients when it all blew up and we had to sell the house and move in here. So now I work in Simmons full-time.'

'I'm sorry, Tracy. Life sucks sometimes.'

'It's not too bad. I'm grateful for the job and you never know what's around the corner, do you?' As she said the words Tracy realized how ridiculous they sounded. She turned away, turned on the tap and began washing the sink.

'You're right, and sometimes things just force you into decisions. Life could turn around for you. You could still have a baby. You're young enough,' said Jeanie.'

'Maybe we'll think about having a child in a few years if the money situation improves. I have big regrets. I wish I'd kept Danielle. I was just a kid and I thought the Fosters were lovely: I thought they were much better than me; they'd do a better job than I could. What did I know about babies? I was just fifteen. But it sounds like she had a horrible childhood. I could have given her better than that. I realize that now.'

'Tracy, when Danielle talked to you about Gerald Foster, do you remember her making any actual allegations against him?'

'She said she and him didn't get on. She said he kicked her out when she got pregnant. She continued to see Marion Foster. I'm not sure if Gerald knew that or approved.'

'Nothing improper though?'

She looked at Jeanie. 'Improper? You think he assaulted her?'

'We don't know anything at the moment, Tracy. We

have to look at this from as many angles as we can.'
Jeanie went across to the table in the lounge and
picked up the bag containing the puppets. 'I think that
it's best to keep Jackson here for now.'

Chapter 32

Carter walked down the corridor to Bowie's office. Bowie looked ready to leave.

Carter popped his head inside the door.

'You off?'

'Yeah, but not for ten minutes. Come in, Dan.' Carter closed the door behind him. 'Sit down and tell me how it's going with the undercover operation.'

'It was test day today, so she's had a lot to cope with, getting her legend right, juggling a lot of balls in the air at once but she'll be okay. She's home now so I'm off the hook for the evening. I need to go home and get some rest.'

'Fancy a drink?'

Carter shook his head and laughed. 'I'm too tired.'

'Yeah, we both know that's a lie. You're under the thumb.'

'Maybe. But I have to give my relationship with Cabrina my best shot. What I don't need is complications.'

'If you change your mind text me.'

'I have to go.' Carter stood, took his buzzing phone from his pocket and looked at the message on the screen. 'I would say I hear my conscience screaming in my ear but it's actually Robbo – just got a message he wants to see me. Have fun.'

Robbo was on his own in his office when Carter walked in. Pam and the other two researchers had gone home.

He looked up as Carter entered.

'I was double-checking the timeline of events. I thought it looked familiar – check out his address.' He showed Carter a piece of paper. 'Remember the man who was there when the boys discovered Emily Styles' body?'

Carter looked at it and squinted for a few seconds as he thought about it.

'You're kidding me?'

Carter parked up outside Gerald Foster's house and watched for a few minutes from the street. The place looked unlived-in; it was dark but Foster's van was in the driveway. It was just gone ten. He rang Robbo again.

'Any news of the hit-and-run driver who killed Niall Manson?'

'None.'

'I'm tempted to get a forensic team over here to check out Foster's van.'

'Discreet for now,' answered Robbo. 'If he is Hawk the main thing is to get Danielle back. We scare him off we could blow it. He hasn't done anything wrong that we can book him for.'

'He's connected to two parts of this inquiry.'

'Could just be coincidence.'

'There's no such thing as coincidence. I'm sure I learnt that from you!'

Carter walked up the drive and as he did so he took a good look at Foster's van as best he could in the light from the streetlights. Even in this light he could see it had been recently repaired – there was fresh paint and a new bumper. Carter took out his phone and photographed the repair work. The flash lit up the night. Foster appeared from around the side of the house.

'Can I help you?' he said frostily as he stood watching.

Carter walked around the van.

'A fair bit of damage on the bumpers?'

'It's a works van. It doesn't have to look pretty. What can I do for you, Officer? Have you found Danielle?'

'Not yet. I believe you were there when the young woman's body was pulled from the canal? Can we talk about it? Can I come in?' Gerald Foster grunted and opened the front door, led the way inside the house. He flicked on a light in the hallway. Carter followed him in. 'It must have been pretty horrible.'

It was dark and cold inside. *Not exactly homely in here.* Carter was thinking how there was no way Foster had been in the front of the house for a good while. He peered into the rooms either side as they walked through to the back of the house. It had a forgotten feel and smell. Foster put the light on in the kitchen.

'The lad found her. I was just there.'

'What were you doing there?'

Foster looked at Carter with contempt. 'What do you think I was doing there? Do you think I always hang about canals in the hope some body will float to the surface? I was working. I was making my way to the Canal Museum to start my tour. I show people around. I told you I'm a guide.'

'Of course. I remember. I didn't realize you were also an expert on the canal system in London.'

'Yes. I normally show people around, take them up the canal on a barge, but it's been impossible for weeks. I like to do a job properly; I like to be thorough. I can walk people up the towpath instead so I like to think of as many interesting facts relating to that as I can. I wanted to take a look at the ice.'

'So you were with people when the boys were playing on the ice?'

'No, the weather meant people cancelled. I was merely checking on things. I saw the boys larking about. Bloody hooligans; should have been at school. I shouted at them to stop throwing rocks on the ice.'

'They didn't listen, obviously.'

'No, then one of the little bastards got pushed on the ice. I thought for a moment I was going to have jump in if the ice cracked.'

'Would you have?'

'No. But there's a lifebuoy. I might have thrown that for him. If he was lucky.'

'Sensible. Did you suspect anything was in the canal there?'

'What do you mean?'

'You told my colleague, Detective Willis, that you

know every inch of the canal; maybe something had caught your eye in the last week or so?' Foster shook his head and stuck his hands further into his pockets as he stared hard at Carter.

'No. Is that where you think Danielle is? Is that what this is about? You think I had something to do with that young woman's murder and that I have even more to do with my own daughter going missing?'

'We believe Danielle is being held against her will. There is still time for someone to release her; still time to get her home to her son Jackson. It isn't too late.'

'Why are you telling me?'

'Because you're right – it's quite a coincidence that you were there when a friend of your daughter's was pulled out of the canal and now your daughter goes missing. But coincidences are a rare thing in my job.'

'I didn't know she was a friend of Danielle's?'

'Yes. She was. Can I just ask you something else about your work showing people around the sites of London?'

'Look, I've had enough. I've told you all I know, now please leave.' He almost pushed Carter backwards.

'One minute, Mr Foster.' Carter didn't move. 'It can be here or at the station.' Foster backed off. 'Do you ever take people to the Heath?'

'Hampstead Heath?'

'Yes, you know, a tour of the parks, that kind of thing?'

Foster bristled with irritation. 'I have done in the past. I do private work where I drive tourists round and show them the sights. Hampstead Heath is sometimes on the list, depends what they want. Is that it? I want you to leave my property.'

'When were you there last?'

'In the summer.'

'You haven't been there in the last week?'

Foster didn't answer; he stared at Carter then waited for an explanation.

'Another body was found there. I think you need to call your lawyer, Mr Foster.'

Chapter 33

The next morning Ebony sat in the housing office with a ticket number in her hand. Archie was asleep in the buggy. Archie had seen Ebony a few times plus he was a good baby and used to going to nursery whilst Cabrina worked for an accountancy firm, so he never minded strangers. Archie was a serious baby; very sparing with his smiles. Ebony thought he could just pass as her child. He had the look of the sun about him: Cabrina was Greek, Carter was half Italian so the mix had produced a stunning baby with a double dose of shiny black hair. Carter had told her what she needed to know to look after him for a few hours and he'd dressed him all in blue today.

She and Archie had been waiting for an hour when her number was called. She went up to the booth. The young man waited for her to sit. He looked at her file.

'You've been sent over to us from our Luton branch?'

'Yes.'

'Can I ask why?'

'Just had some personal issues. I wanted to make a new start.'

He nodded, barely interested. He just needed an answer that corresponded to a question on his form and a box that needed ticking.

'Any preference where you'd like to live?'

'My college is in Holloway, so I don't mind as long as I can reach it by bus. Somewhere where there's a park would be good.'

'Where are you staying now?'

'We're sleeping on a friend's floor.'

Ebony knew what the file said. Robbo had shown her and it was faultless. It said she was to be given priority. The lad shrugged, looked resigned. It was no skin off his nose if she queue-jumped. Someone somehow thought she deserved it.

He picked up a sheet of available flats.

'I have something I can offer you by Beacon Park in Hackney Wick. It's a two-bedroomed apartment on the sixth floor.' He looked at Ebony's expression. She was mulling it over, thinking about the location. 'There's a lift,' he added. 'Can't guarantee it works but flats are few and far between – I'd take it if I were you. It's on a bus route to Holloway. It's near Victoria Park – kiddies' playground.' She nodded.

'Thanks.'

'Do you want to take a look?'

She shook her head. 'No need. I'll take it. Thanks.'

'Okay.' He left his desk and returned with an envelope. 'Here are the keys. Here's the address. The housing officer will be in to make sure it's all working for you.'

'Thanks.'

Ebony negotiated the heavy exit door with

Archie's buggy and stopped outside. She took out her phone as she pushed the buggy one-handed and rang Carter.

'Have just secured a flat.'

'Did you enrol in the classes?'

'I'm on my way there now. You sure Cabrina doesn't mind about borrowing Archie?'

'Nah ... Free childcare. Plus, it's an outing.'

Now Ebony knew he hadn't asked Cabrina. 'Not exactly an ideal activity recommended for a nine-month-old.'

'He'll love it. Buy him a Big Mac.'

Ebony shook her head, couldn't help a smile; she knew Carter was joking. She knew he loved Archie to bits but she also knew Carter had some growing up to do. Still, it left her feeling hungry; she was now obsessing about a Maccy D's. As she hung up the phone and peered around the front of the buggy. Archie's bright brown eyes looked back at her. Ebony was beginning to think Archie was the perfect child for her. He observed the world and occasionally demanded some attention but it was never for anything unnecessary or frivolous; he never grizzled; he never asked for something he didn't really need. Archie smiled at Ebony.

'Fancy a McFlurry?' She shook her head; *better not.*

She steered Archie's buggy awkwardly through the revolving college doors. There a rather tacky Christmas tree with flashing lights just inside the reception area and hanging swathes of tinsel looping down from the light fittings. She walked up to the reception desk.

'I would like to talk to someone about enrolling on a teaching course please.'

'Have you got an appointment?' Ebony shook her head. 'Okay.' The receptionist smiled. 'Let me see if someone's free from student advisory to talk to you.' She winked at the other receptionist as she pressed the extensions number on her switchboard. 'Let's see who we can drag out of the Christmas party.' She smiled mischievously at Ebony as she covered the phone with one hand whilst she talked to Ebony in a stage whisper. 'The college will be closing for Christmas in a week. We've all had our parties today.' She waited for a response from Ebony but got none so she screwed up her face irritably and swivelled her chair round to the desk adjacent, with her back to Ebony as she waited for someone to answer the phone and then gave up.

'First door on your left, corridor straight ahead, down there ...' She turned back round and waved her hand in the direction of a corridor leading off from the reception area. 'They're not expecting you but they're all free.' She smiled coldly. Ebony didn't register it. She was too busy thinking about her cover story and about whether Archie might choose now to get restless. Plus Ebony was used to people mistaking her lack of response as rude when really it was just what it said on the tin.

Ebony tried to redeem herself with the receptionist by overdoing the thanks and then pushed Archie past the Christmas tree and down the corridor. She followed the noise coming from a busy office on her left.

Inside, there was excitement and the smell of mulled wine hung in the air. A young woman honed in on Archie. She knelt by the buggy and breathed mulled wine and turkey dinner into his face.

'You look just like your mummy,' she cooed. Ebony smiled at the thought of what Carter would say to that.

'Yan, there's a client here.' The young woman giggled, stood and called across the office. She winked at her colleague – 'No peace for the wicked.' A geeky-looking lad with glasses and what looked like a leftover attempt to grow a moustache for November smiled at her. He had a 'just got out of bed' look going on with his hair.

'Great.' He grinned sheepishly at Ebony. 'You thinking of enrolling in a course?'

'Yeah.' She nodded. 'I just really wanted to talk things through.'

He reached out for the slip of paper and held Ebony's gaze.

'Of course. Come with me.' His glasses were dirty. He looked at the piece of paper. 'Ebony?' She nodded.

He steered her towards the far side of the room to a quiet corner booth. He sat beside her and steered Archie's buggy in for her when it got jammed on the leg of a chair. Archie started grumbling, just enough to warrant paying attention to. The grumbling began to include a few trial screams.

'If you need to feed him I can find you somewhere quiet?' Yan asked as if breastfeeding was an everyday occurrence in his world. Only when Ebony didn't seem to get it did the red come to his face.

'I expect he's hot.' Ebony stood and pulled back the covers on Archie's buggy, taking off his hat to reveal a shock of black curls.

She also reached inside the pram cover for the bottle she'd left there.

'Oh, okay. Do you want me to heat that up?'

'Please,' answered Ebony.'

'No problem.'

Yan took it from her and disappeared into the rooms at the back of the office. Ebony was really glad she'd listened hard to Carter's instructions as she took Archie out of his buggy and stripped him down. He was hot, but easily pacified. He stared at Ebony and the surroundings; he seemed to be taking it all in. She was hoping he wouldn't suddenly think to himself: *hang on a minute*! One of the women stopped to talk to him and he smiled his near toothless grin back at her.

Yan came back and Ebony didn't have to do much beyond screw the teat on the bottle and check it as Archie grabbed with two hands and started drinking. Ebony was aware of a clock ticking in her head. Things went in one end – they came out the other after a short interval. She was quite taken aback with the fact that Carter knew a lot more than he let on about Archie's routines. He'd shown her how to change a nappy with such precision: it was typical of Carter to have bought himself a special set that included disposable gloves and three different kinds of wipes. Ebony still didn't feel she could do it – what if Archie started to howl and she got poop everywhere?

'Let's start with form-filling,' said Yan as he sat back behind his desk.

Age?'

'Twenty-five.'

'Ethnicity?'

'Anglo-Caribbean.'

He looked up and smiled. 'Lucky you. Do you go to the Caribbean much?'

She nodded. 'I lived there for just over twelve years.'

'Whereabouts?'

'Kingston.'

'I know it well. Whereabouts?'

Ebony felt heat come to her face. 'Just near the Adventist church on South Side, Manning Street?'

He shook his head. 'No, don't know it. Kingston's a great party town. What made you come over here?'

'I was born here. When I had Archie, all the gang shootings in Kingston got me thinking I'd rather live back here. '

He looked at her address. 'What, in super-safe Hackney? I'd rather be in living in the sunshine any day.'

He looked towards Archie, who was holding the bottle for himself as if he'd worked out that Ebony was probably not an expert. 'I guess you have to think differently. The partying gets curbed for a bit.'

'You've lived in Jamaica?' *Shit*, thought Ebony.

He nodded, grinned. 'Lovely. Spent time there when I was young.' *Phew – when he was young. Won't remember*. She relaxed. 'My mum was one of those hippy types,' he said. 'She believed in education on the move. We travelled a lot.'

She smiled; she could picture him on a boat, the salt

spray on his glasses. Some people were funny when they opened up to her for no reason. Sometimes Ebony thought it was because she left a lot of silences in the conversation so that people thought they needed to fill the gaps with snippets about their lives. Robbo said she would make a good counsellor. Carter said she should concentrate on being a good detective and ask more questions.

'You must have loved it?'

He nodded his head. 'Most of the time – it was a kid's dream. No school, no restrictions. Seems a world away now. This is the stark reality of working for a living.' Archie pushed the bottle away and struggled to sit more upright on Ebony's lap. He pulled off his shoe and threw it across at Yan. Yan caught it with a lightning reflex.

'Little boy blue has lost his shoe.' Yan laughed and handed it back to Ebony, who struggled to put it back onto Archie's foot, which seemed to have the ability to change size and shape at will.

'Your name is interesting,' Ebony ventured, trying to mask her incompetence. 'It's not very British-sounding.'

'As I said, my mum loved anything foreign.'

He looked back down at his desk and picked up his pen ready to resume filling in the remainder of the form.

'What about qualifications?' Ebony looked at him dumbly. 'Schooling? That kind of thing?' She'd gone blank for a second. She'd forgotten what it was she was supposed have.

'I took Cape examinations – A levels basically.'

'Okay, great, well that will save you some time – a year of training at least. Okay, now for a few personal details to start. Married or co-habiting with a partner?' He kept his eyes on the page as he waited, poised to fill in the blanks.

'Single parent. I live on my own.'

'Okay, good.' Ebony looked up from tickling Archie's palm with 'round and round the garden'.

'I mean you'll be entitled to the most help,' he said. 'It makes the form-filling a bit longer but it'll be worth it.' Archie burped loudly. Yan grinned.

Ebony blushed. 'Sorry. Thanks for your help. I appreciate it.'

'It's no problem at all.'

Ebony kept her eyes on Yan as she tickled Archie's other hand.

'Yes. It is. I'm looking for a new start. New flat, new life for me and Archie. Just us.'

'I'm sure you'll make it. Well ... if I can help in any way?' He looked ready to conclude the interview. Ebony thought she'd handled the worst of it – now she could relax somewhat and try to work on Yan a little. He seemed the sympathetic type.

'Is this a good college to come to for single parents?' He looked momentarily flustered and blinked behind his glasses. 'I mean, is there some social life here? I'm not much of a party girl but I would like to meet people, you know? Make a few friends. My family aren't around. It's just me and Archie, as I said.'

'Oh yes. I see. It's a good place if you make an effort. There's a fair bit of socializing via Facebook, that kind of thing. There's a Christmas party going on in the canteen right now. We could butt in if you like? Just say hello. Some of the people you'd be doing the teacher training course with will be in there. Some have been studying for a year or two. Would you like to meet them?'

'Love to. I'm a bit out of practice with socializing. Since I had Archie I haven't really been out much.'

'Perfect chance then – nothing too scary, I promise. Follow me. I've already been in there with one group for lunch but ... what the hell ... After all, it's working in the broad sense of the word.' He walked back through the office and called across to his colleague on the way. It was the same woman who'd directed Ebony across to Yan in the first place. 'Just showing a new student where the canteen is and introducing her to the group – okay?'

She looked up from her desk, grinned and rolled her eyes.

'Go on then.'

She winked at Ebony as if she were used to his liberty-taking. He turned back to Ebony with a smile.

'Wish it was Christmas every day. It's a miracle what a couple of lunchtime drinks will do.'

Ebony followed Yan through the office. She caught the buggy on the leg of a chair. He steered it expertly out of the way.

'I'll push if you like. I'm used to negotiating buggies through the office.'

'Thanks. Have you worked here long?'

'I've been here three years. I came here like everyone else to try and catch up on missing qualifications. Which I did, and then I applied for a clerical job here

and worked up to being an advisor. I wasn't expecting
to like it that much but I find it a really worthwhile
job. It's nice to help people. I mean, I don't intend to
stay here for ever.

'What do you want to do?'

'I don't have any idea what I want to do long-term.
But then hardly anybody does, do they?'

'No. I don't.' Ebony was thinking how strange it
must be not to have a twenty-year plan. Her goal was
to take her sergeant's theory exam next year, in March
and work in the different departments within MIT,
including Organized Crime and Vice. She wanted to
learn more about major fraud cases. When she felt
ready, she'd take her inspector's exam. That was her
main aim – she wanted to be an inspector in the
Murder Squad within ten years. At the end of twenty
years she wanted to be a superintendent at least. None
of the plan involved a marriage or babies.

'Do you have a lot of single parents coming
through?' she asked as they walked along.

He turned back to her and smiled, nodding. 'A lot
of people wanting to get off the treadmill they're on.
It's the nice side of my job, when people come back a
couple of years later and their circumstances are really
changed – you know? They're happy. It's a lot about
self-esteem.'

He looked back at her with a quick glance then
manoeuvred the buggy effortlessly through the office,
out into the corridor, left before the reception desk
and down towards the smell of a canteen.

Ebony looked at posters advertising job opportu-
nities on the walls on the way.

'Yes. Must be satisfying, your job. Helping people change their lives around, learn new skills?'

'Yes it is. I won't lie though – I'd rather be lying on the deck of a boat in the sunshine. Or drinking rum in ...? Where's the newest place to go in Kingston?'

'Oh ... there are so many, aren't there?' Ebony looked nervously at the people they were approaching. She was hoping she'd managed to cover her tracks a bit and confuse him into thinking she was anxious about something other than remembering all the facts she'd had hardly any time to learn. She'd definitely look them up later and find out what was current in Jamaica.

'Here they are – meet the rabble.' In the corner of the canteen a group of mainly women were chatting noisily, with kids running around unchecked. Some were standing, bouncing fractious babies on their hips. He steered Archie's buggy across to the group and Ebony followed. The canteen looked like it had seen a fair few parties that day. The cleaners were sweeping up party streamers from the floor.

One of the women standing, rocking a buggy whilst holding a glass of wine in her hand, turned and called out to Yan as they approached:

'You can't keep away, can you?'

Someone else echoed it with a: 'What? You back again?'

He gave an exaggerated shrug and rolled his eyes in embarrassment.

'It's a dirty job but someone's got to do it. Meet Ebony.' He turned and waited for Ebony to come level with him. 'Hopefully, she'll be joining the group after

Christmas.' There was a chorus of hellos and the end of the table opened up as people made space for them to sit down. An Asian woman with a gold stud in her ear and enormous beautiful eyes poured a glass of red wine and handed it to Ebony from across the table.

'Sorry, there's only red left.'

'Red's great, thanks.' Ebony took it from her and took a sip. 'Cheers.' She raised her glass and then put it back on the table. There was shrieking and howls of laughter at the other end of the table.

'I told you they were a rowdy bunch.' Yan settled Archie's buggy next to the table. Archie was sleeping. 'Let me introduce you ...' He worked his way around the table, calling the women out by name. 'I'll leave you to chat now. Call and see me on the way out if you need to, otherwise ring me in a couple of days. I'll have done most of your paperwork by then. I'm on Facebook if you feel like chatting.'

Ebony smiled and nodded as Yan stood and, amongst a few friendly tipsy attempts at berating him for leaving the table, he went on his good-humoured way.

The woman who had first greeted them sat down next to Ebony. She was young, elfin-featured; her name was Sammy.

'You joining the group then?'

Ebony nodded. 'Hopefully.' She'd watched Yan go, thinking about how he'd be checking out all that she had said. Her existence, national security number, her housing association history. All of it had been set up meticulously by Robbo. Now they would see how well it worked. 'You all seem to get on well?'

'Yes. It's quite a social group as well as hard work,' answered Selena, a friendly-faced woman with a shock of tumbling curls and a peasant blouse, long silver earrings. She had black kohl eyeliner around her pretty green eyes. 'We support each other – have to, a lot of us are single parents.'

'Teaching seems the ideal job.' Ebony looked around. Down the other end of the table there was one man in the group. He was joining in with the laughter.

'That's Christian. He's the token man on the team. His little girl is so sweet,' said Selena.

'Is he the only man on the course?'

'Yeah. He's been on it since the beginning. He's been studying here for years.'

Selena leaned towards Ebony in a stage whisper. 'Most of the women fancy him; he has a new one every week. The person he's most in love with is himself.'

Ebony made a face that said 'Really?'

Selena laughed and nodded. 'Not me personally but the women who are talking to him now – they *really* like him.'

Just then the women stopped laughing and looked their way. The man, Christian, had been half eavesdropping into Ebony's conversation. He excused himself and walked down the outside of the row of chairs, stopped by Ebony and held out his hand.

'Christian.'

'Ebony.'

Ebony tried to stand to shake his hand. She got her leg caught in the chair.

'No, don't get up; I didn't mean to interrupt, just came to say hi to the new girl. And to tell her not to believe everything this lot say. This is the naughty end of the table.'

'Yeah, right.' Selena laughed.

'It's nice to have you on the course. Are you going to do computer skills and word processing?' Ebony looked unsure. 'Oh well, I'll see you in there if you are. Nice to meet you.'

'You too.'

'If you need anything you can Facebook me. I'm Christian Goddard.'

'Okay.' She smiled. Christian walked back along the row and continued his raucous conversation with the women at the other end from Ebony. There were shrieks and giggles on his return.

Selena was grinning when she looked back.

'Never takes him long to hit on the new girl.'

Ebony rolled her eyes. 'Doesn't he have any competition?'

'We had a couple.'

'Men?'

'Yeah, there are a few around. But Christian seems to be the Alpha male.'

'He dates exclusively single mothers,' said Sammy.

'I suppose he's got a child. He wants to find someone in the same circumstances?' Ebony said as she sipped her wine.

'It doesn't seem to get them very far with him,' retorted Selena. 'It doesn't do them any good either. Some of them end up dropping out of the course.' She looked across for confirmation from her friend. 'I was

thinking of a couple of women that dropped out –
what was her name?'

'Who?' asked Sammy.

'The girl from IT who dropped out, or she just
didn't come back. Not sure why?'

'There've been a few,' Sammy answered. 'One was
called Emily.'

'What happened to her?'

'Did you see the news? She was pulled out of the
Regent's Canal.'

Chapter 34

Robbo went to get a cup of water from the water dispenser by the door. He could hear a couple of officers talking way down the hall. He heard Bowie's nervous cough. The one that sounded like he had a lump of phlegm in his throat which he hadn't been able to shift for a decade or two. Every few moments he tried again.

Robbo knew he had gone past the point of being able to close his eyes. Now, he would have to knock himself out with sleeping pills to sleep and then he would sleep for a week, getting up only to eat, staying in his bedroom, sleeping so solidly that he wouldn't even dream. But for now, he needed to be as mad as it took to see all the layers of the women's suffering, to see into the mind of the man who caused it.

He got his water and went back to his desk; there were four pieces of jewellery in front of him: the charm bracelet, two rings and the chain. He ran the chain through his fingers over and over. He watched it coil onto the desk. It was mid-afternoon. Pam was watching him out of the corner of her eye. She was worried about him. She knew he needed to sleep so badly but she had seen him this way many times and she knew he would only catnap now until it was over and then he'd collapse for a week.

Robbo sat listening to the noise of the chain, a shushing noise that became loud in his head. He was waiting for HOLMES to finish a check. He picked up Emily Styles' ring and turned it over in his hand. The sharp edges worn dull from years of use. HOLMES was finished; he printed off the pages he needed and smiled across at Pam, as taking the ring with him, he stood and stepped out into the corridor.

He felt calmer in the corridor. He walked down towards Bowie's office. Robbo had no love for Bowie. Years ago they had worked together in CID. But Bowie had gone undercover and helped to end one of the biggest paedophile rings in the country. Robbo had been part of the surveillance team watching Bowie as he integrated into the ring. He had his methods but Robbo wasn't always convinced they were by the book. Robbo was also not sure that anyone could do five years in undercover work and come out of it the same way they went in.

'This is the new search that takes in the jewellery connection plus other things: age of kids, geographical location to college and within a mile of Hawk's phone radius.' Robbo slid a file across Bowie's desk. On it he had the names of five women; clipped to their names were photos.

'These women fit all the criteria. Three missing, two dead. All of these women are linked by the fact they are all in their twenties, they are single mums living in North London and they were all attending classes of some kind in order to retrain.'

Robbo handed him the print-out from HOLMES. 'Two years ago this woman—' he pointed to the photo of Charlotte Rogers – 'disappeared and a year later her body was found in woodland belonging to the National Trust.'

'What was the coroner's verdict?'

'Open verdict. The only thing on her was the bracelet but her mother didn't recognize it. This is Sophie Vein.' He pointed to another photo. 'She was found decomposed in a forest in Rickmansworth, Hertfordshire in February 2011. She'd been lying there for an estimated nine months. She disappeared a while before that, in the August of the previous summer.'

'Anything found on her?'

'Examination of the organs was not possible as they were too badly decomposed; there was evidence of deep ulcerated wounds, causing infections in the bone. Her mother said she always wore a small pink ring on her little finger. Could be the one we have.'

'We'll ask Harding to take another look at the post mortem results and get some re-analysis of the samples taken at the post mortem and the burial site. Was there nothing before 2010?'

'Not that we can uncover. None of the women on the list who might possibly be a victim. If he follows the normal pattern of starting to kill in his early twenties then he is thirty at least.'

'Something happened in the lead-up to that year then. Something flicked his switch,' said Bowie.

'He searches out single mothers; they have to have children. All the women have been described as strong women, determined, not easily fooled. None of these women were registered junkies. None of them were thought to be users of class A drugs.'

'What were the ulcerated sites on the women's bodies then? asked Bowie.

'The results are still not in. But it's certain that whatever it was started under the skin, localized; it ulcerated and then necrosis occurred,' answered Robbo. 'Harding said there was evidence of antibiotics in Pauline Murphy's hair sample. Her doctor hadn't prescribed them at the time of her disappearance – it's the same scenario as Emily Styles. I think Hawk tries to control the infection.'

'Did he infect them with something himself?' Robbo shrugged.

'I don't know but I'm beginning to think it likely.'

'He introduces it and then tries to control it?' asked Bowie. 'As in experimenting on people, watching them die? What is he, some type of Doctor Mengele?'

'Could be,' answered Robbo. 'Every body is different and some organs will fail before others. When they can't last any longer he finishes them off. He chooses the time for them to die.'

'Do we have a DNA sample of Hawk from Pauline Murphy's body?'

'Yes we think we do. He left semen on Pauline Murphy's body but he's not a match for anyone in our system.'

'All these women went to colleges within the North London college umbrella,' said Bowie. 'But we can't bring in every male attending and working in the North London college network.'

'I've worked out the dates for these missing women. They don't just overlap; he doesn't just replace, he keeps them together. They all cross over. Right now Danielle won't be alone.' He showed Bowie the last woman on the list of three.

'Top photo is of Jenny Smith. A single parent with one child. She was attending a computer course at London Metropolitan University while staying in bed and breakfast accommodation. She left a little girl with friends overnight and failed to come in the morning to collect her. That was two years ago and she hasn't been seen since.'

'Eighteen months mean she would have crossed over with Pauline Murphy. Why haven't we found her remains? He's been leaving the others where they will be found.'

'That's a thing he's grown into. Maybe that's why he did it – because we never found her body. He wants attention. He wants recognition. What's the point in going to all this attention to detail if no one knows about it?'

'Yes, you could be right. Or maybe she hasn't been killed yet.'

'He gives a piece of jewellery to those he kills, doesn't he?' Bowie picked up the chain and turned it over in his hand.

'Yes, but we don't know what makes him choose a particular piece of jewellery to give to the women. We just know that it must be when he has decided to kill them. The chain around Emily Styles' neck was enmeshed in her hair, caught at the back of her head where the clasp had become entangled with her hair and torn some out by the roots. The hair was torn from living flesh not dead. So he goes through a ceremony before death: mask of make-up, jewellery. He arranges them for death. I looked back through her file and Jenny Smith always wore her grandmother's antique engagement ring. We have a photo of it.' Robbo scrolled down the images on his laptop and stopped at the photo of the ring and then he opened his hand and placed the ring on the desk in front of Bowie. He turned it to show Bowie. 'It's the same one we found on Emily Styles.'

Robbo went back to his office and laid the two rings and the chain on the desk in front of him. He couldn't stop staring at it. Something wasn't right. He didn't know what, though. He sat back in his chair and tried to close his eyes, tried to rest. More than anything Robbo had the image of Danielle Foster in the coffin. He started hyperventilating when he thought about it. He could see the body of Pauline Murphy in all its horror, inside the box. He saw the mask of make-up and a chain around her neck. The chain was enmeshed in her flesh and Robbo was trying to pick it out but it was so messy his fingers kept sliding. He looked up at Pauline Murphy's face but suddenly it wasn't her face he saw. It was Ebony's.

'Robbo?'

He opened his eyes; the smell of apple shampoo surrounded him and he saw Jeanie frowning at him, standing next to him at his desk. The next thing he heard was the almighty clamour of coffee beans being ground. He shot forward in his chair. Carter sniggered.

'I told Jeanie not to creep up on you.'

'Bastard.'

Robbo rubbed his face, picked up a handful of Haribo sweets and fed them into his mouth.

'I saw your update about the ring,' Carter said.

'Yeah, the main thing we learn from that is that he wants to carve his name in history, have them include him in the book of serial killers. He's making sure we know it's him. He's got a massive ego. He thinks he's better than anyone else. He may have a string of short-term relationships but he can't stay with someone long. He's easily bored.' Robbo slid his chair along the length of the desk and then stopped dead as he began furiously tapping on the keyboard. 'Plus, he has a massively inflated idea of his self-worth; he's callous, manipulative. These women he killed meant nothing to him as human beings, they were just vehicles towards his notoriety. He's also irresponsible, impulsive. But he wanted us to find the rings.'

Jeanie picked up the chain and looked at the rings on the end. 'The chain just doesn't look right,' she said.

'He had no choice but to put them on a chain,' Carter said as he made coffee. 'They would have fallen off when the fingers were lost to pond life.'

'Why didn't he just put plastic bags over the hands like he did with the head?' asked Jeanie.

Carter shook his head. 'If her wrist was already opened by a wound, which it was, then it would have been got at quickly by feeders and she may have just lost her whole hand somewhere in the bottom of the canal, plus these rings were not hers, they probably didn't fit her hand.'

'So he had to put them on a chain. Any old chain?'

'It's never any old anything with him, is it? He takes months to kill, he's not going to be rushed into anything, the smallest details matter to him,' Robbo answered.

'Then he chose a chain that doesn't match the rings. It doesn't look feminine,' Jeanie said.

'From another victim?' asked Carter. 'Or from him then?' Carter had stopped making coffee and was focused on Jeanie. 'Something which was his?' Robbo was nodding.

Carter looked at his watch. 'I have to go and meet Ebony. She's making her way to my house.'

Jeanie's eyes stayed on Carter as he got up to put his coat on. He looked her way and waited.

'The more we find out about Hawk, the more nervous I become about Ebony undercover,' Jeanie said eventually, looking from Carter to Robbo.

Carter put on his coat and stood for a few seconds in the middle of the office. He gave a small nod of the head.

'That's why we need her to succeed more than ever.' He looked over at Robbo.

Robbo was swinging the chain from the ends of his fingers. He had a smile on his face.

'Maybe we have a little piece of him here. Maybe this is his first mistake.'

Chapter 35

Carter met Ebony outside his house.

'I would have stayed longer but I think he needs a change,' she said.

Carter shook his head with mock disapproval. 'I showed you how to do it.'

'Yeah, but I know how fussy you are about things. I couldn't risk getting it wrong.'

Archie woke up and grinned sleepily at his dad.

'Hello, little man – handsome little devil.' He turned to Ebony. 'Hope you got a lot of compliments.'

'Yeah – I did. They all thought he was the spitting image of me.'

Carter shook his head in disbelief.

He turned his key in the front door and then came back for the buggy. He unstrapped Archie and handed him to Ebony to hold as he folded the buggy and in one move lifted it and took it inside the house. He stacked it in a purpose-built cupboard behind the front door. She followed him into the house, trying not to look like she was holding Archie at arm's length even though she was – he smelt. Archie was wriggling to see his dad. Carter took him from her and went to change him. He brought him back in a new stripy suit and held him on one hip as he called Ebony into the kitchen.

'Come and talk to me while I get him some food.' He put Archie into his high chair whilst he began banging about in the kitchen. 'Tell me, what did you find out?'

'Emily Styles was known to the group I've enrolled in.'

'She and Danielle Foster were both at the college – we know that,' Carter said as he searched for Archie's bowl in the dishwasher. 'Robbo said that they crossed over in a couple of their subjects.'

'It's a friendly group,' said Ebony as she perched on a kitchen stool and played with Archie who was getting impatient for food and banging his hand on the table of the high chair. 'They do a fair bit of socializing. I think it will be easy to get inside it. I have a couple of numbers; the women seemed really friendly. I'll be meeting one of them tomorrow – she's going to help me prepare for the course, catch up.'

'Any men on the course?'

'There's one I've met so far – another single parent, Christian Goddard. He seems to be everyone's answer to Brad Pitt, has the pick of the women. He's a good-looking, natural dad type. He told me to look him up on Facebook. I think he probably scores with most of the new women. Robbo's still working on a Facebook profile for me now. I don't want to risk getting it wrong.'

'Yep. No problem. Robbo left some stuff here for you. Plus he wants me to take some photos of you and

Archie.' He stopped stirring Archie's food for a moment, went into the lounge and came back with a buggy. 'You take this buggy – it's an older version of Archie's. And we got you a realistic doll.' Carter unwrapped the doll and held it in his arms as if he were burping it. 'It's one of those realistic feeding, pooping ones that they give to teenagers to put them off having kids.'

'Actually that's not bad.' She smiled. It was a mixed-race doll with black hair. 'As long as no one wants to talk to it.'

'You're just going to have the best behaved but permanently wrapped-up baby there is.'

She looked across at Carter, who had put the doll on the worktop. 'How's Tracy coping? What's happening with the investigation?'

'We confirmed that it's Danielle's voice in the background when Hawk called Tracy. The phone call came from a mile radius of Tracy's house. We can't narrow it down any further. The phone is a pay-as-you-go mobile, bought in Swindon. We're talking to colleagues down there just in case they've had missing women who might fit the bill. We might get lucky. They might have a suspect for us.'

'What's that you're feeding Archie?' Ebony screwed up her face. 'Looks like puke.'

'Sweet potato, sweetcorn and cod. I freeze it in batches. He loves it.'

'Yuck.'

'Ebb – you okay with this UC work?'

'I think so, Guv.'

'We'll be with you every step of the way.' She nodded.

'And you have good friends on The Dark Side. You know that don't you, Ebb? We care for you.' She looked puzzled. 'Not just Tina. I care. You know that?' She nodded. She wasn't sure where that came from.

'Has Tina got a tattoo?' Ebony was used to Carter's random thought process.

'You thinking about the Norse saying, the one on Emily Styles?' He nodded.

'Tina's always threatening to get one but then she remembers there's pain involved. She's a big pussy when it comes to pain.'

'What would she have – a shamrock?'

Ebony laughed. 'How did you guess? She was talking about a four-leaf clover.'

Carter laughed. 'Better put it on her bum, might bring her luck – she might get laid.'

'Oy! Don't be mean.' Ebony looked away and was trying not to smile. 'Besides, Tina is never short of male attention in the canteen.'

'Yeah, that's because men are greedy bastards and she's dishing out the food. Ah, she's a lovely girl, so she is.' Carter tried an Irish accent. 'I know I couldn't manage if Tina didn't help me out looking after Archie sometimes.'

'She adores Archie,' said Ebony. 'She goes on about him when she's been with him. She's always disappointed if he doesn't wake up.'

'You and Tina are like chalk and cheese. You're great friends though, aren't you?'

'Yes. It's funny how it just works.'

'I reckon she mothers you.'

'Yeah, she tries. She has an inbuilt maternal mechanism she can't switch off. I don't mind – most of the time. The rest of the time I pretend I haven't heard it when she tells me to remember my hat and scarf as I'm going out the door – it's a bit annoying.'

He sighed as he finished washing up Archie's tea things and went across to the high chair to wipe Archie's face with a wet flannel. Archie was instantly furious.

'Who'd have thought this time last year that things would have so changed for me, Ebb?' He ruffled Archie's hair.

'Cabrina would have been a fool not to come back to you, Guv. You so missed her. You drove me mad talking about her all the time.'

He chuckled, embarrassed. 'It took a lot though, didn't it, Ebb? I put it down to her being pregnant at the time: hormones and shit. Now we have Archie and Cabrina is back and everything's changed.' He swivelled on his heels and looked around the kitchen that had been transformed from a bachelor's pad to a baby's nursery. 'To think I worked so hard to get all this?' Carter kissed Archie's head. 'Don't mean it, do I, little man? I wouldn't change this for the world. Now I just have my poor dad to worry about. Poor bugger, I can see how scared he is. He starts another round of chemo this week. It's going to be a difficult Christmas, him watching us eat. But if we don't go it will be worse. But . . . if it is to be his last Christmas I intend to make it a good one. What are you doing? Are you going to see your mother?'

'They don't allow visitors on Christmas Day. I'll see her in the week after.'

'Would you go if you could?'

Ebony looked down at her lap; she had clenched hands without realizing as soon as he began asking about her mother. 'I would go because I'd feel it was my duty but I wouldn't want to.'

'So you'll be spending Christmas here?'

'Yes.' She breathed out; her hands relaxed; she lifted her head again and smiled across at Carter. 'With Tina and her brother Dermot who's coming over. He's supposed to be a really wealthy, self-made millionaire car dealer, but for some reason he wants her to buy his ticket over. That doesn't seem right to me, but ...' She shrugged. 'It's not my business. I'm really looking forward to it anyway. Does Cabrina mind going to your family for Christmas?' She looked across at his profile. He shrugged.

'She's happy not to have to do anything. Working full-time *and* doing the lion's share of looking after Archie is really hard on her but what can I do? I can't help my hours. I can't ever be a nine-to-five and week-ends-off type of guy. Now that I'm an inspector there's more pressure than ever.'

'She knows what you are. She accepted it when she came back to you.'

'Yeah – you're right' He winked at Ebony. 'I am ninety-nine per cent perfect – got to make allowances for the one per cent.' She laughed, rolled her eyes. 'Ebb – how is the flat they got you?'

'I haven't been there yet. I'll go there in a minute. It doesn't matter what it's like. Hopefully it'll be warm. But I'll manage whatever.'

'Of course. You won't be in there for long. But, just

in case, I dug these out for you and Jeanie contributed.' Carter handed her a sleeping bag. 'And a ground mat for putting on the floor. This will do for tonight. Buy what you need tomorrow and expenses will cover it.' She nodded. 'The buggy is to have a camera and microphone attached. Here ...' Carter opened a packet and pulled out a toy puppy. 'The camera's hidden inside along with a microphone. You need to leave this attached to the rain cover at the top of the buggy and have it pointing forwards; leave the microphone on at all times. When you don't have the buggy with you, you can clip this camera to your bag or your coat. You have your GPS?'

'Yeah.' She touched the pendant around her neck. 'Robbo had the guys in PTU make me this piece.' She held it up to show him the Tiger's eye stone set in onyx.

Carter studied it for a few seconds.

'That's really clever. Is it a transmitter?'

'Yes. But not the only one. I have one in my shoe, one on the phone. I have a radio in there but basically you're going to hear whatever I say from almost every angle.'

'Good. Here's a mobile phone Robbo asked me to give you to use undercover – give out this number.' He handed her a phone.

She looked at it. Her eyes lit up. 'Can I keep it afterwards?'

'No. You can't. Get yourself a smartphone for Christmas, Ebb. Give out this number and we'll monitor it. Get in with Danielle's peer group as fast as you can now and let's get this man out into the open. Get across to the flat. Take this laptop from work – Robbo's waiting on the other end. I want you to keep in constant contact with me if you can but at least phone in to me at frequent intervals during the day. The flat's going to be a safe place to phone from. Now, you ready?' He handed Archie to her and took out his phone to take some photos. 'Smile.'

Chapter 36

Ebony caught a minicab back to her flat. She couldn't be seen to be using a car and she certainly didn't feel ready to manage a bus with all her things plus a buggy and pretend baby. Ebony didn't have a car anyway. When she drove she borrowed a police vehicle. She'd never had much call to drive a lot: she'd lived in London all of her adult life and the only time she left it as a child was when she was sent to foster homes or children's homes outside London. When she lived with her mother they had lived in and on the outskirts of the city.

Ebony got out of the minicab inside the courtyard. It was five o'clock and already looking like night-time. Her eyes scanned her surroundings as she unloaded her things from the minicab. The wind hit her as it found a channel between the tower blocks and rubbish gathered and swarmed, catching on the buggy's wheels. When she was a kid she'd moved around with her mum and some of the places had been high-rise. The place took on a sound, a light, an atmosphere all of its own. This was one of the older estates.

'Do you need me to help you?' The kindly Somalian

driver had a face that belied his kind nature; it was so harshly scarred that one side didn't match the other.

'No. I'll be okay thanks.' She gathered her things together as he drove away.

Ebony knew that the block in front of her was the right one. She had the slip of paper with the address and the keys from the housing association in an envelope in her pocket. She stood for a few seconds gathering her bags and her thoughts then headed towards the main door of the apartment block. The lift was out of order. She began dragging the buggy up six flights of stairs. She bounced it up the first two flights of stairs and then carried it up the remaining four. The pretend Archie doll was safely wrapped away inside her backpack. If anybody had noticed her arrival and the empty buggy she intended to use the 'aunt' Carter had suggested, who helped with childcare and who would be bringing Archie later.

Above her was the echo of footsteps on concrete. The noise brought back memories as she climbed upwards. She remembered the sound of kids shouting to one another, running along the walkways that joined the buildings. She hadn't reckoned on feeling a mixture of uncomfortable nostalgia. She was used to arriving with Carter or another detective to an estate. It was so different on her own. She had to remember this wasn't her life, this was work, just like it was at other times. Only now she was working alone. She walked along the sixth-floor landing, reading the numbers on the doors. She slipped the key in the lock, turned it and stepped into darkness lit only by the orange light from the landing outside.

Her phone went. Someone had jammed leaflets under her door; it wouldn't open fully.

She walked through the lounge and stood at the window, overlooking other tower blocks and the trails of car lights as rush hour continued. She was grateful for the fact that the housing association had been in and her boiler was working. She had heat in the flat. She phoned Tina as she put the kettle on.

'I'm working away for a bit, Teen. You can leave me a message on this phone and I'll be in contact when I can.'

'Will I see you in work?'

'No. I don't think so. Not for a little while anyway. I'm doing a Family Liaison Course out on the North Circular. I'm staying in a motel there.'

'Is it nice?'

Ebony looked around her. 'No expense spared. But I'll be back as soon as I can.'

'Okay, but I can tell what you're really saying and it sounds like it's pants. Well if you need me, Ebb, you call, and stay safe. Wrap up warm. By the way – I think I've got a date for Saturday.'

'Who with?'

'The one I told you about. That good-looking inspector that's in MIT 15.'

'I know the one – you said he always has hot chocolate?'

'That's the one. Looks like the Hoff.'

'He's married, Teen.'

'No way.'

'Zoe told me. He tells everyone he's separated; everyone except his wife.'

'Oh God,' moaned Tina. 'I knew it was too good to be true. Dan Carter asked me to babysit. I may as well then if my hot date just went up in smoke.'

'I have to go. Speak later.'

'Wait – Ebb? What about ordering a turkey?'

'Let's have an M&S Christmas ready-meal.'

'No feckin' way. Ebony Willis, you're the limit. I've put you down for making a pudding, and it better be a good one. None of that pre-bought shite.'

'No problem. I found this recipe on the web. It's a cake in a mug. It takes five minutes in the microwave. Bye, Teen.' Ebony could hear Tina choke back the expletives on the other end of the phone. She smiled to herself. Ebony closed her phone and put it to one side. The smile on her face disappeared when she thought about another call she really had to make. Her mother would talk about Christmas again. Could Ebony ask them if her mother could come out for Christmas Day? Could she *just* ask?' Ebony rubbed her face with her hands and looked at the phone as if her mother was waiting inside it. She looked at the time – six – it was the time for calls. They ate dinner early. Her mother might be sitting by the phone waiting. Ebony finished making herself tea – strong builder's tea. She sat on the rolled-out ground mat and sleeping bag that Carter had given her; that would have to do for now. The housing association had done some decorating in the flat – they'd stripped out the carpets and there was hardboard down waiting for the new tenant to afford to lay carpet. She pulled the works laptop next to her, switched it on and then realized she'd delayed long enough; she picked up the phone and dialled the number then held it tightly to her ear. She could visualize her mother sitting by the phone: fretting, tutting, scowling at passers-by. Telling people her daughter always let her down. She got through to the switchboard and was put on hold for ten minutes. Then the operator came back on the line to say:

'Sorry, it's not possible to connect you right now. Mrs Willis is not able to take the call.'

'Is she ill?'

'Sorry – I don't have details. Phone back later to speak to someone then.'

Ebony got up and went to the window again. She stared out at the continuing tramlines of orange lights as cars inched their way home. She heard the noise of feet in the flat above her and a television being switched on. Someone was returning to their lonely apartment and needed the noise of television to make it feel like home. Ebony knew what that was like. It had been a massive step for her to move into a shared house with strangers. She'd chosen the room at the top; the furthest away from all of them. Gradually she'd got used to the sounds of them coming and going. Slowly she'd got used to the way she could differentiate between one person's tread or another's on the steps outside leading to the house. She knew who was coming home. She'd felt reassurance in the knowledge that she was in a house with people and yet they didn't require her to socialize; she'd spent her childhood dreading the sound of her mother's steps outside the door. She felt safer when she was far away. Her mother had never visited her unless the authorities were building up to sending Ebony home. Then her mother was required to look like she wanted Ebony back and could cope. But Ebony always knew there was an ulterior motive for having her home. If it wasn't money in the form of benefits then it was accommodation. Sometimes it was just that her mother had run out of attention. What Ebony had never reckoned on was that she would feel secure enough in the shared house to let her guard down and care a lot for another human being. She'd made the mistake once when she was in a care home and Micky had become her best friend. She still dreamt of Micky. Still her heart ached when she awoke to find that she wasn't still friends with him. She had no idea what had happened to him after the scandal at the care home after she left; she thought he must have been one of those abused because he had been unlucky all his life. He once said to Ebony that he counted her friendship as the only piece of good luck he'd ever had. When she dreamt of him she woke up happy just to hear his voice again but then the sadness of losing him kicked in. When she'd heard Tina moving around in the room beneath her she felt comforted. Tina was a great friend. Tina had eaten into Ebony's heart and Ebony was grateful for it.

She made herself a Pot Noodle and came back to the makeshift bed to sit and eat it. Then she remembered the doll was still in the bag and the buggy by the front door. She wheeled it into the bedroom just in case someone should knock, not that she had any intention of making friends with the neighbours – that wasn't in the brief. Head down, low profile, was what she needed. She got the doll out of the bag and strapped it into the buggy. She wheeled it into the bedroom and closed the door to keep the cold out and the heat in the lounge. She wouldn't be sleeping in the bedroom. She preferred just to use one room. She'd stay in the lounge for now. Besides, the sleeping bag was also the sofa. She settled down onto her bed and saw Robbo's avatar flashing on her screen. It was a Stan Hardy lookalike: a fat guy with glasses.

Ebony typed:

'You managed to find an avatar that looks like you?'

'Ha ha. You ok?'

'I'm good'.

There was a pause. She could see the speech bubble on the screen that meant Robbo was writing but kept stopping. Whatever it was he wanted to say he wanted to choose his words wisely. He settled on:

'How's life in the vertical world?'

She smiled to herself. What had he crossed out? She could visualize him at his desk. He would have his leopardprint wrap around his cafetière and he would have his packet of Haribo.

'So far, so good. Have you managed to get my Facebook account up and running?'

'Oh yes.'

She smiled again. She could visualize Robbo's face. She knew he would have enjoyed making a new identity for her. He would have done it well – down to the very last detail. But Robbo wouldn't be clocking off. He would be sleeping at his desk tonight. He would not let her face this time alone. That thought stuck in

Ebony's throat. Being in MIT 17 meant being in the MIT family. It had only just dawned on her that that's what it was.

'*Was it tricky?*' she asked.

'*I had to think of my daughter's account then add all the extras. You don't have enough photos. You're going to have to say that you had a controlling boyfriend that didn't let you have a Facebook account. You're going to have to say you're still loading photos and that you haven't really been doing it that long. It will look like you've been doing it for a year. It will look like you're a loner.*' There was a gap and then Robbo said as a jokey 'aside' – '*Some things I haven't had to make up.*'

Ebony didn't take offence. She smiled to herself. Robbo was in his element. Ebony looked at the Facebook page he'd created for her.

There was the photo Carter had taken earlier. Ebony hated looking at herself but she had to admit it wasn't bad. Archie looked cute with his curls and dark eyes. She looked like a doting mum, squashing her face against his and looking gooily at the camera. There were others of Archie from when he was born to the present day.

'*Need some more photos of you, Ebb.*'

'*I have a few Tina took when we went away to Ireland in the summer.*'

'*Send them to me and I'll get the boffins to super-impose Archie into them.*'

Two hours later the profile was complete. Ebony was ready to try it out. She searched for Christian Goddard and sent a friend request and she contacted two of the women she'd met at lunch: Selena, with the curly hair and earrings and Sammy, the elfin-faced girl. She also did a search for Yan and sent him a friend request.

Yan came back to her first to accept her as a friend. She took a look at his profile. He had photos from all over the world. When he was in them at all, he was alone in them. Most of the pictures were of scenery and wildlife. No girlfriend in sight. Status – single. Ebony didn't know why but she was pleased to see that.

A message from Yan sprang up on her screen. *'How's it all going? Did you enjoy meeting the rest of the bunch?'*

'Yes I did thanks. Looks like it's going to be fun.'

They chatted for a while then Ebony had a notification that Christian had accepted her friend request and wanted to chat on Messenger. Ebony cut her conversation with Yan short.

An Instant Message came through from Christian. *'You got anything planned for this evening?'*

Robbo was watching the conversation.

'Accept the offer if he wants to meet up, Ebb.'

'Not much. Don't have Archie tonight as my aunt's got him, so just chilling.'

'Fancy meeting up?'

'Yes. Sure.' Ebony was thinking how much easier it was to meet men when you were pretending to be someone else. Ordinarily she'd have given up before she began. Making herself available and looking interested was a new thing for her. The few boyfriends she'd had were mostly policemen. She fell into dating

because she worked alongside them every day. She'd never had a one-night stand or been picked up in a bar.

She got ready. An hour later Ebony walked into the pub and saw two of the women from lunch: Selena was there with another woman who Ebony recognized from the college but couldn't remember her name. They waved her over.

Selena made room around the table for her. 'We thought we'd join you. Hope you don't mind? We usually end up seeing Christian here on a Thursday night when he doesn't have Elsie. He said you were on your way.'

Christian was at the bar. He waved at her and picked up a bottle of white wine as a question. She smiled back and nodded her reply as she sat down at the table.

'This is Julie.' Selena introduced her to the other woman. Julie was looking a little too glamorous for a pub setting, with false eyelashes and a spangly micro-dress. 'You remember her from lunchtime?'

'Yes. I remember seeing you there.' Ebony smiled at her. She didn't seem too smiley in return. 'We didn't get the chance say hello; it was all a bit hectic. Looks like you're both still in the party mood?'

'Just getting going,' laughed Selena. Julie's laugh was overly loud but her eyes were elsewhere. Ebony looked up to see what she was watching and she saw Christian approaching with the bottle of wine and two glasses.

'I thought you two could use your own glasses,' he said, setting the bottle down in front of Ebony and pulling up a chair near her. Selena flashed a disgruntled look towards Julie, who knocked back her wine and held her glass out for Christian to fill it. He poured out the contents of the bottle between them.

'You coming with us? We're off to a club down the road,' Selena said.

Christian looked across at Ebony. 'I'm happy here; but if you'd like to go?' Christian seemed nervous.

Ebony shook her head. 'To be honest it's been a busy day for me. I think a couple of glasses of wine is about my limit tonight.'

Julie smirked at Christian. 'Boring ... Well, Christian ... if you change your mind and fancy a late night you know where we are.' Ebony saw how Julie didn't take her eyes off Christian. He was the reason she'd dressed up tonight. Now she was satisfied, after taking a good look at Ebony, that she was no threat and hardly worth acknowledging, she could flirt if she felt inclined. Julie knocked back her drink and stood. Selena picked up her coat from the chair next to her.

'Nice to see you again, Ebony,' she said. 'See you tomorrow. Not too early. About eleven? May see you later then, Christian. You know where to find us. Usual place, be strutting our stuff till two and then who knows? The world is our oyster and thank God for babysitters.' Selena waited for Julie to get her coat on. Julie leaned very close down to Christian to whisper something in his ear and then they left. He looked as if he wanted to squirm but tried to cover it with a friendly smile.

After they'd left Christian turned to Ebony. 'I'm sorry about that.'

She shrugged. 'About what?' She looked like she didn't really understand what he was getting at.

'They're a couple of party animals. I bet they won't be alone long.'

Ebony frowned. 'Looked like Julie was hoping you'd be meeting up with her later.'

'Huh ...' he scoffed, embarrassed. 'She can hope all she likes.' Ebony smiled into her drink. 'Okay ... I admit it. We have a tiny bit of history, me and Julie.

Ebony's eyes opened wide. 'Really?'

'Yeah.' Christian laughed. 'No need to take the piss.'

She smiled.

'You've made a habit of dating the women on your course then?'

He shrugged and gave her a sideways glance, grinning. 'Seriously? What can I say? I'm in the market for a relationship.'

'You don't have any trouble finding them – obviously there are lots of willing victims?' He grinned but his eyes had turned hostile. Ebony tried one more push. She wanted to see what buttons he had and how much they took pushing. 'You are a grass greener type?'

He took a drink, his eyes fastened on hers as if he was trying to read her and the atmosphere became a little strained.

'I've had a few relationships along the way. Just not found the one I'm looking for yet but I don't believe in giving up.'

'What are you looking for?'

He shrugged irritably. 'Not looks.' He flashed her a

look which said *obviously*. 'It's about personality, compatibility, making each other laugh – great sex.' His eyes stayed on hers, they had softened again. Ebony blushed and looked away. Even though she was getting the attention by false means it didn't stop it feeling a bit too real. He smiled at her embarrassment. 'I have lots of boxes that need ticking – I have a kid, after all.'

'Is that why you choose single parents?'

'Whoa ...' he scowled – getting irritated. Ebony thought she'd pushed too hard.

'You make it sound like I prey on them.' He took a drink. 'Which, of course, I don't. I don't *just* date single parents. It just so happens that I'm at college with a lot of them.' He started playing with his beer mat, beginning to look over her shoulder and around the bar.

'Sorry, not my business.' She took a drink.

'Look – bottom line.' Christian smiled and nodded, relaxed. 'I date women on my course as well as others – it's no big deal. I have great respect for anyone who wants to change their life around.'

Ebony was nodding, thinking of what to say. Christian stared at his glass and flashed the odd glance towards Ebony to gauge her reaction.

'I never intended to split with Elsie's mum. It wasn't just up to me. I really tried to make it work. I know what it's like not to have a mum on the scene full time. My mother didn't exist for me. She went off to fuck her way around Europe. She left me in boarding school and when I got chucked out of there, I lived with my dad, who couldn't have cared less either.'

He paused; finished his drink and poured the rest of the bottle into his glass and then looked across at her and smiled.

'The college, the people on the courses, they are my friends. I get close to some of them and we end up having a bit of fun together – where's the harm in that? It's all fun. I don't usually have to justify myself this much?' He raised an eyebrow and gave her a cheeky smile.

Ebony turned away, smiling, but wondering whether she should ask him how he felt about breaking hearts that had already been broken in some cases, and preying on the vulnerable. But she resisted. She had to remember who she was supposed to be. She thought about the character traits that Hawk had exposed. Could Christian kill, torture? Could he hate women that much? Hawk was clever and manipulative. He had a warped sense of women and motherhood. Christian fitted the bill.

'How long have you been on the course?' she asked, leaving those thoughts for the moment. She felt as if she were floundering a little. She needed to give herself time to recover and get back into seduction mode.

'Seems like forever,' he answered, a little deflated, bored. 'I never seem to get to the end. I change my mind about what I want to do and then start in a new direction.'

Like you do with women, thought Ebony. 'Sounds expensive,' she said.

'It is. But I don't have many overheads and I'm lucky enough to be good at poker.' Ebony raised an eyebrow. 'I play it online. It fits into my lifestyle and

Elsie's. But it's a bit of a lonely existence.' He paused, played with his glass, looked at Ebony. She wondered if *I'm lonely* was one of his standard pick-up lines.

'What about Elsie's mum?' she asked.

'We share childcare. I have Elsie for half the week and every other weekend.'

'And normally you're out clubbing with Selena and Julie on your "other" weekend?'

'No ...' He laughed. 'I can see you've formed the wrong impression of me. I like to have fun now and again but Elsie is my life and everything I do is for her. I don't have time for much else. Yeah ... I went back to Julie's a couple of times and we had fun but she isn't my type and I'm not hers if she's honest. What about you? You're just starting dating again then?' She nodded.

'Yeah – it's scary but it feels right.'

'What made you call it a day with Archie's dad?'

'He was abusive. He was in trouble in Jamaica. He was controlling. He got nasty with me. I just decided I didn't want to live my life bullied. Archie needed me to be strong.'

'You seem like the naturally strong type to me. Can't imagine you put up with much shit.' He was staring straight at her. Ebony thought she'd been doing well up till then. She needed to dig deep inside her past to come up with what it felt like to take abuse. She didn't have to search her memory for long before she was back, cornered by her mum, by the bullies in the care home and the staff who were cruel, taking the pain; blaming herself for not stepping out of the way quick enough. Blaming herself for leaving

it just that one second too late to run away. The less
she struggled the sooner it would be over. The care
home could be very tough. She'd been in three different ones altogether. In between that she was with
foster carers or back with her mother. Anywhere
Ebony looked there was trouble of one kind or
another. The only respite she ever had was when she
went to a foster couple called the Bennets; they had
grown-up kids. They spent their lives giving tempo-
rary homes to kids like Ebony. The one thing Ebony
always knew was that she wasn't unique. There were
thousands of kids like her in the UK. The day when
she had to leave the Bennets was a sad one but she
swallowed the sadness and she didn't cry. It felt like
one more kick in the stomach. Then she turned up in
the home and things were bad, worse than they'd ever
been, until Micky came along.

'I learnt to take it,' she said to Christian.

'Sorry. I didn't mean to make you so sad. I can see
how much it still affects you.' He put his hand on
hers. She looked at it. Was it a hand that strangled?
They were strong hands and they felt rough. Not
poker player's soft hands. He saw her hesitate.
'Sorry – rough hands. Been making Elsie a dolls house
for Christmas.'

'Ahhh.' Ebony said responding as required. She
turned his hand over and saw the ring of a blister. 'Is
that a burn?'

'Yes.' He withdrew his hand. 'The things you do for
love, huh? That was welding the tiny iron railing for
the front of the house. Did you decide enough was
enough with your ex? Thought you could do better?'

He tilted his head back as if studying her. She nodded and he sat back and continued staring at her, his arms folded across his chest. 'You're a strange one, if I'm honest. You're not what I expected. Maybe it's because you have spent your adult years living abroad, you just don't seem to fit here, that's all. You are a hard person to get close to, but a nut worth cracking, I think.' He smiled. 'If you'll let me?'

Ebony smiled. He leant across the table and kissed her softly on the lips. Ebony resisted the urge to shudder. Something about Christian made her worry about what she was going to catch, even when he touched her hand. She pretended to look away bashfully as she took a drink of wine to wash it away.

At the end of the evening Ebony left Christian with another kiss at the Underground and made sure she wasn't followed as she got off the Tube at the next stop and onto a bus. She walked the few minutes to her estate. Already she was beginning to feel more at home in the vertical village. The bangs and shouts of people on the landings and stairs echoed as she climbed the flights to her floor. She passed the groups of kids on the way up on the stairwell. Back inside the flat she rang Carter.

'How did your cover hold up?'

'Not bad. Christian senses I don't quite fit but thinks it's because of my life in Jamaica. He's watching me. I'm the new girl to conquer.'

'You're finding it easy to keep in character?'

'It's not perfect but it's getting easier. The accent is not a problem, doesn't have to be that broad, but I worry that I'm not hitting the nail on the head with some aspects of parenting.'

'Remember, keep talking about your baby.'

'Yeah, but these women are in college to get some identity back. They don't spend all night talking about their babies; they want a life beyond motherhood.'

'You've got to know some of them?'

'Yeah – a couple. It's all a bit of a cliquey inner group in the college.

'Alarm bells ringing?'

'Plenty. He's not someone I'd choose to spend time with.'

'Did you get to talk to any of his conquests? We need to know what he's capable of when he lets his guard down.'

'Lots of them fancy Christian. It's cut-throat between them. I'm definitely considered a target both by him and by the women he's had flings with.'

'What kind of man is he?'

'Ruthless. Selfish. He sees himself as a saviour to single parents, giving them a bit of excitement in their lives – that's what he says. Doesn't for one minute feel remorse for the trail of broken hearts he's left. He just shouts *NEXT*. And someone always steps up to take the bait. Women do seem to like him. He's a charmer, easily bored. He's devoted to his little girl, or so he says. Could be just another ploy to pick up women.'

'Any mention of having tried a bit of weird sex stuff like asphyxiation on any of them?'

'Give me chance, it's not the kind of question that rolls off the tongue. I'm trying to meet up with a couple of the women on their own, get them really talking. There's a coffee tomorrow morning with Selena, the one helping me catch up on my course. What's the plan about interviewing college friends regarding Emily Styles' death and Danielle's disappearance? If Christian is Hawk he will be expecting it. He'll know we've made the connection to the college. It won't seem right if no one comes to interview.'

'Yes, but not too soon. I can't risk scaring him off. I'll contact the college tomorrow and ask for names and addresses of their friends on the list. Who's the one to talk to there?'

'Yan Stevenson. He's the one they all seem to connect with.'

'Okay. Good work, Ebb. Glad you're back in the flat. How's pretend Archie?'

Ebony rolled her eyes. 'You're such a slushy bloke, Guv. Archie Two is not as cute as the real one but he smells a lot better.'

Carter laughed.

Chapter 37

The Heath was still dark at seven a.m. the next morning. There was a dampness in the air and the snow was patchy on the grass. Janet was out jogging. She hadn't been to the Heath since the morning she'd found the body. She kept to the paths. She would never get over the sight of the dead woman in the copse but she had to try and get her life back. She passed another jogger, didn't recognize him. His woolly hat was pulled down over his ears. *Good body* thought Janet. She couldn't see the face properly. His eyes met hers and she smiled. He looked about to speak but then jogged on. She began thinking about a route where she might bump into him again.

Hawk ran around the corner and up over the brow of the hill, then he veered left along a side path that he knew would take him down to the pond. He knew every inch of the Heath. He ran on the spot and waited until he heard the jogger's feet on the path, coming his way, then he ran into her path and, just before he reached her, he tripped and landed on his hands and knees. He laughed, embarrassed.

'Are you okay?'

He heard the feminine voice and felt warm breath on his face as she bent over him. He felt her body next to his and her hand on his back. He got onto one knee, shaking his head and smiling. Halfway up, level with her, he grabbed her and smothered her mouth with his hand as he dragged her back into the bushes. He took out the flask from his pocket and poured petrol over her head and shoulders.

Janet heard the screams. She looked up towards the brow of the hill and she saw a raging flame light up the sky.

Tracy was giving Jackson his breakfast when the phone rang.

Back in his office Robbo was waiting for her to answer it. He, too, was surprised at the early morning call.

'Morning, Tracy.' Hawk's familiar deep voice rolled out.

Tracy didn't answer him.

'Morning, police team listening in.'

Robbo held up his hand for Pam to stop typing so that he could listen better.

'Bowie, Carter, Vincent? Who else? The press conference was interesting. I know you're full of tricks. But you'll have to get up early to catch me out. Some of us have already been out jogging this morning. I'm getting bored with always being one step ahead of you imbeciles. But, I intend to take another victim. This last one I take will be my *pièce de résistance*.

Every drop of pain will be extracted. This one will be written in the history books and you'll remember it personally, Mr Robinson.

'You have the power – you said to me, Tracy. Yes I have. I can choose who lives and dies. You have disappointed me Tracy. You've caused me to become a little hasty. I will not be rushed. This is my game and my rules. But you have entered my game from the sidelines. You have become part of the play. I now control you just as I do your daughter. I have your life in my hands. I can kill you when I choose.'

Tracy dropped the phone.

Robbo didn't move. The office was silent.

Ebony fired up the laptop and made herself breakfast of a Pot Noodle. Robbo was waiting for her. She sat on her sleeping bag and opened her laptop.

'How's it going, Ebb?' Robbo's face was in the corner of her screen.

'Good, thanks,' she said between mouthfuls.

'I see you're keeping up your healthy eating regime?'

'Yep.' She lifted up the pot towards the webcam at the top of her screen and tipped the last of it into her mouth.

He watched her flip open the top on a can of Coke; she crossed her legs and frowned at the screen as she read her messages.

'You looking at your Facebook?' asked Robbo. He pushed down the plunger in his cafetière.

'Yeah. I can't believe how some people's whole life is on Facebook.'

'If you really were a single parent living in that

high-rise hell, you'd thank the heavens for Facebook,' he said.

'Yeah, you're absolutely right. I couldn't have made this many contacts on the courses this quickly without it.'

'Right. Today I've sent your friend requests out to thirty more people who are connected with the course. I've seen a lot of photos of Christian on other people's pages. He seems to be the male student everyone has a photo with.'

'Yes,' agreed Ebony. 'Although on his own pages most of his pictures are with his daughter.'

'Although he does have pictures on his page of him with Emily Styles and Danielle Foster – he's there in photos even if there are no obvious couple shots. Do you know much about the way he lives? Does he go to the gym?'

'Yeah – he runs. I know because he told me. He also told me he makes a good living from playing online poker.'

'Entrepreneurial,' said Robbo, drinking his coffee. 'I've checked him out. He travelled a lot at one time. He ran a bar in Thailand; he's been a roadie for a rock band. Before he came to North London five years ago, he was the manager of an online exotic pets store based in Brighton.'

Robbo sat back in his chair and looked at her.

'Do you think you're getting anywhere with him, Ebb?'

Ebony took a drink of Coke and thought before she answered.

'Yes. I think he goes for the new girl every time.

I just happen to be that. I don't think it's hard to get somewhere with Christian. I talked to one of the girls that knows him well but I need to talk to one of his exes to find out what he's really about.'

'Keep vigilant Ebb. Keep your wits about you. Never relax. Never presume it's safe.'

'Of course.'

Robbo came off the phone and opened a new pack of Haribo's. He pulled out the jelly rings and lined them up on the top of his keyboard. He thought about what was best for Ebony now and the job she had to do. From now on he wouldn't share all the information with her.

Carter came into Robbo's office.

'Did you hear the phone call?'

Robbo nodded. 'Did you listen to it?'

'Yeah, and earlier this morning a woman was attacked, petrol thrown in her face and she was set alight – it happened fifty metres from the spot where we found Pauline Murphy. It's got to be Hawk, he spelt it out for us,' said Carter. 'He said he's been jogging.'

'Did anyone see him? Did we get a description?' Robbo asked.

'Not from the woman who was attacked. She never saw his face. No one else has come forward. What's he doing, Robbo?'

'He's showing us he's all-powerful.'

Carter hung his coat on the hanger by Pam's desk and loosened his tie. 'It's almost like he's a bit bored and wants to see how much trouble he can cause.

And, Robbo? He mentioned us by name in the call.'

'Yes ... he saw you at the press conference. He could have found me as the crime analyst assigned to MIT 17.'

'He could have and he did. He randomly sets fire to two people and he promises a *pièce de résistance*. He's escalating till even he can't control it,' Carter said.

'We need to concentrate and stay calm and focused with this. Our panic will feed his ego. I've decided it's better we don't tell Ebony any more than necessary.' Carter was nodding in agreement. 'We need her in there more than ever but we don't need her to be scared witless.'

'I agree. But I wish I'd never said yes to her going undercover.'

'We have to bring this to an end fast. This is the only way now. Ebony has to make it work. Everything we can do to help her is vital.'

Carter looked up as Jeanie came in the office. She had heard the news.

'You all right, Jeanie?'

'Yep – let's get on with it and catch this bastard.'

'Christian Goddard.' Robbo turned the screen to show what he was looking at to Jeanie.

'Alias Mr "I have a passion in my pants and I'm not afraid to show it". He must consider it his best feature; he's obviously keen on showing it off. He sent this picture to Ebony. We just got hold of his phone records. He had some recent conversations with Danielle Foster. It looks like she phoned him on the day she went missing.'

'Who else did she phone?'

'A number that isn't registered and it's out of service now.'

He turned the screen so Carter could see the photo. 'That puny thing?'

Carter winked at Pam, who hid a smile as she turned and busied herself at her desk.

'Must be,' answered Robbo. 'Because he sends this and another twenty or so pictures just like it to all the women he knows. He texts pure filth to just about anyone. Goes way beyond sexting.'

'Interesting,' said Carter. 'Does he get it back?'

'Yeah, he does. A lot of the time anyway. Danielle was pretty good at it actually. Before her, Emily could have knocked Fifty Shades of Grey right off the top off the bestseller list. She wrote whole scenarios. Very talented,' said Robbo.

'Any of the texts get into violent stuff?'

'No. Some smacking, bondage, humiliation. But no violence.'

'There's some things don't translate well into text speak,' said Jeanie.

'So – do we think he's capable of more?' asked Carter.

'Narcissistic, sex addict. Anyone who thinks only of themselves is capable of seeing things very differently to the rest of us,' answered Pam as she looked over her bifocals at Carter. Carter looked back in mock offence.

'Huh ...?' said Jeanie, shaking her head as she caught the conversation. 'Narcissistic sex addict – got you down to a T, Carter.'

'Very funny. What do we know about Goddard's background?' he asked.

Pam went back behind her desk and clicked onto her screen.

'Christian Goddard: aged thirty-three.'

'So he's older than he looks?' said Jeanie. 'And he's dating much younger women.'

'Yeah, but they're not teenagers,' Carter chipped in. Jeanie gave him a semi-hostile look.

'What? What is it with the women in this room and me?' Carter lifted his left hand. 'I am innocent till proven guilty.'

Jeanie turned her attention to Pam and ignored Carter's theatrics.

'What have you found out?'

'He dates all ages,' said Pam. 'According to his text messages he's even had a few flings with the older members of staff in the college and two receptionists.'

Robbo had been waiting to speak. He sat back and rocked in his chair as he lined up the Haribo jelly men in a row.

'He may not like himself or others, especially women,' he said. 'But he is a man who sees through people. I think, somewhere along the way, he's had his trust broken. Someone's let him down badly so he puts on a front to the world, that's why he can look behind other people's masks. That's the kind of partner he craves, someone who is as deep and complicated as himself. He wants them but, at the same time, he wants to destroy them.'

'You get all that from looking at a photo of his cock?' asked Carter, shaking his head and rolling his eyes.

'He preys on the most vulnerable: women who have

a history. They've been hurt, messed about, often suffered physical abuse, and he understands that enough to entice them in. He knows what they're looking for and he gives them just enough to con them into trusting him.'

Carter and Jeanie left Robbo's office together.

'I have to go and see Tracy.' Jeanie wanted to go. She had stood too close to Carter for too long. It was beginning to feel like they were a couple again. 'See you later, Dan,' she shouted back over her shoulder as she left him in the corridor outside Robbo's office.

'Wait. How's it going apart from the phone calls?'

'It's getting fraught. She's not Superwoman. I want her husband to come back home to support her now. Security-wise I think it makes sense. I don't know what you think about that?'

Carter was nodding. His eyes were soft as he stared at her. Jeanie realized he hadn't added anything to the conversation.

'Dan, are you listening to me?'

He shook his head. 'Sorry.' Carter turned on his heels and walked away down the corridor. 'Leaving the Dark Side for half an hour – I need air.'

Chapter 38

After Breakfast Ebony pushed pretend Archie to the shops on the edge of the estate as soon as the kids had gone to school and the estate had calmed. She made sure the doll's face was hidden. If anyone asked she was going to say the baby had chicken pox. She spent an hour on Facebook when she got back. She confirmed Selena's invitation for coffee – it was changed to one instead of eleven. As she was about to sign off Yan came on line.

'How's things? How's it going with the form? Need any help?'

'I do. Can you spare the time? It would be great just to chat through my options'.

'Options are my speciality. What about coffee this afternoon at three in the café opposite the college?'

'Sounds good. I appreciate it. Thanks.'

Ebony signed off with a smiley face :-) She heard a message come through on her phone.

Yan added: *'I have texted you my number in case you change your mind.'*

Ebony picked up her phone from the floor beside

her and read the message. She was just wondering how he got her number.

In case you're wondering – I got your number from the forms you filled in ;-)

Ebony texted back: *'See you at 3.'* She sat looking at her phone. Interesting, she thought, unprofessional, even to take her number. She hadn't expected that.

'Nice place,' said Ebony as Selena opened the door to her.

'Thanks. Come in. Glad you could make it. How's Archie?'

'He'll be okay, thanks.'

'Been here long?' Ebony asked as she went inside.

'About a year.'

Ebony followed Selena through the flat to the kitchen at the back of the house. She walked straight over to the window, which overlooked a small garden with a kid's swing and a bike.

'It's a bit overgrown,' said Selena. 'I'm going to tackle it by the time spring comes.'

'It looks great – loads of potential. It's just great to have a garden.'

'Yeah, I feel lucky. I'm sorry it's a bit cold though. I can't afford to have the heating on when I'm here alone.'

'Of course. It's the same as my place. I don't mind the cold.'

'I thought you'd really feel it coming from Jamaica?'

'Yeah . . .' *Shit*, thought Ebony. She'd let her guard down. 'Surprising how quickly you can adapt to a climate.'

'Do you miss it?'

Ebony nodded, shrugged. 'Yeah, but I'm better off here.'

'Because of Archie's dad?'

'Yeah, Archie's dad. Plus, this is my home. I was here till I was twelve. It always felt like home. After I had Archie I felt the urge to come back – the homing instinct.' She remembered what Jeanie had said about wanting to go home when she had Christa.

'Did you grow up in London?'

Ebony relaxed a little. Now that conversation had returned to London she could use her own life as a reference point. She only had to be truthful.

'Here, there, everywhere. I was in foster homes and kids' homes in between going back to my mum but she moved all over London. I spent more time away from her than with her.'

Selena was filling the kettle. She turned and smiled at Ebony.

'I'm sorry. It must have been really tough.'

Ebony shrugged. 'Some times were worse than others.'

'You must have really missed your mum.'

Ebony didn't answer. She'd already said more than she'd ever usually tell anyone, and to a complete stranger. What was it about being undercover that meant she was beginning to open up about her own life like that? Did it feel safer because it was like playing someone else, even when she was telling the truth? 'What about you? Are you from London?'

Selena shook her head. 'I'm originally from Bristol. I came up here to work in a graphic design studio in Islington. I did a degree in it, and then I got pregnant. I decided to keep the baby. I am retraining now. I miss the money I used to earn and the social life I had; but it was all worth it. She's called Imogen.'

'I saw her photos on Facebook – she's so cute.'

'Yeah, I think so. Tea?'

'Yes, please. Milk, two sugars.'

'You don't have many photos of you and Archie on your Facebook page?'

'I'm just loading them. I haven't been doing it for long. Social media wasn't so popular in Jamaica.'

'Oh, of course. Yeah, it's quite time-consuming to start a new account and load everything on.'

Ebony looked about her at all Imogen's drawings and toys everywhere. Selena caught her looking.

'Yeah – sorry about the mess. Imogen has taken over my life really. I try and keep a balance but she's everything to me. Must be difficult for you, twice as precious, having Archie when your own childhood was difficult? Did you ever think that you'd do it? Considering your past?'

Ebony nodded. 'I wondered if I'd be a good mother.'

'I can see you are. You were lovely with him when I saw you together. It's a shame he's poorly. Lucky you have a babysitter.'

'Yes. My aunt lives in London. I've roped her in to help.'

'Ideal. Leaves you free to date?'

Selena grinned. She sat opposite Ebony at the kitchen table. 'What's happening with you and

Christian? I thought you might have gone for Yan – the nerdy quiet type – still waters and all that. But which would you say is more your type?'

Ebony shook her head, embarrassed, and tried not to smile. 'Christian tries it on, doesn't he? I'm the new girl. But seriously? We're just friends. What do you think of Yan?'

'Complicated. Deep. He gives so much then he backs off. He seems to be always looking for something, someone. He looks like a sweet-natured nerd but he must have seen and done a lot; he's been all over the world with his hippy mum.'

'Did he tell you about that?'

'He doesn't seem keen to talk in depth. He's really kind to me, comes over and puts up shelves for me, that kind of thing.' Ebony was sure she detected a flush coming to Selena's face. 'Christian and him have an odd friendship where you think Yan is always cleaning up Christian's mess. Kind of like Christian is his wayward brother. They even look alike sometimes – wear the same type of things.'

'They that close?'

She shrugged.

'No, not really. They know each other well. They maybe tolerate one another; they have to – I suppose; they hang about with the same people a lot of the time. I'm not sure what else Yan does when he's not working or helping out. In many ways he's quite a private person.'

'What about girlfriends?

'Yan? Never seen any. He gets close to people. Christian pinches them.'

'Did he pinch you?' Ebony watched Selena's reaction over her mug of tea.

A grin spread across Selena's face. 'Oh, so you were more than friends?' said Ebony.

'We thought about it.' Selena gave Ebony a look that said *that's all you're getting for now.* 'How did it go last night?' she asked.

'I was home by ten.'

Selena looked surprised. 'That was fast work even by Christian's standards – back to yours for an early night, hey?'

'No. No.' Ebony laughed. 'Absolutely not.' But Selena gave her a knowing look.

'That's what they all say, but he usually gets what he wants. Christian fancies himself more than he'll ever fancy anyone else. He has women fawning over him all the time. He's never going to settle for just one.'

'Have you dated him, Selena?'

'Me? No way. He's not my type. We had a snog last Christmas, when I was drunk, but that was it. He got pushy. I had to tell him to back off. He sent me filthy texts for weeks. I got sick of it. Every time I opened the phone there was another dirty message. Plus, he went further, videoing himself masturbating. Really yuck.'

'Gross! He looks like he could be into all sorts.'

'Oh yeah, that was another thing: did I have a girlfriend that we could have a threesome with? You know – the usual.'

Ebony tutted. 'Did anyone else ever say he tried something weird with them?' she asked.

'Like what?'

'I don't know, something they didn't like, dangerous maybe? It's just that, well … you think he has a temper? I know what that's like. I had enough of that with Archie's dad.'

'Oh yes. He definitely has a nasty streak if he doesn't get his own way. He's just a big baby really. He doesn't get what he wants he stamps his foot till he does. He uses the fact he has a child to score with women. The only time he pushes the buggy is when he sees a good-looking woman in the park. I met his ex once, she looked really harassed by him. I reckon he's been a wife-beater in his time.'

'Julie's dated him, hasn't she?'

'Yes, well she likes to think so – it was two nights at best, hardly dating. She's really pissed off that he's made a move on you.'

'Do you think she really likes him?'

'Julie always goes for the bad ones. She's been beaten up by most of the boyfriends she's had. Seriously, Ebony; I'm not just saying it to put you off him – he'll bring you nothing but trouble.'

Ebony left Selena's house and walked down to meet Yan in the café near the college as arranged. She was early. She ordered a coffee and looked at his Facebook page whilst she waited. He was everything she wasn't: adventurous and daring. He'd swum with dolphins, gone into bat caves, he'd ridden on elephants in Thailand. Ebony realized she was slightly in awe of him and his free spirit. All her life she'd felt a massive weight of responsibility and never once had she been able to say she was carefree. She was beginning to regret that this was just an operation; that at the end of her time undercover she would not see him again. She wondered if he might still want to be friends after it was all over – maybe more than friends.

Tina called Ebony on her personal phone as she waited for Yan in the café opposite the college.

'Hey, Teen.'

'You all right, Ebb?'

'Not bad.'

'Really? The course you're on, the accommodation? The hotel is shite, isn't it? I can tell it in your voice. You sound tense.'

'It's not meant to be a picnic. I'm fine, honestly, Teen. Busy, that's all. Anyway it has its plus side.'

'What? Tell me. Ebony Willis, have you met a man out there?'

'No. No way.'

'OMG, you have. I can hear it in your voice. You're lining up some nooky.'

'Tina, pack it in. Just work, that's all. I'm feeling good about it – positive.'

'Hmmmm, well, nothing's happening here. The house is still standing. My brother Dermot's talking about staying for New Year's now when he comes. I suppose that's okay?'

'Sounds great. Not sure whether I'll be working or not – I said I would. You can share with me and Dermot can have your room.' There was a silence. Ebony could hear Tina thinking.

'Head up, Ebb. Christmas is coming. We're going to have a blast.'

'Can't wait, Teen. Better go now.' She spotted Yan

in his three-quarter-length overcoat which was turned up at the collar. He waved to her then tucked his head down against the cold. She watched him walk towards the café.

'Ebb ... you keep safe. Love you, mate.'

'And you, Teen.'

Ebony closed her phone and pushed it to the bottom of her bag.

'How's it going?' Yan said as he walked in, smiling bashfully.

'Going well, thanks. Thanks for agreeing to meet.'

'It's a pleasure.' He hesitated before he sat down, looked around as if expecting to see something. 'Is my coffee on the way?' Ebony shook her head confused. 'Don't worry. I just texted you about getting me a coffee, that's all.'

'Oh sorry. Let me order one for you.'

'Don't worry, I'll get it. You were busy talking on the phone; I expect the message will come through eventually. It'll be in a few hours and it'll say please get me a mocha latte with extra sprinkles.'

'Really sorry.'

'No probs. Do you want anything?' She shook her head. Yan went and got a drink and brought it back to the table.

'How's it been going with you?' he asked. 'I see you've mastered Facebook. You seem to be always on there.'

'Do I? God, I'm addicted already. I suppose it's because it's on my phone, makes it easier.'

'It does everything but give you my texts. Sorry – only joking.'

She laughed. 'Are you getting ready for the Christmas break? Does the college close?'

'We close for two weeks.' He smiled but Ebony could see he was bothered by something. He looked nervous.

'Sorry I couldn't join you yesterday evening,' he said. His eyes fixed on hers, watching her every expression. 'Did you have fun?' His face betrayed the fact he was pretty sure Christian had made a pass.

'Yes.' Ebony smiled and gave him a sideways glance as she sipped her coffee. 'We just had a drink or two. We met up with a couple of women from the college: Selena and Julie?'

'Christian's exes.'

'Selena gave me coffee at her place earlier and she had quite a bit to say about you and Christian.'

'Me?'

'Actually, mainly about Christian. He seems to have quite a reputation. She thinks highly of you.' Ebony watched and waited as Yan took his coat off and hung it on the back of his chair. It was expensive, Urban Outfitters. Must have been at least three hundred quid, thought Ebony. Jeanie had shown her some things from there and then decided that someone on Ebony Wilson's supposed budget wouldn't be able to afford them. 'Has he dated a lot of women on the course?'

Yan paused, turned his eyes skyward as he thought about the question.

'A fair few over the couple of years I've known him. Not Selena though; she's one of a rare breed.'

'Doesn't he have any competition? He can't be the only single dad at uni?'

'He's the one that does the socializing and organizes things via social network sites. He makes an effort. You must have noticed.' She sipped her coffee and watched him sip his. He had a plaster on his hand and she clocked dirt beneath his nails.

'What happened?' Ebony could see the plaster peeling, two puncture wounds beneath it. 'Looks nasty.'

'Don't worry, I've had my tetanus booster – staple gun; been doing some DIY for a friend.' He looked sheepish. Ebony shook her head. Inside, her stomach flipped a little as she wondered whether Selena had really wanted to know about any designs Ebony might have had on Yan rather than Christian. Had Ebony missed the point? It wouldn't be the first time. She was rubbish at judging things like that. Christ, how did she ever expect to be a good detective when a whole part of her knowledge of life was missing? She could read a zillion books on how people behave but she couldn't tell what it really added up to. She couldn't put it into practice.

'Does she always call you to help with her DIY?' He looked surprised at the question and gave her a smile.

'Me? No. I'm far too busy. Plus I'm not boyfriend material for her. I'm not ready for fatherhood. There's a lot of the world I still want to see.'

'You don't want any responsibilities?'

He shook his head. 'Why would I? Way too imma-ture. I want to spend my money on myself.'

She smiled. 'I noticed the coat – very nice.'

He looked like he'd been caught out.

'Yeah – I'm lucky. I don't have to worry too much. I got left a house. I rent out a couple of rooms in it to pay the bills.' He looked apologetic. 'You've had it tough, I take it? Difficult childhood?' His eyes had hardened slightly, as if he'd heard it all before and was hoping for something different from her.

She smiled, shrugged. 'It's all comparative, isn't it? If I was a child growing up in Sierra Leone I'd think my childhood over here was a piece of cake. But – yeah – it wasn't ideal.'

He looked at her curiously; his smile was back. His eyes were focused on her and affectionate.

'It's how things affect you personally, isn't it?' he said. She nodded. 'And ... it looks like it didn't do you any harm. You're doing the best you can for Archie.' He looked around. 'Where is Archie?'

'My aunt's looking after him for me. He's got chicken pox.'

'Un-lucky. Does she live far from you?'

'Not far.'

'Will you be able to get out again? It's just that there's another really nice group who you didn't meet and they're meeting up tomorrow evening for a Christmas drink if that's any good for you? It will start at the Pear and Peach on Upper Street. Saturday nights are always quite lively in there. Could be fun.'

'Yeah. I should be able to get out. Shall I let you know on Facebook?'

'Or text me. I don't really like spending hours on Facebook. I've got better things to do with my time.'

'I know what you mean. I'll message you,' Ebony answered.

'I better get back to work now.' He looked at his watch. 'Coffee break is over.'

'Of course. Thanks for meeting me.'

'Not at all. I'm glad you're going to be around next year. Should be fun.' Ebony watched him as he struggled to say something. 'You know, I didn't mean I wouldn't date someone with a child. I just meant ... well ...' He shrugged. 'You know?' She nodded. 'I'd like to ask you out. I'm into opera – don't laugh ... or we could take in the ballet if you'd like? The Nutcracker is on at Sadler's Wells?'

'You picked the only one I know! I'd love to, Yan, but I can't at the moment.' She shook her head. 'I'm sorry.' She could see it had taken a lot of guts to ask her out. 'Could I get a rain check on it?'

He smiled, embarrassed, and disappointed.

'Of course. I understand. Christian seems to get all the women.' He has a right to be pissed off, thought Ebony. 'Be careful of him, if you know what I mean,' Yan added. 'I'd hate it to put you off coming on to the course – you know, if things went badly?'

She nodded. 'Point taken. Just friends. I'm not going to hurry into anything.'

'Yeah – wise choice to stay friends. His girlfriends have a habit of disappearing from the course and one of them was in the news recently – Emily Styles?' Ebony felt a surge of adrenalin but tried not to show it. She frowned and played with her coffee cup.

'Yeah, well, it was so sad. I wondered what happened to Emily. I thought she'd just dropped off the planet.' Yan was putting his coat and scarf on. 'She turned up in Regent's Canal. Such a shock. I wonder where she's been all that time. Her Facebook page is open. People have posted things on there. We all thought she'd just had enough after it didn't work out with Christian but all that time she was in real trouble.'

'That's really terrible. Did you know her well?'

Ebony knew that Yan was in group photos with Emily.

'Yeah, I saw her all the time, at social events. Lovely girl. She was a bit mad and a lot of fun. But not my type.' He blushed.

Back at the flat Ebony skyped Robbo. Ebony thought how tired he looked.

'Phone records are in,' he said. 'Christian Goddard seems to be the common denominator with our victims. On all of their Facebook pages.'

'Has anyone posted anything new on Emily Styles' page since the news broke about her death?'

'Yes, there are over twenty messages. Just basic RIP ones.'

'Did Christian post?'

'No. Yan did, though. How did coffee go?'

'It went okay. He seems to have a low opinion of Christian Goddard.'

'That's a male ploy to big himself up in your eyes. Men always slag one another off to women. We're like builders. We always blame the last man on the job. I am getting your GPS signal by the way.'

'My pendant?'

'Yes. And the transmitter in your shoe.'

'So you heard the conversation anyway. Why did you ask about it then?'

'I didn't want to appear rude.' She smiled to herself and rolled her eyes. 'You're doing a damn good job, Ebb. Keep it up.'

'I'd rather be back in Fletcher House in my comfort zone.'

'You're doing a great job and you've responded really well to everything. You are the one who has a real hope of finding Danielle in time.'

'I understand, Robbo. I'm going to do everything I can. I met one of Christian's conquests yesterday evening – Julie. I think she'd open up to me.'

'Julie Lynton, friends with Selena Tibbs? I see they're friends on Facebook. Yes, she confirmed your friend request.'

'I'll see if she's on chat.'

'Yes she is. IM her. Instant Messenger is definitely the safest way to ask sensitive questions. Any direct messages might be read if you're hacked into. Facebook hang on to data, even deleted messages sometimes. They've had criticism for it in the past. You ready? I'll chip in if I think it's helpful.'

'Okay.' Ebony typed a message in the chat box:

'*Hi Julie, any hangover?*'

'*Not too bad. What about you?*

'*No. I had an early night.*'

'*Are you coming out tomorrow night?*'

'*To the Pear and Peach?*'

'*Yes.*'

'*I think so – finding out about a babysitter.*'

'*Who else is going, do you know?*'

'*Not sure, sorry. Yan told me about it.*'

'*Christian?*'

'*Don't know. Is there a thing between u 2?*'

'*Sort of.*'

'*Oh. Didn't know, sorry.*'

'*Don't worry. Don't think you're his type.*'

Ebony smiled to herself. She knew Robbo would be hiding a smile behind a coffee mug.

'*What about Danielle Foster, people say they are seeing one another? Do you know her? I haven't met her.*'

'*I heard her name mentioned in connection with his. They def were not together. I haven't seen her for a week or two. Who knows? Maybe she's seeing someone else? She missed her classes.*'

'*You care about Christian?*'

'*Not care as in love. Just think we're good together.*'

'*A player isn't he?*'

'*Yeah – bad boy – always fall for them. LOL. He isn't really that bad. He's a really nice guy underneath.*'

'*Have you spent some time with him? Been to his house?*'

'*He came to mine.*'

'*Why didn't he take it further?*'

'*He hasn't yet.*'

Ebony could see Robbo on webcam giving her the 'wind it up' sign. He was telling her that Julie was going to take more time to loosen up. Christian had just come on as available to chat.

'*Got to go now, Julie, Archie's crying. Glad we had a chat.*'

'*And me*'.

Christian was waiting to talk to her.

'*You going out tonight?*'

'*Yes. Joining Yan and a few others at the Pear and Peach on Holloway Road. Are you coming?*'

'*Yeah. I'll be there. How's Archie? I heard he had chicken pox.*'

Yep, thought Ebony, that's the power of social media – word gets around.

'*Who told you that?*'

'*Yan. He also said to leave you alone. LOL he wants you for himself. Take a photo of Archie's spots. I want to see if it's as bad as when Elsie got it.*'

'*Okay – will do.*'

Ebony was trying to work out if she could get Tina to paint some spots on Archie's face when she babysat.

'*Christian, can I ask you something?*'

'*Ask away.*'

'*Are you seeing anyone at the moment?*'

'*Nope. I'm young free and definitely single.*'

'*Yan mentioned you were seeing someone on the course named Danielle?*'

'*Danielle who?*'

'*Very funny – the Danielle who's with you in several photos.*'

'*You've been checking up on me? ;-)*'

'*Not checking, just making sure I know what I'm dealing with. Julie has already staked her claim on you. I don't want to be in a queue.*'

'*No queue. Julie is a bit of a bunny boiler.*'

'*She knew about Danielle.*'

'*Yeah. I know who you mean but Danielle wasn't my type.*'

Ebony looked across at Robbo on the webcam. 'I noticed he said "wasn't?"' she said to him.

'Yes interesting,' he replied. 'Let me take over the typing for a minute.'

'*So you haven't seen her?*' Robbo typed.

'*No. I told you. She's dropped out of the course. I think she's left. She's a nice girl but not my type.*'

'*Do you have a type?*'

'*I like dusky maidens with deadpan expressions who look like they trust no one.*'

'*Can't be many of those around.*'

'*LOL, tell you what. I'll be happy to give my medical opinion about Archie. I make home visits. What's your mobile number?*'

Robbo signalled to Ebony to take over again. She typed in her number and then finished the conversation with Christian.

'What do you think?' she asked, looking back at Robbo on the webcam.

'Yeah, he described you quite well. He is bright. Astute. He's definitely keen. You have to keep it on the simmer, Ebb. There must be no sign of entrapment. Not that I think you'd allow it to go too far anyway.'

'Absolutely no chance of that. He makes me feel slightly queasy when he comes near me.'

'Does he make you feel scared?'

'Not so much. But he's good at this part – the chase.'

'Yes. I guess if he is Hawk, he probably has this part

of the game off to a tee.' Ebony's other phone rang from her bag across the room. 'You answer that. I'll take over for you,' Robbo said, as Ebony got up to answer the call.

It was from the institution where her mother was being held. Ebony listened to the member of staff telling her that she needed to visit more often and that her mother had started self-harming.

Whilst Ebony was on the phone Yan came on to IM and wrote Ebony a note.

'Still coming tomorrow night? How's Archie?'

Robbo answered for her.

'Archie's not as bad as he could be – a bit miz, but I'll make it tomorrow – you had a good day? You been talking to Christian about me?

'Just general chitchat. He's interested if you are!!! You and Christian? I said he had no chance; he seems to think otherwise. Which is it?'

'Maybe,' replied Robbo.

There was a longish gap with no reply.

'Who'd have thought it?

Ebony finished her phonecall and came back over to her laptop as Yan replied: *'Shame.'* And signed off.

Ebony looked at the screen and what Robbo had written.

Bugger, she thought. She knew Yan would wonder why she said that. Maybe he'd question whether he'd understood her at all. She was just as shallow as all the others then.

Robbo watched her reaction: he saw her face drop as she stared at the screen and what he'd written.

'You understand what's at stake here, Ebb? I've sent

Christian and anyone else who's interested, a clear message that you're a maybe. If he's the killer he'll need it. He has to think you're ready. He might like a bit of superficial competition but he also likes a conquest.'

'Do you think Christian could be our man?'

'Yeah, I do. He's working a familiar pattern through picking up a certain type of woman attending the classes.'

'Do you have an address for him?'

'Yes. We can't risk getting too close to it. I think he'll spot surveillance if we're not very careful.'

'Do you think he'd risk keeping the women at his house?'

'Not there. He could have a lock-up somewhere. We are having him followed. We have a surveillance team on him. The injuries on the women suggest that they didn't get fed, looked after regularly: they were starved and dehydrated. Someone could be visiting them less than three times a week.'

'What do you want me to do?'

'Gain his trust. Go so far. Keep a GPS signal transmitting and for God's sake keep your wits about you. He loves to play games. He loves to hurt. He may say he does, but he doesn't have a "physical type", only an emotional one. All the women had in common was their circumstances in life. All of them deserved better than life dealt them and they were realizing it, they were striving for a better life and going it solo. They let their guard down with him. I don't know why. Maybe his good looks, charm, some flattery that they never got. I expect most of them had trust issues like you. Most of them would have been wary. But as tough as these women had had it, they still craved acceptance, adoration from a guy like him. That's the kind of women he goes for – ones where he understands their weak point.'

Chapter 39

Tracy opened the door for Jeanie. Jackson went to sit at the table. Jackson picked up his crayons and began drawing. Jeanie called Tracy into the kitchen to talk. Tracy spoke first before Jeanie had chance to:

'Can I go out? I need to go and see Steve. I'll be about an hour and I'll be back by the time Jackson's ready for bed.'

'Okay, Tracy, if it's important to you then you must go, but take the phone and try not to stay out too long. It's much better if Hawk thinks you are here when he calls. If he does call, try and quickly find somewhere quiet to speak.'

'What should I say?'

'Try and make him feel like you could be a friend – a mother figure. Try and think of him as a victim, Tracy. As hard as it is I need you to be kind to him. I need you to be motherly.'

Tracy nodded. She looked down to see Jackson, who had come into the kitchen and was mirroring her own worried expression.

'Jackson needs some fresh air, I think. We'll go for

a little walk, maybe to the library to read some books,' said Jeanie.

Jackson nodded his head but his eyes stayed on Tracy, worried.

Tracy watched Jeanie get Jackson into his suit. Even Tracy missed Scruffy. She was even thinking of trying to entice the neighbour's cat in for Jackson to play with but she wasn't sure if it had fleas. She went over to him and knelt down and hugged him.

'Have a nice time with Jeanie. Nanny will see you when you get back.' Jackson nodded, put his arms around her neck and gave her a hug.

Tracy waited until they had closed the door behind them and then she put some clean shirts and under-pants in a bag for Steve and locked up. She picked up the phone with a sense of loathing. It felt like she was a prisoner on death row, waiting but never knowing when the call would come. She closed the front door behind her and got into her car, drove out of the drive-way and headed towards Steve's work. She thought about calling him but it was getting near to the end of the working day now. She thought he wouldn't mind if she just turned up.

She pulled into the company car park and looked at the vans parked up there. There was a main reception area in front of the warehouse. Tracy walked up to Betty who had worked on the reception desk for as long as Tracy could remember.

'Hi Betty; is it all right if I say hi to Steve?'

Betty's smile was fading fast; she looked nervously towards the main office, where Tracy could see people moving behind the glass window.

'He's not here, Tracy. I'm sorry.' She shook her head and looked embarrassed. Tracy laughed nervously.

'Oh. I thought he was working today?' She frowned. Once again Betty looked towards the office. A man who Tracy didn't recognize was watching them.

'New staff member?'

Tracy smiled at the man watching her. He smiled back.

'Uh, yes.'

'Okay, well, I guess I'll talk to him later then?' Betty nodded. Tracy was almost out of the door when Betty called to her and came around the desk to speak to her.

'Tracy, the thing is, he doesn't work here any more.' Tracy looked at her as if she were making a joke. Betty reached out to put her hand on Tracy's arm, Tracy stared at it and then back up at Betty's face.

'The thing is, Tracy, he was suspended.' Tracy didn't answer. Her eyes flitted over Betty's face and then towards the office where the man had turned away.

'That . . .' She looked towards the office door and the back of the man's head. 'That's his replacement. Steve didn't deserve it, despite the allegations.'

'What do you mean?'

Betty took a deep breath. 'Look, Tracy, I know you're not going to like me for being the one to tell you but the thing is, I would want to know – so woman to woman, I'm telling you what I know. He was said to have got over-friendly with a couple of the clients we have – big customers. He made a bit of a nuisance of himself.'

'In what way? I don't understand.'

'One of our clients is a college – you know what men are like – like boys in a sweet shop – he was seen hanging about a bit too often there, staying a bit too long. Some of the female students complained.' Tracy started shaking her head. 'It wasn't just that, Tracy ... he was also accused of trying it on with the boss's wife; made a play for her, whatever you call it. They didn't want to sack him and risk him taking it to a tribunal; my guess is they wouldn't be able to prove it.'

'The boss's wife?' Tracy shook her head, still not able to fully take in the news. 'Why would they accuse him of that?'

'Because ... because ... the truth is, Tracy, that he did have a bit of a wandering eye. None of the younger girls wanted to work with him.' Tracy looked at her, horrorstruck.

'Look. I've told you all I know. Six months ago he walked out of that door and I haven't seen hide or hair of him since. Although I know he still comes here to a lock-up.'

Tracy frowned, shook her head. 'Six months? That can't be right. He's been going to work every day just like he always does.'

Betty rubbed her hand on Tracy's arm.

'He's been lying to you, Tracy. If you see him, tell him he has to return the keys to the warehouse; he has to bring the van back. Things will get very nasty otherwise.'

Tracy walked back out into the car park in a daze. Just then Hawk's phone rang in her bag. She pressed the 'accept call' button and held it to her ear.

'Hello, Traceeeeee.'

'Hello.' His voice made her shiver as she stood in the quiet of the dark yard. She heard the classical music again; this time it was louder.

'Why do you think I call you, Tracy?'

'I don't know. I think you need help. It's not too late. You should hand yourself in. Let my daughter go.'

He rolled out a deep laugh. 'I call you because you need to learn a lesson, Tracy. Just like your daughter. She should be grateful to me; I have indoctrinated her in a new family. She no longer needs a mother, a child; all she needs is me, her God.'

'Let me talk to Danielle, please. How do I know she's still alive?'

Tracy heard him walking, breathing. She heard the sound of someone else.

'*Tracy?*' It was Danielle's voice – distant, fading, broken, as if her throat was raw.

'Danielle? Oh thank God you're still alive. Keep hope, Danielle. Be strong.'

'*Jackson?*'

'Yes. Yes, don't worry. Don't worry about Jackson. He misses you but he's okay.'

'*Kiss my baby for me.*'

Tracy heard a noise in the yard behind her. Betty had come out to close the shutters and have a cigarette. She was looking at Tracy with a smile that said, *I'm sorry for you but you need to go away now*. Tracy felt a surge of anger so strong she nearly threw the phone through a window.

Tracy heard him laugh as he mimicked: '*Kiss my*

baby for me. Now here's the price she had to pay to talk to you.' Tracy heard a deep gravelly scream, primeval pain as if Danielle had thrown back her head in agony. The sound vibrated down the phone in a piercing scream. Then she heard Danielle pleading for him to stop as she gasped for breath.

Tracy shouted down the phone: 'Stop it! Stop it! You sick bastard. Leave her alone. That's my daughter you have there. She's worth a billion of you. Danielle is her name, Danielle Foster. Got it? I gave birth to her and I went through agony and I love her. You'll never know love. You are a vile creature. You don't deserve to be loved. Stop all this now. Stop it. It won't be long now before the police find you.' Tracy heard Danielle scream again and then the phone went dead.

Tracy closed her eyes and clutched the phone to her. *Oh God. What have I done? He'll never let her go now. I've ruined everything. It's all my fault. Now he'll come for Jackson.*

Tracy had a need to get home as fast as she could. She wanted to see Jackson, make sure he was safe. She felt too exposed out in the open. Her head and heart pounded as she drove. The place was empty when she got home. It was too quiet. She stayed at the lounge window, looking for Jeanie pushing Jackson home to her.

Jeanie was walking back home from the park. She was still a few streets away from the house. The streetlights shone down. The pavements were wet from the thawing ice and snow clung to the sides of the road. She turned down a side street. Her mind was on getting home to Pete. She hoped Tracy would be home soon so that she could go. She had to go via the office and catch up with the latest developments from Carter first. Jeanie stepped off the kerb and waited in front of the parked cars to cross when the road was clear. Carter had been on her mind a lot recently. It didn't do either of them any good to have to work so closely with one another. It was years since they were together but it had taken a lot to move on. They had drifted in and out of a relationship for a year before they both decided it was best to split. But there were many times Jeanie wondered, if they had just made that extra commitment to one another, if they had taken the plunge, would it have worked? Did she meet Pete on the rebound?

She was just about to step out when lights blinded her and she heard the squeal of tyres as a vehicle accelerated towards them. She heard the scream of grating metal as a van came from nowhere. It crashed into the sides of the two parked cars to the left of Jeanie and Jackson then it mounted the pavement to Jeanie's left and came straight for them. Jeanie screamed as it dragged the buggy from her grasp.

Chapter 40

'You okay, Jeanie?' Jeanie?' She had closed her eyes and was clutching the front door frame of Tracy's house without realizing it.

Carter got to Jeanie as fast as he could. He arrived and gave her a hug. She was still shaking.

'I saw the SOCO team in place. You were very lucky to survive that.'

'No shit, Sherlock! Is it me, or have I got *kill me* written on my back?'

'Of course not.' He held on to her for an extra hug and then drew a little way back. 'But to be on the safe side I'd rather we didn't stand so close.'

'Did you get a look at him?'

'No. But it was no accident. We came this close.' She pinched her thumb and forefinger in the air. She was shaking from the shock and the cold.

'You need to get in the warm.'

She shook her head. 'Not yet. I need fresh air. Is Jackson all right?'

'He's fine. The doctor's checked him out.'

She shook her head. 'It happened so fast. We were just walking home. We were about to cross the road. There wasn't a car in sight. The van came screeching across the road and up on the pavement. He must have been waiting for the right moment. The buggy's totalled. Did you see it?' Jeanie was shaking.

'Yeah. I stopped to take a look at the scene on my way. You did well to save him, Jeanie. You did a good job.'

She nodded, leaned back against the door. She turned to look back inside the house; Tracy was giving Jackson his tea. She lowered her voice: 'It's possible they thought I was Tracy.'

'Or?'

'Or Jackson was the target and Hawk didn't mind who died with him or who he killed to get to him.'

Carter nodded. 'Yeah. Maybe he regrets leaving him alive.'

'Perhaps Hawk thinks I'm getting somewhere with him,' said Jeanie.

'And are you?'

'Yes, I think so. Every day he seems to edge closer to being able to tell us who it was.'

'I'm going round to Gerald Foster's now to see if his van is there and if he's got any new damage.'

Jeanie left Carter and went to find Tracy, who was running a bath for Jackson. Jeanie stood and watched her. She was battling back the tears.

'It's all right, Tracy, Jackson is okay. We are all okay.' Tracy nodded but didn't speak. 'All we have to worry about is getting a new buggy.' Tracy nodded – short, sharp nods – she looked like she didn't dare speak in case she started crying. She undressed

Jackson and got him into the bath. Jeanie came over and knelt by the bath and blew bubbles at Jackson. He was playing with the toys that Jeanie had brought over from Christa's collection. She knew Christa wouldn't miss them. She was spoilt for choice. It hit Jeanie then that she'd missed another bathtime with Christa. Pete would have his disappointed face on. She wouldn't tell him that she'd nearly been killed again – not a good move. He'd want her to give up working there altogether. But even if she wanted that too, she couldn't. She was the higher earner. She was nowhere near ready to go home yet. Carter would be waiting for her at Fletcher House after visiting Foster and they would be working late for as long as it took. She was in it till the end now; they all were. Carter was right – her job came first for now. After today Jeanie realized that she had to be here for Tracy and she had to get the information out of Jackson as fast as she could. Whoever Hawk was, he had changed his mind about killing a child. Nobody was safe from him.

Tracy put Jackson to bed and then she joined Jeanie in the lounge. Tracy poured herself a large glass of wine.

'You okay, Tracy?'

Tracy breathed in deeply through her nose and shook her head. She looked at Jeanie, her face beginning to crumple again. She fought back the tears. The glass of wine in her hand was shaking.

'He phoned again – the man who has Danielle: Hawk.'

'Did he?' Jeanie was shocked that Tracy hadn't said

earlier but then maybe there hadn't been chance.
'When you were out?' Tracy nodded. 'What did he
say?'

'He said I had a lesson to learn. So did Danielle.'
Jeanie waited for her to continue. Tracy walked across
with her glass of wine and sat on the sofa next to
Jeanie. 'I got angry. I called him a sick bastard. I heard
Danielle screaming in the background. She paid for
what I said. Maybe the attack – Jackson and you –
you could have both been killed and it would have
been all my fault.'

Jeanie watched Tracy as she tried not to cry but her
shoulders shook. She put her glass down. Jeanie
reached out and hugged her.

'No, Tracy. He's a madman. You didn't cause him
to hurt Danielle. You did what comes un-naturally to
you. You blew your top. Who knows whether it will
have had a good or bad effect but it won't have
altered his path. I'll listen to the conversation in a
minute on my way home. For now try and forget
about it, please. We're okay. Jackson and I are here
and safe. Did you see Steve?'

Tracy looked embarrassed. She shook her head,
reached across and picked up her wine.

'He was too busy. I'll talk to him later when he
phones.'

Jeanie smiled but she kept her eyes on Tracy.

'You are coping well, you know, Tracy? Much
better than most people could. You're a lot tougher
than you think. You will get through all this.'

'But nothing will ever be the same,' Tracy interrupted.

'No.' Jeanie shook her head. 'Nothing will.'
'Is he going to kill us?'
Jeanie shook her head.

Chapter 41

Carter drove through the evening rush hour and spent an hour nose to tail through busy streets. He cut down all the side streets he knew but ended up snagged in bottlenecks. His father had been a cabbie, retired only three years ago. It was when he retired all his health problems came, thought Carter sadly. His father had loved the cabbie lifestyle, meeting up with his mates, starting the day with a cup of strong tea and a bacon sandwich at five in the morning at a cabman shelter.

At just past nine, Carter arrived at Gerald Foster's house; the van was parked there; there was a large scratch, down to metal on the driver's side. There were no lights on in the house. He walked around to the side of the property, jumped up and held onto the top of the side gate as he peered over into the back garden. He saw a light flickering through the bare branches of the trees at the end of the garden. Someone was working in the shed. Carter jumped back down and brushed down his coat. He cursed to himself. If there was one thing he hated it was getting his clothes dirty. He shook his head and steeled himself as he leapt once more up to the top of the gate, gripped, pulled his weight up and swung his legs over. He paused before dropping quietly down to the ground the other side. Apart from the faint light from the shed, the garden was in total darkness, shadowed by large overbearing trees.

Carter crept down the side of the garden. He kept to the old row of overgrown shrubs for cover. He watched the lights from the shed window as he approached. There was a blackout blind pulled down over the window but a slight breeze inside the shed was lifting it and a bright light burned inside, dimming occasionally as someone passed between the light source and the window. Now as Carter got nearer he realized that it was much more than a shed. It was a substantial-looking outbuilding. It went far back into the trees and must have been sixteen feet long. There was heavy-duty electric wiring up the side of the shed. Whatever Foster did in there, he didn't like it to be compromised by power cuts.

Carter walked around to the back of the shed, one careful step at a time. There was music coming from inside. The shed radiated warmth. He listened hard and heard the sound of someone planing wood. Carter tripped over one of the wires leading to the shed and just managed to stop himself from falling but not before he snapped the overhanging branch of the tree as he grabbed for it. Then the planing and the music stopped as someone had also paused to listen. Carter looked upwards and saw a camera watching him from the trunk of the nearest tree. He crouched beneath its range and dodged the trees as he moved towards the back of the stand of trees that encased the shed. He heard the sound of the shed door opening and footsteps coming over the frozen ground towards him. Carter set off towards the edge of the garden beyond the trees and doubled round until he came level with the open shed door and slipped inside.

Chapter 42

Jeanie left Tracy and decided to pay Steve Collins a visit and find out for herself what was going on. Tracy said he was too busy to see her that evening. Somehow it wasn't sitting right with Jeanie. She drove to the hotel in King's Cross where he was staying. She showed her badge to the receptionist who told her the room number but also said she'd find Mr Collins at the bar.

The smell of cheap food – stale fat and reformed meat being fried – greeted Jeanie as she walked away from reception and past a lounge area and then turned left into a bar. Football was on a big TV screen at the far end of the long bar. Several men were sitting at that end watching it. A few others were dotted around the bar eating dinner or catching up on a bit of work. She went up to the bar and asked the woman serving, a tired-looking Eastern European, if she knew Mr Collins.

'Steve?"

'Yes, Steve Collins.'

The barmaid pointed to a man sitting on the far side of one of the tables beneath the TV screen.

Jeanie recognized him from the photos on Tracy's lounge walls.

Steve Collins was halfway through a pint of beer and enjoying the football when Jeanie stood in front of him, blocking his view of the TV.

'Mr Collins?' He looked her over. 'Can I have a word please?' She showed him her warrant card. He studied her for a few seconds as if trying to gauge the severity of her expression. He nodded and picked up his pint. As he picked up his phone from the table Jeanie saw there were three missed calls from Tracy. He slipped from his stool and followed Jeanie to a table away from the noise of the TV.

Jeanie sat opposite him as she introduced herself.

'Sorry to interrupt your evening.' He didn't answer. Jeanie was getting the feeling that he liked to stare at women a little too much. 'I'm Detective Constable Jeanie Vincent. I'm the Family Liaison Officer who's been staying with your wife and part of the team investigating the kidnapping of Danielle Foster. Just wanted to update you and talk about how we propose to go forward with the investigation. First of all I want to thank you for you cooperation in this.'

'I don't really have a choice.'

'It must be very distressing for you?' Jeanie smiled; her eyes stayed boring into his.

'I don't know her.'

'I see. Even so, what affects your wife affects you?'

He looked away as he shook his head, sighed.

'I told her – can of worms.'

Jeanie looked at him curiously.

'Excuse me?'

'That's what she opened when she let that girl into her life.'

'I know it must be difficult for you but . . .'

'It's not difficult because I'm not going to let it be. I've already told Tracy I'm not coming back till it's sorted.'

'I'd like you to reconsider that please. I'm here to tell you we'd like you to go back home now. We need you to be aware of a few things.' Jeanie stopped mid-sentence when he saw Steve shake his head and take a long swig of beer.

'I'm not going back. I've decided. Not till it's all over. I'm better off here, away from it all. I wouldn't be any help to Tracy.'

'Oh.' Jeanie pretended to look surprised but in her heart, she'd been half expecting it. 'We think you would be a lot of help to Tracy, Mr Collins. It would give her both moral and physical support, plus security. She's often on her own with Jackson.'

'You stay with her then. That's your job, isn't it? What do you expect me to do?'

'She doesn't need me in the evenings after Jackson goes to bed. She needs you. We believe she might be in danger. Jackson, the little boy, might be a target.'

'That's the point. I have got enough on my plate at the moment without becoming caught up in this. I'm sorry and all that but I don't want to get involved.'

'Okay, Mr Collins. I am, of course, disappointed by your decision. If you've really made up your mind not to help then I'll not waste any more of your time and I'll go.'

Steve looked her over as she stood and buttoned up her coat.

'Sorry I couldn't help,' he said. Jeanie didn't answer him. 'Can I just ask though? Is there any compensation for loss of earnings?'

'You have a good job though, don't you, Mr Collins?'

He looked defensive.

'Yes, but Tracy's earnings.' He shrugged. 'They may not be much – but we need them.'

'I'll get it looked into. I'll make sure I talk to Tracy about it. Thank you for your time.'

Jeanie muttered '*Takes all sorts*' as she left the hotel.

Carter looked around the shed as he kept one eye on the door. The place had a slightly stale, muggy smell, as if someone stayed in there most of the time. Here was where Gerald Foster preferred to be. This was where he actually lived. There was a bed in the corner, lying on a raised wooden box. There was a chest of drawers. Above the bed there was a curtain covering the wall behind. Carter walked across and lifted it. He found himself looking at pictures of Danielle. He turned to see Gerald Foster standing in the entrance to the shed with a hammer resting in his hand. Foster stepped inside the shed and closed the door behind him.

Foster drummed the head of the hammer into his palm.

'How dare you come in here without a search warrant?'

'I just saw the light on.' Carter stood his ground whilst scanning the shed for something he could use as a weapon.

'This is private property. I would be well within my right to kill you.'

'I think you'll find that that's not strictly true,' answered Carter with an attempt at a smile. 'I just want to talk, Mr Foster. That's a pretty bad scratch you have on the driver's side of your van. Looks like you dragged something.'

'Wasn't me. One of the lads used it.'

'Lads?'

'I lent it to someone down at the Canal Museum. They borrowed it to move their son. Apparently one of his friends was larking around and drove it into some metal contraption. Bloody typical irresponsible behaviour. Last time I lend anything.'

'Would you be able to provide me with a name and address for the person who was driving your van today?'

Foster squared up to Carter. He nodded. 'I'll get it for you and ring you tomorrow. Goodbye.'

Carter pointed to the wall of photos. 'You seem to have quite a shrine to Danielle here.'

'Not to her. To happy times. To Marion and me. They were our best times,' Foster repeated as he looked at the photos. 'We were happy then. Just for a brief time.'

'Thought Danielle brought you nothing but trouble?'

'But for a while we were the perfect family. Then all Marion's time was taken up worrying about Danielle and she grew sick with it. She worried herself into an early grave. But these years . . .' His face softened as he looked at the photos. 'These were the best years for all of us: Marion and me – we were happy then.' Carter looked back at the wall; behind each smiling face of Danielle there was Gerald or his wife. 'Search the place if you want.'

Carter pulled out drawers and lifted up the lids on the boxes and trunks around the cabin. He left the bed till last. He was looking at the way it was raised and resting on a wooden box. He lifted the corner of the mattress, a futon, and knocked the base. There was an echo. Carter knew he was sweating. He knew he was breathing hard as he tried to stay calm and think of all the things he should have thought of before now – *too late* was what popped into his brain. *Too frigging late.*

'Can I see what's beneath?'

Foster shrugged.

'Sure.'

Carter stood back.

'Can you lift it for me please?'

Foster lifted the bedding right back, folded it into a neat pile. He folded the mattress back. Then he prised up the corner of the box enough to get his hand beneath. He paused, turned towards Carter and, at that minute, Carter was deciding his options. He had already taken a step nearer the door and had made a note of anything he might use as a weapon. He knew he was faster than Foster but was he stronger?

'I need a hand.' Foster nodded towards the foot of the bed. 'Here.' He handed him a wrench. Carter slid the end beneath the top of the box and together they lifted it. Carter stood back and looked at Foster. Foster nodded.

'Go ahead, open it.'

Carter knocked on the lid and then slid it across. Beneath it, lying in the bottom, was a shroud and an urn.

'Marion.' Foster looked at Carter. 'I have left instructions that I want our ashes to be joined and scattered at Margate. That was where we used to take Danielle for day trips. Happy times.'

'Why do you live out here?'

'I can't bear to sleep alone in the house.'

'People get ill, Gerald. There is no blame attached to cancer. People cope with it in different ways and families manage it as best they can. Danielle wouldn't have wanted Marion to get ill. She couldn't have given her cancer as you suggest. There's no justice with cancer – and no blame.'

'I know. I know. I'm not a fool. I didn't cope with it as well as I could have done. When I think of those teenage years with Danielle I just see my wife getting sicker and my life spiralling out of control. It all seemed to go so wrong. All the plans, all the hope we had for the future came to nothing and the one person I loved in my life is gone. Danielle took all my energy that I should have given to my wife in her dying years.'

Carter reached out and patted Gerald Foster's shoulder.

'You did your best.'

He turned to Carter. 'Maybe. I wish we'd never

adopted her. I wish we'd just had each other and not hankered after a child so much. But ... I hope you find her. I hope she does make a good life for herself and the little boy.'

Chapter 43

Harding was sitting at her office desk in one of a suite of rooms in the basement of the Whittington Hospital, which housed the mortuary and post mortem room as well as her laboratory. She looked across at Mark, who was fishing a brain out of formaldehyde ready for slicing into centimetre-wide slices, and wondered if tonight was the night she should make her move.

She phoned Robbo. It was very late – he could have gone home a few hours ago, but instead he had stayed to work on the case.

'Results are through on examination of the ulcerated sites and necrosis on Pauline Murphy's body. I'll be over in a minute. I can't get hold of Carter – his phone is switched off. I'll come across and see Chief Inspector Bowie instead but I'll send you the results first – they're interesting. You may want to get researching.'

Harding got out of her protective work clothes and pulled on her fur-trimmed floor-length coat as she picked up her car keys.

'I'm going across to talk to Chief Inspector Bowie. Will you be okay working late tonight?'

Mark looked up from his work and nodded.

'You driving?' he asked. 'It's really icy out there.'

'I am driving, yes. I refuse to allow a bit of ice to stop me; plus I thought I'd pick up a couple of bottles of something for later, just in case we get thirsty.' She waited for him to look up again from his work. He didn't.

Harding parked outside Fletcher House and punched in her passcode at the door. She took the lift up to MIT 17 and arrived at Bowie's office at the same time as Carter.

'Doctor?' Carter waited until Robbo and Harding were settled and ready to speak.

'As you know we took samples from the ulcerated sites. Results are back.'

'Yes?' Bowie was looking as rough as he always did, thought Carter.

'They're caused by spider bites. Those were the needle-like wounds. They were spider's fangs.'

'Ordinary spiders?' asked Bowie.

'No, they're not ordinary in this country. We have spiders that can bite but ...'

She turned to look at Robbo, whose enthusiasm was unleashed.

'Doctor Harding asked me to look into the types of spider that would be a match for the venom. There are a couple of possibilities, none of them native to this country. We do have spiders that can bite – even the house spider can nip you if cornered – but none of ours would be able to cause infection like this.'

'We have now identified different sized fang bites on

the victims,' said Harding. 'Hawk has more than one type of poisonous spider.'

Robbo started a slideshow of spiders on his laptop.

'What happens when you're bitten?' Bowie asked as the images flashed up.

'Within a couple of hours it starts to itch and swell,' answered Harding. 'And within a few days, left untreated, the ulcers form and start eating away at the flesh. There is no cure for that.'

Robbo clicked on images of bite wounds. There was a sharp intake of breath from Carter. 'Christ.'

'The wounds have been recorded at twenty-five centimetres in diameter,' Harding stated. 'Bacteria creeps in and then infection from these bites is common. Limb amputations are the only answer as gangrene sets in.'

'There's no cure?' asked Carter. He stared at the photos of the wounds and his face paled.

'There's anti-venom.'

'What about the antibiotics you found in her blood?' asked Bowie. 'If he knows a lot about these spiders he knows that he can't cure the ulcerated sites with antibiotics. So he plans to kill them slowly, giving them small amounts of antibiotics just to prolong the agony. Is that what it looks like, Doctor?'

Harding nodded.

'The antibiotics would only have prolonged life but not enough to halt the necrosis or prevent renal failure. All of the victims were about to go into kidney failure. Their organs were in a dire state from the poison in their systems.'

'We'll contact pet shops in North London and start asking for customer lists.'

'There's an exotic pet shop near me. I'll go and ask some questions,' said Carter.

Robbo closed his laptop. 'It would be worth ordering in some anti-venom just in case we have the pleasure of meeting the man and his pets.'

Harding got back to the Whittington and found Mark still working. She had a bottle of wine in her hand and another in her bag.

'Thought we could do we a little R&R?' She planted the wine on the table and threw her coat over the back of the chair.

Mark looked worried. 'Just realized I haven't sent the debris from Emily Styles' hair off for analysis.'

Harding's expression instantly changed to one of annoyance.

'Did you sift it?' she said brusquely.

'Yes.'

'Where is it?'

'Still in the fridge waiting to be sent to the lab.'

A flash of anger crossed Harding's face. 'You better call them now and you can get it across to them yourself.'

'Yes, Doctor.' Harding walked through to the specimen store, a room off the post mortem room, and opened the fridge. Inside were labelled bags and plastic pots and trays. She found the set of specimens belonging to Emily Styles and pulled out the packet labelled hair residue. She took it back to her desk and tipped the contents into a clean tray.

'What are you looking for?' asked Mark as he came to stand behind her.

She was momentarily distracted by the nearness of his body. His leg was against hers as he watched what she was doing.

'We may as well do the first part of the analysis ourselves to save time. I want to dry it off. We know so much more about our man now. I want to make sure we didn't miss anything. I'll just keep it thirty minutes then you can go.' She turned to see if he was okay with that and found him so close that she couldn't breathe. She turned back to the desk and began picking through the debris with tweezers.

'What's that?' Mark pointed to a small silver object on the tray.

'It's a fish scale.'

'No it's not – it's too big, wrong shape.' Mark pulled on a fresh pair of gloves and Harding tapped the scale onto a slide. He took it across to the microscope.

Harding joined him as he looked at it then stood back for her to see.

'Snake.'

She nodded. 'Well done. What kind?'

Mark took a few minutes to look it up on the laptop.

'It's a python – a very big one. This size of scale you're looking at, one over twelve foot.'

Harding sat down at her desk and brought the X-rays of Emily Styles' neck injuries up onto the screen.

'Here's our tourniquet. So wide it crushed her neck, not just the vertebrae, severing her spinal cord but also her jawbone and her trachea. It pushed her jawbone back into the cranium.' She phoned Carter. He was on his way home to get a few hours' rest. He had the phone on speaker.

'While you're in the pet shop find out all you can about any owners of very large pythons in the area. We've found a scale in the debris from Emily Styles' hair. There's no doubt it's what strangled her.'

Carter finished the call and pulled into his street, parked up and walked into his house. Cabrina had fallen asleep on the sofa and Archie was next to her. He picked Archie up as Cabrina opened her sleepy eyes.

'Hello, babe – didn't think you'd make it back.'

Archie didn't stir. Carter took him upstairs and put him to bed. By the time he'd come back downstairs Cabrina was in the kitchen; she had poured him a glass of wine and was heating up some food for him. He came up behind her and put his hands around her waist as he nestled into her neck.

'Sorry – do I smell like baby? Archie and I had a bath.'

'Lucky Archie.' He moved her hair away from her neck and kissed the soft line of her neck that he loved.

She closed her eyes. 'I've missed you, babe.'

'Good.' He smiled and held her tighter. 'Promise you'll never stop missing me.'

'Please. Please, I'll do anything, don't hurt me any more.'

Hawk stood over Danielle and pulled her upright by her wrists.

Danielle felt nauseous. Now that she could open her eyes she realized that her vision was blurred. Her heart was racing. The room was unbearably hot. She watched him move in a distorted fog around her. She listened to his speech from some distant place. She vomited bile; her stomach retched and strained and he turned up the music. He lifted her out of the coffin and held her close to him as he swayed to the music. He began carrying her towards the back of the room and he ducked his head under the rafters. Danielle could not stand. Her head was spinning. She felt herself being lowered. He held her under her shoulders as he dangled her in mid-air and she felt the cold and damp close around her. He dropped her into a pit.

He waited until she finished vomiting to speak:

'Tracy messed up.' He turned to Danielle. 'You all mess up. Like mother like daughter – whores and bitches.' The pain shot through her back as she lay on the bottom of the dug-out hole. She looked up to see him peering down at her over the edge of the hole, ten feet above her. He shone the torch at her and it reflected off the walls around her. She looked at the scratches. White flecks of nail and flesh were embedded in the earth.

Chapter 44

Next morning, Carter pushed open the door of 'The Exotic Pet Shop' on Caledonian Road and was pleasantly surprised. He had been dreading setting foot inside any place that had things that scuttled or slid, but the woman sitting on a stool behind the counter to his right smiled and he instantly felt better. She was pretty, with feline eyes and a mane of black hair that started as a loose bun on the top of her head and then tumbled down till it reached her waist. She had long false eyelashes and pouting pink lips. She looked like she'd stepped out of a Sixties girl band in a leopard-print mini-dress.

'Hi. My name is Detective Inspector Dan Carter.' He showed his warrant card. 'I need some information.' She didn't seem to object. 'What's your name?'

'Silky.'

From the corner of his eye Carter spied movement. Stacks of boxes containing jumping insects, labelled 'crickets', 'locusts'. Silky kept her eyes on Carter as he bent low to look at the insects.

'Funny type of pet. Not so scary as I imagined.'

'They're just food for the others.'

Carter stood and took a step towards Silky, who had a tattoo of a snake running up her arm and flicking its forked tongue into the crevice of her neck.

'Who eats those then?' Carter smiled, embarrassed at his mistake but at the same time wondering if Silky was wearing knickers; somehow he didn't think so.

'The spiders.' She sat back on her stool. 'Is it a spider you were interested in?'

Carter tipped his head to one side, swivelled on his heels and shrugged.

'Possibly. Actually I need some information about some of these *pets*.' She didn't seem to object. He glanced around the shop at the tanks and cages.

'Do you have a favourite?'

'Yes. That's easy,' she answered as she got out of her seat, eased down her dress from where it had lodged at the top her thighs and swivelled her hips around the side of the cash desk as she appeared by his side. 'I'm a tarantula type of girl.' She walked over to the wall full of glass containers. Carter followed her and stood eye to eye with a six-inch-wide, hairy spider. He stepped back.

'Are they venomous?'

She smiled, amused. 'All spiders are venomous. Some more than others.'

Carter tried not to shiver. He was worse than Cabrina when it came to spiders. He was going to have to stop being a wimp about it if he didn't want Archie to be the same.

'Have you ever been bitten?'

The woman nodded. 'A few times.'

'But some spiders can kill?'

'Of course. I keep a stock of anti-venom in my fridge.'

He moved away from the spiders.

'What about for snakes?' They moved on to the far end of the small shop and a large tank with a coal-black snake inside.

'Snakes eat mice, rabbits – small mammals of some kind. It depends on the size of the snake.'

'Do they eat them live?' Carter bent to peer in at the snake.

'No. Not any more. Well, not unless you have a snake that won't feed otherwise. They are farmed, killed humanely and we sell them frozen.'

'Do you have regular clients?'

'Yes. We have our regulars. Once you buy one pet you tend to want more and the same people come in to buy feed for them.'

'Do you have a newsletter that people can subscribe to on your website?'

'We notify people of offers – that kind of thing.'

'Can I get a copy of the list of subscribers for that?'

She shrugged. 'I don't see why not. It's not a private thing.'

Carter bent down to look at the snake sliding its underbelly up the glass as it slid up towards the top of the tank.

'I bet you know all the real spider and snake enthusiasts around North London?'

'We tend to know one another, yeah. People need advice, that kind of thing. We keep in touch.'

'Do you think you know everyone around the area who has a large snake?'

She thought about it and shrugged again. 'That's a hard one. I doubt it. Someone could source their food from someone other than me, like online. They could be self-sufficient and breed their own insects. If they bought a snake from me then I keep a record.'

A young woman passed them as she came from a door at the back of the shop.

'Just going downstairs – mind the till for me, Barb,' she said as she passed.

'Okay, no probs.'

She turned to Carter: 'Would you like to see a big snake?'

'Love to.'

She led the way through the door and down the stairs that turned sharply around to the left. Downstairs they walked into a small hot room with a massive tank running the length of it. Inside was a snake that fitted it.

'Jesus! How big is that thing?'

'*That* is Lulu and she's about sixteen feet.'

'How much does she weigh?'

'About nine stone.'

Carter walked over to the tank and came level with the curled snake.

'She's a python,' said Silky. 'I've had her for ten years but she's just too big for me to have at my house now.'

He shook his head, impressed. 'Yeah – I bet. Do you handle her?'

'Sure, I get her out most days. Except when she's hungry – like most women she gets bad-tempered then.'

'And how often does she get hungry?'

'Once a month.'

'Then what? Half a dozen rabbits?'

'Just one.'

'If she eats that then she won't eat again?'

'Not for a month.'

'She won't bother to kill?'

'No. I mean I still wouldn't handle her alone. Once she coiled around your neck, you wouldn't be able to get her off. She might not even be looking to eat you, just to defend herself or to feel stable, just to get a hold on something.'

'Could she eat you?'

'Lulu?' Carter nodded. 'I'd be too big for her but she could eat a baby, a small child. In the wild they have been known to eat people. They can grow to fifty feet and can weigh one hundred and thirty-five kilos.'

'Would she eat another snake?'

'No. But a decapitated snake can bite itself. A snake's body can go on moving for hours.'

'Jesus – that's evil.'

She laughed. It was beginning to feel uncomfortably warm and small in the room. They seemed to be standing awfully close. He looked at his watch.

'Thanks so much for your help – if I can have that list now.'

'Yeah, sure.' She led the way back up the stairs and stopped halfway. She caught Carter staring at her bum. 'Do you want to give me your number? I can ring you if I think of anything else you ought to know about spiders or snakes. Maybe you could buy me a drink sometime and I'd let you pick my brains?' He followed her back to the counter.

'I'd love to but police business, rules and all that – you understand.'

She cocked her head to one side and smiled. 'I understand. She's a lucky woman.'

Chapter 45

Carter drove to the office and took the lift up to MIT 17.

He had the mailing list of pet owners in his hand. He went straight to Robbo's office and handed it to James.

'Check out everyone on this list and see if Hawk could be one of them please, James.'

'Will do.'

Robbo stopped working and waited for Carter to report back about what he'd found.

He shook his head.

'It seems anyone can own a spider that bites or a snake that can strangle. If you wanted to breed your own food for it, you need never go near a pet shop or a vet's, I suppose.'

Robbo nodded. 'James has been contacting all the vets in North London. We've found three people with registered snakes and we've sent officers round to check them out . Meanwhile I've been looking at the CCTV footage of the roads around Tracy's home; looking for the van driver.'

Jeanie walked in at that moment.

'May I?' she asked as she picked up Robbo's fresh cafetière from on top of the cupboard.

'Yes. Help yourself, pour me one.'

'I'll do it.' Carter said. He walked across to Jeanie and put his hand on her arm. 'You okay after yesterday?'

She smiled. 'I'm fine, honest.' Carter could see she wasn't. 'Okay, I'm a bit shaken but I'll be all right. What's worrying me is what if it was Hawk who tried to run us over, and what if he knew it was me – a police officer. Then he tried to kill me, personally. He knew who I was.' Robbo rocked in his chair. He looked across at Jeanie and Carter.

'Yes – if it was Hawk then we know he knows who is on our team.'

'But does that mean he knows Ebony?' Jeanie asked.

Robbo shook his head.

'He can't know about her. He knew about you from the press conference. He knows about me because he's looked into crime analysts in the MIT teams and maybe he takes a lucky guess.'

'Maybe he's very smart,' said Jeanie.

She sat in Pam's empty chair and watched Robbo scan through grainy black and white images of a night shot of the local shops near Tracy's home.

'I went to see Steve Collins about returning to the family home to provide extra security for Tracy and Jackson,' said Jeanie. 'It was the weirdest meeting with him. He's not interested in moving home. He wants nothing to do with any of it. I'd say Steve is preparing to do a runner.' She joined them at Robbo's desk and pulled up a chair. 'I'd like to give him the benefit of the doubt but I'd say he's a player. Tracy told me he has a history of bad debts. I wonder what it would take for him to jump ship. This might be the excuse he's been waiting for.'

'He works for a storage company, right?' Robbo asked.

'Yes, area manager – Tracy says.'

Robbo started typing: 'Let's have a quick look at what the company say about him.' He clicked on the relevant division and scrolled the list of employees. 'Surprise, surprise, he's not on the list of current employees. Let's try twelve months ago ... Yes. There he is – Stephen Collins. I don't know why but he lost his job and he hasn't told his wife.'

'Could he have known something?' asked Carter.

'He could have been watching the house in the build-up to Danielle going missing,' said Jeanie. She was trying to think back to what Tracy had said about Steve. 'He's pretending to go somewhere to work because she irons his shirts, has his suit dry-cleaned. Tracy thinks her husband is finally making good from having fucked up and smashed her dreams of owning her own beauty salon. They already lost their home because of his bad debts.'

'He hasn't wanted to put yet another nail in the coffin of their relationship maybe.' Carter shrugged.

'What's that?' Jeanie pointed to the CCTV footage.

'It's just over a week ago,' answered Robbo.

Jeanie watched the screen as a young, slim female figure in a fur-trimmed coat came into view. She was pushing a buggy. Jeanie pulled her chair close to the screen.

'That's Danielle,' she said. 'Freeze it for me, zoom in. Yes, that's Danielle, I'm sure. We'll need to look at the footage more closely but it looks like the photos I've seen. There's Jackson.' She touched the screen. 'Look! You can see Scruffy's tail. It's definitely them.'

'What's she doing?' Carter moved in close to Jeanie as he stared at the screen.

Jeanie turned to Robbo. 'What day is this?'

'It's the day Danielle disappeared,' he answered. 'Hours after this was taken she was abducted from her flat.'

Carter looked at them both and back to the screen. 'She came to Tracy's house that day?'

'Tracy didn't mention it. She definitely didn't know. Can we follow her route, Robbo?

They watched Danielle cross the road by the shops and turn down Tracy's road.

'There's no way that she's going anywhere else,' said Robbo.

'So why would Danielle visit Tracy a day before she was due to meet up with her anyway?' Carter sat back from the screen to think.

'Did Tracy invite her?' asked Robbo.

'No. Tracy was working. She told me how busy she was because of the Christmas rush,' said Jeanie. 'She could only meet Danielle because she was on a late shift that day.'

'So for some reason Danielle decided to pay Tracy a visit, or just come and see where she lived maybe?' Robbo moved the image on.

'Wanting to see if Tracy's house meant she had money?'

'We know she tried to ring. She didn't get through on Tracy's phone. Tracy told us Steve said the home phone wasn't working. Either she tried there and didn't get through and decided to come and see Tracy or she got through to Steve and made an arrangement to come over.'

'So she went there and either Steve saw her hanging about outside or he knew she was coming? He recognized her from the description that Tracy had given him? He saw Jackson?'

'And what? He invited her in?'

'Maybe.'

'He was there because he hasn't got a job any more, so he waits till Tracy leaves and then he returns home and lies low till she returns.'

'But Danielle was still fine when she left there because she called in that afternoon for her lessons in college.'

'Ring Tracy,' said Robbo. 'See if she remembers something.'

'No, don't,' answered Carter. 'Let's bring Steve Collins in.'

Robbo nodded his agreement.

'What about outside the college on the day Danielle disappeared?' asked Jeanie. 'Can we place him anywhere else?'

'No. We didn't see him there, but then we weren't looking for him at the time.'

'Run through the footage again while I ring Steve's workplace.' Robbo got through to Betty on reception. They listened to his one-sided conversation. He finished up and told them:

'She says Steve Collins was suspended six months ago. He still has the keys to the warehouse and a set of keys to a works van.'

'Why haven't they got them off him?' asked Carter.

'It's all a bit tricky, according to the new manager. It boils down to Collins' word against the boss's wife and she's a slag, according to Betty. They're frightened he'll go for unfair dismissal so they're taking their time. Everyone's jumpy. Plus he has paid for storage facilities there and he's entitled to use them.'

'So shall we bring him in, Guv?' Jeanie asked Carter.

'No, change of plan. We'll go talk to the new manager again and get hold of the keys for the van and the warehouse where Collins has stored stuff. We'll get inside there and have a look around.'

'Now?' asked Robbo.

'Yes. Now. Jeanie, can you come?'

Jeanie looked Carter.

'Wouldn't miss it.'

Chapter 46

It was nearly five p.m. when Ebony started getting herself ready to go out.

She stood in front of the bathroom cabinet mirror above the basin and made a face at herself. She was tempted to say 'tart' to her reflection but didn't. Why did she have such a problem with putting on make-up, creating another look for herself? Maybe because her mother had so many faces and only Ebony knew which one was real. It was the bi-polar condition in her mother that sent her high as a kite or down into the depths of despair. She was unable to take care of herself, let alone another. 'You can go home and live with your mother' had never been an easy thing for Ebony to hear. 'She's stable now. She's taking her meds.' Ebony had packed her bag in silence and her foster mother Mrs Bennet had come into the room and said, 'It'll be all right, Ebony. Things will be different this time.' She had kept her eyes on the ground as she shut her heart once more and prepared to meet the mother no one else knew except her. Ebony looked in the mirror and she saw herself as an eight-year-old, make-up on her face. Her mother dancing round the room drunk on cheap red wine that turned her lips crimson red. Ebony watching from the corner of the mirror.

'That'll do,' she said to herself as she turned away from the mirror and shuddered. Now they said her mother was ill and undergoing tests and they would be able to tell her more shortly. Ebony felt worried but she didn't know what for. She knew she didn't love her mother when the thought of her death made her feel nothing but relief.

Mike Holland, the new district manager at the storage company, was waiting for Jeanie and Carter with keys outside the office reception.

They took the keys from him and asked him to stay where he was.

'Just to clarify,' asked Carter. 'The van that Stephen Collins has keys for . . . is it here in the car park now?'

He looked around. 'Yes. It's that one over there.'

'Have you seen him here today?'

'No. He comes here most days, stays for a while. I'm not usually here when he leaves. I think sometimes he stays most of the day in there. Don't know what he does. I mean he's entitled to come and sort out his stuff when ever he likes.'

'Is it his lock-up? His stuff?'

'Yes, he took it on when he first started working here. Him and his wife sold up and downsized in a hurry. He put the contents of their old house in here.'

'Has it got a water supply? Electricity?'

'Oh yes. It's comfortable enough – I mean, you couldn't live in there.' He laughed. 'I wouldn't anyway.'

'Thanks. We'll drop the keys back to you once we've had a look. I'd be grateful if you didn't allow anyone else to come into that area for now.'

Carter and Jeanie walked towards the compound behind the main office block. There were twelve large storage facilities units. The place was well lit to discourage thieves.

'You and me out on surveillance duty together. Feels like old times, Jeanie.' Carter looked Jeanie's way. 'That's when we first hooked up, do you remember?'

Jeanie looked across at him. 'How could I forget? I notice you didn't include the word good when you said old times.'

'They were good.' Carter looked across at her as he held the keys in his hand.

'Really?' asked Jeanie. 'Good for whom?'

Carter didn't answer. He waited until Jeanie was in place ready behind him and then he unlocked the door.

In the darkness the massive empty space opened out around them. Jeanie shone her torch into the warehouse and looked at the locked containers. The sensor lights started coming on as they stepped further inside.

'Which one has he got the keys for?' Jeanie shone a torch down at the list she'd been given.

'Third row to our left. Row J. Container 2037.'

They walked along until they cut down left and walked along the dirt floor until they found the relevant row.

Carter slipped the key in the padlock and turned it. The lock dropped to the floor. Jeanie moved it out of the way as Carter pulled back the right-hand door. They felt the heat coming from inside.

The corners of the container were not lit. Fluorescent strip lighting flickered on and off. Carter shone his torch into the container. All around him were cases stacked high. There was furniture stacked to the ceiling, three-piece suites upside down on top of one another. At one side was a laid-out living area, a foldaway bed and sleeping bag. There was a mini fridge and a microwave.

'Someone's been fully living here.'

Carter shone his torch down towards the far end and it was there he saw eyes glinting back at him. A stuffed fox looked poised to strike. The place was a jumble of belongings.

'We need to search the place thoroughly. We'll split up. You start on the left of the door. I'll start on the right.'

Chapter 47

Tracy thought it would be Jeanie at the door when someone rang the bell. Jeanie had promised to come back and check on her and Jackson before she went home to her own house for the night. Tracy had put Jackson to bed early – he was so tired. She was just about to settle down for the evening. She called at the door to ask who was there before she opened it.

'Steve.'

'Steve?'

'Yes – your husband. It's my house, remember? I've already been quizzed by the police outside; now let me in.'

She opened the door straightaway.

'Sorry. Just a bit jumpy. I didn't think you wanted to come home?'

She looked at him and looked back towards the inside of the house and Jackson's room. Something was making her nervous. She didn't know if it was the amount of booze she smelt on his breath.

'You all right, love?'

'Yes. Why wouldn't I be?' He strode into the lounge and sat in his favourite chair. He turned to glare at her, his eyes red-rimmed. 'I'm starving. Have you got anything here to eat?'

'Of course. I'll make you something.'

Steve picked up the remote control and turned the television on loud. Tracy looked towards Jackson's room. She wanted to tell Steve to turn the volume down. But she didn't.

Tracy walked into the kitchen and put the kettle on. She looked at Steve. There had been times when she'd learnt about what he'd done that made her wonder if she'd ever really known him. Now was one of those times.

Tracy made him a sandwich and a cup of tea and stood in the lounge doorway with the tray in her hands. She looked to the chair; he was gone. She looked to Jackson's room and saw the door was open.

She quickly put the tray down, opened the bedroom door and saw Steve sitting on Jackson's bed. Jackson was sleeping soundly.

'What are you doing, Steve?' Tracy's heart started racing.

Steve turned to look at her. His eyes were shining in the dark.

'Poor little fella. He's had a tough time of it, hasn't he?' He looked from Jackson to her.

'Yes.' Tracy stepped forward. 'Leave him alone now, Steve. Don't touch him. He needs his sleep. He's just a baby.' Her voice was beginning to rise in pitch.

Steve didn't move. He reached out and stroked Jackson's head. Jackson's face twitched in his sleep and he turned over.

'I want you to leave him alone.' Tracy was surprised

at the tone of her own voice. It was deep now – steady, calm. 'Get out now, Steve.'

Steve turned and looked at her as if he didn't recognize who was speaking.

'Tracy? What do you think? Do you honestly believe I would harm him?'

'I don't know you any more. You've been lying to me for months, maybe years. You could be capable of anything because I don't know who you are. I went in to your work and talked to Betty.' Tracy felt her anger rise even though she was trying very hard to keep control of it. 'I got the whole story how they would have liked to sack you but they couldn't, even though you were screwing the boss's wife, letching after college students.'

He shook his head. He was still sitting on the bed. Jackson was beginning to wake up. 'I wasn't, Tracy … I admit I kept things from you but we'd been through such a lot and you've been so strong through it all but I know there's only so much you can take. It's all lies, especially about the boss's wife. I've been waiting to see what they'd do about reinstating me. I will take them to a tribunal otherwise. I swear to you, Tracy, that I would not be unfaithful to you.'

Tracy started to back out of the room. 'Leave Jackson alone then. He doesn't know you; he'll be frightened if he wakes up and finds you sitting on his bed.'

'Why would he be? I've met him before.' Tracy stared at him as she shook her head.

'Danielle came around here looking for you when you were at work. I saw him then.'

'Why didn't you tell me?'

'We had enough things on our plate.' She shook her head. Tracy wasn't ready to believe what Steve was saying. 'I admit it, Tracy; I've been depressed. Every day for six months I've been sitting in the warehouse, waiting for you to leave for work so that I could come home. I've been hoping that things would work out on their own. The last thing I thought we needed was this.' He looked at Jackson. 'But maybe it's a blessing in disguise.' Jackson opened his sleepy eyes and looked at Steve and then at Tracy, who smiled and nodded her reassurance. Jackson looked back at Steve and gave him a big smile.

Jeanie and Carter walked back in to see Robbo behind his desk.

'It was just bits of furniture and a collection of all kinds of junk,' said Jeanie, taking off her coat. 'Memories – it looks like his whole life is in there. He must have been living there in fear of really telling Tracy what the matter was.'

Carter shook his head. 'I think he's had a breakdown, looking at the stuff in there. He's collected all sorts of junk. Must have spent a fortune on it: stuffed animals even – a weird collection. If that's what's in his head – he's lost the plot.'

'You searched all the way through it?' asked Robbo.

'We opened every box.'

'Bowie thinks we should bring Christian Goddard in now,' said Robbo. 'He thinks it's time to get heavy-handed.'

'What do you think?' asked Carter.

'It's got to be him. From what we know of him he will be aware of how far we've got because he's fed us all the clues. If he thinks we're getting too close to him we run the risk that he'll go out in a blaze of glory and take Danielle, and whoever else he might have in there, with him. I've been looking into his history.' He showed them the page of search engines he had working on Goddard. 'There must be something on him somewhere. He needs to have had a journey to this point. You don't start killing overnight.' Robbo looked at his Facebook page. 'He's travelled a bit. I'll run a check with Interpol again.'

'Okay.' Jeanie scrolled through his photos.

'It says he's been to Thailand, Laos, Fiji, Australia, New Zealand. He must have learnt about exotic pets in Australia; he worked in a zoo there. He was back here in 2010 – that's when he set up the online pet business and also registered for his first course in college. I think we should bring him in. We can't risk another minute of him being out there if he's Hawk.'

Jeanie pointed to an image of a street and someone walking in a small camera.

'Is that Ebony's camera?'

'Yeah. She is meeting Goddard tonight. I've been thinking about what you said about if there's a possibility that he knows Ebony and I don't think we should take the risk.'

'I agree. We'll have Goddard brought in and get a search warrant for his house,' said Carter.

'What do you want Ebony to do?' asked Robbo.

'We'll salvage the evening. Tell Ebony to arrive late at the pub, after Goddard's been picked up, and then see if she can get any extra information on him from some of his ex-girlfriends.'

'Where is she going?'

'For drinks to a pub called The Pear and Peach – it's on Upper Street.'

Ebony stepped into a doorway to take the call from Robbo.

'It looks likely he's Hawk. We have to find out where he's holding Danielle.'

'Okay, Guv.'

'We're bringing him in for questioning but we don't know where Danielle is being held yet and we need more evidence. Arrive at the pub thirty minutes late. People will still be there and you can pick up what information you can. We are still not sure of an address for him. He doesn't seem to be living at the one he gave. He may be using a second premises.'

Jeanie took a call from the officers outside Tracy's house.

'Steve Collins is back home.'

'Okay, give Tracy a call and make sure she's all right.'

She phoned Tracy.

'You okay, Tracy?'

'I'm okay. Steve is here.'

'Yeah, I was just told. Have you spoken to him about things?'

'He's been living a bit of a lie.'

'I know. We found out about his job. Carter and I went to see where he's been holing up. It isn't a pretty sight. He's obviously been going through a difficult time mentally. Is he going to stay?'

'Jackson seems to be okay with him. He got a smile. That means a lot, I think. At least we know he's not Daddy Pig.'

'Yeah – you're right.'

'Are you any nearer to finding Danielle?'

'We have someone we are going to bring in for questioning. He's a man who we know she was seeing as a friend and more. We are getting closer. I'll be over tomorrow morning but you can phone me any time, Tracy.'

She heard Tracy sigh. 'Thank you, Jeanie.'

Robbo was still searching Interpol when Jeanie returned to his desk.

He looked up as she approached. 'A couple of interesting cases came though from Australia. Two women died in Perth, both in their twenties. Both left a baby. Another three women disappeared in New Zealand, again all three left a child. There was one older woman in her forties found in 2006 in familiar circumstances to our women in a remote farm five hundred kilometres southeast of Adelaide. She was found with a garish mask of make-up on her face; she'd been strangled. Her body was wrapped in spiders' webs by the time they found her.'

'She was forty?'

'Forty-five. No small child anywhere. She was from Britain. I don't know a lot more at this stage. I'll keep looking and I'll get in touch with the police out there.'

Robbo took a call.

'They've picked up Goddard outside his house and

are bringing him in here to Archway Police Station; officers are in there searching the house now.'

'Tell them we are looking for a possible second premises,' said Carter. 'There might be some correspondence with some other address on it -- electricity bill, that kind of thing. I'll get ready to interview him. Robbo, you need to prepare some questions for me specifically about this history.'

Chapter 48

Ebony took a detour on the way to Islington. She was glad that it had been decided to bring Christian in. She would do all she could that evening to find out where he could be holding the women if the police search of his home didn't find them. She needed to talk to some of his less forthcoming conquests just in case more information was needed. She got a text on the way. It was from Yan.

'*There's been police here asking about Christian and Emily Styles, the girl he was dating. I just thought I'd warn you. I really think there's something not right about him. I've decided to invite everyone to mine instead – that is, the people from the course I was telling you about. Where are you now?*'

'*About to get to The Pear and Peach – the pub,*' she texted.

'*Well, go past it, take the next left, walk down that road till the end, I'm across the street, second from the end, number 130. See you in a minute.*'

'*Shall I bring something?*'

'*No, don't worry. Just bring yourself, that will be enough.*'

Ebony glanced into the pub as she passed. Selena and Julie were there. Ebony didn't need to talk to them again. It didn't look like there were many others unless they decided to nearly all go to Yan's.

Ebony walked down to the end of the road and crossed over at the end, then she stood opposite the house. It was a narrow four-storey Victorian terrace that looked in need of repair. The houses either side looked like they'd been renovated but not this one. *Typical student accommodation*, thought Ebony. Yan had said he let rooms out. There were two windows on each floor, overlooking the street. There were black railings at street level and steps leading down to a basement that looked like no one had used them in a long time. An ash tree had taken root in there and was now so tall that it obscured the first-floor windows. There were lights on in the upper two floors. She walked up the steps and looked for a bell, gave up and knocked. She heard the sound of feet approaching. She felt a trickle of excitement in her stomach. She realized she was looking forward to seeing him.

Carter sat across from Christian Goddard and his lawyer. 'Interview commencing at seven p.m. on Saturday December 21st , December 2013. Thank you for agreeing to give a DNA sample.' Carter watched Goddard. He was establishing a baseline. His breathing was deep and calm. He sat still, his hands folded in his lap.

'What's it for?' The pitch of his voice was low, measured. He used his hands very little when he talked.

'Exhibit number eighty-three.' Carter pushed a photo of two women across the table. 'You knew Emily Styles and Danielle Foster well?'

Goddard reached out to pick up the picture and look at it closely.

'Yes. Quite well.'

He was right-handed.

'When was the last time you saw either of these two women?'

'Emily? It was at the festival in Finsbury Park – the Fields festival. It was May sometime – the twenty-fifth.'

'And Danielle?'

'Danielle? A week or so ago. We saw one another at college.'

Carter watched Goddard answer; he was thinking about the dates. His eyes went up towards the left. He was remembering something that was real.

'You have had a few girlfriends from the college?'

'Yes, sure. That's not a crime, is it?'

'But what is a crime is they have ended up dead.' Carter took out the photos of Emily Styles' injuries from the autopsy.

'Do you recognize those wounds?'

'No.' His voice lifted a little in pitch. His body moved forward in his seat. He looked to his right. 'Why should I?'

'I thought you might have because they are spider bites left untreated. You keep spiders as pets, don't you?'

'I do. But that's not against the law.' His voice was creeping up, stressed.

'What about snakes?'

Carter watched the sweat glow on Goddard's upper lip and forehead.

'I haven't owned a snake for a while.' He stopped fidgeting. He put his hands on his lap.

'But you like exotic pets?'

Christian shrugged. 'Depends what you mean by that. Is a fish exotic to you? Maybe it is. Yes I own pets that might be termed exotic.'

'Spiders?'

'I already told you I have spiders.'

'What kind? Venomous?'

'A couple are, the rest just bite if they're threatened. But I would never let a spider bite someone like that. I have anti-venom. Anyway, it just wouldn't happen. I wouldn't let it.' He turned away, unable to stomach the images in front of him. 'I liked Emily.'

'When was the last time you saw her?'

'I told you, at the May Fields festival. We broke up before that – before the holidays.'

'Were you dating? For how long?'

'I wouldn't call it dating. We had had a few nights together.'

'So you felt nothing for her? What about Mary Rogers? Pauline Murphy? Do these names mean anything to you?'

'Yes. They were friends.'

'More than?'

He shrugged. His body remained tense. 'I suppose so – yes.'

'What about Danielle Foster?'

'What is this about?' His voice rose. 'Where is

Danielle? I don't understand. What happened to all these women?'

'When was the last time you saw her?'

'Two weeks ago. We had talked about meeting up.'

'When was the exact time you saw her?'

'Monday the eighth. She had a babysitter. Her mum was looking after Jackson for her.'

'So you met up?'

'Yes.'

'Alone?'

'No. There were other people from the college there.'

'Did you discuss the body in the canal?'

'Yes. A little bit. We had no idea it was Emily. After we heard the next day, then the phone calls started and people posted stuff on Facebook. We were all completely in shock. Emily was such a nice girl.'

'Had you had sex with Danielle?'

The lawyer answered for him: 'My client doesn't need to answer that.'

Christian waited whilst Carter returned with the file that Robbo had printed out for him.

'Have you ever been to Australia?'

'Yes.'

'Were you there in the year 2006?'

'Yes, I think I was.'

'Yes or no?'

'Okay.' His eyes went left. That meant his brain was recalling something real. 'Yes. I was there then.'

Chapter 49

'Come in. Lovely to see you.'

Ebony stepped into the hallway and then she stopped to listen to the music that was playing from inside the house somewhere. 'Ah, the Nutcracker Suite – as I said, the only piece of classical music I know.'

Yan closed the door behind her.

Ebony stopped and turned to look at Yan properly; when he had first opened the door she'd been embarrassed like a schoolgirl; she'd blushed and turned away and covered up her embarrassment and excitement by talking about the music, but then she looked back at Yan's face. She looked at his glasses. They were round, with thick black frames. She knew where she'd seen ones like that before: when she babysat for Jeanie's little girl Christa; when they watched children's television together. They were the ones Daddy Pig wore.

In the darkness she made out his smile. She looked back to the door; her body started to run. She saw only white in front of her eyes and felt the crack of pain to the side of her head before she sank in slow motion, in a dream, to her knees and into unconsciousness. In a dream she felt herself pressed against a wall, hands undress her. She felt pain.

Robbo looked at his screen. His breathing began to come shallow and fast. He couldn't take in enough oxygen. He pulled himself up straight and breathed in deeply through his nose but it wasn't reaching his lungs. He felt his lungs deflate with every breath. He heard them collapse.

Ebony's camera had entered a blackout zone. He tried resetting the connections. Her GPS had lost its signal.

He looked across at Jeanie, who was at another desk checking the information about the cases in Australia. He couldn't breathe; he was about to enter into a panic attack. He wanted to scream with the fear of it. He wanted to run from the room but he was too scared to move. His eyes stayed on the screen. There was a photo from Yan's Facebook. It was Yan on a sunny beach in Australia looking like every other gap year kid – around his neck was a chain.

'You all right, Robbo?' Jeanie looked up.

He shook his head. He stood up and then sat back down and tapped again on his keyboard. His lungs were wheezing. His face was scarlet. His peripheral vision was gone; now he was running down an ever-narrowing tunnel. But somewhere behind him something was pulling him backwards. It was holding him fast in the real world where he was needed.

'Ebony's in trouble, Jeanie. Her signal's gone. Something's wrong. Tell Carter.'

*

Ebony was dreaming of pain, of someone hitting her head with a hammer. She felt her body being jolted, felt it turning around in the air. All the time she heard laughter and then silence, darkness. Her hands shot upwards instinctively before she realized they were tied together at the wrist; they banged against a solid surface just a few inches above her. She passed out.

Carter looked up as the door opened and Jeanie entered. He could see by her face that something was very wrong.

'Detective Inspector Dan Carter leaving the room.' Carter signed himself off and left Christian with his lawyer whilst he stepped outside with Jeanie.

'It's Ebony. Her camera's not working and neither is her phone. GPS signal is lost,' said Jeanie.

'Where was she headed?'

'The last thing we know is that she was going to see Yan and meet some other members of the group after Goddard was brought in. Robbo says there's a photo of Yan on Facebook wearing the chain from Emily Styles' body.'

'Have you got a phone number for him, or an address?'

'We have a phone number but it's dead and it's not registered, it's a pay-as-you-go phone. We've tried college records and council tax, utilities. Either the address isn't the right one or the name of the person is wrong. The college have several addresses for him but his wages are paid in through a bank account that is proving impossible to trace. He seems to have covered all the angles. We need an address from Christian.'

Carter stepped back inside the interview room and sat back down across from Christian.

'What do you know about Yan Stevenson?'

'I've known him for a few years. I first met him in Australia when I was travelling. He was living out there.'

'We need to find him. Do you know where he lives?'

Christian Goddard shook his head.

'I helped him get some animals – spiders, snakes – he wanted once but he was insistent that I never came to his house with them. He collected them from me.'

Chapter 50

As Ebony opened her eyes the pain shot across the side of her head. She shut them fast and tried to breathe through the pain and nausea. She couldn't risk vomiting; she had a gag across her mouth. She opened her eyes again slowly and could see nothing but darkness.

She lay there trying hard to remember how she got wherever she was. She could smell: wood, urine and sweat. She listened hard. Against her back and buttocks she felt rough wood. She knew she was inside a coffin. Her fingers stretched upwards and her fingertips ran along the grooves that other nails had dug. Waves of nausea surged upward. Pain shot across her skull. She tried to calm herself. She could breathe – air must be coming from somewhere. She must try and come out of the pain and fog – try and think – it was her only chance.

She stopped as she heard movement above her. She heard him unlatch the first of the three locks on her box.

Ebony opened her eyes as she heard the box being opened. Three locks, to her left. The sound of music again. She held her breath, waited. As he opened the box, she was temporarily blinded by the light. He shone a torch in her face. She saw Yan's face loom close to hers as he pulled up her eyelids and examined her. He pulled her to a sitting position by her wrists. Her eyes squinted as he directed the light straight at her. A hot bulb shining on her swollen face. He pulled down her gag.

'Welcome to my world.'

His voice chilled her. It was a voice she knew well but she had never heard it in those tones. Now she realized she didn't know him at all. He was bare-chested, had on a pair of combat trousers and was wearing black leather gloves on his hands. He lifted her from the box by her wrists, pulled her over his shoulder and carried her out of the room.

She grimaced in pain as he squashed her bruised ribs and almost ran along the corridor. Try as she might, Ebony could not clear her head and was dipping in and out of consciousness. She tried to focus on where she could be in the house. She looked at the floor and the edges of doors: four, five. He carried her along a low-ceilinged corridor. It felt like they were underground. Suddenly, Yan stopped at a door on their right.

'Welcome to your new home. I've been waiting for you. I've been busy spinning my webs and you walked straight into them, my little fly.'

'Let me talk to you, Yan.'

He didn't answer as he opened a door. Inside she felt the temperature drop. It was completely black and there was the rank smell of something rotting. She felt the air flow over her body as he tipped her from his shoulder. She landed on a mat covered with grit and dirt.

When Ebony opened her eyes she shuffled forward in the dark. She had no sense of time or place. She didn't know where she was. The floor was crunching beneath her palms, something was sticking to her hands and knees. Her shoulder brushed against something that moved back and forth, banging, tapping her lightly. She recoiled quickly as she thought it was him, then in the silence that followed she inched forward again and reached out with her hand to touch the hanging object; her fingers touched a woman's feet covered in silken thread.

At the same time as she recoiled the lights went on and she saw that all around her on the floor, the crunchy paper particles were dead insects and above her, hanging from the ceiling, was a woman's body embalmed in spiders' webs. In the corner of the room she saw a woman she recognized as Danielle, suspended by her wrists from a hook in the ceiling; she was gagged, staring at Ebony. Her eyes were glaring at her, willing her to understand something that she couldn't say.

Ebony couldn't focus, she tried to keep her head very still as she crawled towards Danielle. Danielle began whimpering. Her eyes were fixed on Ebony; the nearer she got to her the louder the sounds she made. Ebony stopped where she was. She kept her head very still as she focused on Danielle and saw why she was crying. Yan was watching them. He had slipped into the room.

'What's this? A party? We need some music.'

Classical music started blasting out from a speaker on the wall. Yan moved to the middle of the room and held onto the hanging corpse as he pretended to waltz in a small circle. He lay on the floor breathing hard and laughing as he looked across at Ebony, who was retching now as the pain in her head distorted her vision and took away her balance. She couldn't stand; she swayed on her knees.

'Ebony, Ebony, Ebony.' She watched him as he circled her. She realized that she only had underwear on and it wasn't hers. It was a red metallic bikini. Her pendant was gone. She glared up at him.

'Yes, you're angry, I know. You fell for the oldest trick in the book, didn't you? Oh Ebony, I can be your boyfriend.' He simpered then laughed loudly. 'You're all the same. You're all pretenders: selfish liars, mercenary cheats, uncaring, ruthless in your pursuit of selfish dreams. And you, Ebony, are the lowest of the low. I intend to put all my skills to use on you. You are my *pièce de résistance*.' he said flamboyantly, waving his arms in the air as he struck a dancer's pose.

Ebony closed her eyes and sank to the floor. *How could she have messed up so badly?*

She heard Danielle try and say something to her from the corner of the room.

'You jealous?' He danced across to Danielle and ran his fingers slowly down her body whilst she twisted from his touch.

'Your turn will come.'

Ebony looked around the room, trying to get her

bearings. There was no window. She thought they must be in the basement. Her heart sank – no way of tracking her anyway, all her devices were gone. If she was ever going to get out she had to outwit him and this place had to become as familiar to her as it was to him.

'I've been waiting for them to send someone to try and trap me. I knew if I left enough clues you'd narrow it down to the college but there were so many choices in there. I wouldn't have known for sure it was you if you hadn't failed. You didn't know a basic fact about your supposed home town. In the café, you didn't get my text because you were on a different phone, which I saw you stuff into your bag. But don't feel bad, I saw you way before that. I saw you from the bridge the day that Emily rose to the surface. For weeks I'd been coming this way and that, different routes, different viewpoints. I had a feeling something would happen that day. I felt her beginning to rise beneath the surface. I saw you walk along the towpath and you didn't see me. You had your eyes on the man with you – Detective Inspector Dan Carter. With his expensive clothes and his black shiny hair like a raven's. That's all you were worried about. "*I'm not your mate . . . you all right Guv?*"' He mimicked them both. 'If you had walked up onto the bridge, past the press, you would have seen me. But I saw you. And you know what? I'm glad you're here now because we are going to play a special game, just me and you and Danielle and Jenny here. Just the four of us. We have plenty of time.'

Yan walked across to the side of the room and

picked up a box. He came across to Ebony and slid open a door at the front of the box. It came level with Ebony's face. She tried hard to focus. Inside she could make out something hanging, wrapped in silk. It had a tail, an ear poking out of the white bag that wrapped it. She focused on the mouse first, its beady little eyes watched hers. Then her eyes shifted to the right and she saw the massive spider that had wrapped it in white silk. He began swinging the box in front of her face.

The spider moved to the back of the box. It began to rear and sway; in the dark she saw its bright yellow markings.

'Tell me, Ebony, does the brown recluse spider always bite?'

'No,' Ebony whispered, keeping as still as possible.

'No. That's right,' he said, allowing the spider to stay still in front of her face. 'Very good, Ebony. But this isn't the brown recluse spider, this is the jumping tree spider, highly venomous and aggressive and she ...' The spider reared onto its back legs and showed two red fangs. '... does.'

'Tell me about Australia.'

'My client ...'

Christian Goddard turned to his lawyer to indicate he wanted to speak for himself.

'Look, I've got nothing to hide here. I'll tell you what I know about Yan but I'm not sure it will help. I am fond of Ebony and Danielle. If I can help I will.'

'How did you meet Yan?'

'In a bar in Adelaide. He was with his mother. She

was a hippy type. They'd travelled the world. By the time I met them they weren't getting on very well. His mum had a really wild side and a habit of sleeping with Yan's mates.'

'Including you?'

Christian shrugged. 'Actually no – it didn't work for me.'

'What were you doing at the time?'

'Drifting, working where I could. I got work in a bat sanctuary and then a zoo. That's when I learnt about looking after pets.'

'And Yan?'

'They had enough money sent over by his dad to keep them going but they lived very frugally. They rented out shitty old places and lived like tramps. Yan had been brought up like that. Ever since his mum left the UK supposedly to find herself and left Yan's dad and never came back. By the time I met Yan he was bitter and angry and seemed to be on the brink of just flying back to the UK without his mum. Then his dad died over here and it seemed to be a massive blow to him. All he ever talked about was his memories of his dad. He talked about getting back here and making up for all the lost time. He really hated his mum then.'

'What happened to them then?'

'I didn't see him for a while. The next time I met him out in a bar on his own I asked after his mum. He told me she was back at the farm they were renting. She was pretty ill. He said he was waiting for her to get better then he was definitely coming back to the UK and he had inherited his dad's house.'

'Where – did he say?'

'Yes, off Upper Street somewhere. I didn't see him again until he contacted me on Facebook and I found out he was working at the college. I decided I would take a couple of courses and it just snowballed from there.'

'So you are friends?'

Christian shook his head. 'Not really. I don't like him and he doesn't like me.'

'Would it surprise you to know that his mother died in that remote farm outside Adelaide?'

'Not really. How?'

'Strangled. By the time they found her she was cocooned in spiders' webs.'

Chapter 51

Ebony's face felt like it didn't belong to her. The bite was throbbing. She raised her hands to touch the swelling on her face. She could feel the poison working. Her ribs were in agony when she breathed. She had passed out after killing the spider – she hadn't meant to but her instinct was to crush it in her hand. He'd beaten her unconscious for that.

Her wrists were bound together. She must have slept. Her vision was slightly better although her face throbbed. She looked around her. The corpse he called Jenny was still hanging, mummified and cocooned, from the hook in the ceiling. As she focused on it she could see that beneath the white web there was movement – hundreds of spiders had colonized the body.

Danielle was watching her from her place, strung up by her wrists, her legs opened and chained to anchors in the floor. There was blood dripping down to her feet. Yan was in the corner of the room. A bottle of vodka was open beside him. Ebony looked at the photos on the walls. There were large prints of a young boy with a man. She recognized Yan from the photos.

'My dad,' he said, looking up. 'The dad my mother never let me be with. She should have left me with him. I loved him. He would have looked after me. I could have nursed him back to health when he got ill. I never saw him again after we left. She was taking me on holiday, she said, taking me away for the summer, but we never came back and I missed all those years with my dad. Women shouldn't have kids selfishly like that. They shouldn't just up and leave the man who gave them that child. Women are fickle and vain and only think about themselves. They entrap a man with their looks, cover themselves in make-up, but inside they are worse than spiders, worse than the female spider for taking what they want and then destroying the mate that gave it to them.'

He looked at Ebony. He picked up the vodka and swigged it back. 'Did you really think I wouldn't know that the police would try and trap me? I'm not going to let you stop me from finishing the game. I know that this will be my last game and I chose to end it here with you two – my last players. Danielle, you will die on my first mark ... Ebony on my second.' His laughter started deep and ended in a shrill squeal that left him doubled over and breathless. 'We are going to play the game called "tighten the noose".' He got to his feet slowly – with deliberate precision he then walked across to Danielle; he walked like a ballet dancer. He took every step as if he were on stage – in a performance.

'Ebony, you have to answer questions. If you get them wrong then I tighten the noose around Danielle's neck.' He took his mother's scarf from his pocket and tied it around Danielle's neck, looping it twice around and taking up the slack in his fist. She twisted and thrashed against his grip as the scarf tightened around her throat.

'Here's the question ... ready?'

'Leave her alone,' Ebony shouted out.

'What is your worst nightmare? What do you fear most?'

'Pain. I fear pain most.' She couldn't bear to see Danielle struggling to breathe.

'Liar.' He squeezed the scarf and twisted it around his fist.

'Being alone.'

Yan shook his head, tutting, and gathered more of the scarf in his fist. Danielle started to lose consciousness.

'Stop ... stop ... Okay – my worst nightmare is something I don't understand. It's dark. I hear my mother. I'm being touched ... I feel violated, vulnerable ...'

He released the scarf and Danielle slumped forward and her shoulders rose and fell as she snatched the air back into her lungs. The gag was sucked into her mouth at each breath.

'Good.' He waited a few minutes for Danielle to recover. He turned to look at Ebony.

'It's all black and white with you. Did no one tell you the world is grey?' He pulled the scarf tight around Danielle's neck again. Her legs began to shake. Her chest rose and collapsed. Then he released the tourniquet.

'Second question: have you ever betrayed anyone?'

'No.'

'Liar. I looked you up. I found you. Wilson equals Willis. Ebony Willis – right age, right mixed-race kid from children's homes and a fuck-up mum. I looked you up and I thought, you know what? We have a lot in common but still you were sent to trick me and you accepted the challenge willingly.'

'I didn't know it was you. Please stop. No. I don't know what you want from me. I have never betrayed anyone.'

'What about your own mother? You arrested your own mother.'

'I had no choice. It was my job. She killed someone. Please. Please ... let Danielle go. We can talk ... yes, you're right, we have a lot in common. My mum was sick. She did things.' Ebony was fighting to think straight. She didn't know what she could say to save Danielle. She would give anything to do that – even her life.

'You betrayed her. You couldn't wait. You hated her.'

'Maybe.' Ebony looked at Danielle and saw the urine run down her legs. 'I am telling the truth.'

He released the tension on the scarf and he took off Danielle's gag so she could breathe better. She gasped and her lungs squealed and sobs erupted from her raw throat. 'Please. Please, I've had enough; let me die,' Danielle begged.

'Not till I'm ready.' He turned to Ebony. 'Do you wish your mother were dead, Ebony?'

'No.'

'Yes you do.' He snatched up the slack from the scarf.

Danielle twisted in the air and her feet beat against the floor as she tried to get oxygen and failed.

'Yes. Yes ... you're right. I hate her. Please ... please ... Danielle doesn't deserve it, kill me not her. Yes my mother doesn't love me ... is that what you want me to say? My mother doesn't love me. Never did and never will.'

Danielle's legs stopped twitching and her body slumped. He pulled the scarf away and she stayed the way she was. Ebony watched helplessly. She was here to save Danielle and she had failed.

Yan was angry with himself. 'You did this – you made me lose concentration. You made me rush.'

He reached down and pulled Ebony to her feet and threw her over his shoulder again. Ebony started to retch. She was sick over the floor as he walked. She looked up as they were leaving the room; Danielle was stirring, coming round. Ebony felt the hope in her return. It wasn't too late. Yan carried on walking, almost jogging along the corridor. Ebony felt the cold air rush as she stared at the floor beneath her. Her stomach heaved. She counted the doors, she knew the direction. She was back where she started. He opened a door and the mustiness, the heat in the room hit her. He laid her back in the box and left her for what could have been days. She had no idea how long.

She closed her eyes inside the coffin and tried to rest. She was thinking of Micky when she heard Yan return. She heard the three locks on the coffin being undone. As her eyes adjusted she saw him standing over her, something moving in his hands. Her eyes focused and she saw he was holding a rat; it was trying to bite him through his gloves. He held the rat one-handed as he reached into the box and pulled her up to a sitting position by her wrists. Then he dropped the rat in the box with her.

Ebony struggled to breathe through the panic as she felt its warm body and its sharp claws scratch her as it scuttled nervously around the box. He reached in and lifted it out by the tail. He dangled it in front of her face. It squealed as Yan pulled and twisted – dislocated its back legs. Then he dropped it back in. She watched it drag its mutilated body around the box.

Yan left her and walked to the corner of the room; she couldn't see what he was doing but she heard the slide of a heavy glass lid being opened and the musty smell in the room intensified. He moved slowly back towards her carrying a huge snake coiled around his arms. Its girth was as thick as a man's leg. He carried it looped over his shoulders and across his arms, walking slowly with the weight of it. Its head rose in the air as it smelt the room with its tongue.

'Now this is my interpretation of a well-known classic: three blind mice. But this is one crippled rat and it isn't the farmer's wife coming after him, it's my lovely Miranda.'

Ebony breathed hard as the snake's head appeared over the side of the box. It was watching both her and the rat.

'Stay still – I would – because she gets very jumpy when she's hungry. She'll strike at anything, even me. She has scores of sharp-as-needles teeth. The wound on my hand that you thought was made by a staple gun was actually Miranda's teeth.'

Ebony stayed still, slowed her breathing and watched. She felt the snake's body against her own as it dropped into the coffin with her and she sensed its tongue against her legs as it slithered its way slowly along. The rat didn't seem to know what was about to happen to it. It edged closer to the snake as if curious. Miranda moved across Ebony's legs, slowly inching its way towards the rat until their faces were almost touching and then she made her strike. She bit into the neck of the squealing rat and wrapped her coils around it as it fought to escape. Yan didn't move – he was watching Ebony. She could feel it – she had to play his game now if she had any chance of surviving this and helping Danielle. She turned her head away, disgusted, and refused to look at the rat whose feet paddled in the air at the crack of its spine.

'Please let me go, Yan. I can help you. I'll tell them you were kind to me – please don't kill me this way.' Yan smiled. He was pleased to see Ebony so upset.

'Take a good look, Ebony. Every time the rat exhales she constricts tighter; imagine her squeezing the life out of you.' Ebony shuddered.

'Please, Yan. Please stop this.'

She watched as Miranda opened her mouth wide and began taking the rat inside.

'My game. My rules. I say when it's over for you and Danielle. Stay here. Don't move. You move and Miranda will strike.'

'Please don't leave me with it. Yan, please . . .'

Ebony heard his footsteps as he left. She listened to

them outside the door and counted his steps. She knew he'd gone into the room where Danielle was. After a few minutes she heard the door open again and his footsteps climbing stairs.

Ebony didn't dare breathe as she lay listening to the cracking of the rat's bones and the sound of a door opening to the upper floor. He was planning to kill Danielle on the next floor of the house. If he'd left the door unlocked then Ebony could make it.

She looked back at Miranda. The rat's body was slowly disappearing and now half of it was already jammed into Miranda's throat. It was time to make her move. Ebony began biting the binds on her wrist.

She looked at Miranda. The snake was watching her, but she reckoned it wouldn't be able to spit the rat out and that gave her time to work on her bonds. Ebony wiggled her legs slowly out of the crushing weight of Miranda's coils and then she began working at her wrists against the sharp ends of the catches on the locks that held the coffin closed. All the time keeping her eye on the snake's head, she gently pushed its coils off her. Ebony knelt and applied her weight until the rope began to fray and give way.

By now only the rat's tail was still showing from Miranda's mouth. Ebony stepped carefully out of the box and made a circuit of the room. It was a dug-out basement area that had been crudely extended. It had low ceilings and bare rafters, concrete floors. The basement had been used as a wine cellar at one time. It was barely lit. There were shelves still there where the wine rested. She walked cautiously forward. There was a crudely dug pit to her left. She peered inside. It smelt of urine and earth. On the far side of the room she found Miranda's empty tank.

Ebony moved slowly backwards away from the tank and found a sturdy metal pole, with a hook on the end – a snake hook – then she crept towards the door. She watched Miranda drop off the side of the coffin and onto the floor.

Chapter 52

Robbo was in his office with Jeanie, Pam and James. He sat despondently and stared at the screen. He was trying every way to reconnect with Ebony's GPS but it was dead.

'Christ almighty, why isn't it working? Come on, Ebb – talk to me.'

'Out of range or inside a building?' said Jeanie as she put a hand on Robbo's shoulder. He looked up at her, exasperated.

'I'd like to think so, Jeanie, but I think it's more likely Hawk's found it.'

'We have to keep trying, Robbo. Ebb won't give up. She's a fighter.'

'She'll need to be, Jeanie.' Robbo looked exhausted.

James stood to retrieve something from the printer.

'I have a list of Yan's closest friends now,' he said to Robbo. 'The ones he talks to most on Facebook.' He gathered up the printed pages. 'I have their addresses and phone numbers.'

'Good – start phoning, and make a list of any you can't get hold of and I'll send officers around there. One of them must know where he lives.'

'Can't we trace his address through his father and the details of the house ownership?' Jeanie asked Pam.

Pam shook her head. 'I'm trying but I'm having no luck so far. I don't think he had his father's name. I don't think they were married.'

'What about his birth certificate?'

'It gives his father as Joseph White, but I can't find out any more about him. I'm trying every angle I can think of,' Pam said. She looked fraught.

Jeanie smiled at her. 'I know you are ... we're all so worried but we need to stay calm and focused.' Pam nodded.

'How's Carter getting on, Jeanie?' asked Robbo.

'He's throwing everything at it that he can think of. We have a hundred officers walking around the streets off Upper Street doing house to house.'

'Yan's not going to answer the door though, is he?'

'No, but they might get lucky – see something suspicious. They're also looking for vans and checking out the owners with vehicle registration. We've even got a heat-seeking helicopter up looking for the snake tank in case it's on the upper floor.'

Robbo rubbed his face with his hands.

'We need to put more officers out there. No squad cars, we need plain-clothes officers out looking for her. We don't want to scare him into finishing the game too soon, before we have time to find her.'

'Is that what you think will happen?'

Robbo nodded. 'He is not going to hand over control of the game or have it taken away from him. He won't allow that to happen. He'll end it first. End it on his own terms. Ebony is his *pièce de résistance*. He's had this worked out for some time. I can't imagine he hasn't thought of everything.'

Ebony crept past the room where Jenny's corpse was hanging. The corridor took a sharp right before an old stairwell and a door to the next level. Her feet creaked on every step. At the top of the stairwell she turned the door handle and stepped into a kitchen. It hadn't been updated since the Fifties. She could hear music playing. She heard Yan talking as she crept forwards.

Yan was humming to the music as he prepared Danielle's face. He applied a layer of thick foundation to her pale skin. He drew red circles on her cheeks and painted blue eye-shadow in a block above her eyes. He worked methodically, slowly.

'Stay still,' he said to Danielle, who was shaking violently. He held her head steady whilst he painted on spidery eyelashes up past her eyebrows. It was then that he heard the turn of the handle on the cellar door. He listened for footsteps along the corridor. He knew it was dark. She would have to feel her way. He strained to catch the tiniest movement. He thought he heard a sound the other side of the door.

'You can run. But you can't hide. This is my lair. I'm coming, Ebony. Run. Run!'

Ebony flew up the stairs to the next floor and up again. She tried the windows at the top of the house but they were shuttered and she couldn't open them. She turned to listen to the sound of him coming up the stairs. She was cornered; she ran into a room and immediately she felt trapped; the smell of decay and death was ripe in the air. A chandelier hung down from the ceiling and allowed a sickly light to shine on photos of women, their emaciated bodies posed in provocative poses. Their skeletal bodies were clothed in bikinis like the one she was wearing. There was nowhere to hide in the room. She could not stay in there. She felt as if she were already dead. She heard him standing outside. He rattled the door handle. She stood, both hands gripping the pole, and waited for him to open the door but instead he locked it.

'My game, Ebony.'

She heard his footsteps fade. She looked around her in a panic. She had to get out of there. She'd become like the women she saw all around her.

Yan went back to Danielle in the front room and stood back to look at his handiwork.

'One more thing and then you're ready, my dear.'

He tied Ebony's pendant around her neck.

Robbo leant towards the screen.

'What is it?' asked Jeanie.

'For one second I thought that Ebony's GPS signal was back.'

'Can you trace it?'

'No, it's gone.'

Ebony tried the handle but it wouldn't budge. She kept telling herself she had to get out to save Danielle. If she stayed in that room they would both be dead. She looked around for anything she could find to unscrew the lock. She looked at her snake hook and tried prising it under the brass plate but it wouldn't go, it was too thick. She couldn't see properly in the gloom. The chandelier didn't throw off enough light – it was broken, bits hanging off it. Her eyes stayed on it. She hooked the pole over it and dragged part of it down. She smashed the fitting and was left with a bulb holder. Ebony took it across to the brass door plate and tried to slot it into the top of the screws to undo them but it was too thick. She turned it over in her hand until she found the narrowest part, made of tin, and she bit it hard between her teeth. She tried again and managed to loosen one of the screws a little until the top of the plate was free and then she hooked the snake hook inside and levered it out into the room. It crashed down and the door splintered and swung open. She stood listening for any sound from below. She picked up the snake hook and held it in her two hands as she edged downstairs in the darkness.

At the end of the street Carter was examining a van that had the college logo on the side. There was a deep scratch along the side. The bumper was dented on the driver's side, *soft impact*, thought Carter. He knelt down and ran his hand around the inside of the wheel arch and looked at the residue on his fingers. Dried blood. He rang in.

'Robbo, I've found a van which looks like it could have been the one used in the attacks on Jeanie and Jackson, and Niall Manson.' He gave him the registration number. 'Find me the address.'

'Okay.'

'Any sign of her, Robbo?'

'I thought I had a signal but then it went.'

'Jesus! Okay, I'll keep going. Let me know if you find anything.'

Carter continued up the street. He knocked at a house five doors up from Yan's.

'Did you ever hear of anyone with a pet snake living in this area?' The tenant shook her head.

'Has it escaped?'

'No, nothing like that. Do you know of a man name Yan Stevenson?'

She shook her head. 'Sorry.'

Ebony got back down to the kitchen level. The music had stopped. She knew he was waiting for her but she didn't know where. Gripping the pole with both hands, she edged along the corridor. She knew it would take all her strength to knock him hard with it. She wouldn't get a second chance. She had to hit him and make it good.

'Ebony?' She gasped. Out from the shadows he appeared, his face smiling in the gloom. The scarf was in his hand. He came towards her, twisting it between his hands. Ebony swung at him but missed him in the dark. She turned and fled back through the kitchen, tried the back door and couldn't smash it, and then she ran back down the cellar stairs, along the hallway and into the room with the coffin. He came slowly down the cellar stairs after her.

Ebony unscrewed the light bulb from its pendant fitting and hid behind the coffin in the dark with the snake hook in her hand. She had to focus – to keep

calm. She heard him calling from outside the door. She
heard the door opening slowly and a small shaft of icy
air came into the sweltering hot room. He had a torch
in his hand. He shone it around. Ebony started crawl-
ing around the room. From the corner of her eye she
could see Miranda near her. The snake was coming
her way. She dashed to the other side of the room and
the torchlight flashed across her.

Leaping forward, she knocked the torch out of his
hands with the snake hook. It rolled and clattered on
the floor and pointed a beam of light towards the far
wall and then went out. He made a grab for her and
just caught Ebony's arm as she lunged forward. He
held on tight. She smashed his forearm with her fist.
He let go and made another grab as she threw herself
forward. He held on to her ankle.

Ebony dragged his weight forwards as well as her
own as he smashed his foot down into the back of
her knee. She turned and kicked him with a sweep of
her foot and caught him off balance as he hit the
ground and she scrabbled forwards in the dark.
Ebony whipped her upper body round and smacked
him hard with the snake hook. She heard it contact
with something hard. She heard him groan and he
seemed to slip back. Ebony lashed out at him again in
the same place and the pole hit and slid over the top
of his head. She heard him fall backwards into the
pit. But not before he had grabbed hold of her leg and
pulled her with him. Miranda paused to listen, she
smelt the air with her tongue and turned towards the
pit.

*

Danielle lifted her head to listen to the noise from the cellar. The pendant shifted slightly where it rested on her collarbone.

Robbo leaned towards the screen, hardly daring to breath or blink in case it disappeared.

'Signal, Jeanie. We have a signal. Get Carter. It's finding an address. Go, go!'

Carter got the call and whistled to his officers on the street. He sprinted up the steps to the house and began breaking the front door down. Wood splintered as they kicked through the panels.

Inside the hallway he took out his revolver and held it ready as he came to the room on his right and nudged the door open with his foot. Danielle was suspended from the ceiling, her face made up, her body clothed in a bikini.

'We're police officers. Where is Yan? Where's Ebony?'

She could hardly speak. She nodded towards the hallway.

'There's a kitchen. A cellar.'

Carter signalled to an officer to phone for an ambulance at the same time as he said he was going down alone. Carter understood that Yan would not give himself up. He would take Ebony with him if she was down there. Carter on his own might work – Carter and an army of police officers never would.

He pushed open the cellar door and stepped down one stair at a time. When he reached the bottom he stood listening and heard nothing. He pushed open the door on the right; the light was on and he saw the corpse covered in webs hanging from the centre of the room. It was against all his instincts that he stepped into the room to make sure she was the only one in there. He had a hard job talking himself through it. He knew if he hadn't been looking for Ebony he would not have gone in there – nothing else mattered to him now. He had to find her. He came out of the room and walked on down the corridor. He checked three other rooms, which were empty, and then he stopped at the last room on his left and turned the handle. He smelt the musty smell of people and animals and fear. He put his gun away. In the darkness he couldn't be sure of shooting the right person. He stood in the doorway.

'Ebb?'

He heard a moaning coming from the middle of the room on the left-hand side. He opened up the torch on his phone and shone its bright narrow beam towards the sound and saw nothing. He walked further inside towards where the noise had come from. He was almost in the hole before he saw it. He shone his torch downwards and saw Ebony staring up at him, her body covered by Miranda's coils.

He stared, speechless.

'Guv?' Her voice came out breathless – squashed. 'Guv . . . get this off me.' Carter reached inside the pit and took her hand as he hauled her out. He took out his radio. 'Tell everyone we found her. She looks okay – yes I can confirm.' He looked at what she was wearing. 'She's okay. Get me a snake handler and another ambulance. The suspect is not looking so good.' Carter shone his torch back into the hole and saw the snake coiled around Yan.

Carter looked back at Ebony. He took off his coat to put round her. She was shivering.

'Like the outfit. Thought you were in trouble – didn't realize you were having a holiday.'

'Yeah, funny. Is Danielle okay?'

He nodded. 'What about you, Ebb?'

She felt too overwhelmed to speak. It wasn't like her to cry but she was in danger of doing so. Carter hugged her as officers passed them and spread out through the house.

Chapter 53

'*Away in a manger, no crib for a bed.*'

The whole of the cast stood as the audience applauded at the end of the show.

Tracy was sitting in the front row next to Danielle. Jackson beamed at them. He was dressed in his bunny suit and stood fidgeting at the entrance to the stable.

Tracy looked across at Danielle and smiled. She reached for her hand and gave it a squeeze.

They walked outside into the bright cold night and Tracy picked Jackson up in her arms.

'What are you going to do?' Danielle asked.

'I've applied to be a beauty therapist on a cruise liner and been accepted. I'll send tickets back for you and Jackson to join me whenever you can along the way.'

'What about Steve?'

'We have come to the decision that we won't divorce for now but we'll go our separate ways and see how we find it. I'd like to think we could start again but we need time and space for now.'

'I'm sorry, Tracy.'

'No, don't be. It's a relief for us both. Steve will be

able to find out what he wants in life. Instead of always trying to be what I wanted him to be. And maybe we'll fall in love again – who knows?'

'What about Christmas?'

'Steve's going back to his family for Christmas and I'm hoping for an invite from the two people I really love more than anyone else in the world.' She gave Jackson a kiss. Danielle smiled. Tracy reached over and kissed Danielle's cheek. Danielle's face still bore the scars from the suffering she'd endured. 'I feel like being a mummy and a nanny to two people I think the world of, if that's okay?'

'No problem.'

Jackson shrieked as he struggled to get out of Tracy's arms.

'Anyone want a dog?' Jeanie pretended she hadn't seen them.

Scruffy was still bandaged around his trunk but able to move his legs. He was ready to go home.

Christmas Day

Carter held Archie up and blew a raspberry into his neck. Archie screamed with delight. Carter looked across at Cabrina, who was unwrapping a present that Carter had bought her. She jumped up and kissed him.

'Thank you, it's lovely.' She held up the necklace and looked at it. She did her best to look pleased.

'I know, I know.' Carter smiled, shook his head. 'I've kept the receipt.'

Ebony lifted her shot glass and smashed it into Dermot's.

'Cheers, Ebb, I hope your face gets better by New Year otherwise you're going to be disappointed when it comes to twelve o'clock.' Dermot winked. Ebony laughed. 'Though – I might rethink that after a few more of these.' He held up his glass again.

'Christ, Ebb.' Tina hid a scowl inside a smile. 'You'll break the other leg. If you don't sit down, you'll fall down.'

'It's not broken, Teen, just bruised. Cheers,' Ebony said as she took Tina's help to manoeuvre her bandaged leg onto a stool and sit down. She felt like getting drunk. It took the pain away from her throbbing face and her bruises. But the pain the drink took away was not all physical. She had a lot she didn't want to think about.

'Happy Christmas.' She smashed her glass into Dermot's again.

Ebony's phone rang. She had a sense of dread as she looked at who was calling and then she answered it quickly.

'Happy Christmas, Jeanie.'

'Just ringing to make sure you're okay. How's the head and the leg?'

'All much better for a few drinks thanks, Jeanie.'

'That's the way to go, Ebb – let your hair down. The hospital said Yan will be able to answer questions in a couple of days. He has crush injuries from being strangled. The van proved positive for both attacks – the one on me and Jackson and the one that killed Niall Manson. He must have been worried that Manson would identify him after he saw him with Danielle. You have a good day, Ebb. Love you loads.'

'And you, Jeanie. Tell Christa to save some of the chocolate for me.'

Ebony's phone rang again. She looked at the number and shuffled to her feet to take the call in the hallway, away from listening ears.

'Hello?'

'Miss Willis?'

'Yes.'

'I am ringing to tell you that you have been granted special permission to visit your mother due to her injuries. She has several deep wounds and required over seventy stiches. We think it would mean a lot to her to see you.'

'Why?'

'Why? Well, naturally, this is a special case and she is a patient of ours.'

'She is also a manipulative killer who is able to run rings around you.'

'I beg your pardon?!'

'I am sick of her making me feel guilty all the time. I need to rebuild my life. I will come and see my mother when I choose and not when she cuts herself so badly that you feel sorry for her. Tell her I wish her a speedy recovery. Tell her Happy Christmas.'

Ebony came off the phone and walked back into the lounge. She held up her glass for Dermot to pour a refill. She felt like she was in danger of crying but at the same time she felt enormous relief. Things had changed forever for her now. In her heart she knew that she had opened a door into her memory bank that she wished had remained closed. It held pain and guilt and darkness, but she would keep the door ajar and deal with whatever crept out. She knew the main thing was that she was alive and that was more than could be said for the women who'd worn the red metallic bikini before her.

'Teen?' She looked up at Tina, who was busy being hostess and handing out sausage rolls and mince pies.

'Yes, Ebb?' Tina had been pretending not to be watching Ebony but she had taken it all in and could guess who the phone call was from.

'I could do with a holiday. Fancy coming?'

Tina beamed. 'You? The workaholic? On holiday? Never thought I'd see the day!'

'Never thought I'd want to get away so badly.'

'I understand. You're on. Can't wait to put my bikini on.'

'Yeah – you know what? Think I'll get a swimsuit.'

Acknowledgements

My thanks and gratitude go to all the people who helped me write this book:

Detective Inspector Dave Willis (retired), Neil Rickard, Frank Pearman, Crime Analyst Catherine Ash. All the police officers who happily answer my questions. The Canal Museum staff in Kings Cross. My family, who help me with medical queries. The unsung heroes: friends and family, who listen to my ideas for stories and are invaluable in their feedback. They are: Norma Saunders and Noreen Carew, Beccy at Visage, Della at True Colours, mum, sisters Clare and Sue and kids Ginny and Robert. They are all invaluable in helping to push me over the bumps on my story road.

Of course, I wouldn't have got off the starting blocks without the massive help of my agent Darley Anderson, and the team, and Emma Lowth and the whole Simon & Schuster team, who have made me very welcome.

Big thanks to all my readers who email me with their ideas and suggestions and especially their support.

Lee Weeks

Dead of Winter

Victim, suspect, policeman. When the lines blur, who do you trust?

When two bodies surface in the garden of a rented house in North London, Forensics discover fingerprints which link back to an unsolved crime that no one in the Metropolitan Police wants to remember.

More than a decade ago, in an isolated holiday cottage in Sussex, a family was found brutally slaughtered. The prime suspect was Callum Carmichael, the father of the family and a police officer from the Met's own ranks. But without enough evidence to arrest him, the case was hushed up and the trail left to go cold.

Now, with fresh proof that the killer is still out there, rookie DC Ebony Willis is sent to find Callum Carmichael. But Carmichael is an unknown entity and, with every piece of information she tells him, she risks leading a dangerous man closer to his prey.

Paperback ISBN 978-1-84983-857-3
Ebook ISBN 978-1-84983-858-0

Craig Robertson
Witness the Dead

Red Silk is back ...

Scotland 1972. Glasgow is haunted by a murderer
nicknamed Red Silk – a feared serial killer who selects
his victims in the city's nightclubs. The case remains
unsolved but Archibald Atto, later imprisoned for
other murders, is thought to be Red Silk.

In modern-day Glasgow, DS Rachel Narey is called to a
gruesome crime scene at the city's Necropolis. The body
of a young woman lies stretched out over a tomb. Her body
bears a three-letter message from her killer.

Now retired, former detective Danny Neilson spots a link
between the new murder and those he investigated in
1972 – details that no copycat killer could have known
about. But Atto is still behind bars. Must Danny face up to
his fears that they never caught their man? Determined
finally to crack the case, Danny, along with his nephew,
police photographer Tony Winter, pays Atto a visit. But
they soon discover that they are going to need the
combined efforts of police forces past and present to
bring a twisted killer to justice.

Move over MacBride! *Witness the Dead* is the compelling
new thriller from Scotland's hottest new talent.

Paperback ISBN 978-0-85720-420-2
Ebook ISBN 978-0-85720-421-9

Lynda La Plante

Backlash

Two unsolved murders. Three confessions. One suspect.

**But is the man in DCI Anna Travis's custody a
serial killer ... or just a compulsive liar?**

It is late at night on a notorious council estate in
east London when the police pull over a van.
Inside, they discover the body of a young woman.

The driver confesses, not just to one murder – but to three.

Five years earlier, a 13-year-old girl disappeared in
broad daylight on a busy London street. The unsolved
case has haunted DCS James Langton ever since.
But when the case is reopened, it falls to Anna
to investigate and bring the killer to trial.

Meanwhile, the murder team is hard at work,
verifying the details of the van driver's confessions
and desperately trying to uncover the identity
of his second and third victims.

And then he changes his story ...

Paperback ISBN 978-1-84983-336-3
Ebook ISBN 978-0-85720-185-0

Mary Higgins Clark
Daddy's Gone A-Hunting

A dark family secret puts the lives of two sisters in grave danger

Hannah Connelly is plunged into a nightmare when she learns that Connelly Fine Antique Reproductions, the family business founded by her grandfather, has been levelled by a huge explosion.

The ashes reveal a startling and grisly discovery. Could the explosion have been deliberately set? And what was Kate, Hannah's sister and a highflyer in an accounting firm, doing in the building in the middle of the night?

With Kate lying in a coma in hospital, it is now down to Hannah to discover what truly happened. But little does she know that someone will do anything they can to prevent Kate regaining consciousness. Will Hannah find out the truth before that person kills to save himself?

'I adore Mary Higgins Clark' Karin Slaughter

Paperback ISBN 978-1-84983-026-3
Ebook ISBN 978-1-43919-987-9

Camilla Grebe & Åsa Träff

More Bitter Than Death

Sometimes reliving the past revives old demons …

In a Stockholm apartment, five-year-old Tilde
watches from under the kitchen table as her
mother is brutally kicked to death.

Meanwhile, in another part of town, psychotherapist
Siri Bergman and her colleague Aina meet their
new patients – a group of women, all of whom
are victims of domestic violence.

From Kattis, who was beaten by her boyfriend and lives
under the constant threat of his return, to Malin, the
promising young athlete who was attacked by a man
she met online, and from Sofi, the teenager abused by
her stepfather, to Sirkka, an older woman who had a
troubled marriage – each woman takes her turn to
share her story in the safety of the sessions.

But as the group gets closer, it is not long before the
dangers lurking in the women's lives outside invade the
peace with shattering consequences. And somehow, the
fate of five-year-old Tilde is intertwined with that of Siri
and the other women, so that what started out as the search
for peace will swiftly turn into a tense hunt for a murderer.

Paperback ISBN 978-0-85720-950-4
Ebook ISBN 978-0-85720-951-1

Penny Hancock
The Darkening Hour

A middle class woman at her wits' end.

A struggling migrant worker with few options for survival.

When tensions boil over, who will be the first to snap?

Will it be Theodora, finally breaking under the pressure?

Or Mona, desperate to find a way out?

Two women. Two stories.

Who do you believe?

'The author skilfully plays with [the two narrators']
versions of reality – as this dark and brooding novel races
towards its genuinely scary conclusion' *Sunday Mirror*

From the author of the Richard & Judy Bookclub pick,
Tideline, comes a story of two sides and with
darkness at its very heart.

Paperback ISBN 978-0-85720-625-1
Ebook ISBN 978-0-85720-626-8